I'm Right Here

Yvonne Cassidy was born in Dublin in 1974. She studied English and Economics in University College Dublin. She has worked in the field of marketing communications and fundraising in London, Dublin and New York.

Yvonne enjoys teaching creative writing and teaches extensively in New York, where she has developed writing programmes for homeless and other marginalised writers. She lives in Manhattan with her wife, Danielle.

www.yvonnecassidy.com
@YvonneCassidyNY

Previously by Yvonne Cassidy
How Many Letters Are in Goodbye?
What Might Have Been Me
The Other Boy

YVONNE
CASSIDY

I'm Right Here

HACHETTE
BOOKS
IRELAND

First published in Ireland in 2017 by HACHETTE BOOKS IRELAND

1

'Heaven' reprinted with permission of the University of Georgia Press from *Boy: Poems* by Patrick Phillips (2008)

Cataloguing in Publication Data is available from the British Library.

ISBN 9781444744187

Typeset in Arno Pro and Caslon Antique by Bookends Publishing Servies, Dublin

Printed and bound in Great Britain by Clays Ltd, St Ives plc

Hachette Books Ireland policy is to use papers that are natural, renewable and recyclable products and made from wood grown in sustainable forests. The logging and manufacturing processes are expected to conform to the environmental regulations of the country of origin.

Hachette Books Ireland
8 Castlecourt Centre, Castleknock, Dublin 15, Ireland

A division of Hachette UK Ltd
Carmelite House, 50 Victoria Embankment, EC4Y 0DZ

www.hachettebooksireland.ie

For Annette and Barry, who will always be ‘right here’

HEAVEN

Patrick Phillips

It will be the past
and we'll live there together.

Not as it was *to live*
but as it is remembered.

It will be the past.
We'll all go back together.

Everyone we ever loved,
and lost, and must remember.

It will be the past.
And it will last forever.

Prologue

CASSIE

Did I ever tell you how Grandad used to say that he had lived two lives? I remember him saying that, and I always thought he meant his life here, in Ireland, and the one after, when he moved to New York. The other day, driving from the airport, I was the first one to see the sign for Donegal. It was ancient looking, white with black writing in Irish as well as English, and it made me think of that – Grandad's before and after life. I started to talk about that, to explain it to Mom and Ryan, but before I could, Mom interrupted and said that he didn't mean Ireland and America, he meant his life when he was drinking and the one after, when he got sober.

I couldn't see her eyes behind her giant sunglasses but I don't think she was saying it just to disagree, I think she was saying it because she thinks it's true. I was tempted to argue; I almost said that ever since she's back in A.A. she thinks everything is about people getting sober, but something told me to let it go. I didn't want the memory of seeing Grandad's hometown for the first time to be tied to a memory of an argument with Mom. I've enough of those memories already – you know that – and I'm starting to think that even when I win, I still lose.

Maybe it's not about who's right anymore, maybe it never was. And since Grandad's been dead almost half as long as I've been alive, it's not like we can ever know what he meant for sure.

There are things I do know for sure – things I can tell you. I know that I'm glad to be out of Redfern even though it was kind of scary leaving in the end, which was weird after wanting to get out of there for so long. I know that here in Donegal 'summer' doesn't mean anything – that it can be sunny and rainy and freezing all in one afternoon – and that I wish I'd brought a woolly hat like the Kangol one Ryan's been wearing ever since we landed. I know that even though I've only been here for three days, that in some way this place isn't new, that I already know it. The air is different, the feel of it on my face, and the light is different – how it stretches so long in the evenings into the sky – everything is so different from Brooklyn, different even from when we visited Limerick and Dublin all those years ago. But even though I am experiencing this light and this air and this place for the first time, it's all familiar too, like it was inside me all along, just waiting to be found.

I know that Grandad is glad the three of us have come together back to where he was born. I can feel him here, on this beach, on Trá Mór, with me. He knows why Dad's not with us – he knows everything that's happened since he died. I feel a sadness, his sadness, like he's sorry that passing on his gift to me caused so many problems, but I'm not. I wouldn't have it any other way. Despite everything that happened I'm still glad you came to me. I want you to know that – that I don't regret any of it, not a single minute.

Thinking about you makes me think that even though I'm only nineteen, I suppose in a way that I've lived two lives already too – yours and mine. And I can't pretend that I'm not scared about writing to you again, because it's been so long and I'm not even sure I still know how to do it or what might happen if I start again. I'm scared I'll have forgotten everything but I'm scared of remembering everything too, and if we were talking the way we used to talk you might laugh and say that's just like me to be scared of two completely opposite things at the very same time.

The shrinks in Redfern asked so many questions about you, had so many different terms for you. You'd laugh at the names they called you – a delusion, a split-self, a disassociation, even a ghost.

No one just called you by your name; no one just called you E.L.

I'm sitting on the sand now and I can feel the hard indents underneath me from the ripples of waves that must have gone out hours ago because I can hardly see the white tips of them from here. I don't care that it is damp, that the wind blows at this paper. I've wanted to write this story – our story – for a long time and I don't know how I know here is the right place, but I just know it is. I know that here is where I write our ending.

I can hear the shrinks' voices in my head – not like I used to hear yours – I hear memories of their voices, one voice, a hundred voices, all layered over each other, overlapping, all asking the same thing.

How does it feel, Cassie?

Tell me, Cassie, tell me what it feels like.

Can you describe the feeling, the sensation, Cassie?

Where do you feel it in your body?

You know me, if someone asks me something, I answer honestly, I try to – or at least I did in the beginning. I told them all of it, how it started with the dreams, the dreams that turned out not to be dreams but memories. Your memories. I tried to explain how I knew that, what it was like, how vivid they were and then, waking up, how I could hear your voice and how scary that was until I learned how to talk back to you.

That's what sunk it for me, when I told them about talking back to you. I learned the hard way that you can be too honest, that some things are better off not said and that people who say that they just want to know the truth really mean they want a version of the truth they can understand.

A seagull is walking really close to me now. It's not afraid, I don't think it is. It looks curious. Curious and hungry.

You know what? I'm curious too, curious about what it will be like, now, after all this time, to write out everything that happened, to have you tell me your part all over again, even though I know it already. And maybe I don't need to be so scared about remembering and forgetting. Maybe it's not even about one thing or the other, maybe it's about being able to do both.

Maybe, somehow, with your help, I'll be able to do both, at the very same time.

Part One

CASSIE

This story starts five years ago, when I was fourteen, the year Mom's memoir came out. Four years after Grandad died. The shrinks go further back than that, of course, so according to them it might have started when I was five or two or in Mom's womb. Or maybe even back further again to when Mom was five or two or in her mom's womb. That's the problem – one of the problems – with therapy. If everything can go back and back and back, then where's the start of anything? And if every question has a nice neat answer, then what happens to the things that can't be explained, like magic and ghosts and the afterlife?

These are the questions I used to ask to the shrinks in Redfern and to Alice before then. They'd nod and say, 'how interesting, Cassie', but no one would ever answer.

But since all stories need a starting point, let's say it started when I was fourteen, because that was when we went to Charleston and that's where I meet E.L.

Mom and Dad were still together, I know that, although that is harder than you would think to know because their breakup came in little slices way before the big break. Like when Mom started working on her memoir on Sundays even though Sunday had always been family day, no matter what. Or when they started sleeping in different rooms – because he snored, they said – and then when he needed his own overnight place in the city, close to work, just for during the week. You buy those things when you're a kid – or at least I bought those things – because part of you wants them to be true even though another part of you knows deep down that they're lying. But sometimes lies are easier than the truth, it turns out. Sometimes I think it would've made life so much easier if I'd just lied about E.L. from the start.

So there we are, Mom and Dad and Ryan and me, in Charleston, staying in a guesthouse that's a big, old, white house with a wraparound porch and a courtyard out the back where we eat breakfast outside and listen to the sound of the birds. No one has said that, unless things get better with Mom and Dad, this is the last family vacation we're all going to go on together, but we all know it, and the silence somehow makes the stakes even higher.

If I was fourteen, then Ryan must have been eleven, which makes sense because I remember the first argument of the morning was about him having his Nintendo at the table.

'Ry, I told you to put that away,' Mom says. 'You can take it out later, when we're in the car.'

Dad is helping himself to honey. He doesn't see the bee on the other side of the pot and I don't tell him. I can tell he's going to disagree with Mom before he does.

'He's not harming anybody,' he says. 'How is it any different than letting Cassie read through every meal we sit down to eat together?'

Mom tries to blow her hair out of her face but it sticks to her skin, already sticky in the heat. It was still long then, still blonde.

'Books are different, Joe. Educational.'

It's six months since Mom's memoir came out, a month after she's first been on *Oprah*. None of her novels ever made it on *Oprah*. None of her novels had even come close.

Dad makes a face. 'Harry Potter? Hardly educational. Haven't you already read that one?' It's a question but he doesn't give me time to answer. 'When I was fourteen, I was reading Hemingway. Mark Twain.'

'Jesus, Joe.' Mom pushes her chair back and the metal makes a screeching sound on the flagstones.

'What?' he says. 'What's wrong with the great American writers?'

'*Great American writers.*' She shakes her head, pulls a cigarette out of her pocket book and lights it up.

'You're going to smoke at the table now? Over breakfast? Before you even eat anything?'

She turns her head, blows smoke the other way. 'Why not? It just gives you something else to be self-righteous and judgemental about.'

Ryan looks up from his Nintendo and we catch eyes for a second before I go back to Ron and Hermione. Dad's right, I have read it before. It's *The Goblet of Fire* and it's the last one Grandad bought for me; he bought us both copies so we could read them at the same time.

My eyes scan the words but I don't take them in because I'm waiting for Dad to respond. He'll ask her what that's supposed to mean or he'll defend himself or he'll accuse her of being the one whose self-righteous – that's how it works. But he doesn't do any of those things. Instead he just looks at her and puts some more honey on his toast, spreads it around.

And that's scariest of all.

He gave me *The Adventures of Tom Sawyer*, Dad did, after Grandad died. Grandad taught me how to read before I even went to school. By the time Mrs. Pikowski was teaching us the ABCs Grandad had me reading the *New York Times* front page. All the books on the shelves in my room were from Grandad up until Dad gave me that book. He'd wrapped it up really nicely and inside there was a note about how it was his favourite book growing up and that he hoped I'd love it too.

I never read it. I don't know why, I knew it was a big deal to him. Maybe it was even *because* I knew it was a big deal, or maybe it was just because it was hard with all the funny old-fashioned words and the way that Jim the slave spoke. If Grandad had read it to me like he read all the Tír na nÓg books, it might have been different, he might have brought it to life, but Grandad wasn't there – that was the whole point. Dad asked me every few days if I was enjoying it and if I'd finished it. I lied a few times and moved the bookmark deeper in, but when he'd try and talk about a bit of it, then he knew. And after a while, he stopped asking me.

Sitting in the heat of that Charleston courtyard, starting the same sentence about Ron and Hermione over and over, I have this crazy idea that if I'd read *The Adventures of Tom Sawyer*, then none of this would be happening. This argument, all the other arguments, everything unravelling might be down to that one moment. That maybe if I can somehow engineer the day so we can get to a bookshop and I can get another copy and read it as fast as I can, then I'll have something to talk to Dad about again. He'll know I wasn't ungrateful and that I loved his present and that I loved him for giving it to me.

But I don't say anything. I read instead. Mom smokes. Ryan plays Nintendo. Dad eats toast and honey. And after breakfast we get in the car and drive to the cotton plantation that Mom had seen in the guidebook, the one Ryan wanted to go to, and I had too, until this morning.

Maybe if I'd insisted about the bookshop, maybe if I'd refused to go to the plantation, then things would have turned out differently. Maybe I could have stopped Dad leaving, at least for a while.

But then again if we didn't go to the plantation, then I'd never have met E.L. And then there'd be no story at all.

E.L.

They calls me E.L. Cassie use a'ways ask what that stand for and I say what Charity a'ways say – that E.L. stand for me and that all I need to know.

Charity not my mamma but she like my mamma. She my mamma's friend from when they was little girls like me and Miss Ellen. My mamma and Charity, they came here t'gether. My mamma passed but Charity stay 'live. Cassie ask me a lot of things I don't know no answers to. I don't know 'bout addin' up numbers or 'bout music and even though Charity teach me to read and write some, I don't know these books Cassie a'ways talkin' 'bout.

But I know how to read the colours in the sky and how much time it gone take b'fore they all come in from the field. I know how the wind feel b'fore it rain and which snakes you got be 'fraid of and which you don't. I know the diff'rent looks in the Master face a'most b'fore he make them – the one that mean he gone pick me up and the one that mean I need to run fast through the kitchen and down the steps and hide under the porch. I know the Mistress don't like me none, that she don't like when the Master nice to me. I know where to get the best wood for the fire – better than any of the boys.

I work in the big house for Miss Ellen and she a'most a whole year younger than me but she act like she older. The big house got its own name – Riverside Hall. The whole plantation called that. Outside the walls is South Carolina and in South Carolina there som'place called Charleston where the Master go to get new slaves and do bus'ness. I ain't never been there 'cause I'm a girl and only the mens get to go outside on Sundays sometimes or days when Nagle wants them to work som'place else.

Nagle the overseer but I don't want to talk 'bout Nagle. 'Stead I'll tell you 'bout the mens. They all stay in one cabin – Big Bill and Little Bill, John, Benjamin, Sullivan, Walker, Elijah, Carlton, Harry and Paul.

In our cabin is the womens: Charity and me, Linda and Marjorie and Rose and Nelly. Sometimes Big Bill comes in to see Charity and I pretend to be sleepin' and I never say nothin' to no one 'cause he a'ways gone in the mornin'. Linda married to John but I ain't never seen him in our cabin.

Juba work in the house and she sleep there too. Juba older than anyone else here. She r'member the old Master – the Mistress Daddy – and she a'ways talkin' 'bout what it like here back then. One time, Miss Ellen ask the Mistress if I can sleep in the house too and she say that the cabin good 'nough for me and that she ain't havin' me in her house all night. Juba hear her sayin' all that and she smile like she better than me. When I tell Charity, she say that house slaves like Juba the dumbest of all 'cause they think white folk look at them diff'rent when ev'ryone know that white folk look at slaves like they all the same.

Firs' I don't know Cassie white and when I find out it like it make e'erythin' worse, it make me think she some demon in my head. It diff'rent for me than for her. I don't know nothin' 'bout me bein' in her dreams and she ain't in mine. No one ain't ever in my dreams 'cause I don't ever dream nothin'.

What happen for me is that I start to feel her there – feel somethin' diff'rent. It hard to 'splain what it feel like but I can tell you 'bout the day I firs' notice it – the feelin'. I can tell you 'bout the day somethin' change.

That day, I in the clearin', visitin' Dolly. Dolly use belong to Miss Ellen but after the Master break her when he throw her at the wall, Miss Ellen give her to me. Dolly Miss Ellen's fav'rite – I know that – and she say she want me to treat her right and take care her so she don't get hurt worse. I don't take her to the cabin 'cause I don't want Marjorie to take her and I don't want Charity to see her neither, case she get mad that I take somethin' from Miss Ellen, even though she give her to me. So I hide her in a hole in one of the trees 'round the clearin' – 'bout half way down the trunk. Inside there some moss – real soft. That moss Dolly's bed.

That night it a'ready gettin' dark, but it easy to find the tree even without the sun. Under my feets the grass cold. One time Miss Ellen take her shoes and stockin's off to see how the ground feel and she don't like it none. She made me put her shoe on and I don't like that none neither. I like to feel the earth, the grass, with my feets. I like to know what type of ground I standin' on and to know it ain't no snake.

The night Cassie come – the night it a'ready dark – when I reach in for Dolly she ain't there. I put my hand down deeper into the hole in case she fallen even though I know she can't have fallen. She ain't there, only moss there. And my heart beat real fast then like I been runnin' 'way from Nagle's dogs and my breath fast too like I gone cry. And that's when it come. The firs' feelin'.

At firs' it feel creepy, like someone watchin' me but when I turn 'round there no one there.

'Hello?' I shout out, make my voice braver than I feel. 'Who there?'

There ain't no one there, only the moss blowin' a little bit in the wind. I shiver then even though I ain't cold and if it ain't for Dolly bein' missin' I woulda done run back to the cabins. But she is missin' and she Miss Ellen's fav'rite b'fore she give her to me and now she mine and I want to take care her. And even though she only a doll I don't want her bitten by no snake the way Little Bill was when he nearly die.

I gets down on my knees to look for her, in case she fell outta the tree. The grass longest here, it a'ready damp. I brush my hands through it 'round the roots of the tree and all the while I still have it – the feelin'.

After, Cassie ask me how I knew she there, what it feel like for me. She done ask me that a thousand times and a thousand times I tells her the same thing. That down on my knees in the damp grass, it feel like there someone else down there with me – someone helpin' me look for Dolly. Only that ain't really right 'cause it feel like the feelin' comin' up from inside me – not outside – like the feelin' sometimes I get in Church when we all singin' and I sittin' so close to Charity that our legs and shoulders touch. But it ain't like that feelin' neither 'cause it silent and there only me but with this feelin' it seem like I ain't on my own. And even though it gettin' darker and the dark is when the snakes come out, and even though Dolly still missin' and even though I s'ppose be back at the cabin and have the firewood collected a'ready I don't feel 'fraid no more. And I don't know how I know, but I jus' know ev'rythin' gone be a'right.

I sit 'gainst the tree. I feel the trunk 'gainst my back. My hand skim the top of the grass and I really feel that too. I done skim the grass like that a thousand times b'fore but I feel it like it the firs' time. And I lookin' at my hands and my fingers and my knuckles and it all look new – even the scar where the Mistress have Nagle burn me for stealin' the biscuit even though I ain't never stole nothin' from that kitchen. And it like I never seen my hand b'fore and it real peaceful sittin' there lookin' at it and I think maybe I dyin' – maybe this what dyin' feel like and if it does I ain't never gone be scared no more.

And right when I'm thinkin' that, in a patch of grass right next to me, a patch where I musta looked five or six times, Dolly there, lyin' face down on the ground.

I pick her up, real slow. I put my finger on her face – like the way I seen Miss Ellen do. I run my finger over her nose and her chin and the cheek that ain't broken and the big hole in her other cheek where the Master broke her. I take the longest on that bit and all the time I doin' it, I tippin' her head back and forward so her eyes open and then they close 'gain.

This the way Miss Ellen play with her dolls, but not me. I ain't got no time to play like that with Dolly. I a'ways take her out fast – check her face – put her in 'gain. I ain't got no time and b'sides I don't want no one seein' us. But that night with the new feelin', it diff'rent. Like there ain't no rush for nothin'. Like there ain't no reason to be 'fraid.

I stand up slow and it like someone helpin' me – pushin' into my legs along with me, givin' me they strength, well as mine. When I put Dolly back in the hole and fix the moss all 'round her I close her eyes with my hand and say 'night, night, Dolly' out loud and I ain't scared that someone gone hear.

Walkin' back to the cabins I can feel it goin' – the feelin' – like I leave it there back in the clearin'. If you watchin' you won't see nothin' change – only a girl in a grey slave dress and white head scarf walkin' home none too fast – I won't look no diff'rent to you than I did b'fore. There ain't nothin' diff'rent 'bout the way I walk or the steps my feets take – prob'ly even my face look the same.

But inside it change – like there somethin' full b'fore and now it empty. And it make me think of my mamma and I don't never think of my mamma. Even if I want to I can't 'cause I don't hardly r'member her. And I wish then I didn't never have it – that other feelin' – 'cause I ain't never known I was empty b'fore. I think how I a'ways feel the only feelin' there is.

I get in trouble for havin' no wood but I don't care. Charity ask me if somethin' wrong and even though I don't never lie to her I say no 'cause I don't know what to tell her. And all that night I lie 'wake and I thinkin' it mus' be somethin' to do with Dolly – that she musta done had some magic inside her that I ain't never found b'fore. But when I go back the next day, even though I hold her that same way and stroke her face like I did the night b'fore, it diff'rent. Somethin' missin'. The feelin' missin' – til it come back 'gain.

CASSIE

The first time I had the dream, I thought that's all it was – just a dream. It was the night of the day we'd visited the plantation. The plantation had not been a success. It was hot and there were too many tours and Mom insisted that we do all of them. Southern heat feels different than New York heat – your skin feels slimy all the time, like you're dirty. I wanted to be back at the hotel sitting in a rocking chair drinking sweet iced tea and reading Harry Potter. I wanted to be anywhere but there.

After we did the tour of the big house and the tour of the fields where the slaves picked cotton, we visited the cabins where they lived. There were eight of them, laid out differently and when you hit a button by the door a slave-type voice came on to tell you the story of the family who lived there. But the story wasn't enough for Mom – she had to read every bit of writing on the walls as well. And there was a lot of writing.

If this was a movie, or a made-up story, something would have happened to me in one of those cabins. I might have had some feeling come over me – some presence – or I might have seen the initials 'E.L.' scratched into a wall, really low, in a place where no one else would see it. But I've been over and over that day in my mind and I don't remember anything like that. I only remember the heat in those cabins. And how all the other visitors walked out when the talking part had ended but we stayed, Mom taking photos and reading, Ryan outside in the shade playing Nintendo and Dad leaning against the door, watching Mom.

'Seriously, Lou – do you really need to read every single word?' He gestures at the walls.

'For once can you exercise some patience? It's fascinating. Look – did you see this? An inventory of all the slaves they bought and sold.' Mom takes another photo on her phone.

'What do you need a photo of a slave inventory for?'

'I'm a writer, Joe. This is how you get ideas. You never know, I might decide to write a book about this someday.'

Dad tries to catch my eye, so I'll be on his side, but I look away.

'If you're going to write a book about it then we should have gone to the other plantation – the authentic one. The guidebook said these cabins aren't original – they were built for some movie. That inventory is probably made up.'

I speak before I know I'm going to. 'Why would that bother Mom? She has no problem making stuff up to sell books.'

They both turn and look at me. Mom raises her sunglasses up into her hair.

'What's that supposed to mean?'

She knows exactly what I mean. I shrug. 'Just that I always thought there was supposed to be a difference between writing fiction and writing memoir. That memoirs were supposed to tell the truth.'

Before she can answer, I walk past Dad in the doorway and down the steps past Ryan in the shade.

'Cassie!' Mom says behind me but I don't turn back. I keep walking all the way down to the riverbank. It's not cool there – nowhere in this sweat pit is cool – but it's ever so slightly less stifling than the cabin.

I sit down on the grass and I start to pluck at it with my fingers. There's a chance Dad might come after me. Mom definitely won't.

If Grandad were here he'd leave me for a bit but then he'd come and sit next to me, a little bit away. He'd wait for me to talk first and when I did, he'd listen, really listen and then he'd tell me the truth.

He always told the truth. Mom was the one I couldn't trust, who lied all the time.

Plucking at the grass makes me think about the summer evenings when he would water the plants and dead head the flowers. We did it together, he showed me how and I used to love that time of the evening when the heat was still in the day and it was just the two of us out there, taking our time with the watering can, plucking and pouring and saying goodnight to the plants. It was on one of those evenings when I'd first mustered up the courage to ask him what I'd been meaning to ask him for a long time, what had been on my mind for months.

'Grandad, why do Mom and Dad fight all the time?'

I remember that feeling after the question was finally out – the space I had back in my mind and the relief that brought, until fear washed into it like a wave, about what his answer might be. He might deny it, say they didn't fight, that he didn't know what I was talking about. But I knew he wouldn't say any of that, I knew he'd tell me the truth.

He put the watering can down, sat on the little metal chair in the backyard so we were at the same level.

'People fight, Cass. Sometimes even when they love each other. Sometimes people who love each other fight most of all.'

'But why?' I said. I remember saying that. 'I don't get it.'

He took a minute to answer. He looked sad and I wondered for a second if it was his fault they fought and if that would be better than it being mine. 'Sometimes we expect so much of the people we love. It's not enough for them to love us, we want them to love us in a certain type of way. We want them to fix us.'

His eyes held my eyes and I wondered if he was talking about Nana who died when I was only a baby because once I heard Mom and Auntie Cathy talking about the terrible fights Grandad and Nana used to have. What Grandad was saying was important – he wanted me to understand and I wasn't sure I did but I wanted to, more than anything I wanted to.

'And when they can't? We get angry at them. Mad. But really we're mad at ourselves.'

I played his words over in my head, could hear them as clear as the rushing of the river water, as if he was there, saying them to me, instead of some memory from five or six years ago. And I still wasn't sure I understood. Grandad was the one I'd loved most of all and he'd loved me the most – everyone knew that – but we never fought, not like Mom and Dad. And watching the water flowing by over the rocks and pulling at the reeds I want to have an epiphany, to suddenly get it, but I don't. I'm still not sure what he meant.

I wait by the river for someone to come get me but no one does and eventually I get up and I find them, three cabins on from where I'd stormed off. I don't apologise to Mom, even though I know she thinks I should, and when we finally drive out of the long driveway no one is speaking and the only sound is the click Mom's phone makes as she takes photos of the long line of trees through the back window.

That night we go to an Italian for dinner. Dad wants Southern food but Mom says she's sick of grits and fried chicken, and I'm secretly glad she gets her way. On the way there it rains like I've never seen rain before, a sudden relentless pouring that comes out of the thick sticky air and fills up the drains and makes rivers of the paths and stops as quickly as it came. And I'm pretty sure the argument over dinner was about the rain and whether we should have waited it out under the awning of some gift shop or run the extra block to the restaurant like Dad wanted to. And I'm glad I brought Harry Potter this time so I can half read under the table and pretend I don't notice the fight and I can tune out the stupid waitress who recognises Mom from *Oprah* and keeps talking on and on about how powerful reading her memoir was. And of course when she says that, Mom forgets to argue with Dad and the smiles come out and she signs a napkin and makes a drawing of a love heart next to her name.

Mom drinks too much red wine like she always does and there's a part of the meal where she's fun and Dad is laughing before the part where her teeth are turning that pinkish colour and there's red stains at the edges of her lips. She's slurring by then, saying stupid things and it's not fun anymore. Dad's paid the bill, you can tell he wants to get out of there, when Mom calls the waitress over and smiles, puts her hand on her arm.

She drops her voice like she is whispering her a secret.

'Be an angel and bring me one more glass of the Cabernet, will you? We never got a photo together – we can do that if you like.'

And it's so embarrassing then, I want the floor to open up because it's not the same waitress; it's some young girl who's hardly older than me and probably doesn't even know who Mom is. She looks around. There's only one other table in the restaurant and they are standing up, about to leave.

'We're just about to close,' she says. 'Everyone's left already.'

Dad stands up behind Mom's chair, puts his hand on her

shoulders. 'Don't worry,' he says to the waitress. 'She's fine, she doesn't need it. We're going now.'

Mom snatches herself away from him. 'Since when do you speak for me, Joe?'

He reaches out to touch her, both hands on her shoulders this time, keeps smiling as if she hasn't said anything. Mom takes out a twenty from her wallet, waves it at the waitress. 'Cabernet,' she says. 'Please.'

The waitress stands up straight – she looks like she might cry. 'The bar's closed,' she says. 'I'm sorry.'

Mom composes herself, stands up, smooths down her skirt, smiles. 'Of course. That's no problem. Thank you.'

The waitress bolts from the table, disappears behind the bar. Mom swings her bag over her shoulder and starts to walk to the door.

'C'mon, guys,' Dad says, 'let's go.'

'I need to pee,' Ryan says. 'Can you wait a second?'

'You heard what the waitress said, this place is closing. You should have gone earlier. Let's go.'

He starts to walk after Mom and Ryan's about to follow him when I put my hand on his arm.

'Dad! Don't be a jerk – it's not Ryan's fault. Anyway, I need to use the restroom too. And it *can't* wait.'

Dad turns around and looks like he wants to kill us both but he doesn't question it. He doesn't want to risk getting into some teenage girl territory that he can't handle, just like I knew he wouldn't.

'Okay then, go on. But make it quick.'

We hurry away, walking fast, but in the stall I take my time. I don't actually need to go but I take out my book, read two pages. When I come out, Ryan is outside.

'You were ages.'

'Girl stuff.'

He makes a face. We start to walk back towards the table, Dad is gone now. The whole restaurant is empty.

'Where's Dad?'

'What am I, psychic? Probably outside with Mom.'

We walk past the waitresses at the bar, the one who recognised Mom from *Oprah* and the young one and two others I hadn't seen. They are talking and when they see us they stop. They wave goodnight and we wave back.

'They're going to get a divorce, aren't they?' Ryan says as we walk through the main door.

'Don't be stupid.'

Outside, Dad is standing on the porch, his face lit up by his phone screen as he punches in a text. He never texts.

'Where's Mom?' Ryan asks.

'I don't know. She's not answering her phone. She probably went back to the hotel.'

'Without us?' Ryan sounds close to tears.

'Well, if you two hadn't taken so long in the damn bathroom she probably would have waited.'

I put my arm around Ryan's shoulder. 'Don't blame us just because you two are fighting. We haven't done anything.'

Dad's phone light goes out and I don't know if it's just the half dark but he doesn't look angry anymore – he looks tired. Beaten.

'You're right. I'm sorry, guys. I know I'm being a grouch. Let's just go back to the hotel.'

We were supposed to do a horse and carriage ride after dinner and I think Ryan is going to remind Dad because I know he really wanted to do it, but he doesn't say anything and I don't either. The sidewalks are almost dry despite the crazy heavy rain earlier and the bars we walk past are full with music and laughing and people spilling out onto outside terraces and sometimes the street. I see Dad looking inside each bar, pretending not to, and I'm looking in too, to see if I can see her. Back at our hotel, it's quiet. The tiny bar in the lobby is empty. When Dad opens the door to his and Mom's room I'm praying that I'll see her shape, asleep under the covers of their four-poster bed but I don't. She's not there. I walk through to the adjoining room, the one that Ryan and I share and she's not there either.

'Mom's not here,' Ryan says. 'You said she'd be here but she's not. That means she's missing!'

Dad rubs his hand over his hair, from one side to the other so he leaves a funny bit sticking up at the front.

'Listen, kiddo, she's not missing. She just needed to blow off some steam, that's all. She'll be home soon – wait and see.'

'How do you know?' Ryan asks.

Dad folds his arms and smiles. 'I just know, buddy, that's all.'

That 'I just know' crap doesn't work on me by then but I don't say anything.

'Listen, how about we all get into this bed here – it's big enough – and watch one of the movies on demand. They have *X-Men*.'

'Can we order room service?' Ryan asks.

'No. But there's some microwave popcorn in the minibar, you can have that. And a soda.'

'Awesome!'

Usually we're never allowed soda this late and Ryan drops down on his hands and knees in front of the minibar so he can see what's on offer.

'I'm going to go to bed,' I say.

Dad frowns. 'Really, you're tired?'

'I have as much desire to see *X-Men* as I do to have multiple root canals.'

Dad semi-smiles, and reaches for the remote. 'Okay then, we can watch something else, there's a ton of movies.'

'It's okay.' I shake my head. 'I'm going to read. I'm at a good part in my book.'

I wait for Dad to say something about Harry Potter and start on again how I should be reading something else, but he doesn't. Instead he reaches over and hugs me.

'You're always at a good part in your book,' he says into my hair.

And I go to bed then. And I read. And I hear the T.V. in the next room but I hear Dad snoring and Ryan too and I know they've fallen asleep and I think I'm not going to sleep until Mom comes home but eventually I fall asleep too.

And that's the first night I have the dream.

***

We're running through the grass. I want to say 'I'm running through the grass' but this is her memory, this happened to her, not to me. I don't know this place, the flatness of it, the dirty heat. It is her memory even though it is my feet I can feel bare, on the earth, hot, stony, sore. A sharp stone jabs my skin but my foot is moving too quickly – her foot is moving too quickly – for it to hurt for long.

We're going downhill, the ground underneath our feet is a decline, only a slight one and our legs are moving faster, whirling, out of our control. If our legs were a bike, we'd be freewheeling but there's no wheel, only legs, one set of legs, her legs, mine, running, running, running through the grass, one set of arms out front, two hands, pushing the grass out of the way, making a V in the grass so that every now and then some of it snaps back, too fast, flicks into my eye making it water.

Her eye.

Breath is panting. I can hear it, feel it, just like I can feel my skin – itchy, hot – and I can feel the grass and the sun and the material of this strange dress I'm wearing, heavy on my body, much too heavy for this heat. Why am I wearing this? Where are my shoes?

I stumble and it slows me, just for a second. Back up, my arms stretched out in front of me are thinner than my arms. And they are a different colour than my arms – they are a black person's arms. And I know that this is not me at all.

Something is behind us – someone is – getting closer. I can't see who or what it is because she doesn't look around and I can't hear what they are calling out to us over all the breath but I can feel it, sense it, like a monster in a movie, getting closer and closer and my heart is pounding along with her heart and my feet are wheeling faster over the earth, so the stones and the broken stalks and the uneven bumps of ground barely hurt.

Over the tips of the blades of grass, there is a line of trees with moss dripping from the branches like falling water. Above the trees the sun is like a magnifying glass in the cloudless sky. But we are not running towards the line of trees – we are running at an angle now, towards a single tree at the edge, slightly apart from all the others. That tree is the one we are running towards, the one with a branch that dips towards the ground. The one with something else hanging from it, apart from just the moss.

And right now, right here, I want to stop, to pause and look closer, to see what is hanging there, but this isn't my memory, this is E.L.'s memory. She's the one running faster, who won't look back – can't look back – she's the one who keeps running, running, running towards the tree on its own. This didn't happen to me.

And then, we're close enough. Over the blades of grass I see it. Has she seen it before me? The split second before I do? Or do we see it at the exact same time? The shape that even in the tree's shade is blacker than everything else, hanging from the lowest branch, the one facing away from us. That was how we hadn't seen it earlier – how I hadn't seen it earlier – this shape raised up above the grass, turning, slowly, slowly.

Each stride, every foot on the earth and lifted back up again, brings the shape closer, up over the blades of grass we can see more of it, I can. The ground goes down, our feet in a hole, a wobble and it disappears for a second so there is only grass until we are level again and it is there, in the air, hanging from the tree. Turning slowly.

We're getting closer, it's getting closer, the thing behind us might be closer too or maybe it has stopped because it feels like she is slowing, the strides, the steps are slower, we are definitely getting slower, slow like the slow turn of the shape.

And it's not just a shape. It's a person.

Did she know that, all this time? Did she see straight away? Can our eyes look at the same things and see something that's not the same?

She stops. There is a wind. I hadn't noticed the wind before. The grass bends. The shape turns. The person, the body. It is wearing some clothes and there is red on the clothes and on the face. Blood. Slowly turning I see its hands are tied behind its back. The head isn't bloody, the head is on one side, leaning on the shoulder, like it's only sleeping.

It turns.

The head is facing us, straight on. The face. Her face. It's not an 'it', it's a woman. Her eyes are open. Across the grass she sees the open eyes, I see the eyes before I close my own. Open my mouth.

I couldn't see birds but I know that my scream is making them fly from the bushes and the ground and the trees where they have been resting up until now. I know the scream that rips my throat can be heard by them, by animals everywhere even if not by people, even if I can't hear it myself.

But maybe some people can hear it. Through the walls of their houses. Through the thick heat, through time – through seconds and minutes and decades of time.

Some people can hear the scream.

Hear us.

Hear her.

Hear me.

E.L.

We in the barn. We all sittin' in a circle 'round Charity. She want us all see the book. Her finger move real slow, 'long with her words 'cross the paper.

'The Lord is my shepherd, I shall not want.'

It dark and hard to see the black marks on the page. She done 'splained a'ready 'bout letters makin' up words and words makin' up sentences but ev'rythin' look the same to me.

Next to me, Little Bill laughin' at somethin' and he poke me in the ribs. I lift my hand to hit him not takin' my eyes off the page.

'E.L., Little Bill! Pay 'tension!' Charity say. 'And hush. You don't want the Master findin' us, do you?'

'No, ma'am,' says Little Bill.

I shake my head.

'You know what'll happen if we caught, don't you?'

We both nod at the same time. We ain't laughin' no more. Charity start readin' 'gain.

'He make me to lie down in green pastures.'

Then Marjorie shake her head and look at me like she all grown up and she never gone laugh and risk us gettin' caught and I wish Little Bill ain't never poked me.

'What a pasture?' Benjamin ask.

Charity look up, smile. She never get mad when we ask questions.

She say she like it and sometimes I think Benjamin ask questions to make her like him the best. 'Pasture jus' 'nother word for field.'

Benjamin laugh. 'This mus' be som'place else 'cause there ain't no one restin' in no fields 'round here!'

Marjorie start to laugh 'cause she laugh at ev'rythin' Benjamin say, and Charity laugh too but then she stop all a sudden. I go to say somethin' but she put her finger to her mouth and then we all hear what she hear – a noise outside. Footsteps. Through the gaps b'tween the wood I can see someone there – a man – and then the door bust open and the light 'splode in.

I close my eyes, squeeze them tight.

'What the hell goin' on in here?'

I open my eyes. Big Bill standin' in the doorway so tall his head nearly bump the top. He step inside, close the door b'hind him. No one says nothin'.

Charity jump up real fast to her feet, try to hide the book in her skirt but he seen it a'ready. He go to grab it out her hand but she too fast and she snatch it 'way.

'I can't believe you still doin' this – what I done told you? What gone happen when Nagle find out?'

Big Bill grab for the book 'gain, miss 'gain.

'Nagle ain't gone find out,' Charity say. 'He ain't gone find out 'cause no one gone tell him.'

'You know that for sure? Huh? What if I been Nagle? What if I been the Mistress?'

He ain't shoutin', he whisperin', but his whisper feel loud as a shout. My heart thump like I been runnin' all the way from the cabins to the big house 'stead of jus' sittin' here on the barn floor.

Charity fold the book in front of her chest like a shield. 'Well, you ain't Nagle. You ain't the Mistress!'

'I coulda been – what you say if I had been?'

'I tell them it Sunday, that we lookin' at the Bible. Like in Church. What the diff'rence?'

'What the diff'rence? You mean that – what the diff'rence?' Big Bill move in close to Charity. His face real dark – much darker than hers – so all I can see is the white part of his eyes.

'You a smart woman – you know the diff'rence.' His fingers reach 'round the Bible, take it from her hand, throw it on the floor. 'They find out you can read? That fifty lashes right there. Teachin' these chil'ren? A hundred. More, maybe. That what you want? That what you want them to see?'

Little Bill musta done stood up 'cause he standin' now but real close to me so his leg push 'gainst my arm. Charity flick her head so her hair fall back off her face and you can see the shiny scar at the top of her forehead.

'They can give me three hundred lashes. Five hundred. Hell, they can give me a thousand! No matter how much of my blood end up by that whippin' post they ain't never gone be able to take 'way from these chil'ren what they a'ready know.'

She pick the Bible up from the floor, dust it off. My heart beatin' faster and I 'fraid I gone relieve myself right there on the floor.

Big Bill walkin' 'round in a circle. His voice louder than b'fore but still low. 'You can't be so damn hot-headed all the time. What good you gone be to these little ones if you sold or worse? If you want teach 'em somethin' teach 'em how to pick cotton, skin a goat. Set a fire. What use they ever have for readin', for writin'? None, that's what.'

Charity holdin' the Bible to her, huggin' it to herself 'gain. She shakin' her head with ev'rythin' Big Bill say. She look at me, at Marjorie, at Benjamin. 'He don't mean it. He jus' sayin' it. He don't mean it.'

'The hell I don't!' Big Bill forgettin' to whisper now. 'Teach 'em to work hard. To keep their tongues. Not to cry when they gettin' beat 'cause that make it worse. Teach 'em those things. What do they need readin' for? To read the notice at the auction when the slave trader comes? To see how much they life worth?'

That when Charity hit him, right in front of us. She hit him with the Bible, hard, two fast thumps 'round side of his head. He grab her wrist and they struggle, she try pullin' 'way from him from him but he hold her too tight.

'Don't never say that. Don't never say that 'gain! Readin' give you ev'rythin', readin' give you somethin' they can't take. Readin' give you freedom!'

She shoutin' out now – loud – and Big Bill pull her tighter. Nobody else speak and there no other noise except for the scuffle of they feets on the floor. And then I hear it – the other noise – we all do. It a rhythm, far 'way, then closer. It the sound of a horse.

Big Bill freeze, let go of Charity. She put her finger on her mouth 'gain even though she don't need to. We don't speak, don't fidget, don't hardly breathe – jus' listen and wait. We like that for a minute, for ten minutes, and my chest hurt and I close my eyes 'cause I don't want to see the door open 'gain and Nagle standin' there.

The horse noise get louder and louder and right when it like it gone bust inside the barn it turn and it not quite so loud as b'fore. And then it get further 'way – little by little – until it only a soft noise and then no noise at all.

I feel somethin' wet on my arm and when I open my eyes I see Little Bill movin' 'way and there a wet patch down his pantaloon. Marjorie got her knees up to her chest. Benjamin standin' b'hind her and he walk up to Charity, put his arms 'round her waist. Her hand rub his hair, his neck and I want to go to her too only I don't think I can stand up.

Big Bill touch the side his face where Charity hit him with the Bible. When he talk 'gain his whisper lower than b'fore. 'You think you givin' them somethin' they can't take? They can take anythin' they want. Anytime. Even these chil'ren know that. 'Specially that one – she know most of all.'

He point at me and Charity look at me too. And I see then that she got tears on her cheeks that run right the way down under her chin. I think maybe she gone argue. To say somethin' else. But she don't, she only take one hand out of Benjamin's hair and she hold it out to me. And I stand up real slow and walk over and hold on to it real tight, like I ain't never gone let it go.

And Big Bill don't say nothin' else neither. He walk over to the door, real quiet and open it real slow so that for a second you can see the whole barn – the loft and the weighin' machine and the ladders and the carts – and then he close it b'hind him.

And after the brightness of the sunshine it feel darker then after that, in the barn, darker than it ever done feel b'fore.

CASSIE

I want to tell you that I had the dream every night for the rest of the vacation but I want to tell you the truth and not exaggerate, and that might be exaggerating. Maybe I had it one more time or maybe twice on vacation, but it's really back in Brooklyn that I remember the dream taking hold. Every time I had it, it seemed longer, more vivid. Sometimes when I closed my eyes at night it felt like I fell right into it, like it had been there all day, waiting for me to come back, as if it never really left me at all.

It always started out the same – running through the grass, the tips flicking back into my eyes – and it ended the same way too. Every time I woke up, my heart was beating way fast and my throat was hoarse like I'd been screaming for real. Waking up was like being dropped into my room from some other world – some other planet – and it took longer and longer to recognise where I was, for my breath to be able to come into my body again, for me to reclaim my own life.

I developed a system to help pull me from the dream, to get things under control again. Every night before going to bed, I needed to make sure my glasses were on the nightstand. As soon as I woke up I had to put them on straightaway and turn on the light, ideally all in one movement. Next, I had to focus on the bookshelf at the end of my bed. They were in order on the shelves and I knew the order better than I knew anything. The Dr. Seuss's came first and then the Irish ones from Grandad all together – the *Irish Legends* series: *Oisin and Tír na nÓg*, *The Children of Lír* and *The Salmon of Knowledge*. After that came *The Secret Garden* and *A Little Princess* and *Harriet the Spy* and the *Long Secret* and *Sport* and after that came all the Narnia books and *Call it Courage* and the Judy Blumes and the Harry Potters. From bed I couldn't read all the names on the spines but I didn't need to – I knew the colours and the shapes and what came next. The trick was not to rush, to say the names slowly in my head before moving on to the next one and make myself breathe at the same time.

Usually, by the time I got to *The Secret Garden* my breath was slowing down and by Harriet it was nearly normal again, but sometimes it took until I got to *The Lion, the Witch and the Wardrobe.* Once I knew I was okay, I'd reach down for my feet and run my fingers over the soles and between my toes so I'd know they weren't cut. I knew by now that they only felt like that, that it was impossible to get cut or hurt from a dream but they always felt like they were bleeding so I always had to check. By the time I got to the Harry Potters I was able to lie back down and pick up whatever book was on my nightstand and feel calm enough to read it until I fell back asleep.

I guess you might be wondering what I was doing with all those kid's books on my shelves – *The Secret Garden* and Harriet and all that – but the truth was that when I fell in love with a book I could never throw it away. Mom was always trying to get me to give some away to Goodwill, she even tried to sneak out my Dr. Seuss books when I wasn't looking one time, but I found them in a box by the kerb and I took them back inside, even though they were wet from the rain.

After I'd finished reading, when I lay back down in bed, I'd vow to tell someone about the dream the next day – but I never did. One day I came close to telling Gabi on the walk to school. She was my best friend and you were supposed to be able to say anything to your best friend but one time I'd tried to tell her about Grandad's gift I knew by the look in her face she thought I was making it all up. I didn't want to see it again – that look – and besides, the only thing she wanted to talk about lately was some new guy in our grade called Scott Stroller.

One night after making my way through all the books, my heart is still racing and I make fists with my hands and hit the bed, once, twice, three times, each time harder than the last. It's right there inside me, the anger, and it's worse because I don't know who I'm mad at –Mom or Dad or Gabi or even Grandad, but that makes no sense because Grandad is dead and you can't be mad at a dead person. Especially when I was never even mad at him when he was alive.

'Where are you?' I say that out loud. 'Are you there? Can you hear me?'

I'm talking to Grandad – I think I am. Maybe I'm mad at him because he's the person who I would have told. Maybe I'm mad at him for not being there, right when I need him to be. For the millionth time my mind, goes back to trace over every detail of the day he took me to Brighton Beach, the day I was off sick from school. That was the day he told me I'd inherited his gift – that I'd always be able to see him, feel him, talk to him. Both fists hit the bed again. It was five years since then – more – and I'd never even felt his presence near me, let alone seen him, even in a dream. Maybe Mom was right, maybe all those things she wrote were true. Maybe I should never have trusted him.

This time my legs pound the bed along with my fists. 'If you can hear me, please help me. Please tell me what's going on.'

I listen but the room is silent. The anger is a bit less than before but guilt washes in to fill its place: guilt that I could question Grandad, guilt that I could believe Mom's lies, that I could take her side.

It had to be my fault, I had to be doing something wrong. Maybe these dreams were part of the gift, maybe something was happening and I was so dumb I didn't even know it. Grandad had never mentioned dreams, he'd certainly never mentioned nightmares, but maybe it manifested itself in different ways in different people. Maybe I just had to be patient.

I don't remember what time I eventually fell asleep that night but these were the kind of thoughts that chased each other around my head every night by then. The more I thought the more mixed up everything got, twisting tighter so I was further away from figuring anything out than when I started. And so the dream stayed in my head, just a dream. And so long as it was in my head, so long as I didn't tell anyone and I had my system to get back to sleep, everything was fine. Because unless I told anyone about it, then it wasn't really real, I had it all under control.

And I did have it all under control. Until I didn't.

***

I need to back up, to tell you more about Granddad's gift. I'd always known about it – I don't remember anyone ever telling me, it was just something I knew about him like that I knew he was from Donegal and that the only thing he could cook was sausages and that he always wore three piece suits, even in the summer. It didn't even seem that unusual to me – Grandad could communicate with dead people and that's all there was to it.

It might seem strange, reading that, but it wasn't strange to me – it made sense. Ireland was a place of fairies and magic and people who lived for hundreds of years, all the books said so. The people who came to our house to meet with Grandad – the old women and younger ones and even the men who came sometimes – knew he had some of this magic in him. They came because they had lost someone and they wanted to talk to that someone, just one last time.

Even though Mom rolled her eyes and Dad did too, it seemed normal that no matter what time these people arrived Grandad would bring them to his room and close the door. From my hiding place on the stairs when I watched them leave again, they always looked happier than when they came.

It might sound bizarre to you, but we never really talked about his gift, like somehow I knew not to ask too much about it. So that day on Brighton Beach I'm not expecting him to bring it up. I'm off school that day – I'd had a cold but I was feeling better by then – and I'd persuaded him to bring me on an adventure. More than anything I loved our adventures, the little smile on his face that he knew where we were going and I didn't. That day the beach is windy – it's cold, not officially open yet for summer – and I'm glad he made me take my hat. He hands me the box with the pizza slices and puts the cans of Coke on the sand while he lays his suit jacket down for us to sit on with the lining part down against the sand.

'There,' he says. 'Perfect.'

'Why did you polish your shoes to come to the beach, Grandad? Aren't you worried about them getting messed up?'

He shakes his head. 'My father always said it was important to have polished shoes wherever you were going. And I can polish them again tomorrow.'

I sit down on his jacket, put the pizza in front of us. Grandad hardly ever talked about his father and I wanted to know more.

'Did he have polished shoes?'

'He did. He only had one pair that I remember but you could see your face in them.'

'Did he wear them to the Trá Mór?'

Trá Mór is the Gaelic name of the beach in Donegal where Grandad grew up – it literally means big beach and I'm proud that I remember it. Grandad laughs and his laughs turns into a cough that seems like it'll never stop. When it does his eyes are watering but he hasn't forgotten my question. 'I never in my life remember my father going down to Trá Mór.'

'Why not?'

He shook his head. 'I don't know. He was away a lot. Working. And anyway, the beach was for women and children. Not for men.'

I stand up to help him sit down because I know it's hard for him to get down on the ground even though he never told me.

'Thanks, love,' he says. 'You know how to read your old Grandad's mind.'

'You're not old. Gabi's Grandad is eighty-two. *That's* old.'

'That is old.'

Eating the pizza, we don't talk, we watch the waves instead. Looking back, they were some of the best bits of time together, sitting, not talking, only I probably didn't know it then. Twice, I suck my Coke too fast through the straw so it fizzes out and onto my hand. Mom would be mad at me for that about getting things sticky and messy but Grandad only laughs and I wipe my hand on my jeans.

'I love our adventures,' I say, after I've eaten. 'This was worth being sick from school for.'

He smiles, his eyes crinkle. 'We just better make sure we get home before your mother or this might be our last adventure.'

Mom is out with her editor and then her agent. I know she won't be home for ages. I want to get back to talking, for him to tell me more about his father. About Donegal.

'Someday we'll go to Donegal together, won't we, Grandad? We'll go to the Trá Mór?'

I remember looking at him and he's looking at the waves and he takes a while to answer. When he turns to me he's still smiling but it's a different smile.

'I hope so.'

I don't like his answer. 'We will, Grandad. I know it. We definitely will.'

He takes out his hanky, blows his nose before he speaks. 'If we don't get there in this life together, we'll get there in the next.'

'What's that supposed to mean?'

He looks at the sea again and back to me. 'I don't want to lie to you, Cass. I can't say for sure that we'll get there together. That Dr. Harvey, he's been at me to do some tests on my lungs. I'm sure it's all grand but, sure ... you never know.'

I start to cry. I don't have time to hide the tears – they're not there and then they are, just like that.

'Ah, come here, child.' He shifts closer on his jacket, puts his arm around me. 'I'm sorry, I didn't mean to upset you. I'm right as rain, so I am."

'Don't die, Grandad, don't leave me. Please don't die.'

He holds me tighter. 'Sssh. I'm grand. I shouldn't have said anything. And sure, aren't we all going to die – you know that. We've talked about that.'

'Yes ... but ...'

We had talked about it after Mrs. Schneider next door died and Gabi's granny did but it was different, this conversation, when it might be about him.

'I shouldn't have said anything. I only meant that you never know what's going to happen. I don't want to make a promise that I can't keep, Cass. I'd never lie to you. You know I'd never lie to you.'

'So you're not dying?'

He squeezes my shoulder. 'Let's just say it's not on my agenda for today.'

'Or tomorrow?'

He laughs. 'Or tomorrow. Hopefully not for a long, long while. And anyway, whenever I do – hopefully a long way from now – you don't need to worry because you'll see me again.'

'I will?'

He nods. I check his expression to make sure he isn't joking but he's serious, he's telling the truth.

'You know about my gift, don't you?'

I nod.

'Well, I hadn't planned to tell you this today but I need to tell you sometime.'

He pauses, he knows he has my full attention now.

'What Grandad?"

'I think you have it too. I think you've inherited it from me.'

He watches my face, waiting for my reaction. I'm not sure how I'm supposed to feel.

'How do you know?'

'I've watched you. I know you better than anyone, Cassie. You're sensitive to things, you pick things up – feelings, energies. The same way I do.'

Mom tells me all the time I'm too sensitive and I wonder is that the same thing.

'You know when we talk about *Tír na nÓg,* or the stories from Ireland, it's like you really really feel them. Your brother, he likes them, enjoys them – but with you, Cass, it's different.'

It makes sense, what he's saying. I did feel things in a different way than Ryan, I thought I did. Sometimes when Grandad was telling me stories the smell of the turf fires was so strong it was like a taste in my mouth. When he talked about Trá Mór I could feel the wind from the sea on my cheeks – gentler and cleaner than the wind in Brooklyn.

'My gift – it's not really mine. It's passed down from generation to generation. My mother had it and her father before her.'

'What about Mom? Or Auntie Cathy? Do they have it?'

He shrugs. 'Sometimes it skips a generation. Sometimes the person who gets it isn't open to it. They shut down. It can be too much. A burden. You have to want it, Cassie. You have to stay open to it.'

'I want it,' I say. 'I'll stay open to it.'

He pulls me in close to him. The can in between us falls over but it's empty by then so it doesn't matter.

'Good girl,' he said. 'I know you will.'

The sea is calm, making small waves on the hard, packed sand. The sun is in my eyes. Grandad's cough comes back and he turns around to cough in the other direction. I count the waves until he finishes.

'So when you die – if you ever die – I'll be able to talk to you? Is that what having the gift means?'

'That's it. And it means you'll be able to help other people too. The walls between the real world and the spirit world are very thin, but only some people have ears that work on both sides of the wall and yours will.'

It sounds so simple, the way he says it and I imagine that the beach around us isn't empty, that we're surrounded by spirits of Russian men and women, even children who've come and gone before we have and for a second it's like I can feel their chill.

He fixes my hair back, from where it had escaped from my hair band. He holds it behind my ear. 'Don't be scared, love. There's never any need to be scared. They're only ever people, like you and me. They'll have a message, that's all. And once you get their message they'll leave you be.'

'But why will they come to me?'

'Because you're special. Don't ever forget how special you are, Cassie, sure you won't?'

'No.'

'Promise me.'

'I promise, Grandad.'

He nods, satisfied. Like something has been settled. I think he's going to take out a cigarette then and smoke it before we go, but he doesn't. Instead when he stands up he takes my hand again and we walk down all the way to the shore, to almost where the waves wash over our shoes. By then it's getting really breezy and when I look at my watch I get scared, in case I'm wrong about Mom and her agent, in case she'll be back already and there'll be a fight when we get home.

And like he did so often before, he reads my mind. 'You're right, time to go. And don't worry your mother won't be home. This adventure will be our little secret.'

He was right, she wasn't home. And it was our little secret because I never told anyone what he said to me on that beach. Not Mom or Dad, not Ryan, not Gabi. Up until Mom and Dad take me to see Alice, I never say a single word, not to anyone.

E.L.

I under Miss Ellen bed. If I put my ear to the floor – flat on the wood – I can hear the Master talkin' downstairs and Miss Ellen too. I think I hear her laugh. I waitin' for Juba to come with a plate. I think I hear her on the stairs.

It one of the good nights. Some nights me and Miss Ellen hide under this bed and we ain't laughin' but today the Master in a good mood when he come home from Charleston. He bring presents for Miss Ellen – two new dolls and he tell her she has to let me play with one. He say it right in front of me and she pout even though she pro'bly let me play with it anyway, even if he ain't said nothin'.

He bring home silk for the Mistress so she can make a new dress and barrels of whiskey that Big Bill and John unload from the back of the cart and put in the storage cellar next to the kitchen.

'That'll last us through the whole winter.'

He say that to the Mistress earlier this afternoon when we all watchin' them roll the barrels down the two planks they got rigged up at the back of the cart.

She don't say nothin' and he turn to look at her. 'You hear me, dear? I said this will last us through the winter.'

She sniff the air as if there somethin' to smell but I don't smell nothin'. 'I hope so,' she say. 'I sure do hope so.'

The Master look sad then and I hate the Mistress for makin' him sad when he happy like he is now and sometimes after he get sad he get mad as well. She barely look at the silk he give her and when he ask if she like it, she say the color pink look good on her sister, Abigail, but she like green on a lady better herself.

After Big Bill and John put the barrels 'way the Master say it important to have somethin' call 'proof of purchase' and he make me and Miss Ellen come with him so he can taste the whiskey. Usually I 'fraid of the storage cellar – in case of snakes – but it feel better with the Master tellin' us 'bout his trip and the folks he saw and how he stop by the store where he use to work b'fore he marry the Mistress.

'My mother got me that job,' he say to Miss Ellen and me, both of us sittin' atop the other barrels where he lift us up. 'Old man Sinclair who owned it – he'd have done anythin' for my mother – your grandmother. Did I ever tell you that?'

Miss Ellen nod up and down and I do too even though it her he talkin' to, not me. The Master take another drink from his cup and lean 'gainst the barrel.

'She was the most beautiful woman in all South Carolina. Ellen Joyce. My father said he didn't know a man whose heart didn't beat that little bit faster when he heard the name Ellen Joyce.'

'Ellen is my name,' Miss Ellen say, kickin' her legs 'gainst the side of the wood.

'It sure is,' the Master say. 'And men's hearts are going to beat faster when they hear your name too.'

Miss Ellen blush and giggle like she a'ways do when he say that. And he say that a lot – things like that, talkin' 'bout his mamma and how he love her so much. Miss Ellen tell me there a big paintin' of her in the parlour, only I ain't never seen it 'cause I ain't 'llowed in there.

I don't know how long we stay in the storage cellar but when we come out it nearly dark. On the porch there a smell of somethin' cookin' and my mouth water real bad.

'Daddy, I'm hungry – can we have dinner now?' Miss Ellen say.

He pick her up. 'What? You're hungry? Hungry for dinner?'

He spin her round till she laugh and put her back down 'gain.

'What about you, E.L.? Are you hungry?'

'I a'ways hungry.'

I think he gone laugh more when I say that only he don't laugh and when he pick me up, he don't spin me round like he sometimes do, he jus' hold me there. I wish he spin me like he done spin Miss Ellen – I wish he do anythin' 'stead of jus' holdin' me and lookin' at me all sad like that.

And then the door bust open. It the Mistress. The Master drop me so fast I ain't got time to get my legs ready and I fall right on my rear, hittin' the deck hard.

She look at me firs' then the Master and there ain't 'nough words for hate to tell you how much hate there in her eyes.

'It's past our daughter's dinner time and I don't want her going hungry,' she say in a voice that don't sound like her.

The Master smooth down his shirt, fix his hat.

'No one's going to be going hungry,' he say. 'We're coming in now.'

He reach 'round her, hold open the screen door. Miss Ellen walk in b'tween them. The Mistress go next. She turn 'round to look at me like she think I gone follow her in there – like she think I don't know no better than that. She wait in the doorway, watchin' him.

'I'll be right there,' he say. 'I'll join you and Ellen in a moment.'

The screen door close over then and even though I can't see her, I feel her eyes and her ears like she right out there on the porch with us.

The Master get down on his hunkers so we at eye level.

'Will you do something for me E.L.?'

I nod. I can smell his whiskey. His chin scratchy like it get when he don't shave.

'You go on upstairs and you wait in Miss Ellen's room. I'm going to ask Juba to bring up a plate of dinner, but she can't know it's for you so you have to hide – under the bed or in the wardrobe, you understand?'

I nod. I und'stand.

'I'll get her to leave it there, say that it's for Miss Ellen to have later and when she's gone, you can come out and eat it but you can't let anyone see you. All right?'

I nod 'gain. He smile. He stand.

'You're a good girl, E.L.'

There ain't no clock in here and even if there was I can't read no time anyways so I don't know how long 'go he say that. But I know I cramped up from bein' under this here bed so long and I so hungry I suckin' on my fist and Juba still ain't come. And I know that Charity gone be worried 'bout me and that the herrin' and cornmeal ain't as good as the plate Juba gone make for me, that it better than no plate at all.

I push my ear into the floor so flat it hurt. This time I don't hear no laughin'. I hear the Master and he singin' the same line of the same song over and over. And I hear the Mistress and she angry – she shoutin' at him to stop singin' and the louder she shout the louder he sing and the louder she shout 'gain. I wonder if Miss Ellen still with them or where she at 'cause I don't hear nothin' from her. And I think maybe she gone be the one to come bring me food if Juba done forget. But I wait and wait and she don't come and Juba don't come, and by the time I done sneak outta the house and back to the cabins, the food there all gone and I don't get nothin' to eat there neither.

CASSIE

The reason I can tell you how often I had the dream is because I started to keep a diary about it. It's August when I start the diary, two months after the dream started, and by then I'm having it twice, three times a week.

At the bottom of my bookshelf I find the old diary I started to keep after I read *Harriet the Spy*. Grandad gave me *Harriet the Spy* the Christmas that I was eight and he gave me the diary too. It was the perfect present. After reading the book I decided I wanted to be like Harriet; I wanted to *be* her. I wanted to find out things like she did, I wanted to solve mysteries, I wanted to find out the truth.

Sitting cross-legged on my bedroom floor, for the first time in two months I forget about the dream as I read my blocky eight-year-old writing. There's a lot about Mom and Dad, and turning the pages I see that was when I first started to count their fights – how many days between each one, whether a fight was really over or if it was just in hiding. I read about the clues I'd taken note of, whether in the morning they were calling each other 'honey' or 'baby' or 'Lou' and 'Joe' – that things were really bad when Dad called Mom, Louise. I count the empty wine bottles by the sink, the number of days Mom has coffee instead of granola, the number of days we go without having milk for cereal. Everything can be a clue – the way Dad clears his throat, the click of the door closing when he leaves, when Mom pauses in her sentence, the pitch of her voice – these are the ways I can tell whether it's going to be a good day.

I put the diary down on the carpet. I don't want to read anymore but another part of me does, another part wants to read it all. So this was where I learned it – to read the type of silence in the room, to know whether it was a quiet cosy silence or the kind of brittle silence where walking into the kitchen was like walking on a sheet of ice, waiting for it to crack.

I skip ahead. My writing changes, it is joined-up writing now. Grandad's name is there more and more – about his cough lasting all winter, the doctor coming in the middle of the night. Conversations behind the closed doors of the living room. I want to see when I knew he was dying, what I wrote – if I put anything in the morning he died or the day of his funeral but there are only blank pages where that should all be. After the blank pages there's more about Mom and Dad. It seems like the fights stopped for a while but then they came back. Mom had started writing her memoir by then and I know that Granddad is going to be in it. I thought things were okay because there were no bottles of wine by the recycle bin anymore, but one morning Ryan shows me three in the garbage. Dad isn't happy about whatever Mom is writing, one night I hear him yelling at her about the impact it will have on the kids. In my notebook I've circled that with green marker and put a bunch of question markes beside it. At the bottom of the page I've written another line underlined in red with smiley faces on each side:

> ☺ I don't care what Dad says, I'm glad Mom is writing about Grandad. Reading her book will be like seeing him again!! ☺

I read that line twice, three times, four. I wait for tears to come, to feel something – anger, injustice, embarrassment for seeing my childish hope laid bare so colourfully on the page – but I don't feel anything, just kind of numb. And so I rip them out, those pages and all the ones before, ripping, ripping, ripping until the book is clean and ready to start again and all those wasted words are in the garbage.

The first entry in the new diary is August 11th and according to the diary I had the dream 116 times between then and Christmas. The columns track what day of the week it was, what time I went to bed, what book I was reading, what time it was when I woke up. There's a wider column at the end for me to record anything new that happens in the dream but page after page that's empty. Month after month, nothing changes about the dream – I never get any closer to the tree, I never wake up before I see the body, no one else ever comes into it. It's all the same. The only thing that changes is how long it takes me to get back into my own world afterwards.

The night before Christmas Eve I have the dream twice. I've never had the dream twice in one night before and I'm scared to go to sleep the third time, in case I have it again. Lying in the dark, I decide I'm going to tell Mom and Dad, that I have to. For the rest of the night half of my brain argues with the other half. It's not the right time to tell them, this close to the holidays, that somehow it's going to lead to some kind of argument that will spoil everything. But the other half just says quietly that I haven't been left with any other choice.

In the shower I figure out what I will say, how I'll say it, casually, so they won't worry. I don't want to make them worry. I know the first thing they will ask is why I didn't say anything before now so I might not let them know it has been happening as long as it has. Maybe I'll say I've had the dream for a few weeks, or a month even. The details aren't important, the important thing is to tell them, to tell someone.

In the shower I'm convinced, I'm going to tell them, it will be easy. Walking downstairs I organise the words in my head. I'll tell them when I open the fridge to get the milk out, if the milk is already on the table then I'll get juice even though I never drink juice. It will be easier to tell them if I'm not looking at them – the trick is to downplay it, keep it casual, light.

Easy.

As soon as I walk into the kitchen, my resolve falters. Something is wrong. Something more than just the usual something. Dad is at the table, the paper open in front of him but you can tell he isn't reading it. Mom is drinking coffee, looking out into the garden. It looks like a holiday card with the dusting of snow and the birds on Grandad's bird table but the water in the fountain is thick and frozen. As thick as the silence in the room.

I open the fridge and take out the milk, pour a bowl of Cheerios. I will myself to speak but the words have vanished.

Mom turns around from the window. Usually she'll smile – even a fake smile – she'll ask if I slept well, but this morning it's like she barely registers I'm there. Dad takes a sip of his coffee, turns the page of his paper.

I sit down opposite him with my cereal, put my book on the table.

'Look, Dad, see what I'm reading?'

He looks up and his eyes seem to take a second to register what he is looking at – the copy of *The Adventures of Tom Sawyer* that I'd brought downstairs.

'Tom Sawyer? That's great, baby. My little bookworm.'

His words sound like a script, something he is supposed to say – has said fifteen hundred times before. His mouth makes the shape of a smile. His eyes go back to his paper but on the way they glance to the table and I see there's a magazine next to the butter. It's the *Oprah* magazine and Mom's name is one of the ones on the front.

'Oh wow, is this the one we're in?' I say, but no one answers.

I open it anyway, flick through the pages. And there we are, a two-page photo of Mom and Dad and Ryan and me all in the back garden, all wearing plaid shirts, leaning into each other, smiling. That was the photographer's idea – the plaid – and she'd brought all these extra shirts in different sizes and colours in case we didn't have any of our own. Mine is green with black and Ryan's is red and Mom's and Dad's are lighter and darker blue. We're all smiling and the smiles look real, even though the photographer had been saying goofy things to make us fake laugh. The colours jump out – the plaids, the brown of the tree bark, our smiles, Mom's lipstick. Usually I hate myself in photos but I don't hate myself in this. I don't hate any of us. The headline is in bold letters, white in a green box. 'The holidays with Louise Lazzaro and her family!' it declares. There are Christmas cartoon baubles linking the Ls in Louise and Lazzaro.

I turn the page. There's a bunch of smaller photos – Mom in her room, writing, me and Ryan and Mom in the kitchen with a rolling pin and flour all over the counter. Mom and Dad kissing under the mistletoe with their eyes closed. I can't remember the last time I saw them kiss. When I look up from the article Mom has left the room and Dad is looking at me looking at the mistletoe photo and he gets up and leaves too.

They didn't make it through the holidays. I guess at some point admitting the truth about the family we really were, became easier than trying to pretend to be the family in those photographs. I don't know for sure if that had anything to do with it, but I do know I was glad I didn't tell them about the dreams that morning, because I knew then, that it wasn't because of that. That they didn't split up because of me.

I guess there's no good time for your dad to leave but I can tell you from experience that Christmas Day is not a good time. Even now, whenever I hear a cheesy Christmas song or see the first commercials on T.V., I can see Mom, standing at the top of the stairs throwing Dad's jeans and his ties and his shirts still on their hangers down into the hall. Funny, it was one of the only Christmases we'd stayed in Brooklyn because usually we went to Pennsylvania to Nana and Grandad Lazzaro but that year Mom had said she could't take the time away. That had been another argument – a big one – in the run up to the holidays and I wonder if Dad had taken us on his own like he had threatened to, if they might have made it through.

I don't remember the argument that started the end of it that day, but that memory of her throwing the clothes comes as automatically as blinking. I can picture her face, the redness high in her cheeks, her hair wild, see him, running around, half-heartedly catching things, running upstairs towards her and back down again calling out at her to stop but she doesn't stop and eventually he runs right past me and Ryan out the front door. He leaves it open and I think he's going to come back in and Mom keeps on throwing things and Ryan and I just stand there until a gust of wind catches the door and slams it shut so hard I think the glass panels are going to smash.

He came back a couple of hours later. Mom was still in her room. We were watching a movie and eating dumplings from the take-out carton – Ryan and me – sitting close on the love seat even though the couch and the recliner were free. Dad sat on the coffee table so his knees nearly touched ours. He was going to stay in his place in the city, he said. He and Mom needed some space but things were going to be fine – just fine. Ryan wanted to go with him, I could tell, and I did too, even though I didn't say it. A tear slid down the side of Ryan's face and he wiped it away quickly and we all pretended we didn't see it. Dad looked at me and I knew he needed me to be grown up and adult, to side with him, so I did. I agreed with him that we'd be fine, that it was just a bad patch, that all families went through this and they just needed space.

We helped him pick up his clothes and fold them up, put some in a bag that he put in the back of the car. He gave me a hundred dollars in twenties and I put it in my back pocket and made a joke to Ryan about how rich we were now and he laughed even though it wasn't funny. We played on Ryan's new Xbox while Dad tried to talk to Mom through the locked bedroom door and I turned up the volume really loud because for once I didn't want to record the evidence. I didn't want to remember at all.

That night going to bed I saw that we'd missed one of Dad's Nike golf shoes. Somehow it had wedged between the two last bars at the bottom of the banisters, two steps up from the end. I couldn't even remember him ever playing golf. I was too tired to move it that night so I left it there and the next morning I didn't move it either and Ryan didn't move it and neither did Mom when she finally came out of her room. So it stayed there all through the holidays, until Angelina came to clean on New Year's Eve. When she finally pried it out, there was a scratch on one bar, where the spikes from the sole had gouged out the paint.

No one painted over it. It was close to the bottom near the carpet and you wouldn't see it unless you were looking.

Unless you knew it was there.

E.L.

I make a mistake. Miss Ellen and me lyin' on the floor in her room and she readin' her Bible and I read the next line without thinkin' 'bout it. I shoulda been more careful. I shoulda known better than trustin' her – Charity tell me often 'nough not to go thinkin' Miss Ellen my friend. She say that she ain't gone tell her mamma and I don't think she mean to, I think she make a mistake too. And I don't think she know her mamma gone be mad as she is. I don't think neither of us ever seen her mad as this.

'If you're so good at reading, then why don't you read this?'

The Mistress voice so close and so loud it like it the only voice I ever gone hear 'gain. Her hair 'scape from where it tied back so it hang round her face like moss from a tree. Her veins in her cheek look broke and red as the barn outside. Juba say the Mistress sister Abigail prettier than the Mistress but she never come 'round so I ain't never seen her. But it ain't hard to b'lieve 'cause the Mistress one ugly white woman.

'Ellen loves being read to. Don't you, Ellen?'

Miss Ellen sound like she cryin' and I 'fraid to look at her. She think it her fault but it my fault. I the one who made the mistake.

'What's the matter, girl? The words too big for you?'

My legs hurt from where the she tie them to the chair legs. I look down, like lookin' down gone take the pain 'way and she yank my face back up, so as to look at her. Her breath smell bad, like somethin' sour. I ain't never seen no white person's face this close up b'fore. Not even Miss Ellen. Not even the Master when he swing me round in his arms. Her spit land on my face. The corners of her lips gloopy sticky white.

'Did that whore teacher of yours not get as far Hawthorne?'

It ain't a proper question and I don't answer. Charity a'ways say it best not to answer.

'Answer me!'

She swing the book back real fast and hit the side my head. It so fast I feel it b'fore I even see it. She hit hard and the pain like a flash in my skull.

'Mamma!'

I open my eyes and Miss Ellen jump outta her seat and she run to get b'tween her mamma and me.

'Sit down, Ellen!' The Mistress yell at her a'most as loud as she yell at me. 'You've made this bad enough already, don't make it any worse!'

Blood beat a pulse in my head where the book hit me. The side of my eye sting. Now she holdin' the book open so the paper in my face. The words too near to see even if I know what they mean.

'Read it!'

The paper so close make it hard to breathe and maybe it a good thing my hands tied to the chair 'cause if they free maybe I push the book real hard back in her face. Maybe I hit her with it. Maybe I take it and rip the pages and stuff them all into her stinkin' pink mouth.

'I said, read!'

She pull the book 'way and her scream in my face feel like worse pain than where she hit me and suddenly my anger all gone. There only fear. I want to pee real bad. I scared I might cry. Charity say cryin' make it worse, cryin' don't make them stop. Charity a'ways say don't never let them see you cry. I push back in my chair, far as I can. I close my eyes.

Miss Ellen cryin' harder now. I keep my eyes close but I hear her. I feel the Mistress real close. I feel her breath. When I open my eyes she take a step back but she lookin' at me all over – at my arms tied to the chair, the V my dress make where my legs tied too. And then she take the book and hold it up in the air, over her shoulder and then she let go, like a cat'pult. I move my head to the left and the book skim my right ear and smash into the wall b'hind me, hard. Maybe hard 'nough to kill a person.

'Come on, Ellen,' she say. 'Forget her. She's useless. Why are we bothering?'

Miss Ellen stand up but she don't move. The Mistress hold out her hand.

'Don't just stand there, dammit! Come on!'

Miss Ellen look like she don't want to take the Mistress hand but she take it anyway. She look back over her shoulder and then they gone.

At firs' I glad they gone. I sit and breathe and wait for my heart to be normal 'gain. It feel wet on the side of my face and I mus' be bleedin' only I can't reach up to tell. I think that when the Mistress go lie down that Miss Ellen gone come back and untie me but she don't come. No one come. A long time pass till I hear someone in the hallway and Juba there, carryin' a tray. I call out to her and she act like she don't hear and I think 'bout what Charity say 'bout house slaves and they think they better than us. But maybe Juba tell Linda and she come. We share a cabin. She ain't gone leave me here like this. She gone come untie my hands and feets. That what I thinkin' but I wrong 'cause Linda don't come neither.

The room get dark, the house quiet. There no sound of dinner or nothin'. My legs hurt more than my arms, the way she tie them, my hip kinda twisted 'round. I need to pee so bad, it feel like I tryin' to hold a knife inside me – that what the pain like. And Miss Ellen, she ain't comin'. And Linda ain't comin'. And I think 'bout the Master and that maybe he gone come home soon but then I r'member what Miss

Ellen say 'bout the fight they had last night and how he say he never comin' back 'gain. That what made me make the mistake – when she start cryin' and all. I hate seein' Miss Ellen cry and I done think that readin' the Bible to her gone make her feel better, the way it do when Charity read to me.

Thinkin' 'bout that make the pain worse. Not jus' in my legs and arms but in my heart. 'Cause it only then I think 'bout Charity. And how she be comin' in from the field right 'bout now if she ain't come in a'ready. And I think 'bout what Big Bill say in the barn the day he catch her teachin' us.

And that when I get real scared. 'Cause I know whatever the Mistress do to me, it ain't nothin' compare to what they gone do to her.

CASSIE

I don't know I'm sleeping until I'm awake. I don't know if it's the jerking of my arms that wakes me up or if I wake up and then I jerk my arms. I only know that the jerk knocks my books onto the floor. And that Mrs. Palomino is walking down the narrow aisle between the desks towards me.

'Cassie, are we keeping you up?'

When I sit up I have drool on my cheek and I try to wipe it casually but Justin Caldwell must see because he makes a slurping sound and everyone laughs. Behind me I even hear Gabi laughing. My breath is fast like when I wake up from one of the dreams and I know then that that's where I've been.

'Settle down, everyone,' Mrs. Palomino says. She's stopped by Justin's desk, but her eyes are on me. 'Cassie, do you want to give us your thoughts on Holden Caulfield as a narrator?'

I nod. I hear the question. I want to answer it – more than anything, I do – I am here in English, my favourite class. But I am somewhere else too, I am in a darkening room, my arms and legs tied to a chair.

'Would you say he's reliable, that you can trust him?'

The class is silent now. It's not like me not to answer, to have nothing to say about a book we're reading in class, especially *The Catcher in the Rye*. Mrs. Palomino has started to walk towards me again and she's doing that thing where she juggles a piece of chalk between one cupped palm and the other one. And that's when I notice the feeling on my leg: warmth – a spreading warmth on the inside of my thigh and down my calf.

I should have stayed silent, I know that by now, but in front of me heads are starting to turn around to follow her walk down towards me and I think saying something will make her stop and put the focus on someone else.

'Yes,' I blurt out. 'I think he's reliable.'

'Really, Cassie?' Behind her glasses she frowns slightly. There are no wrong answers in English class until you give the wrong answer. 'You didn't ever get the feeling that there were things he wasn't telling us? Or things he was telling us that weren't a 100 per cent true?'

The warm feeling on my leg is different now. It's cold. Wet. Right as I register that, I notice the smell.

Mrs. Palomino is two desks away now. Tammy Davis is at the desk in front and she turns around to face me. She's got to smell it too.

'Well, Cassie?'

Another step, two. Mrs. Palomino is next to Tammy, in front of me. Tammy wrinkles her nose, looks around. She's smelled it and Mrs. Palomino is going to too. Any second she's going to notice, to say something.

'I'm sorry, I don't feel well. Can I be excused?'

In front of Tammy, Leo Schultz is turning around now and out of the corner of my eye I can see Kristen Silverman whisper something to whoever is sitting next to her. I try to keep my eyes focused on Mrs. Palomino. They all smell it, I know they do.

'We're almost at the end of the period—' Mrs. Palomino starts but something makes her stop. Her nostrils flare. Her eyes are on mine. 'Sure. You can get the homework from Gabrielle.'

My face is burning. I can't look at anyone. I can't look under my desk, can't check if there's a puddle.

'Thank you, Mrs. Palomino – I appreciate that.'

I will get it for being such a kiss ass, I know I will, but I can't care about that now. All eyes are on me, everyone in the class, and I wish I was sitting near the door, not in the seat by the window. And when I bend down to pick up my bag I see it, the dark stain on my jeans, wide inside my thigh and then getting narrower as it goes all the way down to my ankle. And on the floor, next to my Converse, there it is – a puddle.

I don't know how I'm going to get up and out of my seat without anyone seeing, how I'm going to leave the room. And that's when I realise Mrs. Palomino is standing right there, right next to me. Almost like she is covering me.

'Alright everyone, we're going to do a visualisation exercise to finish out the class,' she says.

'A what?' Justin Caldwell says.

Behind me, someone groans.

'A visualisation exercise – you all have to close your eyes and put your heads on the desks.'

'Are you going to hypnotise us?' Leo Schultz asks.

Justin laughs. 'Maybe she's going to go through our pockets!'

'That's enough! Everyone – eyes closed and heads on the desks now!'

Mrs. Palomino's voice is a bark and she never barks like that, like some of the other teachers do and the result is a stunned silence. Half the class's heads go down on the desks.

'Come on – the rest of you too. If I see one eye open then there's going to be two essays for everyone.'

More groaning and the rest of the heads go down. She's not looking at me anymore, not giving me any indication that this has anything to do with what is under my desk. I feel strangely calm as I stand up, stepping around the puddle so as not to slip or make a squeaking noise on the floor. Even though everyone's heads are firmly on their desks I pick up my backpack, hold it in front of me so it covers my leg as far as my knees. It would be quicker to cut through the desks up through the middle but that would mean getting close to Justin Caldwell and if anyone's going to smell it he will so instead I cut through the side, past Kristen Silverman and Chrissy Peters. Danny McGonagle is in the last seat and as I get towards him I see him lifting his head but his eyes are still closed and he just turns it to the other side.

When I get to the door, Mrs. Palomino looks over but she doesn't say anything. The visualisation is actually pretty cool, kind of like a meditation where she is guiding them through Central Park along the same route Holden Caulfield took. My hand is on the door handle. Round, smooth, metal. I can't believe I might be able to make it outside without anyone noticing. I can't believe this is happening.

When I step into the hallway it's empty and for the next few precious minutes it will stay that way. I walk fast. I don't run. I wish I had a coat, something long. I hold the backpack behind me because I can see there is no one in front. Two minutes now and everyone will be out. I speed up, a walk-run past the signs that say no running in the hallways. Past the ads for the chess club and the orchestra and the book that is this month's 'Big Read'. I hurry past the bathroom and past the lockers and down one flight of stairs and then two until I get to the main door and I push through it and down the steps and that's when I start to run.

Once I start, I don't stop. I run out the gate and around the corner. I run up the sidewalk, dodging around moms with strollers, office workers on their lunch breaks, students from my school who shouldn't be out already but somehow are. I run and I run and I run, even when my lungs are bursting and I think I might get sick from running so hard, even when the light on Court Street tells me not to walk I run through the gap in the cars. I keep running, my arms clasping my backpack in front of me, and I don't stop until I get all the way home.

***

We're sitting on the step of a cabin and it feels extra hard – like there is no flesh on my butt, just my bones on the wood. It's hot – that same slimy dirty heat – and those trees are there again, those weird ones with the moss that hangs. It doesn't blow, just hangs. The sky above the trees is a white-grey.

At first we're just looking at that – the trees and the sky – and I think we are alone but then she turns her head and I see the others. They are sitting on the ground around a fire that is really just a wisp of smoke. Two young boys are sitting on the steps of a wooden cabin opposite where I am sitting. No one is speaking. Everyone's eyes are on the plates in their laps and that's when I feel the tin plate in my hand too.

They are all black, the men and women. I know right away that they are slaves. I look down at my plate and I see fingers – my fingers? – picking up pieces of corn. They are black fingers, skinny long fingers. And that's when I get it. She is a slave too.

I don't want to eat the corn – I hate corn – but she is putting it into our mouth and something hurts when we bite down on it. There's a gap where our teeth should be but she keeps biting down anyway and it hurts like hell every time we chew but she keeps chewing, keeps swallowing.

A man walks out of the cabin opposite us, so tall he has to duck to come through the door. He walks past the two boys and they look up at him but no one speaks. The others are watching him too but no one says anything. He walks past the fire, over to a bucket by a low wall to where a woman is standing.

She's pretty – the woman – and we are watching her intently now, her and the man. Something unspoken passes between them. Somewhere in me there is dread, I want to turn away our eyes away, but I can't control that – just like before, she is in control. I can only see through her eyes.

The woman turns and bends forward so that all we see is the curve of her back. She slides the thing she is wearing off – it's more like a rag than a dress – and arches further forward. She slides the material slowly, deliberately. It seems to catch on something and she arches more. Stops. I can't see her wince but it's like I can feel it. We are holding our breath. She pulls it right off, in one motion.

When we see her back I'm glad we can't see her face, glad we can't see both things at the same time.

The lines are criss-crossed – some curved, some straight. They are different colours – dark black ones and fresh red ones and some that are almost a type of green. Her back is like some kind of map, of rivers and contours and mountains. Her back tells a story.

We drop the plate, it slips from our fingers, makes a noise as the tin hits one step, then the next, rolls down onto the ground. Our hand grabs at the corn that has rolled too and we pick it up and put it in our mouth without even cleaning it. Our eyes flick back to them both. The tall man has lifted the bucket of water, lifts it high over the woman's head. He tips it slowly over her neck, her shoulders, her back.

Her poor back.

The corn is covered in dirt – it makes us gag – we spit it out, one mouthful, half chewed, then another. Before I know we are going to get up, we are standing and turning away. I can't see properly and it's only then I realise that she is crying. We are crying. We push open a door and we are inside a cabin where it is darker and hotter with slats of light that come through the gaps in the boards.

Our crying is more intense now, louder – our sobs come from our chest – and our knees hurt as we fall to the floor. We double over, small – chest against knees, elbows against thighs, fists in our eyes to keep the tears back.

Only they don't.

They come.

They keep coming.

Until I wake up.

***

The night of the accident in Mrs. Palomino's class is the first night I have the new dream. It's also the night Mom comes into my room to find out if I'm okay.

I haven't even caught my breath yet, am still going through the books trying to slow my heart down when the door opens really slowly. My breath gets fast again, shallow and quick like I can hardly catch it. And then when the door fully opens I see that it's Mom.

'Honey, are you okay?' she says. 'I heard you crying out.'

I want to answer her, to tell her I'm fine, but my voice doesn't seem to be working.

'Was it a nightmare? You look like you've seen a ghost.'

She's coming over to the bed. She's in her black silk shirt and her long necklace with the tiny diamonds that I thought were fake but it turns out are real. I can smell the vanilla-y smell of her perfume and it reminds me of the Friday nights when her and Dad still went on 'date night' and Grandad used to babysit me and Ryan. As she gets closer I can smell other things too: wine on her breath and smoke on her clothes and even though I hate those smells in a way I'm glad to smell them, because the perfume on its own made it too easy to trick my mind into thinking it was back then, back when I could still trust her.

I find my voice. 'Mom, it's nothing. I'm fine.'

She sits down on the edge of the bed, reaches out to touch my hair and I let her fix it behind my ear.

'Sweetheart, it's going to be all right.'

She hasn't called me sweetheart in years and part of me wants to tell her I'm too old for that but the other part – the part that's winning – wants to stay just like this with her stroking my hair, to be the little girl who was always begging her for a spray of her perfume.

'I was just on my way to bed, coming up the stairs, when I heard you calling for me.'

And it's then I notice it. The glaze in her eyes that are looking directly at me but not really seeing me. That smile playing around her lips even though it doesn't match what she's saying. She's drunk. Of course she's drunk. Why wouldn't she be drunk?

'Calling for *you*?'

I emphasise the 'you' to put as much scorn as I can muster into it and her hand on my hair stops stroking.

'You must have been hearing things, Mom. I wasn't calling for you.'

She pulls her hand away.

'When are you going to stop being mad at me, Cassie?'

'I'm not mad at you.'

She wipes the edge of her eye with her fingernail. 'Sure you are. You can hardly look at me, you never talk to me anymore. You're so impatient with anything I have to say—'

'I thought you came in to comfort me. How did this suddenly turn into you criticising me?'

She laughs. 'See? Your anger – it's always right there.'

She points at her chest, close to where her heart should be. I roll my eyes.

'Dad just left, Mom – it's not even a month since he left. Since you *made* him leave. Don't you think I've got a right to be a little mad? That most people might be a little mad?'

I wait for her to say she didn't make him go anywhere but instead she turns away from me, gazes around the room like it's the first time she's ever been in here. Her eyes stop on a photo on my dresser – the one of all of us at Coney Island – Grandad, her, Dad, Ryan and me. When she talks her voice sounds strange, disconnected, like it's not her voice.

'We both know you've been mad at me since long before then, Cassie. This isn't to do with your dad leaving – it's to do with my memoir, isn't it? It's to do with your grandad.'

'Oh, please. Let's not get into this again.'

She spins back around and suddenly her face is red, angry and her voice is back to being her voice. 'Why not? Don't you think I've a right to be mad too? To be hurt? Have you any idea what it was like when the store manager at Book Haven called me to say that he'd seen you in his store, turning my book around to face the wall – hiding it in the children's section so no one could find it?'

I sit up in bed, pull my knees up to my chest to make space between us. That was a dumb thing to do, especially in the store where she'd had her launch; I should have stuck to Barnes & Noble instead.

'Well, it didn't dampen your sales, did it? It didn't stop you from going on *Oprah*.'

'That's not the point, Cassie, and you know it. You did it to hurt me – to punish me—'

'I did it because I didn't want people reading those lies you wrote about Grandad!'

She's talking over me, interrupting, like she always does. 'And what kind of message do you think that sends, that my own daughter doesn't believe me?'

I want to get far away from her. I want to push her away, out of my face, my bed, my room.

'Thank you, Mom! Thank you for being honest – for once. For admitting that all you cared about was your book sales. Forget about the effects the lies you wrote had on your family – your kids.'

I'm yelling now too, right in her face, and I've probably woken Ryan up and part of me feels bad thinking about that but part of me wants him to hear, wants him to come in and start yelling at her too the way I know he wants to.

She stands up. 'I'm not having this conversation again. If I've told you once I've told you a million times, everything I wrote was true.'

'Everything?'

She folds her arms. 'Yes. All of it.'

'So why didn't you put in the part about your birthday?'

'My birthday?'

'You put the part in about him ruining your twenty-first birthday because he went to the pub and drank the money you'd put down as a deposit, but you never wrote about how he made amends for that – how he threw you the surprise party in Carmine's for your fortieth.'

'Oh, please, Cassie.' She shakes her head.

'What? It's not there. Show me the page where you wrote about that.'

'It's not in there – you know it isn't. You probably know the book better than I do, but just because I left it out doesn't mean it's a lie about the twenty-first.' She talks to the ceiling, not to me. 'That happened, Cassie – I went to put my decorations up with Bessie Morgan and Anna O'Brien and the barman told me that they'd given the room away and there'd be no food because Daddy had drunk the money I gave them.'

I sit up straight in bed. 'Did you ever hear of a lie of omission, Mom? Grandad was sober for twelve years – since right after Nana died. He made his amends for that thing to do with your party. You know how bad he felt about it and you pretended you forgave him. What you wrote wasn't the full story and you know it.'

She's pacing now, one arm wrapped around her middle, the other fiddling with her earring. I have her on the ropes. Two strands of her hair have escaped from where it is tied back and hang down on either side of her face.

'If Grandad had been the monster you wrote about – if he did all those things … beat you and left you without food or heat in the winter … you'd never have asked him to come and live with us. You'd never have let him babysit for me and Ryan every Friday night.'

She stops in front of me, she looks like she might cry. 'I told you already, Cassie, a lot of things came up when I was writing the memoir. After he died. My therapist says that I'd repressed the memories—'

'Repressed?' I make myself laugh hard. 'Come on, Mom. We both know that your editor told you that this had to sell better than your novels. That you needed to spice the story up for them to publish it. You exaggerated what happened – made it worse than it was to sell more books. Why don't you just admit it?'

Her slap is hard and fast and out of nowhere. At first there is only shock – no pain – but then the numbness gives way to a sting. I'm touching my face and she reaches out to touch it too but I pull away, back into the headboard.

'Oh, Cassie. Oh, my God! Are you okay? I'm sorry. Baby, I'm so sorry!'

I'm not crying although I wish I was. I'm okay – I'm more than okay. Her hitting me makes her wrong and me right, no matter what way she tries to spin it. I've won now and she knows it too.

'Just leave, Mom.'

'I didn't mean to, Cass, I—'

'Mom, please.' I hold my hand up. 'Just go.'

She takes a couple of steps towards the door. Her thigh clips the corner of the desk but she doesn't seem to notice. When she turns back around she is crying, her tears making a mess of her mascara.

'You've every right to be angry, Cassie. Watching your Grandfather die – losing him. Then losing him all over again through my memoir – feeling like you're losing your dad as well. You're right. It *is* my fault. All of it, it's my fault.'

I hate seeing her crying, hearing her like this, but that's the point, that I'll feel sorry for her, that somehow I'll be the one who'll end up apologising. She sees me soften, some part of her sees it and she starts to walk back towards me again.

'I hate to see you in so much pain, Cassie. It tears me up. It's not healthy to carry all this anger around – this rage. Why don't we find you a therapist, someone to talk to?'

I pause before answering, just to let what's she's said sink in.

'Let me get this straight – you're the one who comes into my bedroom in the middle of the night, you hit *me* across the face and *I'm* the one who needs to see a shrink about *my* anger?'

I think she's going to have something to say to that – that it'll make her mad again – but she only folds her arms and hangs her head low.

'Forget it, Cass. It wasn't the right time to bring it up. I'm sorry.'

She turns around again, walks back to the door and crazy as this is going to sound, despite everything, more than anything, right then, I want her to stay. Her hand reaches for the doorknob and I think of the new dream, the old one, how I don't want to have any more. I'm scared – that's what I want to tell her – but I don't know how, I don't have a clue how, so instead I do the only thing I know how to do: I start another argument.

'Look at that photo, Mom – the one at Coney Island. I saw you looking at it earlier. We're all happy there, right? Don't say we're not.'

She pauses, looks at the photo on my desk. I want her to pick it up – I will her too – but she doesn't.

'Remember? We rode the Cyclone? All of us, even though Ryan was technically too short. We had fun. It was a fun day, right? Remember?'

My voice is desperate now. I hear the desperation and so does she.

She nods. 'Yes, I remember. It was a fun day.'

I break out into a smile. Triumphant. 'We were happy?'

'Yes.' She nods again. 'We were.'

'You see?' My face is throbbing now, but it doesn't matter anymore.

'See what?'

'If everything you wrote was true, then that can't be true as well. If Grandad ... if he did all those things ... then you couldn't have had a day like that together. Right? Both things can't be true.'

I want her to give me that. To agree with me. But her fingers are still on the doorknob and the glaze in her eyes is back and I know that even if it was true about her being on her way to bed when she heard me earlier, that she won't be heading there now. That instead she'll be going downstairs to have another glass of wine, at least one.

She looks at me, fixes her hair, half smiles.

'Life doesn't always work like that Cass – the truth isn't like a math equation. Sometimes things that contradict each other are both true. Even when they don't make sense. One day when you're older you'll learn that for yourself.'

I want to ask her what she means but before I can, she's already opened the door and stepped through and clicked it closed behind her. And I'm alone again just like before she came with only my books and the remnants of the dream and the last lingering vanilla-y smell of her perfume and I touch my face where she hit me, and it's only then that I let myself cry.

E.L.

I don't know how long they leave me tied to the chair. It the Master who make Linda untie me and I hate that he see me like that, all soiled and dirty. I don't know why Charity ain't come to find me and it only after I get back to the cabin I find out 'bout the beatin' Nagle give her.

Things go black 'round then, I don't r'member too much a nothin', if you want know the truth. I don't r'member what Miss Ellen say to me the firs' day I go back to the house. I don't r'member what I say to her. What I do r'member is that Charity diff'rent. She don't sing no more when she gettin' the fire started in the mornin'. Even on Sunday in Church she don't sing. She look like she singin' 'cause she open and close her mouth but I sit next to her and I know there ain't no sound comin' out. She don't read in Church neither. She jus' sit there with her hands fold on her lap. I don't know what they done with her Bible – if they took it or if she threw it 'way herself but I never seen it no more after that.

But the biggest thing diff'rent ain't the singin'. The biggest thing diff'rent that she don't talk no more. She hardly ever talk and she know I love talkin' with her. She know I love her stories. So I figure she mus' be really mad at me to stop talkin' 'cause that the way she know she gone hurt me the most.

It musta been a few weeks after when we down by the river – jus' the two of us, washin' out our dresses, and it feel real bad 'cause neither of us sayin' a word. Maybe it not even that long 'cause the scars on her back still open when she lean over, the new blood still crack out fresh under the old black blood.

Even though I scared I d'cide I gone talk firs'.

'Did you and my mamma come here and wash your dresses jus' like this?'

She leanin' over with her arms in the water. I can't see her face.

'Sometimes we come here,' she say. 'Other times over the other side of the creek.'

I wait for her to say somethin' else but she don't. Usually she the one a'ways talkin' 'bout my mamma. Usually I the one who don't want to.

My dress jus' 'bout done. It heavy with water and it hurt my arms to pull it out on the bank.

'Why we a'ways come here? We never go the other side of the creek.'

She turn 'round, real slow. Neither of us got no underclothes so we both naked till the dresses dry. Her breasts look soft and beautiful in the sun. When I little she hold me right there in her softness and it feel good. But today, she ain't soft. Even with her breasts hangin' she hard. Her skin hard. Her face hard.

'What the matter with you? Don't you r'member nothin'? Don't you know what happen your mamma over there?'

'What you talkin' 'bout?'

'I ain't tellin' you nothin' no more. What's the point? It ain't like you listen to a word I say.'

I don't know I'm gone cry but the tears, they jus' come real fast. And I know cryin' gone make her mad but I can't help it. She ain't never talk to me like that b'fore and I figure she mus' still be real mad. That maybe she ain't never gone forgive me.

'Sorry, Charity. I'm sorry you got lashed so bad. I know it all my fault.'

I think it gone make it better but 'stead her face get more hard. More mad.

'Don't say that. Don't you ever say that 'gain. You hear?'

My tears comin' hard now. Faster.

'But it true. You tell me never to read in front them. Not to trust any white folks. Even Miss Ellen, that she ain't my friend.'

She scramble closer to me on the grass. Her face so mad it don't even look like her face.

'You listen up, E.L. and you listen good. Don't never say sorry for somethin' that ain't your fault. You hear me? Your mamma done that and look where it get her.'

Her eyes big and flashin', scary bug eyes. She the one tell me b'fore it good to 'pologise and now she say not to. It don't make no sense.

'But – if I ain't read the Bible to Miss Ellen then the Mistress ain't never know 'bout you teachin' us readin' and–'

That when she hit me. Her palm flat and hard and fast 'gainst my cheek. It shock more than it hurt. I put my hand up to my face. It ain't that bad. Not like when the Mistress hit me with the book or Nagle beat on me with the paddle for being too slow. No, this slap ain't hardly nothin' compare to that. So how come it hurt so bad?

'Oh, E.L., E.L., I'm sorry! I'm so sorry, baby.'

She cryin' then too. Her face change back to her face – the hardness gone. She reach out to me but I ain't ready and I pull 'way 'gainst her but she don't let go. Her arms skinny but they strong and in the pullin' she win. I stop fightin'. I let her pull me into her.

'I'm sorry I hit you, I'm sorry I hurt you. I'm so sorry, baby.'

She say that over and over while she hold my head 'gainst her breasts and her fingers stroke my cheek where it sting.

'It ain't your fault, baby. Nothin' of this your fault. Don't never think it's your fault.'

And part of me feel better 'cause she hurt me now, jus' like I hurt her, so maybe that make us even, maybe that make it better. And I right here in her softness like where I want be b'fore. But it feel diff'rent. Even though she feel soft, it feel hard too. Like und'neath it hard. Und'neath she hard. Even here. Even in her softest place of all. And that scare me. That scare me most of all.

CASSIE

I know that Mrs. Palomino is going to say something when we next have class and she does. At first, when she says 'hi' to me like it's any other day and then asks questions, like it's any other day, I start to hope that maybe she didn't notice anything after all, that maybe I've got away with it. But when at the end of the class she calls out from the front of the room for me to stay behind, I know there's no escaping the conversation.

Gabi's next to my desk, where she's been waiting for me. She makes a sympathetic face.

'So long, Cass-a-blanca,' she says. 'See you in the cafeteria.'

'Yup. Save me a seat.'

My voice sounds normal but my insides don't feel normal. Suddenly I feel like I might throw up, right here on my desk. Maybe if I throw up Mrs. Palomino won't make me have the conversation, maybe she'll let me go home.

I take ages putting my books in my backpack, lining them up the way I always do, biggest to smallest from back to front. And then the classroom is empty and it's just me and her. She's leaning against one of the front desks – Lisa Chen's desk. Her arms are folded.

'So, Cassie. Are you going to tell me what's going on with you?'

Outside in the hallway there is a river of kids going by. A boy's voice yells something that could be my name. She reaches over and closes the door. I wasn't expecting her to be this direct, to jump right in like that.

'What do you mean?'

She fixes her glasses on her nose, gestures for me to take a seat but I don't.

'Everything's fine,' I say.

'Really? It didn't seem like that yesterday.'

She stops. She's waiting for me to say something. My face burns. I hitch my backpack higher on my shoulders. I'm not going to say it. If she's going to bring it up, she has to be the one to bring it up.

'I mean I know accidents can happen, but ... it seems unusual.' She fixes her glasses again. 'It made me wonder if everything was okay. At home, I mean.'

'I'm sick.'

The words plop out between us on the floor.

'You're sick?' Behind her glasses, her eyebrows raise.

I've prepared for this, read up all about it last night but I know the trick is to keep it brief, not to go into too much detail – just enough so she'll believe me.

'I have what's called an overactive bladder. My mom took me to the doctor.'

I hold her eyes. I don't look away. Her eyes are a greenish colour – kind looking. I've never noticed her eyes before.

'Oh. Oh, I'm sorry to hear that.' She pauses and I keep holding her gaze. She is working out whether to believe me. 'I'm surprised your mom didn't tell the school – it would be good for us to know about these things. This is something I should let Mr. Freeman know about.'

'No!' I say it too quickly, then slow myself down. 'Please don't. It's so embarrassing, I don't want all the teachers to know. I'm getting treatment and it's working. I guess I got caught short yesterday. It won't happen again.'

She nods slightly. She believes me, I think she believes me. She has to believe me.

'And everything's okay at home?'

The pause between 'okay' and 'at home' is so slight I might have imagined it. Maybe she knows about Dad leaving. But how could she? She's bluffing, there's no way she knows.

'Everything's fine.' I smile wide. 'Everything's great.'

Somewhere outside there's a siren and she waits until it passes to speak.

'I was just wondering – with your mom being so high-profile – on *Oprah*, I mean I can't imagine' – she raises her eyebrows – 'I was just wondering how all of that is for you?'

She's probably read Mom's memoir. She probably thinks it's all true, so there's no point in saying it's not. I'll only look like a child, resentful, too young to get it. The trick is to be happy, proud of Mom, like I'm supposed to be.

'It's really exciting. She's going to be on the show again next season. They've booked her for a regular feature.'

The feature is about healing from your childhood wounds – Mom didn't tell me exactly, but I overheard her talking to her agent about it. I bet Dad doesn't know, he's always asking me and Ryan questions about Mom when we see him at the weekends but I'm not going to be the one to tell him. Suddenly though, I want to tell Mrs. Palomino, I want to tell her all about it but she doesn't ask. Instead she adjusts her seat slightly, against the desk.

'That's wonderful for her. I'm sure it could put a lot of pressure on things though, you know, being in the spotlight. Not just for her but your dad as well. Your whole family.'

Those greenish eyes of hers are really on me, like they can see inside my head or something. I shift my backpack to my other shoulder.

'Not really.'

There's no way she could know about Dad. But then Grandad always said Brooklyn Heights was like a village back home with curtains twitching. Maybe someone saw him leave? Or Angelina – maybe she told someone? It wouldn't be Ryan, I knew that. Mom had sat us both down and explained how important it was to keep Dad's leaving a secret for now, at least until all the press coverage was finished. Ryan would never go against her and anyway, he probably didn't want to tell anyone for the same reason I didn't – that telling someone would somehow make it more true.

Mrs. Palomino is still looking at me. It's not normal to look at a person that long. I look at my Converse and back to her. She smiles. She has a lipstick mark on one of her front teeth.

'You know you can talk to me, Cassie? I don't just mean about schoolwork, I mean about anything.'

For a split second I imagine taking my backpack off, sitting down in the chair in front of her and telling her about Dad's golf shoe in the bannister, about Mom hiring Angelina full-time to cook dinners and everything because she's hardly ever there. About the dreams that come every night now, sometimes twice a night and how it's got to the point where I'm afraid of falling asleep.

'I mean, you're my top student. I know college applications seem a long way off but keeping your grades up now - being consistent - is important.'

So that's what this is about – college, my GPA, probably how it affects her teacher ranking. What a fool I was to think it could be anything else. I look away, down at my book bag in my arms.

'Sure. Yep, I know. You're right.'

'You're too smart to get wrapped up in drugs or anything, right?'

Drugs. I smile. Drugs would be so simple. There are rehabs for drugs, counsellors, twelve-step programmes, books. Alan Matthews went to a rehab on Long Island last year and he's fine now.

I make myself laugh. 'I don't do drugs, Mrs. Palomino.'

She laughs a little laugh too. When I look up, she seems relieved. 'Good, well, I'm glad we had this chat. Have an early night tonight, okay? You look tired. Maybe have your mom pick up a good multivitamin.'

I hold my smile so long that it turns fake but she doesn't notice the difference and sometimes I feel like I've forgotten the difference myself. I picture Mom finding time to go Duane Reade to pick up a multivitamin in between her production meetings and broadcasts and interviews and meetings with her agent.

'My mom's going to be in the *New York Times* magazine on Sunday. The Talk Section.'

'That's great,' Mrs. Palomino says. 'I'll be sure to pick up a copy.'

I don't know why I tell her that, about the *New York Times,* except maybe because even more than anything else this feels like the biggest deal of all, more than *Oprah* even. Maybe some part of me wants to tell her about Sunday mornings and how Grandad would pick up the *Times* on the way home from his A.A. meeting and I would grab it from him at the door and run into the kitchen where Mom and Dad would still be in their pyjamas lingering over breakfast. And by the time Grandad had sat down and Mom had poured him some coffee I'd have found the magazine part and opened it to the Talk Section to tell them who was being interviewed that week. And how when Dad lifted the magazine from me and started to read the questions and answers in that funny voice he put on, that even Ryan would always come in from the T.V. room to hear and that no matter what else was happening that week, no matter what else we all did, those few minutes of every Sunday were something we always did together.

Mrs. Palomino said I could talk to her, tell her anything, and I might have told her all that, only by then she's cleaning the board and I know that means that it's the end of the conversation, that it's over.

And walking down the hall towards the cafeteria, I'm trying to remember the last time we read the Talk Section together. I know that after Grandad died, we started to get it delivered and I'd pick it up from the porch and bring it in, but when Mom started to write on weekends, even on Sundays and Dad didn't seem interested in who was in the Talk Section and even when he read out loud he didn't put on his funny voice anymore and one Sunday when I asked him to, he said we were too old for that and I never asked him to read it again.

If I'd told Mrs. Palomino all that she probably wouldn't have known what to say – she mightn't have said anything. And I'm glad I didn't tell her and I know I'm not going to tell Gabi, which means like most things, I probably won't end up telling anyone at all.

***

We are spinning around, being spun around. We are in his arms – the man with the kind eyes and the scratchy red beard. At first I can't see him, I can only feel that I am in his arms – that I am in someone's arms – that they are holding me, firm and tight. We are spinning, the world is spinning and upside down around us – wooden steps, a red barn, a driveway, a horse, trees, wooden steps again.

We are leaning back, that is why everything is upside down, and the laughing is that out of breath laughing that nearly hurts. I hear how his laugh sounds before I see his face. It is excited-sounding laughter, almost like the way a child would laugh, a laugh all caught up in breath. When he pulls me back up, I can see things properly now – a white wooden house, a window, a porch. Our face is almost level with his face. In the middle of his red beard his smile is wide. His beard covers most of his face, not only his chin but his cheeks as well and even most of his neck, down to his shirt collar. Under the hat he is wearing his hair looks browner than his beard. My hand – our hand – reaches out to touch the red bristles and at first it feels scratchy but he takes his hand and puts it over ours to push it closer to his skin and the bristles start to feel soft.

And then he takes his hand away from mine and hooks it around my back to hold me tighter and starts to spin again, and we lean back again, and the house is upside down again, the trees are, the ground is. And we are going faster but his arms have me – have us – they are not going to let us fall. He is not going to let me fall.

We spin faster. We laugh louder. We scream with laughter.

We are safe.

In his arms, we are safe.

In his arms, I am.

Safe.

***

It is one of those days where the cold is like a physical thing in the air – something that strips your skin away. Down by the ~water the wind makes it worse, like ice knives in my face. My Nike Frees slide a little on the ice, but I keep running, from Columbia Street onto the promenade, away from the bridge. Across the water on the other side the skyline is cold too. Empty. It marks my progress.

Something different is happening; it's been happening since I woke up this morning. Her voice – the slave's voice – is in my mind, mixed in with mine. The more I try and stop it, the worse it gets. It feels like grease – her voice – like it's getting into crevice, every part of me and there's nothing I can do to stop it.

I don't know why the Master gone so long. He never gone this long.

That thought – that voice – it is not mine. I don't have a 'master'. I am not some slave.

This is *my* mind, *my* brain, I have to be able to control it. I focus on the things I can see – the things here around me now. The Statue of Liberty in the distance. The grey water. The man on the bench with the little girl so bundled up in her red puffa jacket that she looks more like an inflatable toy than a little girl.

What if he ain't gone come back? What if he left for good like Linda say to Juba?

It's President's Day. That's why I'm off today on a Monday instead of being at school and I wish I was at school, in Mrs. Palomino's class or in art class. Even math would be better than this.

Anything would be better than this.

Linda say it my fault he gone. 'Cause I make the Mistress so mad 'bout the readin' and then she get mad at him but that don't make no sense.

I'm on Remsen Street now, almost home. Not that it feels like home, especially not today. As well as being President's Day, it's Grandad's anniversary. February 20th. The day after my birthday.

Linda don't like me none 'cause she Marjorie mamma and she thinks Marjorie should be Miss Ellen slave and not me. Benjamin tell me she say bad things 'bout me and 'bout my mamma too.

I run until I can't run anymore, up the steps to the front door. I pant as I unlock it.

'Hello? Anyone home?'

I call out even though I know no one's home because the alarm is beeping for me to turn it off. I call out because I need to hear the sound of my own voice, because I've tried everything and my own voice is the only thing that seems to stop her, even for a second.

I pound up the stairs. Even after my run I still have all this energy, more than enough for one body, it feels like. In my room I put on Van Morrison, *Astral Weeks,* in honour of Grandad. I skip to 'Beside You', leave the door of the bathroom open while I get in the shower.

It's dangerous playing 'Beside You'; I never usually let myself but today is his anniversary and I have to do something. I hear the guitar but the water drowns out the words and maybe I want it to. Maybe knowing it is playing without hearing it is enough.

Today makes it five years – he's five-years-dead today. The first year it was such a big deal with the mass in the Bronx and all his old A.A. friends came and some people from his Brooklyn Heights' group came too. It was kind of funny that we went to mass considering he called himself a 'recovering Catholic' and he said his only church was A.A. But we went anyway and afterwards Mom and Dad paid for everyone to have lunch in a restaurant he'd liked up there – more of a bar really – and we went around the table and everyone told their favourite story about him. When it came around to me I couldn't think of any – I couldn't think of a single thing to say about him. It was embarrassing, the silence around the table, everyone's eyes on me, my cheeks getting redder. Dad tried to bail me out; he told them how I was Grandad's best little buddy and that I probably had too many stories to pick just one, but that wasn't the reason. It was like there was a big hole where the memories should be, nothing there, just emptiness, just space.

It was Mr. Foley who brought up the thing about the gift. He was one of Grandad's friends from the Bronx who brought Irish candy when he came to visit. I'd always liked him, his thick bushy eyebrows that stood out in all directions and his kind smile.

'He talked about you all the time,' he said, 'told me you'd inherited his gift.'

'His gift!' At the end of the table Mom laughed and Mr. Foley turned to look at her.

'You don't believe in it, Louise?'

'No, I don't,' Mom said, reaching for her glass of wine. 'And I'm surprised you do, Frank Foley. It's not right, filling a child's head with nonsense like that.'

Mr. Foley looked like he was going to say something, but he didn't and he left soon after. The next year there was no mass, just a visit to the grave and lunch after with a smaller group of the A.A. people and he didn't come. After that, we went on our own – just the family – to the graveyard and the restaurant, we did that twice. And last year Mom's memoir had come out so she was really busy with that and Dad had a work meeting, so we didn't even go to the restaurant, only to the grave. But at least we did something. At least they remembered.

When I get out of the shower, it's on 'Cyprus Avenue' which isn't as dangerous as 'Beside You' but I blast the hairdryer just in case. Even though I can hardly hear the music, I can still hear the voice in my head which is saying something now about a cat of nine tails and joists.

When I'm done I Google 'cat of nine tails' and a picture comes up of a weird kind of whip. I didn't know that. No one ever taught me; no one ever showed me. How can there be a name for something in my head I've never even heard of before? How can I know what it means?

I think about calling Gabi again but I've already left two messages and texted Amanda and Dan as well. Everyone is away for the weekend. Or busy with their families. Passing by Ryan's room I stop. I open his door and look inside. It's neat as a girl's room – neater than my room – with his sneakers all lined up by colour like soldiers on the floor. I wish we hadn't fought earlier, when he asked me if we were doing anything for Grandad. It wasn't him I was mad at. When he said that we should go ourselves, just us, I made out like that was such a dumb idea but really I think I was mad that I hadn't thought of it myself. We should have gone. I'm fifteen now, practically an adult. In some countries I'd be married with a kid already. I shouldn't be scared of getting the subway to the Bronx, I should enjoy the adventure. I should have just said yes.

What if the Master never come back? What if the Mistress send Charity away?

I slam the door, run down the stairs. I don't know if I'm hungry or not but I want food. Angelina is only off for one day but she's stocked the fridge as if she's away for weeks. Cheese, cold cuts, sesame pita bread, hummus, yoghurts, arugula, parmesan, eggs. For a second I think about cooking something in Grandad's honour – like those pork sausages he used to travel all the way to the Bronx to get and fry until they'd split down the middle and the insides come out. If I'd taken Ryan to the Bronx we could've bought those sausages.

They ain't gone sell her. She pick more cotton than anybody. Even the mens.

We don't have any sausages just like I know we won't. But we have bacon. And eggs. I can make an omelette, add bacon to it. That's close enough.

The eggs are in my hand when my cell phone rings. It's Gabi and I don't think I've ever been so happy to see her call.

'Gabster!'

'Cass-a-blanca! What's doing?'

'Nothing much. You coming over?'

'I can't. The family's on their way. We're having dinner.'

Gabi's family was proper Italian, not like Dad's. The family probably meant about fifty people – most of whom weren't even related.

'Dinner? It's not even lunch yet. You've tonnes of time. You'll get to see me cooking – I'll even cook for you!'

She laughs. 'You? Cooking? What are you making?'

'An omelette. Or omelettes if you can come.'

'Ugh, no thanks.' I can picture the face Gabi is making with her lips kind of curled and her forehead scrunched and too late I remember she hates eggs.

'I can make you something else. Or we can order in. My mom left money. We could get something from Capizzi's.'

Capizzi's is Gabi's favourite pizza place and I can hear her hesitating.

'That sounds awesome but I really can't. Mom will go crazy if I bail when I'm supposed to be helping her.'

'Okay.'

'Anyway, I'm surprised you even want pizza after last night.'

'Last night?'

'Uh – your birthday dinner? At John's? Where you have it every year?'

I fiddle with the egg box lid, trying to decide what to tell her.

'We didn't go.'

'But you go every year.'

'Apparently that is no longer a true statement.'

'How come? Oh, was your Mom working late again?'

That was one of the good and bad things about Gabi, she answered her own questions before you could get a chance to. Right now, it's a good thing.

'Yeah.'

'That sucks.'

Out of nowhere, I'm on the verge of tears, don't trust myself to speak.

'Uh huh.'

There's a pause and I know she's going to say she has to go and that's fine because I want to go to – to get off this phone before I start to cry or something and that's when the voice comes, like it's right there on the phone line.

What if Charity die, like my mamma?

'Fuck!' I say.

'What?'

'Did you hear that?'

'Hear what?'

'Listen.'

The line between us is silent, only air.

'What am I listening for?'

I shake my head. 'Nothing, it must have been a crossed line. Forget it! Enjoy your family dinner. I have to go.'

'Cass, you sound weird. Is everything okay?'

I do sound weird, she's right, but I can't help it.

'Everything's fine. I have to go.'

'You want to come over for dinner later? I didn't ask because I thought your family would be doing something. Not that you need an invite.'

'I can't. But thanks. I'll see you at school tomorrow.'

I hit the red button before she can say goodbye. I don't know how long I stand there waiting to hear the voice but I realise I must have dropped the eggs because when I look down the carton is on the floor and yellow-white slime is leaking out onto the tiles.

'Who are you?'

I say it out loud to the kitchen. To the stainless-steel appliances and the maple-wood cupboards. To the eggs leaking on the floor.

'Who's there?'

There is no answer. Only silence. Only the hum of the fridge. The voice is goading me. It hasn't gone, I know it hasn't. On the counter next to me the knives are in a block. I pull one out before

I know I'm going to, hold the blade on my skin on the inside of my arm.

'Who are you?' My voice is low. Trembling. 'Who the fuck are you?'

The blade is sharp. Angelina has a glove she wears when she's chopping to protect her fingers from its sharpness. The name is printed on the metal – Cuisinart – and as I tilt the knife back and forth the light reflects on it. I don't think it will take much pressure to make a line of blood, just a little more than I am applying right now.

'Leave me alone, whoever you are, okay? Just leave me the fuck alone.' I'm yelling by then – that last part is close to a scream.

Leave me alone or what? That question in my head is my own voice and I don't have an answer. Slowly I lift the knife away from my arm. I slide it back into the block. Seeing it there – where it is supposed to be – I take a deep breath, then another. It is silent, I am breathing, there is no one here.

There is only me in the kitchen, in my own house. My home. There is no voice, no ghost, no slave. Nothing. No one. Just me and a broken box of eggs. There is no one else there at all.

E.L.

Things ain't the same with Miss Ellen no more neither. She don't look at me like she look at me b'fore. And when she talk to me it like she talkin' to Juba or Linda or any other slave. When she talk to me it sound like her mamma talkin'.

'Tidy this room up, E.L.'

'I need more ice tea, E.L. – didn't you notice my glass was empty?'

'E.L. – bring me some coal up for that fire before it goes out.'

We don't never play with her dolls no more. She keep them in a box in the corner of her room and I don't think she play with them neither 'cause it look like no one ever touch that box. One day I ask her.

'You want me take your dolls out for you?'

She look at me like I speak some other language she ain't never done heard b'fore.

'Dolls are for babies, E.L. I thought you'd have known that, seeing as how you're older than I am.

I feel dumb then 'cause she right, I seven months older and I shoulda known better. I look at the floor.

'Yes, Miss Ellen,' I say.

'And besides, I won't have time for much of anything now. Mamma's going to teach me to play the piano – she wants to teach me every day. She thinks with her blood and her mamma's blood in my veins that I might be good enough to play for the president some day.'

She smile like she a'ready playin' for the pres'dent. The Mistress play all them hours ev'ry day and she ain't never played for no one 'cept herself. Not even the Master listen to her play. That what I thinkin' but I don't say none of that to Miss Ellen.

'That sound nice,' I say 'stead.

Even though she say we too grown up for dolls now, I still stop by and see Dolly 'most ev'ry evenin' on my way home. Sometime it make me late and Marjorie or Benjamin have to look for firewood after they come in from the field but when anyone ask I say I doin' things for Miss Ellen and they can't say nothin'. I even tell Charity that when she ask, and I feel bad 'cause I ain't never lied to Charity b'fore.

The thing 'bout lyin' is that once I start, it hard to stop. And b'sides it feel good takin' Dolly outta her tree house and talkin' to her. In the beginnin' I talk to her inside my head but one day I start talkin' out loud and that even better and, anyway, there ain't never anyone 'round to hear. I tell her all 'bout Miss Ellen and how she change and how Charity change too. I tell her how the Master gone to Charleston 'gain and that I thinkin' maybe he ain't never gone come back this time but I 'fraid to ask Miss Ellen.

It feel better talkin' to Dolly even though she don't talk back but then after a while it like she talkin' back to me too. Not out loud or nothin' but in my head it like I can hear her voice. She tell me it gone be a'right. That sometime she scared too. She say she miss her Dolly Mamma and her Dolly Daddy and that she like talkin' to me. She say talkin' to me make her feel better, less 'lone.

One time I hear somethin' in the trees and I scared someone gone hear me talkin' to her and that they gone think I poss'ssed by some kind demon. Juba tell me that happen to a slave jus' five mile from here on 'nother plantation, that the overseer drown her in the lake and when she drown all the black demon spirits come pourin' outta her and turn all the water black. That scare me hearin' that story like she know 'bout

Dolly and her voice in my head. But Dolly ain't no demon and b'sides, since Charity got lashed and Miss Ellen done changed, without Dolly I ain't got no one else to talk to.

Talkin' to Dolly make me feel that feelin' I told you 'bout b'fore – that firs' day I think I lost her. Talkin' to Dolly I fill up inside – like I jus' ate a good meal. I don't feel hungry or thirsty or nothin'. It like I don't need nothin' else.

If I been able to talk to Charity maybe I woulda told her but she still not the same. I woulda like to ask her if she thought my mamma might be talkin' to me through Dolly, if my mamma's spirit might be in Dolly tiny body. But I glad I don't say nothin' to Charity, get her hopes up like that.

'Cause it turn out it ain't Mamma I talkin' to. And it ain't Dolly neither. It turn out I talkin' to Cassie. And I don't know what Charity woulda done said 'bout that and I ain't never gone know 'cause I never got to tell her.

CASSIE

We have more eggs but I don't make an omelette. I don't eat anything – I'm not hungry anymore. I flick around the T.V. channels but there's nothing on – only dumb Disney movies and *Family Feud* and reruns of *Law & Order*. Grandad loved *Law & Order* – the original series with the hard-ass DA Jack McCoy – but these are the dumb *Criminal Intent* ones so I keep surfing till I get to the beginning again.

The voice is there all the time, on a low volume, muttering. I hear names – the same names; Benjamin, Marjorie, Charity, Linda, Miss Ellen, the Mistress. I turn up the T.V. volume all the way to the top but the louder it gets, the louder the voices get and eventually I snap it off and throw the remote at the couch.

I check the time – two fifteen – not too late to go to the Bronx after all. That's where I should be today; that's why this is so hard. For a second it seems like the best idea in the world and I start a text to Ryan before I delete it. He's probably still mad at me and, anyway, he's going to be with all his friends playing video games somewhere. And what kind of fifteen-year-old wants to hang out with her twelve-year-old brother?

Without the T.V. on, I feel calmer – the voice is low, almost gone. It seems to keep lower if I am calm. I leave the living room, take the stairs slowly, I don't run. In my room I turn *Astral Weeks* on again but as soon as I do the voice starts, gets louder and so I snap it off.

Beside my bed is some dumb book Mom got me for my birthday called *Invasion of the Boy Snatchers*, which I started last night, just to make her happy, but I can't force myself to open it up again. I'm about to pick up the first Harry Potter and then I see my backpack in the corner and I remember the homework Mrs. Palomino gave us, to take the first line of *The Catcher in the Rye* but to make up our own character, someone different than Holden Caulfield. It's not due for another whole week and probably no one else is doing their dumb English homework on a holiday, but writing something like that would make me concentrate. And concentrating sometimes made the voice stop.

The Catcher in the Rye is at the front of my backpack and I pull it out, holding my breath. There's silence, only my thoughts, no one else's. I put it on my desk, take out my notebook and put it next to it. Still no voice. I open the notebook to a new page, find a pen. Breathe. I write out the first line, copying it down carefully. Nothing. But right when I think about the next line I'm going to write, the voice is there again.

Charity ain't never gone go. She never gone leave me. I know she ain't.

'Fuck!'

I pick up the notebook, slam it down hard on the desk. Without thinking about it too much I turn to a blank page, write three words.

Who are you?

I watch the paper. Nothing happens. Of course nothing happens. What was I expecting, some words to magically appear from some slave ghost in my head? I put the pen down, spin around in my chair.

When I tell you what happened next you're probably not going to believe me. You'll think I made it up, or that I'm crazy or both. But I can't control that. I can only tell you the truth and leave the rest up to you.

My left hand picks it up – the pen – I'm right-handed, I never told you that. My left hand picks up the pen but it's not like I'm picking up the pen, it's like someone else is doing it – like a Ouija board or something. I look at my hand – the pen is gripped in my fist, not like it's going to write anything. But then it moves – is moved – and I can only describe it like a pulling, a jerking – like some other force is pulling it and I'm fighting it. The other force wins. And here's what it writes:

E.L.

The writing is big and blocky and takes up four lines of the page. There's holes in the page where the periods are after each letter. Almost without thinking about it I put the pen back in my right hand. I write my question slowly.

Where are you?

When I finish, I put the pen down on the paper. A second passes and then my left hand reaches for it again, makes a fist around it again. The words come out slow and shaky.

I'm right here.

When I tell you that that's when my cell phone rings you're definitely going to think I'm making it up but I swear that's what happened next. Right then, right as my brain is digesting the words the phone rings and my heart nearly stops. I'm aware that this is like something that would happen in some dumb ghost movie. But in a movie it would be an unknown number and some heavy breathing and this is only Mom.

'Cassie?'

'Mom?'

'Is everything okay?'

'Everything's fine. Why?'

Even as I answer her I am folding my arm over the paper, as if she can see me.

'I just wanted to call and check in on you. To see how you're doing – to make sure you're okay.'

She never calls to check in on me. I don't know if she's doing it because it's Grandad's anniversary or because of the botched birthday dinner but the answer is the same either way.

'I'm fine.'

'What are you doing?'

'My English homework.' I sound defensive, I can hear it.

'Is Gabi over? Or anyone else?'

I look at the page. 'I'm right here.' I turn it over.

'No. It's just me.'

'Where's your brother?'

'Out.'

She sighs. 'Out where?'

Her questions seem like they'll never end. I flip the page back over to check the words. 'I'm right here.' They're still there.

'Mom, I'm not Ryan's keeper. If you want to know where he is why don't you call him? Where are you anyway?'

I stand up, walk over to the mirror, flick my hair back so it sticks up, pull it back down. I look the same, like nothing has changed. I'm waiting for Mom to yell at me and tell me to stop being a wiseass but she's distracted, talking to someone in the background.

'Call your brother. Tell him to be home by six. Your father's taking you to John's Pizza for your birthday.'

'My birthday was yesterday.'

She's got her hand over the phone now, she's talking to someone in the background, I can tell.

'Are you in a bar?'

'I'm working, honey. I'll be home soon.'

'Are you coming for pizza too?'

In the mirror I don't look fifteen. My hair might, my earrings, but my cheeks are going red the way they always have when I get upset, the same way Ryan's do. In the mirror I look like a little kid.

'After yesterday I don't think it's such a good idea, do you? I'll take you out next weekend. You can have two birthday celebrations!'

She laughs, like that's something great.

'I don't want two birthday celebrations – I want one. You said we could all go together.'

The noise in the background changes and I picture her walking outside, or into a bathroom.

'I know, honey, and I'm sorry.'

'"I'm sorry." That's all you say any more. You promised! You both promised.'

'When we promised we meant it, sweetheart, but things are difficult –complicated—'

'It's your fault – if you hadn't said that thing in the *New York Times* interview about always putting family first the fight wouldn't have started.'

'But I *do* always put you guys first – who's the one who's there every night? In the mornings when you go to school?'

'Angelina?'

'Oh, come on. Be fair, Cassie, so I need some help sometimes. What about your father? Where's he been? He was the one who stormed out last night, not me. I would've gone for dinner. You know that. You know I would have gone, Cassie.'

I turn away from the mirror, sit on the edge of the bed. 'Mom, you don't get it—'

'It's not an easy situation, Cassie, okay? I know it's not easy on you but it's not easy on me either! Looking after you both by myself, all the pressure from my publisher, from the show—'

'What's not easy about pizza, Mom? What's not easy about four people having pizza together? Tell me what's not easy about that?'

The background is getting noisier again. 'Just tell Ryan to be home by five thirty, okay? You know he's always late and your dad is picking you up at six.'

'Mom?'

'I have to go, honey. Have fun with your dad.'

She hangs up and then there's silence. I'm about to hit redial. I want to call her back to finish the argument. I want to tell her how shitty it is not to come out for her daughter's birthday even if it is a day late, and how not everything is about her and her stupid publisher and her stupid shows. I want to ask her if she even remembered it's Grandad's anniversary today, whether she even thought about doing anything to mark it. And all of those things are jostling in my head but then I lie back on the bed and look at the ceiling fan swoosh and all of a sudden I'm exhausted and the anger drops away.

And I do forget to call Ryan because, before I can, my eyes are closing and I must have fallen straight asleep. And for the first time in what feels like forever, I don't have a single dream.

***

This story is going pretty fast and I want to pause for a minute to tell you something that happened way before all this. Something that only afterwards I realised might be important.

It happened in Ireland, the year after Grandad died. Mom was writing her memoir then and she decided it was finally time to make the trip, to meet her family, to research. I was so happy because I thought we'd be going to Donegal, that I could finally see Trá Mór, but Mom said it was too far north and anyway, there was no point because none of the family lived there any more. I was really mad about that and I sulked and threatened not to go. But then I found out Dad wasn't coming either – they told us he had to work – and I could have stayed behind with him so I decided to be happy, because going to Limerick and Dublin was better than not going at all.

On the plane Ryan and I do rock, paper, scissors for the window seat and he wins, which turns out to be a total waste because he falls asleep as soon as we've eaten dinner. I stay awake all night, reading my Tír na nÓg books, but he's still sleeping when they come through the cabin with some funny pastry for breakfast. The stewardess reaches over to lift our window shade and suddenly it's morning and the plane fills with yellow light. Over the wing you can see the sun like a streak in the white-blue sky and down below, way, way down below, you can see the ocean, navy-blue, crashing up against the edge of a coastline, just as green as I'd always imagined.

I turn to make sure Mom is looking too and I nearly bump heads with her because she's leaning so far over, into my seat.

'There's Ireland, Mom! Can you see it?'

She takes my hand, squeezes it. 'I see it, honey. I see it!'

We stay like that, hand in hand as the plane gets lower, low enough that we can make out a rocky shoreline and little fields and then a city getting closer.

'Do you think that's Limerick, Mom?'

'I'm not sure, honey, but I'd imagine it might be. Auntie Maureen said it wasn't far for them to come from the airport.'

Auntie Maureen is who we're staying with, only she's Grandad's sister's daughter, which makes her Mom's cousin, not our aunt.

'Remember that story, Mom, about the man Grandad knew from Limerick? With all the turkeys? That must mean he was there, right?'

She doesn't answer straight away and when I turn around to make sure she's heard she has tears in her eyes and one has escaped down her cheek.

'Are you okay, Mom?'

'I'm fine, honey.' She squeezes my hand tighter before she takes it away to find a Kleenex. 'I was just thinking about that story ... I hadn't thought about it in years.'

'So you think Grandad was here in Limerick, where we're going to be? I mean, it makes sense, right? The man would hardly have brought the turkeys somewhere else?'

She blows her nose and smiles – it's a real smile. 'I think you're right, honey. I bet he was here.'

It starts the second we get off the plane, maybe before then, maybe it starts with the captain's voice speaking Gaelic. It's like everywhere around me I think I'm going to see Grandad; I almost expect him to be in the crowd, waiting for us, alongside Auntie Maureen. There are other men in the crowd who look like him and on the way to the car I see even more – men who walk like him, stand like him, wear their jackets the way he wore his. And after a year of no memories it's like they come back then, all together, all at once, too fast to even tell apart from one another.

Me and Ryan are squashed into the back of the car with Brendan and Fiona who Auntie Maureen introduced us to as our cousins, even though they're actually Mom's cousins not ours. Brendan is twelve, a year older than me, and Fiona is ten, but they both seem younger and they don't say anything. Outside the window, Ireland is going by, just like it is any car ride, just like it is any other day.

'Which is your favourite Tír na nÓg story?' I ask Brendan, because he is sitting next to me.

'Tír na nÓg? You like Tír na nÓg?' He snorts a laugh and looks at Fiona.

She makes a face at him. 'We have to read it at school,' she says. 'It's in Irish so it's not like you'd have a favourite story, you know.'

'Cassie has the books in English,' Ryan says. 'She has them with her.'

'You have them with you?' Brendan makes his snorting laugh again and I can feel my face burn. Right then, at that moment, I feel more homesick for Grandad than I ever have before and it takes everything in me not to cry, to keep looking straight ahead, out the windshield.

From her seat by the window, Fiona leans forward so I can see her. 'I'd like to see one of them later, Cassie. If you don't mind, that is?'

I smile. I make sure the tears aren't going to come before I turn to her, answer her. 'Sure, I don't mind.'

I want them to live in a thatched cottage but Auntie Maureen pulls up outside a house that could be in Queens or the Bronx or anywhere. After we sleep for a bit we get up for lunch, only the meal is thick ham like at Thanksgiving and two different types of potatoes and Auntie Maureen calls it 'dinner'.

Mom hates ham but she doesn't say anything and eats it anyway and every now and then she brings up Grandad, all casual, and asks Auntie Maureen what she remembers about him. I'm waiting for Mom to say it's because of her memoir she's asking – to say anything about the memoir – but she doesn't so I don't either. At first Auntie Maureen says that because he was the youngest and her mom was the oldest she never knew Grandad well, that that's what happens when you have eleven children in the family, but then she looks like she's going to say more and that's when she tells us kids to go outside and play.

No one asks where we're going or when we'll be back and me and Ryan follow Brendan and Fiona into their backyard. There's a swing set and I think we're going to play on there but they walk past it, straight to the corner where there's a mound of dirt and grass piled next to the shed. Brendan runs up the mound first and barely touches the wall as he jumps over in a way that makes it look easy. Fiona goes next, running like he did, but at the top she hoists herself up on the wall.

'Come on, Cassie,' she calls.

The first time I go too slowly so my Nikes sink into the dirt. Mom bought them for me for the trip and I like them clean – box fresh – but I don't want to act all uptight so I don't say anything. Behind me Ryan is laughing but it's a nervous laugh. Fiona stretches out her hand.

'Faster. Just take a run at it, don't think about it.'

I take another run, pushing myself up through the sinking part until my hand reaches her hand, cold and kind of clammy at the same time. I'm up on the wall with Fiona and we are both there to help Ryan but he doesn't need it. He runs up and launches himself at the wall like he does this all the time, like this is how he spends his hours back in Brooklyn instead of playing his Xbox. He jumps down onto the other side, where Brendan is waiting. It's high, this drop into the field, and I copy the way Fiona does it, sitting on the edge, walking her legs down so they are close to the grass before letting herself go. I wonder if she always jumps down like this or if she is doing it for my benefit.

Behind their house is a whole field, a giant one with no fences or animals or anything, just loads of longish grass and trees to one side. And my heart gives a little smile because it doesn't look like Queens or the Bronx anymore, not out here. It is starting to look like Ireland.

'Race you,' Fiona says and she is already running by the time I get what she's saying. She runs past the boys and they start to run too and I am bringing up the rear. Brendan has a stick in his hand and he swipes the top of the grass, takes the lead again. I am a fast runner, a good runner. I catch up with Ryan, run past him. Fiona glances back and smiles, her hair is caught in her teeth, I run past her so I am in between her and Brendan. Behind me Ryan is getting tired of running, his head down. Further behind him the back walls of the houses are further away. I can't tell which is theirs any more. If I had to climb back over the wall on my own I might not choose the right one. Fiona said one of their neighbours had two German shepherds in their yard on a chain. I might climb into that garden by mistake.

Brendan stops running when he reaches the trees and finds a path in between them, hitting the trunks with his stick. I'm hot from running but it's colder here, a kind of damp cold. Above the trees the sky is grey, like a cloud sitting on the tops of the trees. It's been that way since we arrived.

Fiona comes up behind me, panting.

'Where are we going?' I ask.

'Just into the woods.'

'Why? What's in here?'

Fiona links my arm. 'Just for a mess around. Come on.' She smiles and I smile back. And it's funny how earlier they seemed so much younger than us and out here they are in charge. Out here, they are the adults.

The path gets narrower and Fiona goes on ahead. My arm feels cold where hers was and I wish we were linking again. Ryan is between her and Brendan so I am in the back now. I don't like being in the back. How do they know there aren't bears in this forest? Or some pyscho waiting to abduct kids like us? Why aren't they afraid?

In front, Brendan is saying something to Ryan that I can't hear. He raps the branches overhead with his stick so the last of the leaves come floating down. The trees in Brooklyn were still yellow when we left but here nearly all the leaves are gone already. I am figuring out whether this would be an interesting thing to say out loud or not when the path opens up, into a clearing. In the middle there are white grey ashes from a camp fire. Around the edges are beer cans, folded in half, not there long enough to be rusted. Brendan picks one up and holds it up high, tips his head back. Some brown liquid drips out and into his mouth.

'Gross!' Fiona makes a face. 'You're so disgusting.'

'Just because you're too scared to drink beer,' Brendan says. 'I bet Ryan will have some.'

Ryan picks up a can, copies Brendan. When the liquid hits his tongue he gags and spits it out. Brendan laughs.

'What's the matter? Not man enough?'

'Leave him alone,' Fiona says. 'People could have pissed in them or anything for all you know.'

Ryan looks like he might cry and part of me wants to go to him and tell him it's all right but I know he doesn't want me to and it'll only make it worse. He drops his can out of his hand, down behind him as if Brendan won't see. I walk over to the fire, kick it with my toe.

'Who made this? Who comes here?'

'The leprechauns,' Brendan says in a stupid voice. 'The little people.'

I know it's a dig about the Tír na nÓg books earlier but I don't say anything. Before we came I'd imagined conversations about Grandad's gift, had wanted to ask if they had it too but I know now I'll never say anything. At least not in front of Brendan.

Fiona rolls her eyes. 'Don't mind him. It's just the teenagers, they come here to knacker drink.'

I don't know what 'knacker drinking' means but I can guess and I don't want to ask any more dumb questions. Brendan is standing outside the circle, throwing his stick high up into the tree and catching it again.

'Let's do something,' he calls. 'This is boring.'

'Do you know any games?' Fiona asks. 'What kind of games do you play in New York?'

'I like *Grand Theft Auto*,' Ryan goes, 'but she prefers Minecraft.'

'Not those kinds of games, Ry.' It comes out more impatient than I mean. 'Fiona means games we can play out here, like, games we can play now.'

'Oh.' Ryan kicks at the edge of the ashes with his sneaker like I was doing before. He doesn't know any games like that. Apart from computer games, we know Scrabble and Jenga and Pictionary, but I know those aren't the kind of games Fiona means either so I don't say anything.

'Let's climb this tree,' Brendan says. 'I bet you all I can get up the highest.'

He's dropped his stick and is already squirming up the trunk, finding foot holes and hand grips where there don't seem to be any. The tree is tall, the branches shaking in the wind over our heads.

'You climb that tree every day, you'd want to get highest,' Fiona says. 'I have an idea though, there's this thing we were doing at school. It's kind of like hypnotising someone.'

'Bor-ring,' Brendan calls from the tree, pulling himself up higher.

'It's really cool, I swear,' Fiona says. 'You'll do it, Cassie, won't you?'

I don't think it sounds cool but she seems so excited and I don't want her to not like me. And I trust her, I think I do. She stuck up for me in the car and helped me over the wall.

'Sure.'

'Great! So, you need to stand over here—'

Brendan jumps out of the tree, landing on a pile of leaves. 'I want to go first.'

'No,' Fiona says, 'Cassie's going first.'

I shrug. 'It's not a big deal.'

'Cassie, you're first, then Brendan.'

Brendan makes a sneering face. 'You just don't want me to go because you know that you can't hypnotise anyone and I won't let you get away with it.'

So that's how Brendan ends up going first and lets Fiona put in him position, his back against the tree, me and Ryan on either side of him. He closes his eyes when Fiona tells him to and she half closes hers as she starts to hum and make clicking sounds with her fingers, clicking close to one of his ears, then the other. Sometimes as the set of fingers on one hand clicks, the other hand makes a waving motion in front of his face, over the top of his head. In between the clicks, she claps her hands, super-fast like castanets.

'You are falling into a deep sleep,' she says in a fake deep voice. 'You feel yourself sinking, sinking, down, into blackness.'

Brendan is slumping back into the tree. He's faking it, I'm sure he is. But when she takes one of his wrists and ties an imaginary knot around it, his arm twitches a little bit, even though his eyes are closed. And when she starts to pull on the invisible string his arms lift up, jerky at first, then smooth – the kind of smoothness when you are not doing something for yourself. Fiona pulls her hands higher and Brendan's arms are fully outstretched like Frankenstein's monster.

'Cool,' Ryan whispers. 'Can you make him pick up that cigarette butt and pretend to smoke?'

'I'm only supposed to keep him under for less than sixty seconds,' Fiona says, breathless, before letting the strings go so his hands hit into the bark of the tree pretty hard. It must hurt but his eyes don't open and he doesn't say anything. 'It's time to wake up now, Brendan. I'm going to count backwards – three, two, one …'

She claps her hands in front of his face a final time and Brendan lurches to one side, stumbling forward. I grab his arm to stop him falling and when he looks around his eyes are open and he is frowning, confused.

'What happened? What did you do?'

'Don't you remember?' Fiona says, victorious now.

He rubs his left wrist with his right hand.

'What did you make me do?'

'You don't remember anything?'

He circles his wrist with his fingers. 'I don't know, some kind of tugging?'

'What was it like?' Ryan goes. 'Did you know what was happening?'

'He's faking, Ry,' I say. 'He knew the whole time.'

'Oh yeah? So why don't you do it next.'

'Fine, I will.'

Taking my spot by the tree I'm not scared. I saw what Fiona did, there's nothing scary about it, it's not real hypnosis. The only thing I'm scared of is bugs that might be in the trees so I try not to stand so close to the bark.

'Ready?' Fiona asks.

'Ready.'

I close my eyes and I hear her start to hum, the clicking close to my ears. Hearing it without seeing it makes it feel faster, closer than it looked when it was Brendan's turn. I go to breathe but then I realise I'm already holding my breath so I exhale instead. And that's the last thing I remember before I wake up on the ground.

'Cassie?'

Someone is calling me from far away; I don't recognise their voice.

'Cassie? Wake up, please wake up.'

It's a girl's voice, a girl with an accent and when I open my eyes it takes me a second to recognise the face close up to mine, the hair that's dangling down on my cheek. Behind her head there are bare tree branches, the grey of the sky.

'Cassie,' she's saying, 'it's me, Fiona. Are you all right?'

'I'm going to get Mam.' Another voice, a boy's.

'Don't you dare, Brendan Kelly!' Fiona says, flicking her head around. 'She's waking up, she's grand.'

'Cass, are you okay? Cassie, can you hear me?'

This voice I know, it's Ryan's and his face appears next to Fiona, the colour high in his cheeks. I want to tell him I'm okay, that it's all okay, but when I open my mouth to speak my voice doesn't work.

'Give her room,' Fiona says, in charge again now. 'Brendan, go and get her some water.'

'How am I supposed to get water without Mam noticing?'

'Not from Mam, stupid, from the stream.'

'I've nothing to put it in.' Brendan sounds like a little boy now, not like before.

'Put it in one of the cans. Wash it out properly first. Rinse it a few times, then fill it up.'

I don't want water out of a dirty can but my mouth won't work to say that.

'Come on, Ryan,' Brendan says and I hear their footsteps walk away.

'It's okay,' Fiona is saying, 'deep breaths, that's right.'

After a few minutes of lying there like that, I try to push myself up a bit and she helps me sit up, so I lean against the tree.

'Are you feeling okay? You were trying to say something – were you having some kind of dream?'

And then it comes back, the two women in shawls as thin as skeletons. Standing here, right here in this spot.

I swallow, my voice is back. 'What happened?'

She pulls a lock of hair from behind her ear, twists it around her finger.

'I don't know. I was just doing the stuff – you know, like with Brendan – and then you fell over, really suddenly, like just down on the ground.'

'Did I hit my head?'

'I don't think so. I didn't mean to. I was only doing what we did at school, all the girls have done it.'

I feel my forehead for a lump but there is nothing there. One of the women had something in her hand, something dark – blackberries. She was trying to hand them to me. But I wasn't me, I was someone else. She kept calling me Sheila.

Fiona is twisting her hair around her finger so hard, the tip turns white. 'Are you sure you're okay?'

'I'm fine.'

I think about telling her about the women, asking her if she knows anything about them, anyone called Sheila, but then there are footsteps on the grass and we both look over to see Brendan and Ryan coming back towards us. They're not running but they're fast walking and Brendan has a can held out in front of him, water dripping on the grass. He hands it to Fiona and she pours a bit onto her hand, puts her hand on my forehead, the coolness feels good.

'You fainted,' Ryan goes, 'you were unconscious for ages.'

'It wasn't ages,' Fiona snaps.

'Yes, it was, wasn't it, Brendan? It had to be five minutes, more.'

'Easily,' he says, turning to Fiona. 'You're going to be in such big trouble when we tell Mam and Auntie Louise.'

'We don't have to tell them. She's grand now.' Fiona puts some more water on my cheeks this time. 'You won't tell, sure you won't, Cassie?'

Fiona's scared. She'll be in big trouble if I say anything I know she will. 'I'm fine,' I say, pushing myself into a stand to prove it. 'Let's just go home.'

The other three stand up too, but slower. On the way back nobody runs and nobody talks. Brendan's lost his stick somewhere so he doesn't hit the trees. I'm relieved that without talking about it we decide to walk around to the front of the house instead of going back over the wall.

Before we leave the field I glance back, over my shoulder to the trees, and it's like I can picture her, the woman who called me Sheila, a shadow of her, even if she is not there. And it's only then I remember, about the famine, and I want to ask Fiona if people died here, to tell her what I saw and see if she thinks it could be Grandad's gift. But Brendan is standing at the corner, waiting for us, and after his jokes about Tír na nÓg and leprechauns I don't want him to have another reason to make fun of me. So I keep it to myself, I don't say anything more about it.

***

For a while after that day when E.L. wrote me the note, I don't have any more dreams. Dad takes me and Ryan out for my birthday pizza and I'm dreading coming home, dreading the dream, but it doesn't come. It doesn't come the next night or the one after and the voices are quiet too. By the weekend I'm starting to hope – even to believe – that it might have been a phase, that it might be over. And then the dream comes back. It's the original one, the one where we're running through the grass towards the body in the tree, and when I wake up my heart is racing and my breath is fast and shallow like it always is. I put on my glasses, am about to start my system working through the bookcase, but then I try something different – I grab the pen and pad next to my bed.

Who are you? I write.

I put the pen down, wait for something to happen. It's not going to work. This is stupid; maybe it never happened at all – the note from her – maybe I imagined it. And then my left hand picks up the pen and my heart is slowing a little, I think it is.

E.L.

Just like before the periods punch holes in the paper. I wait for more – the rest of a name, but that's all there is.

You told me that already, I mean, who are you really? What does E.L. stand for?

There's a pause. I don't think she's going to answer. But then she does. Each letter takes forever and her sentence gets small near the end where she runs out of paper, as if she doesn't know she can turn the page.

E.L. the name my mamma give me. Charity say it stand for me.

Charity – I've heard her talk about her. Somehow I know she's the woman who I've seen with the whip marks on her back, I don't know how I know that, but I do. I'm figuring out what to ask next but the pen in my left hand is moving again.

What your name?

I don't know why but I'm not expecting her to ask me that – to ask me anything. I answer quickly.

Cassie Lazzaro.

She grabs the pen back, writes faster than before.

What kinda name that?

I laugh. I can't help it.

My dad is Italian and my mom is Irish. Cassidy was her last name before she got married. She liked it so she gave it to me as a first name, but everyone calls me Cassie for short. My brother's name is Ryan because that was her mom's last name before she married my grandad. Mom and Dad wanted us to have Irish and Italian names.

I hadn't planned to write all that, taking up almost a full page and part of me wants to keep writing, to tell her how I've always wondered how I can keep the Irish part alive when I get married and have kids but I make myself stop. This time I put the pen in my left hand straight away instead of putting it down on the paper. She doesn't write anything – for ages she doesn't, two minutes, more – and I think I've somehow broken the spell and messed it up. But finally she starts to write, and this is what she says:

Hello, Cassie Lazzaro.

She's smiling. I don't know how I know that but I do. And I smile too when I write back.

Hello, E.L.

And I'm still smiling when I put the pen down and shut the notebook. My eyes are heavy, my head is heavy on my pillow and I feel sleep coming like a wave, pulling me in, pulling me under. And for some reason I already know there won't be any more dreams that night and there aren't. Just a deep, strong sleep that lasts all the way till morning, and I don't wake up at all.

E.L.

It diff'rent for me. I don't write no letters to Cassie – I ain't got no time for that and b'sides Charity not teachin' us no more 'bout writin' and readin' so it take me a long time to write ev'rythin' out like that.

No, for me it like talkin' in my head. Like the way I talk to Dolly – only now I know it Cassie I really talkin' to. In the beginnin' I go to the tree anyway and sit down with Dolly only then I notice I can talk to Cassie any place, I don't have to be there. So once I start I talk to her in the big house when Miss Ellen havin' her piano lessons with the Mistress and me and Juba beatin' the dirt outta all the carpets out on the porch. I talk to her at night in the cabin 'stead of sayin' prayers the way Charity and me use to say t'gether.

Firs' we talk 'bout me all the time. She ask all these questions – so many questions I can't answer, like what happen my mamma and where my daddy at and what day and month and year it is today. She ask my age and I know that – thirteen – 'cause I a few months older than Miss Ellen and she have her thirteenth birthday a few months back. When she ask 'bout my daddy I tell her what Charity tell me, 'bout how he on that other plantation where Charity and my mamma use be b'fore they got sold here. And when she ask 'bout my mamma I jus' tell her she dead and nothin' more 'cause there ain't nothin' more to say.

One time I talkin' to Cassie when I walkin' through the woods back to the cabin and Marjorie come outta the trees right next to me silent as a snake.

'Who you talkin' to?' she say.

I scared of Marjorie. She ain't never liked me none.

'I ain't talkin' to no one.'

'Sure you was – I seen your lips movin''

My stomach feel sick when she say that but I laugh – I make myself.

'You seen my lips movin'? You hear any sound? Who I gone be talkin' to makin' no sound?'

Her eyes get narrow, mean lookin'.

'So why your lips movin' then? You talkin' to some spirit demon? Some devil?'

She make me think 'bout that woman 'gain, the one they drown in the lake. If I let her see that I scared she gone know she on the right track. She gone know I got a secret – somethin' to be scared for. Charity a'ways say not to let them see your fear – she talkin' 'bout the white folk but maybe it the same for Marjorie too. Maybe that work for anybody.

'You mind your tongue,' I say. 'I prayin'! I out here talkin' to God! Not that it any of your bus'ness!'

I walk past her. Keep walkin'. There a half broke branch in one of the trees and I snap it off and start to swish the tops of the tall grass with it as I walk by.

'They say the Master ain't comin' back,' she call after me. 'They say the Mistress got bills pilin' up! That she gone sell you and Charity to pay 'em!'

I keep walkin', keep swishin'. Somethin' come into my head, maybe some words that Cassie put there, 'cause I ain't never think of somethin' like this to say on my own. I stop, turn 'round.

'If she want to pay bills course she gone sell us,' I say. 'She ain't gone get hardly nothin' if she sell you and your mamma!'

I turn back 'gain, keep walkin' towards the cabins. I shoulda been scared after sayin' that to Marjorie. She older than me and stronger than me. If she take a run at me from b'hind and push me down, gettin' up ain't gone be easy. But I hear Cassie in my head.

Keep walking, she say.

So I do.

It's going to be all right, she say.

And Marjorie don't say nothin', she don't do nothin'. And for right then, Cassie right. Ev'rythin' a'right. For right then it is.

CASSIE

I tried not to write to her. If you want to know the truth, it freaked me out. Grandad never mentioned writing as being a part of his gift – I don't remember him ever writing much, even on birthday cards he just wrote '*love Grandad*' in tiny writing. I didn't want to do it but when I didn't write back her voice just got even louder in my head and I had more dreams about her, all sorts of crazy dreams. In the night, in the dark, writing to her didn't feel so bad – it felt kind of good not to be alone – but in the morning, seeing the notes written back and forth made me feel like I was going crazy.

Most mornings I went to Mom's office before I went down for breakfast, so I could shred the notes from the night before. One morning, the shredder jammed and I started to panic. As I switched it off and on and off again I imagined what she would say if she saw what I'd written, about what she said before about me needing to see a shrink. And even though I get the shredder back on and whirring through the paper, that's the day I swear that no matter how bad things get, I'm never going to write to E.L. again.

I last two days that time. I make it through school and even one whole night of her voice talking to me, I make it through the same dream over and over where two men are killing something outside our cabin in the middle of the night and we almost step in the blood, black like ink on the grass. The next day, during Mr. Conan's geography class, her voice is there, calling my name, I wish I'd never told her my name. Her voice is there through lunch, when I'm listening and not listening to Gabi talking about Scott Stroller.

It's there when we're in the library studying after school and once when Gabi is in the bathroom I open up my notepad, am about to write to E.L. to tell her to stop, to beg her to stop, but then Gabi is back so I never do.

That night, in bed, I crack. Lying on my right side, my left, my back – turning so much the sheets are twisting around me, her voice is there.

Cassie where you at? You still here Cassie? Cassie, I want talk to you!

Cassie, Cassie, Cassie – it's never-ending and before I know I'm going to I jump out of bed, pound to my desk and grab my notebook from my backpack on the chair.

LEAVE ME ALONE!

That's what I write, in big capital letters. I turn the page, write it again.

LEAVE ME THE FUCK ALONE!!!!

My breath is shallow. Fast. My left hand takes the pen from my right. I snatch it back but my left takes it again, almost calmly. Quietly. The words on the page form slowly.

Why you mad at me? I thought we friends.

I scream as I throw the pad across the room. It bounces off the blinds and onto the floor. Around me the house is silent. I wait for noise, for the sound of Ryan getting out of bed or for Mom's door to crash open but nothing happens. It's as if my scream was only silence. I walk across the room, pick up the notepad, get back in bed.

I need you to leave me alone – I can't be your friend.

My left hand takes the pen, writes back.

Why not? I done somethin' wrong?

I snatch the pen.

You're dead. You're not real. I can't help you. I'm sorry. Please, please, please. This is scaring me. Please just leave me alone.

I rip the page out, crumple it up and throw it on the floor. On the next page my left hand starts again.

I ain't dead. And you know I real. What make you think I need help? I ain't the one askin' for help.

I scribble out the words with my right hand – hard spiral scribbles like I haven't made since the third grade. I rip the page out too and throw it on my nightstand. I need to put the pen away, get rid of it, but before I do there are more words pouring from my left hand which is getting faster now at writing them.

There ain't nothin' to be 'fraid of. You know you want be my friend too.

NO I DON'T! I'm not your friend!!!

It's my turn to make the words big so they take up the rest of the page. I rip this one out too and fire the pen into the corner of the room so I can't write any more even if I want to. Even though I know it doesn't work, I put my headphones in, hit play. It's Sigur Rós, an Icelandic band, and of all the music I've tried it's the only one that calms me, even a little bit. I don't know if the words are Icelandic or made up words but usually they quieten E.L.'s voice too – only not tonight.

You think it me you mad at, but it ain't. I'm your friend. I'm the one who help you.

I turn up the volume to the max.

Cassie Lazzaro why you so mad? Why you won't be my friend no more?

I sit up in bed, slam my hands against the mattress.

'Jesus Christ! I'm not your friend! I was never your friend!'

Sigur Rós is still blaring, still flooding into my ears, so I see Ryan, standing in the doorway, even though I don't hear the door open. With the light behind him from the landing, he's a silhouette, and it feels like he's a long way away from me. I rip the headphones off.

'Cass?' he's saying, 'Cass, are you okay?'

I turn on my bedside lamp. Lately he's been wearing oversized Slipknot hoodies but in his pyjamas with his hair all flat and not spiked he looks much younger, like a little boy. A scared little boy.

'Hey, Ry, sure. I'm okay. I'm fine.'

'What's going on? Who were you yelling at?'

'I wasn't yelling.'

'I heard you. You screamed first, then you started yelling about not being someone's friend.'

He's walking closer to the bed now, close to the balled up notes on the floor.

'I don't know, I was asleep. I guess I was having a nightmare.'

From the headphones on the bed the music is still blaring, he can hear it – we both can. There is no way I'd have been able to sleep through that, no way anyone could. I turn it off.

His eyes wander over to the nightstand with the open notepad and more ripped out pages.

'You're writing? What are you writing?'

'Nothing. I'm not writing anything. Go to bed.'

He takes another step. One of the crumpled pages is on the floor, right by his foot. He sees me looking at it and he bends down to pick it up. He opens it.

'Give me that!'

I dive out of bed, over to snatch it from him, but he's too quick, running out of my grasp and around the end of the bed.

'Who are you writing to? Some boy, I bet!'

I grab for the letter again, but he laughs and holds it behind his back.

'Ryan, that's private! Give it to me now!'

He runs on his tiptoes away from me and when I catch his waist he twirls out of my hold and jumps up onto the bed and starts to read aloud.

'"I need you to leave me alone – I can't be your friend."'

'Ryan! Stop it, give it here!' I jump up on the bed too, but he bounces down the other end.

'Wow, who is this guy? He must be some loser if you can't even be friends with him?'

'Seriously, Ryan, you're going to be in big trouble – Mom's going to come in here any minute.'

I'm grasping for the letter but he keeps turning just far enough out of my reach. He's out of breath as he keeps reading and I am too.

'"Why not? I done something wrong?" Geez Cassie, what's up with your writing? It looks like a five year old.'

My lunge gets him this time so we both fall on the bed, laughing and twisting together, like the way we used to play when we were kids, only we're not kids and this isn't a game. My hand grabs the paper and I pull but I only tear off the top part – the part he's already read. His laugh is a victory whoop as he reads the rest.

'"You're dead. You're not real. I can't help you. I'm sorry. Please, please, please. This is scaring me. Please just leave me alone."'

His voice trails off at that last part. I grab the rest of the letter from him, crumple it up in a ball.

'We're going to wake up Mom – she's going to be in here any minute and you're going to be in the shit for causing such a ruckus. For going through my stuff.'

We both know that's not true, that from the wine Mom had over dinner and then later, in her office, that nothing will wake her, but he doesn't contradict me. He sits up slowly, twists so he's sitting on the edge of the bed, his back to me.

'What's going on, Cass?'

'Nothing. It's nothing, Ry, don't worry about it.'

I crumple all the papers together, as tight as I can. More for the shredder or maybe I'll burn them. Maybe I'll ask Angelina to set a fire tomorrow and I'll wait and watch them all go from flames to ash.

'You said you were scared. You said you were writing to someone who was dead. That's messed up.'

For a second I think about explaining, about asking him what Grandad told him about his gift. In the Narnia books sisters and brothers go on adventures together, in Harry Potter too. But this isn't some book; this is real life. And in real life, offence is the best form of defence.

'Where do you get off? Since when do you come into my room and go through my stuff. If anything's messed up that's messed up!'

His shoulders are slumped forward. 'I'm sorry. I was just busting your chops – I thought it was some guy at school ...' He turns around and his face has that flushed look that means he's close to crying.

I crawl across the bed, swing my legs over the edge so we are sitting side by side. For a second I think about putting my arm around him but he won't let me do that anymore and, besides, then he'd know there was really something wrong.

'It's a school assignment, dumbass.'

'What?' he looks up, confused, hopeful.

'In history – Mrs. Fenimore wanted us to really get in touch with a character from history, to be friends with them. So we had to pick someone and write to them – and have them write back.'

He's frowning, trying to make sense of it. 'Who'd you pick?'

'I picked a slave girl, from South Carolina. Remember that time we went to the cotton plantation with Mom and Dad? I imagined she lived there.'

It feels so good right then to mention the cotton plantation. He doesn't register and for a horrible second it feels like he's not going to remember, that maybe even that wasn't real. But then he nods.

'I remember. That was the time you'd a fight with Mom and we all had to look for you.'

'What are you talking about? None of you looked for me – when I came back you were all still looking at the slave houses, I don't think Mom even noticed I was gone.'

He shakes his head. 'No way, she was freaking out. She was about to ask the people who ran the place to make an announcement. I was the one who found you. I knew you'd be down at the river.'

He knew because I told him. I remembered it clearly, afterwards I'd told him about sitting down there, waiting for them to come and no one did. But it didn't matter now and anyway, bickering about details of an old vacation was better than him asking why a homework assignment was making me yell and scream in the middle of the night.

'Whatever,' I say. 'That's the place and that's why I wrote about the girl.'

A beat passes and I hope that's the end of it, that there are no more questions, but Ryan always has more questions.

'What's up with doing your homework at two in the morning?'

I shrug. 'I guess I couldn't sleep. Sorry I woke you up.'

He nods again, pushes down into the bed with his hands.

'You didn't. I guess I couldn't sleep either.'

Looking back, I see now that he was opening a door then. I could've asked him why he wasn't asleep, asked him how he was doing with Mom and Dad and everything. That's the kind of thing big sisters are supposed to do – the kind of big sister I want to be anyway – but the fact is I didn't. The fact is that ending the conversation with him without any more questions or lies was the most important thing, the very most important thing to me right then.

'Okay, buddy, it's time to get some sleep,' I say instead. 'School tomorrow.'

As I'm saying it I know I sound like someone else and it's only when the words are out I realise it's Dad I sound like, he's the one who calls him 'buddy'. And I wait for him to say that, to give me a hard time, but he doesn't. He just stands up and says goodnight and goes back to his room.

And I like to think that he went to sleep straight away then, as soon as he was back in bed. But maybe, like me, he lay awake, looking at the ceiling. Maybe, like me, he couldn't sleep for a really, really long time.

E.L.

When the Master come home it late – we a'ready in bed. I musta been sleepin' 'cause I only wake up when I feel somethin' hit me.

'What that?' I jump 'wake and I see Marjorie there and she musta stood on me 'cause she runnin' 'cross the cabin like it on fire. She run for the door and I see her mamma in front of her jus' b'fore it close.

'What's goin' on?' I call out but they don't answer.

Next to me Charity 'wake and sit up too. 'What happen?' she say.

'I don't know – Marjorie and Linda run out. I don't know what going on.'

'Wait here. I gone go see.'

She pull her blanket 'round her and go out the door too. There shoutin' outside, men's voices and there a woman cryin'. I look 'round and Rose sittin' up like me, next to her Nelly lyin' down sleepin'.

'That Linda cryin',' she say. 'I know her cry.'

'What you think happen?'

Rose shake her head. 'Seems to me the Master might be back and maybe ev'ryone ain't so please to see him.'

I don't know how Rose know that, but when she say it I want go look for myself even though Charity tell me to wait. I pull my blanket 'round my shoulder like she did and I walk over to the door. I open it jus' 'nough to see outside, not the whole way.

It dark but b'side the mens cabin there three white mens on horses and they got torches. One of the mens is Nagle but I don't know the other two. Next to them is Ruby – the horse that belong to the Master

– but the Master ain't on him. I open the door more and creep out on the porch and there he is holdin' a lantern standin' b'side Big Bill. Next to both there another slave I ain't never seen b'fore. He got chains on his hands and on his feets but he so skinny he look like he coulda slip outta them if he try.

Rose right 'bout the Master and she right 'bout Linda too 'cause when one of the horses move I see her down on the ground near the Master feets and she cryin' out: 'No, you can't! Please don't! Massa, please don't!'

It only then I see John on the other side of the slave with the chains, half-hidden by the shadow. Linda crawl 'cross the earth and wrap her arms 'round his feets.

'Let go – let go of him, you filthy bitch!' That Nagle voice shoutin' and his whip crack down on Linda and next to her so the dust rise all 'round her. He hit her twice more till she don't move.

Standin' a bit back, Charity got her hands 'round Marjorie but when Nagle whip her mamma, Marjorie break free and run over to the Master. In the light from his lantern you can see her tears shinin' on her cheeks.

'Don't let them take him!' she cryin'. 'Stop them! Don't let them take my daddy!'

The Master don't look so good. He ain't got no jacket and his shirt dirty and torn. His beard longer than I ever seen it.

'I'm sorry,' he say, 'your daddy has to go now. He has a new owner.'

'No! No! No!' And some demon musta got into Marjorie then 'cause she start hittin' the Master, poundin' on his chest with her fists. 'You can't! You bastard!'

The Master look so shocked he don't do nothin' and her daddy the firs' one to act and he come runnin' and grab her by the waist. Then

Big Bill join in, grab her too and it take both of them to pull her 'way. Nagle down off his horse by then and he take her by the arm so hard he a'most lift her in the air.

'I'll show you what we do with disrespectful nigger bitches like you,' he say. 'Pete! Take her to the stocks.'

'No!' Linda get up but only far as her knees, like she prayin' now. 'Please no – she don't mean no harm. She a good chil'.'

The Master fixin' his shirt. He look embar'assed. 'It's not necessary, Nagle,' he say. 'The girl is highly strung, she's upset – her father–'

'Excuse me, sir, but it sure is necessary,' Nagle say. 'You let a little negress away with acting like that and we got an insurrection on our hands faster than you can say Nat Turner.'

I think the Master gone say somethin' else, that he gone stop Pete, but he only look at the ground and it terrible listenin' to Linda screams and then Marjorie screams gettin' further and further 'way.

'Let's get this done,' one of the mens on the horses say. 'We haven't got all night.'

He jump down and Nagle jump down and t'gether they take the chains off the slave standin' next to Big Bill. He look even skinnier without the chains – his arms and his legs skinnier than a girl and his head look too big for his skinny body. He blacker than any of us – his skin so black it shiny. Next to his mouth there a round part shinier than the rest and it a scar where someone cut him or branded him or somethin'. And it sit part over his mouth that scar so it make him look like he smilin' only the rest of his face ain't smilin'. The rest of his face look mean.

After they take the chain off he bend down and rub his ankle, walk 'round a little bit. That when I see his leg on the left side don't work none too good.

Nagle move to put the chains on John and Linda start cryin' all over 'gain.

'What you tradin' my husband for him for? He lame, he skinny. My husband worth ten o' him.'

The Master look like he go to say somethin' only Big Bill stand close to him and shake his head. I r'member then how Charity tell me Big Bill know the Master since he a little boy – that they grew up t'gether, like me and Miss Ellen.

'Move, woman!' Nagle yell at Linda. Charity come close like she gone try and pull Linda outta there but b'fore she can Nagle kick her hard in the side and she roll 'way close to Ruby, the Master horse, so she rear up on her back legs.

All hell break loose then with the horse rearin' and whinnyin' and Linda screamin' and Charity tryin' to pull Linda up onto her feets and John fightin' Nagle and the other white man tryin' to put the irons 'round his legs. Usually John don't hardly say nothin' and up till now he ain't said a word but when he start it like he ain't gone stop.

'I ain't goin'! I ain't leavin' my family! You can't do this! Jus' 'cause you lost some card game you can't do this!'

That when Nagle start beatin' on John, hard with the end of the whip over and over, and if it ain't for the other white man who pull Nagle off then maybe he hurt John real bad.

'Take it easy,' the white man say, 'he's someone else's property now. I don't want to be bringin' back damaged goods.'

With ev'rythin' that happen I don't see the Master leavin', I only notice the horse stopped jumpin' and then I see that 'cause the Master talkin' in her ear when he lead her to the path toward the big house.

Big Bill run up next to him. 'I take her Master – you a long journey. I take her to the stable.'

'Thank you, Bill.' The Master say his name but he lookin' at the horse not at Big Bill. 'But I'll take her. She's had a shock. I'll settle her down.'

Big Bill nod and stand back as the Master walk her on. B'hind the trees there light in the sky and it not gone be long b'fore the horn blow for mornin'.

The white man got John on his horse now, layin' 'cross in front him. There blood on John shirt 'round the neck part. Linda on her knees but she quiet now too and she look like she prayin'. Her eyes on John and his neck craned up so his eyes on her too and even though ev'ryone else there, it like it jus' the two of them.

Nagle start to push Big Bill and the other mens back into the barn.

'Back inside,' he say. 'Show's over.'

The new slave don't move; he jus' stand there.

'You,' Nagle say, 'get in there with the others. You got a name?'

When he speak his voice deep. Angry soundin'.

'Jasper,' he say. 'My name Jasper.'

I know I shoulda been inside too that Charity gone be mad but I can't make myself move. The firs' white man on the horse give it a kick and turn it 'way and then the second one – the one with John – do the same.

Linda find her voice 'gain. 'John!' she cry out. 'John!'

'Linda!' He twistin' his body up so it look like he gone fall off but the white man push him back down and kick the horse so it move faster. 'Linda! Linda!'

The sound of those horses gallopin' 'way and they voices in the night musta been the loneliest sound I ever done hear. But then they gone and the gallopin' too far 'way to hear and John voice too far 'way to hear and all that left the sound of Linda cryin'.

'Get up!' Nagle go to kick her 'gain but Charity get in b'tween them so his foot get her instead. 'Get her up! Get her out of my sight.'

I run back inside then and I seen Rose been up too lookin' out the door, Nelly the only one still 'sleep, still snorin'. But when I lie down I close my eyes tight like I 'sleep too 'cause I don't want Charity to know I disobey her and I don't want to see Linda neither 'cause I don't know what I gone say to her.

I keep my eyes shut so tight I can't see nothin' but I can't shut my ears too and I hear they feets on the steps and the doors open. Linda not sayin' nothin' but she cryin' real hard and Charity tell her hush that it gone be a'right but when she say that Linda start cryin' louder.

I don't sleep that night. It ain't jus' 'cause Charity ain't lyin' down with me or 'cause Linda cryin' all night – most of the time she ain't even cryin' so loud. It 'cause my mind in so many other places at the same time: out in the stocks with Marjorie and on a horse somewhere with John goin' to some new master he ain't never even met. And it on the face of the new slave that look like he a'ways smilin' and the face of the Master when he stroke the horse 'stead of lookin' at Big Bill.

And it make no sense why he sell John for that new skinny slave and it make no sense that if he the Master that he don't stop Nagle makin' Marjorie go to the stocks. And after all that time wantin' him to come back, now he back, I wish he stay 'way. I wish he never done come back at all.

CASSIE

I know as soon as I walk into the kitchen that something is wrong. First of all, I haven't seen Mom and Dad in the same room together in months – not since the night of my birthday fight – and, second, even when they both lived here, neither of them were ever home this early.

'Hey, Mom, hey, Dad!' I make my voice sound all casual. 'What's up?'

Dad stands up, hugs me. 'Hi, Cass. Your mom and I wanted to have a chat with you.'

He gestures to an empty chair between them and I'll admit it: despite all evidence to the contrary I feel a little bounce of hope in my heart that maybe they are getting back together.

I take off my backpack. Sit down. 'Chat about what?'

I look from Dad to Mom and back again. She's not smiling; in fact her face has that look where her skin is stretched so tight that she looks way older than she is. She covers her eyes with her hand. The hope sinks into some other feeling that I have no name for and I curse myself for letting myself feel it, even for a second.

'You mother and I – your mom and I – we wanted to have a talk. With you.'

'Okay. You said that. What about?'

I'm conscious of my heart beating in my chest, can hear it vibrating in my words. Dad has a cup of tea in front of him and he turns it in his saucer. Looks down into it. He opens his mouth to speak, but Mom beats him to it.

'Cassie, there's no easy way to ask this: are you on drugs?'

The question is like an explosion in the silence of the kitchen. My first response is to laugh. 'Drugs? Really? You think I'm on drugs?'

'Look, just tell us the truth,' Mom says. 'Don't deny it, please don't lie to us.'

'Deny it? What the hell, Mom? Dad, you don't think I'm on drugs, do you?'

I turn to Dad, but he's not smiling anymore.

'We're not mad, honey,' he says, 'we just want you to be honest with us. We know what pressure can be like at school, but we want to help you – there's a lot of help out there.'

'There's addiction in our family,' Mom interjects. 'I told you that before – you need to be extra careful. Some kids might be able to try stuff out – experiment – but you can't risk that. '

This is crazy. They ask me a question and don't even let me answer. As usual they have everything figured out with no input from me.

'I'm not on drugs. I swear.' I look from one to the other. Mom's face is angry; Dad's is afraid, he wants to believe me, I know he does. 'So once there was a joint going around at a party at Justin Caldwell's house and I tried it and it had no effect other than making me feel like throwing up. That's it, that's all I've done. The only time.'

There's silence then. Dad looks at Mom but she is still looking at me.

'If you don't believe me check my room. Ask Gabi. Give me a blood test, I don't know. I'm telling the truth!'

The funny thing is I am telling the truth about the joint and Dad must hear it because it reaches across the table and touches my arm.

'Okay,' he says. 'Calm down, honey, it's okay.'

As soon as I say the thing about checking my room I wish I hadn't.

I've stopped shredding the paper every time E.L. and I write back and forth to each other. I've kept some notebooks and journals. I've hidden some of her notes in between pages of my favourite books.

'It doesn't feel okay, Dad. It doesn't feel okay to walk in here and to be accused of being on drugs. Would that feel okay to you?'

Dad kneads my arm. 'Honey, I can see how this would be a shock. Your mother and I are just worried about you, that's all. We –'

'I spoke to Mrs. Palomino.' Mom says. 'I ran into her in CVS and she asked me how your "overactive bladder" condition was. Obviously I had no idea what she was talking about so she went on to tell me about your "accident" in class a few months ago.'

She makes the quotation marks gesture with her fingers when she says *overactive bladder* and *accident*.

'"An accident"!' She does it again. 'At fifteen years of age!'

'Lou—' Dad says.

Outside the garden is starting to look green again, after the winter. There are buds on the cherry blossom tree, the daffodils are coming up.

'And then she goes on to ask me if anything is wrong. Tells me how your grades have been slipping – that Mr. Conan said he was worried too not only about your grades but because you fell asleep in his class. Twice.'

Mom pays a gardener to keep it looking the way it did when Grandad was alive, but he doesn't keep it as nice, it doesn't look the same.

They're both looking at me, waiting for a response.

'Everyone falls asleep in Conan's class. He's the most boring man alive!' That's when the tears come, when I start to talk, and I wipe the side of my face with my sleeve. 'So my grades aren't top notch, I fell asleep in class. So what? I'm not perfect. It doesn't mean I'm on drugs. You're taking all these unrelated things and ganging up on me. It's not fair.'

I sound five, not fifteen. Without even thinking about it, Grandad's voice comes into my head: *Who said life was fair? You'll spend a lot of time upset if you expect life to be fair.*

Thinking about him makes me cry more. If he were here I could tell him the truth – about E.L. and the dreams and the voices. He'd help me to make sense of it, he'd know it was part of his gift. But Mom and Dad don't believe in his gift and I know saying anything about it will make them think I'm crazier than they already do.

'Talk to us, Cassie,' Dad says, 'we want to help. We know these past few months – since the separation – have been hard on you, on Ryan.'

'Oh really? You know that, do you? Well, how come you didn't just think maybe that's the reason I'm not your usual Grade A student? You have to jump to the conclusion I'm on drugs? Why can't you just cut me some slack?'

'Because of these, that's why.'

Dad's the one I've been talking to but when I turn and look at Mom she's pushing my Marble notebook across the table at me. On top of it there's the pad from next to my bed and on top of that there's a bunch of other pages ripped from notebooks and jotters and journals – all of them filled with writing.

The realisation hits me slowly, then fast.

'You went through my room? You've been through my things?'

'Cass, wait, just listen,' Dad says.

'You'd no right!' I stand up, push my chair back. 'Those are mine! I can't believe you – I can't believe this!'

I lean across the table to grab at the pile of letters, but Mom pulls them back, away from me.

'What were we supposed to do, Cassie? You're wetting yourself in school, your grades are falling. Your little brother says he hears you screaming in your room at night. Throwing things.'

She has to be lying, Ryan believed me – I know he believed me.

'He told us everything, Cassie, how scared he was to find you writing to some dead slave girl, some ghost—'

'Geez, Mom – it was a joke. Besides, since when is Ryan doing your spying for you?'

Mom's on her feet now too, her hands on the table as she leans towards me. 'Stop lying, Cassie. For one minute can you tell us the truth? It's not just Ryan – Gabi's Mom called me, wondering what was going on – Gabi says it's like you're not there, you hardly ever speak to her anymore. You've lost weight – Angelina says you're hardly eating ...'

I turn to Dad but he's the one with his head in his hands now.

'Angelina, now? What the hell? Her cooking sucks. Did you know that? Maybe if you were here once in a while, instead of out in some bar, maybe you'd know that! You might not have to ask the housekeeper what I'm eating.'

'Take that back!'

She's leaning further across the table and I know that something bad is going to happen if I don't stop, but I can't stop now, even if I wanted to.

'Or what, Mom? You'll slap me across the face like you hit me the last time you didn't like what I said? Bet you never told Dad that little secret.'

Dad's face jerks from his hands and I know I'm right.

'Shut up! Just shut up – that's not how it happened, stop twisting things!'

If she could reach me she might have hit me again right then but instead she swipes her hand into the teacup and saucer so they go flying off the table. The cup hits the wall and smashes, tea splashes everywhere. The saucer doesn't break but it skids across the tiles under the fridge.

'Enough!' Dad slams his hands down on the table. 'That's enough!'

I'm looking at the broken cup. It's part of a set of two I got them for Christmas two years ago, in Starbucks. I hadn't known Starbucks did teacups until I saw them. When Dad moved out I had wondered if he'd take his one with him, but he didn't, he left it here.

Dad hardly ever shouts anymore and he looks like he surprised himself. His hand in front of his face looks like it's shaking. 'Sit down, let's everybody just sit down and be calm. Let's start this conversation again.'

I could run out – up to my room or out of the house completely – they couldn't stop me. I could jump on a subway into Manhattan and they'd never find me. But what then? Where would I go? I couldn't believe that Ryan had turned me in. What Gabi's Mom had said. Gabi and I had hung out yesterday in Connecticut Muffin after school; how could she say I never spoke to her anymore?

I sit down. Out of the corner of my eye I see Mom still standing behind her chair. The notebooks and the pages are between us on the table. The loose pages that I'd kept inside *Harriet the Spy* and the Judy Blumes. I couldn't believe they'd found them, that they'd gone through all my stuff like that. It was my own stupid fault for writing to her so much, for stopping shredding them like I had in the beginning. But at some point the notes had turned into letters,

letters I couldn't wait to read and the truth was I couldn't destroy them even if I wanted to.

The silence in the kitchen feels like it's vibrating. Mom's sniffs and the hum of the fridge are the only sounds. When Dad breaks it, his voice is quiet.

'Cassie, I'm sorry if this feels like an invasion of your privacy but we're your parents and we care about you and we need to know what's happening here. Please try to understand.'

His face looks tired too, like Mom's. It's nice to see him sitting here at the table, in his chair. No one else has been sitting in it all these months, it's still his chair like Grandad's at the end will always be Grandad's. It seems chairs last longer than people in this house.

'Talk to us, Cassie. Tell us what's going on.'

He raises his eyebrows, nods to the pile of paper between us in the centre of the table. They've read them all anyway – the notes, letters, whatever you want to call them. They must have. So I may as well tell them, it's not like I'll be telling them anything new.

And even in spite of everything, the broken cup and Mom screaming and Ryan betraying me and all of that, it's kind of a relief, if you want to know the truth. It wasn't the way I would've planned it but some part of me didn't want to keep it a secret anymore. Some part of me – a big part of me – had been wanting to tell them, to tell someone, for a very long time.

And so I take a breath and I reach for the notebooks and I start from the only place there is to start: the beginning.

Part Two

CASSIE

The first shrink is called Alice. She's probably Mom's age but she looks younger because she doesn't wear any make-up and her brown shoulder-length hair looks like it's been that way since middle school. She has an array of long corduroy skirts in different pastel shades. The day of the first family-therapy session, she's wearing the yellow one.

I'm skipping ahead in the story – just a bit – it's probably three months since that afternoon in the kitchen, since I started seeing Alice twice a week.

It's funny, but after not being able to talk about E.L. I found I was dying to talk about her, especially when Alice explained about boundaries and how everything was confidential. She didn't judge me – that was one of the things I liked about Alice at the time – so we chatted about E.L. like she was anyone. I even told her how I was writing to her more, more letters back and forth.

To tell you the truth, Alice was much more interested in talking about Mom and Dad and Ryan than she was in hearing about E.L. And when I tried to tell her about Grandad's gift she'd bring the conversation around to what it was like when he was sick or after he died, which was actually really annoying because I thought she might be able to tell me about other people who had a gift like ours and how to channel it better.

I didn't know how much Mom and Dad were paying her but I hoped it wasn't too much because sometimes she wasted whole sessions on things that were nothing to do with E.L., like the day we spent talking about 9/11, going over every detail of the day. I hardly knew anyone who died in 9/11 – only two friends of Dad's and Jonas Mulcahy's father – and I could barely remember that afternoon on the promenade with Mom clutching me and Ryan on either side of her, watching the people pouring over the bridge to see if Dad was one of them, while the smoke hung over the rest of the skyline like a cloud. And anyway, that all happened years before I ever saw E.L.

We're in a different room for family therapy – a bigger room – all sitting in a circle around a horrible-looking beige rug divided into four with an off-centre purple cross. Alice has messed up and put six chairs around instead of five. I take the one closest to the door, next to Alice and Mom sits on my other side. Dad and Ryan sit next to each other so the one across from me is the one left empty.

'I'm glad you could all make it today,' Alice says. 'I know it's hard to find a time that works for everyone.'

'Tuesday afternoons are good for me,' Mom says. It's raining outside and she's fixing her black-and-white rain mac on the back of the chair but it's too long and drapes onto the floor. She pulls it up and it falls back down again. She gives up, turns around, fixes her hair behind her ear. 'Not that it would matter, I mean nothing is as important as this, as Cassie's health.'

That's a dig at Dad and I wonder if Alice heard it. Last night when I couldn't sleep I came down for a glass of milk and I could hear Mom arguing on the phone in the kitchen. At first I didn't know who it was she was talking to and then I heard something about making time for today and of course she hadn't forgotten and so I knew it was him. The hall stank of smoke and I could hear the pause for her to drink some of her glass of wine as well so I'd crept back upstairs and got some water from the bathroom instead,

Dad is sitting with his arms folded, his legs are crossed at the ankles. Ryan is sitting in exactly the same way. He's jerking his foot – his right one – so his sneakers squeak. Outside a siren goes by. When it passes there is silence and then the squeaking starts again. Squeak, squeak, squeak. And then it stops.

'So,' Mom says, 'what's the agenda? Do you have some kind of update on Cassie's condition?'

Cassie's condition. I hate how she says that.

'It's therapy, Lou,' Dad says, 'not a business meeting. There's no agenda.'

He looks to Alice and shakes his head, as if he is apologising for her.

'Alice knows what I mean,' Mom says. 'Cassie must be at a certain stage in her treatment if you thought we should get together, right?'

Alice has been watching them both and she has that face where it's not a smile but it's not a frown either. A neutral face that they probably teach at therapy school, a face that doesn't give anything away.

'What Cassie's been going through affects the whole family,' she says. 'We thought it would be good to have a space where everyone could air their feelings.'

'You mean *you* thought it would be good!'

It's the first thing I've said and Alice laughs. Dad looks shocked.

'Cassie, don't be so rude!' he says.

'Don't worry, Joe – she's being honest. Today *was* my idea. Honesty is one of the ground rules for our sessions.'

There's silence again, only the squeak of Ryan's sneakers. Alice breaks it.

'Louise, would you like to tell us how you feel about what Cassie's been going through?

Mom sits up straight. 'Me? How *I* feel? Well, I think it's great that she's seeing you. I think things are getting better for her. She seems more settled.'

Alice doesn't say anything so we can all hear what she hears – that Mom hasn't answered the actual question. Alice does this all the time, she's great at it – cornering you so you're forced to say something about yourself instead of other people.

'And what's it like for you?'

Mom flicks her hair behind the other ear. 'I mean – it's a complex situation. Even in the past few months ... seeing a few different people – our primary physician, a psychiatrist, a neurologist. It's confusing, you know, all these different opinions about what's going on.'

In her lap Mom has a tissue and she folds it over and over into tinier and tinier squares.

'At first the doctor thought she'd had a mini stroke!' Mom laughs, like that's hilarious, and she looks like she's waiting for Alice to laugh too but she doesn't, she just looks at her. I can't look at her looking at Mom so instead I look at the off-centre cross on the rug.

'That sounds frightening,' Alice says.

'They were wrong. They did the tests, you know, so many tests. They had her in hospital for two days.'

'That must have been an anxious time for you?'

'We were all relieved when the tests came back negative. It was a strain on Cassie, of course. And on Ryan. He doesn't always show it but he's a sensitive boy. He and his sister are very close.'

We all look at Ryan in his Slipknot hoody and oversized jeans. His sneakers stop squeaking.

'Would you describe you and Cassie as close Ryan?' Alice asks.

He shrugs, a tiny fragment of movement inside the giant sleeves of the hoody. His eyes dart over to me and back to the rug.

'She's just my sister.'

'Have you been worried about her?'

He blows his fringe out of his eyes, looks at the ceiling fan and back to the rug. 'No. I mean, I don't know. So, she's a bit crazy. Who isn't?'

I smile. I want him to look over at me and smile too but he doesn't and that's when Dad leans forward so his elbows are on his knees.

'Of course he's worried about his sister. We all are. What kind of family would we be if we weren't? We've been around the block trying to sort this thing out and we can't get a handle on it. Like my wife said, one doctor tells us one thing, one tells us something else. Schizophrenia. Borderline Personality Disorder. Dissociative Identity Disorder. Post-Traumatic Stress Disorder. One of them even had us believing she was on drugs. And then there was the stroke scare. It's a fucking joke – excuse my French. None of them can agree, but the only thing they can agree on is that it's not normal. It's not right.'

'You sound angry, Joe.'

'I'm not *angry*. I'm frustrated. Wouldn't you be? All this time, all this money, and she's still not any better.'

'Your wife thinks she's getting better.'

Frustration is a type of anger. Alice showed me a chart one time about feelings and frustration was there, linked to anger. I think about saying that but even if I wanted to there's not enough room to say anything because everyone is starting to talk over each other.

'She wants her to be better, so she thinks she is. She's in denial. It doesn't fit her image having a daughter with mental-health issues, just like it doesn't fit her image to be getting divorced.'

'See?' Mom turns to Alice. 'You see what I have to deal with? He thinks this is my fault. He blames me for *everything*. If you were to believe him you'd think I was fully responsible for the breakup of our marriage – that he was always Mr. Perfect.'

'Oh, please!' Dad rolls his eyes, turns away from Mom so he's facing Ryan.

'He can't get in touch with his feelings – that's his problem. And he's consumed by guilt over not seeing the kids, missing weekends because of his job—'

Dad whips back in his chair. 'One weekend, Louise! In six months I've missed *one* weekend!'

Mom continues to talk to Alice as if none of the rest of us are there. She fixes her hair behind her ear, drops her voice to a confidential tone.

'I've always been more optimistic than him, I knew that. From the start, that was one of the problems in our marriage, his negative attitude.'

'Optimistic?' Dad laughs one of his horrible, fake laughs. 'That's one word for it, Louise. Denial – that's another name for it. It's not just a river in Egypt, you know.'

'See?' Mom says, shrugging. 'You hear that sarcasm? How can you communicate with someone like that?'

I look up at Alice to see when she's going to stop it, stop them, and she's looking at me too so I look back down at the rug. She told me the other day that family therapy was a good forum to resolve issues and despite myself I'd let a little hope stir again, which was obviously completely dumb of me. This whole session was dumb.

If this were my regular session I'd be facing the window and seeing the tops of the trees in the park and talking about E.L. So far no one had even said anything about E.L. – as if they'd all forgotten why we were even here.

Alice gathers her corduroy skirt tight behind her knees the way she always does before she comes out with something big to say.

'There's a lot of feelings in the room,' she says. 'I can see that, and that's fine. That's what this space is for, to hold everyone's feelings.'

Mom nods a slight nod. She approves of this. This is the kind of talk she can do, the kind of thing she talks about in her interviews or on *Oprah*.

'I want to know if she's still having those delusions,' Dad says. 'That's what I want to know.'

He looks at me and I'm terrified of what to say next but Alice intervenes.

'If possible, it would be helpful if we can avoid words like "delusions".' She holds her hands out, her palms flat, in a gesture I've come to recognise means letting go.

'Why not? That's what they are. What do you want me to call them? Hallucinations?'

'Words like "delusions" or "hallucinations" or even words like "real" and "imaginary" – they're judgement words. They're labels – assigning a value to someone else's experience. It would be helpful to drop the labels.'

Dad shakes his head. 'But we've got to be able to speak the truth here! This slave girl is a hallucination, she's imaginary!'

'To you, she's imaginary. To Cassie, she's real.'

Alice smiles, like it's perfectly simple. Dad looks to Mom for support but she's looking at her shoes.

'Come on – you have to work with me here. She's either real or she's imaginary! She can't be both.'

Alice sits back in her chair, tips her head so it's almost touching one shoulder. I know that means an analogy is coming and I nearly laugh but I stop myself just in time.

'Let's use an example to help illustrate what I mean. If I have a fear of flying, then it's a real fear, right?'

'I suppose,' Dad shrugs.

'Even if the top technicians and engineers check out the plane before take-off and say it's one hundred per cent safe. Even if that airline has never had a crash – even if the airports that I am taking off from and landing at have never had a crash. Even if no one else on the plane has any fear of flying – my fear is still real, wouldn't you say?'

She tips her head to her other shoulder, smiles wider. Ryan is squinting his eyes the way he does when he is trying to understand something. He catches me looking at him and he stops.

'Yes, but fear is a feeling,' Dad says. 'That's a totally different situation. We're talking about facts.'

'So you're saying this girl – this slave – represents Cassie's fear?' Mom says.

'No, Lou, that's not what's she's saying!' Dad snaps at Mom. 'It's an analogy, it's nothing to do with fear.'

'Cassie tells me her grandfather had a gift,' Alice says. 'That he was able to communicate with those who had passed on. That she inherited this gift from him.'

'Oh, come on!' Mom shakes her head. 'Not that again. My father's been dead almost six years. We shouldn't have to listen to this crap anymore.'

'Wait, Lou – he did always say that, ever since she was a little girl. I want to see what Alice has to say, maybe there's something—'

'Please! My father said a lot of things – he said there was a college fund for me and my sister. He said he'd come to our wedding.'

'It sounds like you're carrying a lot of anger towards your father,' Alice says, but no one listens.

'He was drinking then, Lou, it's not the same.'

'Are we really having this conversation, Joe? Aren't you the one who always said this stuff about his gift was B.S., that you hated that he was filling the child's head with a bunch of superstitious garbage? And now suddenly you believe it?'

Dad's the one shaking his head now. 'I'm not saying I believe it. I didn't say I believed it.'

'You're clutching at straws, you know that? You say I'm in denial but you're so desperate not to believe our daughter has a mental illness that you'd believe anything else. Even that my father passed on some supernatural gift.'

'Can you two cut it out for five minutes? This isn't about you – it's about Cassie!'

Ryan's voice cuts across Mom's and we all look over at him. He looks like his outburst has shocked him as much as it shocked us. I love him right then. I want to run across the room and hug him and muss his hair the way I used to when he was little.

'Can I ask you something?' he says to Alice.

Alice lets her skirt go, gathers it back up. 'Sure, it's a safe space. You can ask anything.'

'Do you believe her? Do you think she's able to communicate with this dead girl, this ghost? Do you think it's possible or do you think there's something really wrong with her?'

It's a great question. I'm glad he asked it. I wish I'd asked it. We're all looking at Alice and I realise I'm holding my breath, that I'm a bit afraid of the answer.

She shifts in her chair, keeps her eyes on Ryan. 'That's a complex question and thank you for the courage it took to ask it. You might have noticed there is an extra chair here in the circle. This chair represents E.L., whether you see her there or whether you see an empty chair, her presence or absence has an impact on this family, on this circle.'

We all look at the empty chair. Ryan looks at me. 'You see someone there?'

If Mom or Dad had asked that I might have got mad, made a face, but something in the way he asks – in the purity of the question – makes it okay.

'No, Ry. I don't see her. That's not how it works.'

He blows his fringe out of his eyes. 'How does it work?'

I look at him, my kid brother asking a question. He's not trying to tell me I'm crazy, he's not trying to make fun of me; he's just trying to understand. Just like I've been trying to understand.

'It's not like I can conjure her up whenever I want to. Sometimes she's in my dreams and sometimes I hear her voice in my head.'

Next to me I feel Mom squirm in her chair.

'And you can write letters to her,' he says. 'Like that night in your room?'

'Yeah.'

'And she answers?'

I glance at Mom, but her head is turned away from me.

'Yeah – she answers.'

'Cool.' He nods, blows his fringe again. 'I think that's cool.'

Dad looks at Alice.

'I think it might be a good time to give your professional opinion here – you know, to answer my son's question as to what you think about these, ah, about this slave girl. You know, to set him straight.'

Before Alice can answer, Mom interrupts.

'I thought you'd stopped writing to her? I thought the goal was for her to stop writing to her?'

Mom sounds mad at Alice who puts her head to one side again. 'It's very early in the process to have hard and fast goals. At this stage of our work, it seems it's important for Cassie to continue writing to her.'

'So you're not scared of her anymore?'

That's Ryan again and I like that he's asking me things. It feels like we're having the first conversation we've had in a really long time and that makes me happy, even if it is in front of Mom and Dad and Alice. I think about it, before I answer, because I want to make sure I'm telling him the truth. It's so early in therapy I haven't learned yet, how dangerous the truth can be.

'No,' I say. 'I'm not scared of her anymore.'

'How come?'

And the answer to that is easy and saying it makes me smile.

'I'm not scared of her anymore because I've gotten to know her. I'm not scared anymore because she's become my friend.'

E.L.

Me and Miss Ellen sittin' outside in the courtyard. It mus' be close to noon and the sun beat down so she sittin' under the archway 'cause that the only shade.

'Come sit by me, E.L.,' she say. 'There's room for us both.'

I know she only want me sittin' next to her 'cause she 'fraid there gone be 'nother rattler over her head like the one Elijah found there last week but I don't say nothin'. It nice when she bein' nice to me, no matter what the reason.

I sit down next to her. Her mamma not gone like her sittin' on the ground but I don't say nothin'. She don't say nothin' neither jus' look up at the leaves over our heads. And it only then I hear the other sound in the quiet – music. It comin' from the parlour window.

'That sound your Mamma playin' piano?' I ask.

Miss Ellen look at me funny. 'You know it is. You've heard Mamma play before.'

I guess she right, I guess I did but I don't never r'member hearin' it like this b'fore. Maybe 'cause I a'ways runnin' or busy or somethin' but sittin' here in the shade the piano sound diff'rent. It make me think of the grey wisp of smoke from the fire in the mornin' when Charity only gettin' it started. Fragile but somethin' you know gone grow strong. Somethin' at the heart of ev'rythin'.

'It sound diff'rent today,' I say. 'It sound beautiful.'

'She thinks I should be able to play Beethoven like that – like her – after a few months,' Miss Ellen sayin'. 'She's played her whole life.'

I listenin' and I ain't listenin' to Miss Ellen 'cause I thinkin' 'bout the music and how it feel like Cassie real close by right then and I wonderin' if she can hear it too. And that make me think 'bout Charity and wonder how I'm gone be able tell her 'bout Cassie without her thinkin' I got some demon inside.

Then the music stop and the silence sound diff'rent like the empty air made for holdin' piano notes. That when Miss Ellen start to fuss – she half stand and then sit down 'gain.

'Miss Ellen, what the matter?'

'He said he'd be home by now. He's supposed to be here.'

'Who suppose to be here?'

'Daddy. He said he was going to teach me how to horseback ride – properly, not side-saddle. But now he's not here she's going to want me to practise again, I know she is! I hate that piano! I hate that that's all she ever wants me to do!'

Miss Ellen agitate' like I ain't hardly ever seen her b'fore. I don't know what so bad 'bout spendin' hours at the piano. I ain't never been inside the parlour but I seen the piano from the hallway. It got wood so shiny it like a refl'ction on the lake on a spring mornin'. I don't know why anyone hate somethin' as beautiful as that.

Inside the house we both hear the Mistress feets on the wood floors. She call out for Miss Ellen but she don't answer, jus' look at me and put her finger on her lips. Then we hear Juba callin' out too – the two voices, her and the Mistress. My heart goin' faster and I want to call out and say we here 'cause I know they gone find us and somehow it gone be my fault Miss Ellen ain't answered.

The back door make a long creak when it open up.

'Ellen?' It the Mistress. 'Ellen, are you out here?'

Firs' she don't see us sittin' there in the shade and I think she gone go back inside, but then she turn 'round and she do.

'Ellen! What are you doing sitting on the ground like some dirty slave! You're thirteen – almost a lady. Get up from there at once!'

Miss Ellen get up slow. There bits of twig and dus' on her dress from the ground and I do my best to wipe it clean without her Mamma seein'.

'Didn't you hear me calling you? I've been looking all over. It's time for your piano practice.'

'Mamma, can we take a break today? We've been practising every day this week.'

The Mistress smile but there somethin' else und'neath too.

'Practice makes perfect, remember? Besides, I used to practice with my mother every day. For hours. And I was glad to. They're some of the happiest memories I have, playing piano with my mother.'

She walk back through the door into the house like Miss Ellen right b'hind her only she ain't right b'hind her.

'But Mamma, Daddy said he's going to come home early. That he's going to take me horseback riding on Princess.'

Miss Ellen don't say nothin' 'bout it bein' proper ridin', not side-saddle, and I don't neither.

The Mistress come back to the door.

'Horseback riding?'

'Yes, Mamma, it's so much fun! He gave me a lesson the other day. You should come with us.'

'Fun? Fun won't get you too far in Charleston, Ellen. It won't be long now until you'll have gentlemen calling on you and I can tell you right now that piano playing will serve you much better at finding a husband than horseback riding.'

Miss Ellen face go red, like maybe she gone cry. Her fists clench. 'I don't want a husband, Mamma. And besides, Daddy says a girl on a plantation should be a good rider. That it's important for daughters as well as sons.'

The Mistress look at Miss Ellen like she gone say somethin' but it seem like maybe at the last minute she decide to say somethin' else.

'Your father ... he says a lot of things. But in any case, he's not here, is he? So come along.'

This time the Mistress wait by the door till she see Miss Ellen start to walk over. She look back at me.

'Can E.L. come?' she say.

I ain't never 'llowed in the parlour so I know the Mistress gone say no. But she don't say no. She look at me and she smile.

'Of course she can. Come on, E.L.'

Walkin' into the parlour that day the rug under my feets feel like the softest blankets or like rose petals or like the softest blankets cover in rose petals. Inside, the parlour even bigger than it look from the hall – more than twice the size the cabin. Even with the piano and the pink and green velvet chairs, there so much space. On the wall, there pictures of white people in gold frames and mirrors that make them all look back at one 'nother. One paintin' bigger than all the rest.

'That's my grandmother – Daddy's mother,' Miss Ellen say. 'I'm named after her.'

I know 'bout her grandma but I ain't never seen the paintin', not up close like this. The white woman in the picture look young – younger than the Mistress. Her hair a golden red colour and it long – it fall all the way down onto the shoulders of her green dress. She got kind eyes.

I want to look more at her, there somethin' 'bout her eyes that make me want to stare but there so much else in the room to look at and the thing I really want to see is the piano. I look over but the Mistress standin' there next to it so I look 'way 'gain.

'You like the piano, E.L.?'

I look up at her and back down at the rug.

'It's all right. You can come closer and see it if you like. It's a beautiful instrument. Look.'

She ain't never speak to me like this b'fore in that voice that soft like honey. Real slow, I look up. She run her hands over the shiny smooth wood.

'It's made of rosewood,' she say, 'and they polish and lacquer it to give it this finish. The keys are made of ebony and ivory.'

She lift up a part of the wood to show black and white parts und'neath.

'Ellen, why don't you play something for E.L.?'

'Mamma, you know I'm no good! It all sounds horrible when I play. I'll never be able to play like you!'

'That's because you don't practice, darling. I keep telling you, it doesn't come on its own; you need to practise. Discipline. If you only knew the hours I practised with my mother. Practice, practice, practice makes perfect – that's what she always used to say!'

The Mistress stretch her hands out over the white and black part. A ripple of sound come out. I smile, I can't help it and the Mistress see me. But maybe it a'right 'cause she smile too.

'You see, dear, E.L. loves it. I bet she wouldn't mind practising, I bet she'd be grateful of the chance to play piano, wouldn't you, E.L.?'

I don't look at Miss Ellen.

'Yes, Ma'am.'

'So come on over here, let me give you a lesson.'

She pat her hand on the empty part of the stool next to her. That part of the stool meant for Miss Ellen only Miss Ellen done gone sit in a pink chair in the corner by the fireplace now and she lookin' out the window and up the driveway.

'Come on, E.L., there's no need to be frightened.'

The walk from where I standin' over to that stool only six steps, less, but it feel longer than the walk from the cabin to the cotton field. The whole time the Mistress look at me and even though she smilin' I waitin' for her to laugh, for her to say I mus' be crazy if I think she gone let me dirty up her piano stool. But she don't laugh and she don't say nothin' so I keep walkin'. And then I next to her and she pat the stool 'gain and I sit down closer to her than I ever sit b'fore.

'All right then,' she say. 'These here are the keys. The black ones are the minors, white are the majors. Each one makes a different sound, a different note. And we start here at this one – middle C.'

She push a white one down and a piece of sound come out. She spread her fingers on either side and like magic, the sound is music.

'Now,' she say. 'You try.'

I too close to her. I so close I feel part of her hair touch my cheek. It soft. I move 'way.

'Come on. There's no need to be frightened.'

I put my finger where she show me, but when I push, it sound hard and ugly. Nothin' like music.

She laugh but it ain't a mean laugh. 'Gently. Like this. Imagine you're stroking a kitten.'

The barn cat had kittens and when I try b'fore to stroke one she swipe me with claws and rip my skin open. I hit the note real fast and pull my hand back 'gain.

This time she don't laugh. 'Stead she take my hand in her hand, put my finger on the key, hold it down and lift it up. It make the same sound she made. Down and let go. Down and let go. Over and over, the same sound.

'There you are. Now, try on your own.'

I try on my own. The same sound, like she make.

'Good. Now try the key next to it, and the one next to that.'

She doing the same thing with her other hand, only opposite, like we in a mirror. I watch her, copy her, make my finger hit the same time hers do. It not music yet, not like what I hear comin' through the window, but it gettin' close.

'Very good. Now, try both hands. Fan out, like this.'

She do that thing 'gain where her hands stretch out and this music r'mind me of the ripple in the creek when we throw stones in. And I get scared all over 'gain 'cause I know when it my turn, it ain't gone sound nothin' like that.

'Just try – good girl.'

She put her hand on my back, low down in the part where the bone dip in and it feel soft and solid, like when Charity put her hand on my shoulder at Church. I look over at Miss Ellen and she pr'tend she ain't lookin' at us and go back to lookin' out the window.

'Go on,' the Mistress sayin'. 'Try with just one hand, start here, stretch out, one at a time. Like this.'

I stretch out my fingers. And I holdin' my breath even though I didn't know it so I let a bit of breath out when each finger touches the key. They feel so smooth, so cool, and I push each one down slow and let go like she show me. And the sound like hers, like the water ripples.

She take her hand 'way and my back feel cold where it was even though the room hot. She start to clap. She smilin'.

'Wonderful, E.L.! You're a natural,' she say. 'Ellen, did you hear E.L. play? I think she's a natural.'

My hand on the keys still and she lift it up, hold it in hers. Her skin nothin' like Charity skin. Her fingers soft like the piano. Smooth like the piano. Her thumb push 'gainst my thumb, then 'gainst my finger and then the next one. She feel each bone, each knuckle, No one ain't never held each of my fingers like this b'fore. No one ain't never looked at my hand the way she lookin' at it and it like I seein' my hand for the firs' time.

'You have long fingers, E.L. Piano-playing fingers. Your mother had fingers like that too. Did you know that?'

'No, Ma'am.'

She ain't never said nothin' 'bout my mamma b'fore. I look at her but she ain't lookin' at me, only at my hand, our hands t'gether.

'Oh yes. She had fingers just like yours. One time I came in here and I found her, sitting at the piano. She was afraid to make any sound but she was touching the keys like she was born to do it.'

Charity never told me nothin' 'bout my mamma havin' long fingers or 'bout no piano. I think the Mistress done be mad if she catch me doin' that but she don't sound mad.

'I bet if you learned, if you practised, you could become very good. You would practise, wouldn't you, E.L.?'

'Yes, Ma'am.'

'If I asked you to, would you practise on this piano every day?'

'Oh yes, Ma'am.'

It hard to breathe. It too much, her holdin' my hand, the shiny piano, what she sayin' 'bout my mamma and that I can do this 'gain tomorrow. And the next day and the next. Her hand holdin' my hand tighter now. Real tight.

'You hear that Ellen? E.L. would practise. She would practise every day.'

She grip my three middle fingers and she squeeze hard and then harder till the top parts nearly as white as hers. And when I look into her face her smile change. It still a smile but this a smile I done seen b'fore and sudd'nly I scared but it too late to pull 'way now.

'You know, E.L., there's something else these fingers would be very good for. You know what, don't you? Picking cotton. Long fingers like these would make you a fast picker, I'm betting you'd pick as much as Charity within a few weeks.'

Charity pick more than John or Walker or even Big Bill but she still get whipped when she don't pick 'nough. Sometimes she get whipped on days she pick too much 'cause it mean she lazy and not tryin' them other days she pick less. Even Miss Ellen tell me one time it ain't fair that Nagle whip her so much like that and I look over at her 'cause I hope maybe she say somethin' but she still lookin' out the window at the driveway. She lookin' for her Daddy, I know she is, but he ain't comin'. There ain't no one comin'.

The Mistress still talkin'.

'I think that tonight I'm going to talk to Mr. Nagle and see if he can't find you a job in the fields, E.L. And, unfortunately, he's going to keep you so busy you won't have any time left to practise.'

She squash my fingers all atop of each other and more than anythin' I want to pull 'way but she got me held tight.

'So, I hope you enjoyed your first piano lesson because it's also your last one. If I ever catch you touching my piano again I'm going to have Mr. Nagle cut these beautiful long fingers right off.'

She say that in the same soft voice she say ev'rythin' else and she lay my hand down, real gentle on the keys. She smooth the skin on my fingers and her touch light. And I wishin' then that I ain't never touch the piano 'cause it gone be hard to forget how it feel – so cool and smooth. And somethin' tell me that tomorrow when I in the fields reachin' for a cotton boil that in my mind I gone be touchin' these piano keys. And somehow it worse knowin' that than never knowin' how it feel at all.

I leave my hand there too long. That what happen. Maybe I want to r'member how the piano feel, maybe I want my fingers to touch somethin' I know my mamma touch. Maybe that why I don't think 'bout why she pull her hand 'way so quick, maybe that why I don't know what gone happen next till it happen.

I don't see her grab the wood lid, don't see her smash it down on my fingers but I feel it, Lord do I feel it. This pain sudden, sharp, like no pain I ain't ever felt b'fore. I don't r'member if I cry out. But I r'member the look on her face, her smile. 'Cause her smile the last thing I see, right b'fore the room go black and after that I don't see nothin' more.

CASSIE

When I wake up, my fingers are sore. Just my right hand. I try and flex them but they are so stiff, I can hardly move them. I comb my memory for a dream but there's none – since we've been writing they seem to have almost stopped. I reach over and pick up the pen, even though my right hand hurts so much I can hardly hold it.

What happened? I write. *Are you okay?*

I put the pen in my left hand. Sit and wait, but nothing happens. I transfer it back into my right again.

E.L? Are you there?

My fingers feel like they are broken, but they can't be broken, there's no swelling, not even a bruise. I pry the pen free and hold it in my left hand. Today it feels like it would be easier to write with that but thirty seconds pass, a minute and no words come, so I put the pen back in my right hand again.

Did something happen to you? Tell me. Are you hurt?

The page between us is silent. Waiting, almost like it's breathing. This hasn't happened before and I don't know how I know this but some part of me feels like she is there, waiting. That she is silent and scared.

E.L., it's going to be all right. Whatever it is, whatever happens, we're going to be okay, you know?

I write that and then I put the pen down. She's not there or if she is there she's not going to answer. And what do I know about things being okay, for her or for me? I've no idea whether or not things are going to be okay again.

***

I'm in a session with Alice. I haven't heard from E.L. in five days. I've written to her at school, in the library, at home but she won't write me back. The pain in my hand is starting to go away and I don't want it to. At my desk I find myself bending my wrist back, pushing into my fingers to make them hurt more. The pain is a connection between us and if I stop feeling it I'm afraid I might lose her completely. Obviously, I don't tell Alice about that part.

'What about dreams?' Alice is saying. 'Are you still dreaming about her?'

'No,' I shake my head. 'No dreams either.'

I think about telling her about the other dreams I've been having, the ones about Grandad but she didn't ask me that, only about E.L.

'What's going on at home?' Alice asks. 'How are things with your mom?'

It pisses me off that every time I talk about E.L. she brings the conversation back to Mom and Dad.

'Fine,' I go. 'Still the same.'

'The same? I would have thought things would have changed a bit now your mom is in A.A. How long is it now?'

'I don't know – a month? Six weeks?' That's a lie. Mom counts her days on the fridge. Today is day fifty-two.

'And there haven't been any changes?'

I shrug. 'She's still out all the time so it's hard to tell. The only difference is she's at meetings instead of bars.'

Alice scoops her skirt up behind her knees.

'That's the only difference?'

I swap the cross of my legs.

'That and she's on her phone even more than before, sometimes even in the middle of the night. I got up the other night when I couldn't sleep and she was on the phone to some guy called Jason.'

I let his name sit there on the rug between us.

She waits for me to say more and when I don't she asks a question.

'How did you feel about that?'

I sit with the question, really try and remember. I remember being in the kitchen, wishing I'd put my slippers on because the tiles are cold under my feet. I remember first of all being annoyed when I saw she was there because that meant I couldn't get the ice-cream without her giving me a hard time. Then I was sure that I'd caught her drinking, that she'd have an open bottle of wine – I remember feeling kind of triumphant and scared all at the same time. When I saw she didn't, that she only had a cup of herbal tea I felt really guilty. And then I heard her say, 'hold on, Jason' as she put her hand over the phone and it made me think that it would've been better if I had caught her drinking after all.

But that's all too complicated to explain to Alice and I don't think these are even feelings so instead I go back to what I want to talk about.

'Five days is the longest time ever that I haven't heard from E.L. Do you think that's she's gone for good? Do you think she'll come back?'

As soon as I ask, I think that I'm going to get a 'how would you feel about that?' as a reply but instead she says something else.

'Do you think it could be to do with your medication?'

Alice looks at me and I make sure to hold her gaze. I'm supposed to take two pills a day, it's been a few weeks now, but except for the first day I haven't taken any. I'm careful not to shift my eyes away, not to blink.

'I guess it could be. I hadn't thought about it.'

'And if it is that – how would it make you feel?'

There it was, I'd known it was coming. I almost smile, but I don't. Instead I put both feet on the floor, my hands on my knees. I go through the list of feelings she taught me and pick the one I'm supposed to feel.

'I guess, I'd feel happy,' I say. 'I'd feel happy, because it would mean that I must be cured.'

***

It's a dream and it's a memory all in one – my memory this time, not hers. We walk into the room and the sun is shining in lines from the window so you can see the dust floating. He's not sleeping in his room anymore because he can't walk up the stairs. This is the living room but it doesn't look like the living room. Mom wanted his bed set up in the dining room at the back but it's darker there and he said he likes the light. She couldn't say no to him because he is sick.

Nobody says he is dying but I know he is. I've known it since before they set up this hospital bed, since before Olivia the nurse started to come every night and Erin started to come every day. I've known it since that day on the beach when he couldn't stop coughing.

Maybe I've known it since before then.

Right now, he's sleeping. We're the only ones up – me and Betty, whose fur feels hot in my hands. Nine going on ten is too old for teddy bears, but this morning is an exception.

Olivia is outside smoking. When she comes in she will spray a spray in her mouth so no one will smell it, but I smell it. I like it – the smell.

I wish Grandad still smelled like smoke and mints instead of this new smell which is in the whole house. Ryan asked Mom what the smell was and she said it's the smell of the medicine and the hospital equipment but I don't think it's that. I think it's the smell of dying.

Grandad doesn't look like Grandad. His face looks smaller – sunken in – without his glasses, and I want to put them on him but I don't know where they are. They should be on the nightstand next to his bed, on top of his books, beside his serenity prayer in a frame. But all that's on his nightstand right now are pill bottles.

If I knew I wouldn't get in trouble with Olivia I'd bring down one of my Tír na nÓg books and read it to him the way he used to read it to me. It doesn't sound the same when I read it, I can't make the pictures in words come out as well as he does but I'd like to read it to him anyway. I'd like to try.

'Grandad.'

It's a whisper. I know he won't wake up and even if he did he won't be able to say anything because of the tube in his mouth but even so, I try again.

'Grandad.'

My whisper is a little bit louder this time. Maybe he won't wake up but maybe he can hear me. Maybe behind his eyes he is already in Ireland, on the beach in Donegal. I wonder how his gift can help him now, if even as I'm watching is he already somewhere else, if there are people helping him come home from the other side.

Under his eyelids his eyes move and for a second I think they are going to open, that he's going to turn his head and take the tube out of his mouth so he can smile at me. I imagine him taking down the railing at the side of the bed and patting the mattress for me to get in and sit next to him so he'll tell me a story.

But his eyes don't open. And his head doesn't turn. I hold Betty tighter so her furry face is next to my face. I hold her too tight, tighter than she likes being held but I can't help it. I know she's afraid.

'It's okay, Betty,' I say. 'There's nothing to be afraid of.'

When Grandad says those words to me I feel better but they don't sound the same when I say them to Betty and I feel her fear through her fur. I am close enough to touch him now but I don't touch him. Instead, Betty reaches up, over the railing, into the bed. Her paw is near his face but she doesn't touch him either. I hear something; the back door clicking. Olivia will go into the bathroom now to wash her hands and clean her teeth and spray that spray. We don't have much time.

I lay Betty down. There is just enough room between his arm and the railing. I push her under the blanket, cover her head over even though she doesn't like her head to be covered. I hope she won't dislodge one of his tubes, make it worse. I hope she won't make anything worse.

I don't know when I started crying, but there are tears on my face and neck and my chest feels cold and empty without Betty. I don't want to say goodbye to her, not yet, but if I don't give her to him now I know I won't be able to again. I don't know how I know this but I do. I know that today is his day to go home. And more than anything I don't want him to have to go his own.

'Bye,' I say. I'm saying to him and Betty. I think I'm saying to them both. 'I love you.'

The neck of my pyjamas is wet and I wipe my nose with my cuff. I hear the click of the downstairs bathroom door opening. On my tippy toes I run into the hall and around the corner and up the stairs.

I take them two at a time. At the top, if I stopped and looked through the bars I could see into the room, I'd be able to see the light and the windows and the bump Betty makes under the blanket next to him.

But I don't look down. I don't look back. I run into my room and close the door and jump into bed, pull the covers over my head as if I'm still asleep. As if I've never been awake at all.

***

She comes back, just like that. One night in my room, when I'm doing my math homework, my left hand takes the pen. And right under where I've written out the equation, her writing appears:

Cassie? Cassie? You there?

You know that expression 'my heart jumped'? I always thought that was just an expression until that moment and it turns out that it's true.

I switch the pen back to my right hand.

Yes, I'm here! How are you? Where have you been? It's been nearly two weeks – I've been so worried!

I'm right here. I been right here the whole time.

I can't get the pen back in my hand fast enough.

Why haven't you written to me? I've been writing to you every day – you never answered. Were you able to hear me?

There's a pause before she answers.

No. I ain't heard nothin' and I been listenin'. I been listenin' the whole time.

I'm about to ask her about her fingers and what happened to them but the pain is totally gone in my fingers by then and so I know she must be better and, anyway, something makes me afraid to ask. Something makes me not want to know the answer.

I remember once Grandad said that there could be a block – some kind of reason why he wasn't able to get through to someone on the other side.

A memory surfaces as I write, of a woman with short black hair and a tweed coat buttoned up to the neck, sitting at his round table under the Black & White Scotch Whisky mirror. Her head is bent but I can still see she's crying. I must have been spying on them – maybe it was one of the times Ryan and me are looking through the crack in the door. I can't hear what she's saying but I can hear Grandad's voice, low and serious, telling her that sometimes there are blocks between the spirit world and ours.

The pen switches back to E.L.'s hand.

The other side? What that mean?

You know – the spirit world. Too late I realise that I shouldn't have written that – *spirit world* – that that will play into her fear of demons and being possessed. *What I mean is energy – there could be some kind of energy field blocking the way.*

The pen is in my left hand for thirty seconds, forty-five, a minute, before she writes and I think I've lost her again, that after waiting for so long for her to come back I've blown it.

I don't know nothin' 'bout spirit worlds or no energy field. The only field we got 'round here the cotton field.

I laugh out loud. I love when she's funny like that and she doesn't even know it. I write down the shorthand I've taught her, wonder if she'll remember.

LOL.

She takes the pen back straight away.

You think that funny? You try bein' out in the cotton field all day and you see how much you laughin' then.

She remembers LOL; I hoped she would. I turn the page, write back fast.

I'm sorry, I'm not laughing at how hard cotton picking is. Just the way you said it. You're funny, you know that? You have a good sense of humour.

Waiting for her to write back I wonder if she knows that, if anyone else has said that to her before or anything like it. And right when I think she's not going to respond the letters come, big and blocky like always.

LOL.

That's the last thing she writes to me that night and it's only later lying in bed reading back over the conversation that I realise she's never said anything before about being in the cotton field, that she's always in the big house. And so I turn the page and start to write to her again.

E.L., are you there? Why were you in the cotton field instead of in the big house? Is something going on?

And I wait for her to tell me, to answer, but she doesn't. So after a while of waiting I put my notebook away and try and sleep. Because if I've learned anything about E.L. by then it's that I can't force her to do anything, to say anything. That she'll tell me when she's ready.

E.L.

That firs' mornin' it excitin' – goin' with them. Like it makes me more grown 'cause I spendin' the day with Charity and Rose and Nelly and Big Bill and all the other mens. And being in the fields means I ain't never gone see the Mistress now.

'You want me tell Miss Ellen hello for you?' Marjorie ask that mornin' in the cabin. She smilin' 'cause she think it gone be easy workin' in the big house with her mamma. She smilin' 'cause she ain't never spent no time with the Mistress.

'Tell her what you want,' I say and then I follow Charity out the door.

Walkin' over to the field it hot even though it still early and I thinkin' that this the firs' day I can r'member when I ain't gone see Miss Ellen. Even on Sundays I see her. Even when she sick and in bed that time I creep into the house and seen her. Thinkin' 'bout that make me feel sad but b'hind me I hear Nagle yellin' and his whip crack and there ain't no time to feel nothin'.

In the field Charity help me. She show me how to tie the bag high up round my neck but it still too long, it still drag in the dirt. She fixin' it when Nagle come over. His whip crack so loud at firs' I think it pain in my skin but it only noise.

'Come on, hurry up! We ain't got no time for laziness out here.'

I next to the cotton then and I grab at the closest boil with my left hand 'cause my fingers still bound up on the right from the piano.

'Come on! Faster! Use both hands!'

I look 'round and that my mistake. Nagle right b'hind me on his horse and he as tall as the sky. His lift his whip and it touch the cloud. With my bound fingers I reach for another boil but when I hold the branch it break in my hand.

Ev'rythin' stop then – it feel like ev'rythin' stop. That crack of the branch louder than the sound Nagle whip make. It louder than the whinny of his horse.

The whip come down so close to my foot I nearly fall. And b'fore I get to move, it down 'gain and it catch my foot this time. I hear the crack. I see the line of blood on my skin b'fore I feel it but then it come like an explosion – pain.

Nagle hat make a shadow on his face but I see his smile. Big Bill say Nagle worse when he smilin'.

'Dumb little bitch! No cotton is going to grow from that branch now. Do you know what that means?'

He flick the whip 'gain but it don't hit me that time. There fire where my foot should be.

'It means all the hard work that your master put in, months of hard work, is all wasted because of you. Because of your stupid clumsy nigger hands. What do you think of that?'

My voice stuck inside. I want to talk but nothin' there. Inside ev'rythin' shake. When I look down my foot cover in blood – not jus' the stripe but the whole top of skin.

'You think you can just ignore me? Not answer? You might get away with that in the big house but that doesn't work out here in the field. Strip! Go on, take that dress off.'

Strip means more stripes comin'. I try and open the button at the collar of my dress but my fingers don't work no better than my voice.

'Hurry up! You think I have all day to waste on you? Take the damn bag off first.'

My hands shake bad. My foot on fire. I gone cry. You ain't never meant to let them see you cry but I might cry all the same. I pull at the strap of the bag and it move lower. Nagle move his horse closer and he so close I scared his hoofs gone stand on my feets.

And then from nowhere Charity there, standin' b'tween me and Nagle.

'You leave her 'lone.'

Her voice loud. Brave. Ev'ryone stop pickin' now. Ev'ry eye in the field on us. On her.

'What did you say?'

I wait for the whip crack but none come and that nearly scarier. I look up. B'hind Nagle the sky blue like the dress Miss Ellen have with the slippers that match. More than anythin' I want to be with Miss Ellen – in her room, hidin' under her bed.

'It her firs' day out here. She don't know yet. She need to learn.'

Nagle tip his hat back off his head. He turn to Pete who there b'hind him now 'stead of up front where he was b'fore.

'Hear that, Pete? This one don't approve of my teaching methods.'

Pete laugh like he s'pposed to but Charity keep talkin'.

'I the best picker you has. The fastest. Let me show her – teach her so she pick like me.'

He pull the horse back and it rear a little. It look like it smilin' too with its big yellow teeth. It a mean smile.

'You want to show her how to pick cotton? To make sure she don't break another branch?'

'Yes sir.'

'Ya'll hear her that she think she the fastest picker out here? What y'all think of that?'

He shout out into the field but no one answer, there only cotton white and tall and still. In it there eyes watchin', ears listenin'. Some hands still stopped but some pickin' 'gain 'cause they knows when weighin' gone happen it ain't gone matter that they spend time bein' audience for Nagle.

He lift his whip high, hold it over his head. He gone bring it down hard, on Charity, then on me. I still wearin' my dress, I ain't done take it off, nor the bag neither and inside it I make my body small so there less of me to hit.

But he don't hit us. He bring the whip down, real slow and then he fold it 'cross his legs. Pull the reins of the horse to the left.

'Fine then, teach her,' he say. 'But you better make sure you pick more than yesterday and then some. Or you'll regret it.'

He yank his horse right the way round and then Pete do too. When they far 'nough 'way Charity put her hand on my shoulder.

'It gone be a'right,' she say. 'I gone show you. We gone do this t'gether.'

And we do. All day she show me what she know: how to hold the boil so the cotton come out easy, which ones I can do with one hand, how to reach 'round the branches so they won't break. I do most the low ones, she do the high and when her sack or my sack full I drag it down the ridge to the basket set up for us at the end of the row.

All day long Nagle up and down on his horse, his whip crackin' only he don't crack it near Charity and me. He leave us 'lone, he don't look at us when he pass.

The heat hotter than any heat I ever known – there ain't no shade and we done drank nearly all the water. Sometimes I think I ain't gone be able to keep goin' with the pain in my hand and my foot on fire where the stripe is and my dress heavy with sweat. But then I look at Charity and she smile at me and knowin' she there – that we doin' this t'gether – make it better and my hand reach out for the next boil and put it in the sack.

When the sun highest we stop to eat cornmeal and drink the last of the water. And when we start workin' 'gain it seem like we have a rhythm – Charity and me – and by the time the sun hide b'hind the trees and the cicadas out I know we gone get through the day, that we gone survive.

When we done, on the way out of the field Big Bill lift the sack from me and put it in our basket and put that on the wagon.

'You done good,' he say. 'The firs' day the hardest.'

He smile at me and it nearly worth it then to have him smile like that and I wonder how Charity feel havin' him smile at her like that ev'ry day.

The weighin' happen in the barn. When Marjorie and me and Little Bill and Benjamin were little we use look through the gap in the walls but we all work now and there no little kids lookin' on and I glad.

Pete get Sullivan and Walker to hoist the baskets up on the weighin' machine. They start at Jasper the new slave. His weigh twelve pounds more than yeste'day. Nagle got the paddle now 'stead of the whip and he walk right up to him. He pat the side of his face.

'Well, well, boy – maybe you're not the Master's biggest mistake after all. For a skinny son of a bitch you can carry your weight. I bet you do even better tomorrow.'

When Nagle take the paddle away it look like Jasper smile but that only his scar make him look like that and I don't think he ever smile none. Not really.

Big Bill next and it take Walker and Sullivan both to pull his basket up high on the machine. Big Bill stare straight ahead like it don't got nothin' to do with him. He don't look scared, he don't look like he even really there.

Pete fix the numbers on the scale and Nagle watch.

'Two hundred, same as yesterday,' he say to Nagle.

Big Bill nearly a'ways pick the same. Charity say she don't know how he know but he do.

Nagle swipe the paddle through the air like he gone hit Big Bill on the side of his head and he laugh when he flinch.

'What's the matter? You ain't scared, are you? Maybe you should be. Maybe if you don't start pickin' more the Master gone trade you like your buddy.'

Big Bill don't look like he hear him. He stand, stare straight ahead. Ev'ryone know that the Master ain't never gone sell Big Bill. And maybe that why Nagle don't say nothin' more 'bout it. 'Stead he turn to Charity and me.

Charity a'ways get more than Big Bill. Charity a'ways get more than anyone and today her cotton and my cotton t'gether in the basket. I too old to hold her hand – I ain't no baby no more – but I want to. Pain beat in my foot like a heart and when I look down the sawdust from the floor stuck to the blood and it swollen so big the skin look nearly white where it stretch.

Walker and Sullivan hoist Charity and my cotton up onto the scale. It look easier than when they put Big Bill basket up there. Pete move the big weight and the little weight till it balance. I don't know numbers yet so I don't know how much it say, can't tell if it good or bad.

Nagle walk up real close so it see it and then he walk 'way real slow. He tap the paddle 'gainst his pants leg while he walk. When he get to the door he stop, turn, walk back to where we are.

'A hundred and ninety-two pounds,' he say. He smile.

Charity don't smile, she look at her feets.

'A hundred and ninety-two pounds,' Nagle say 'gain. 'Pete, can you check yesterday's number?'

Pete opens a book, flicks a page.

'Two hundred and twenty-four pounds,' he say.

'Two hundred and twenty-four.'

Nagle walk over to us, so his boot nearly on Charity toes, so his face right in her face. 'You know how much less you picked today, you worthless bitch? Can your dumb brainless head do the math?'

He grab her chin, his fingers twist her face close when she try and move 'way.

'Thirty-two pounds,' Nagle say, flickin' her chin so it twist. My neck jerk even though he ain't touched me. 'Today there were two of you and you picked thirty-two pounds less.'

My foot on fire. There somethin' wrong with my breathin'. Charity don't say nothin'. Maybe she ain't able to speak 'cause he holdin' her jaw so tight. Maybe there ain't nothin' to say.

'And you' – he let go Charity then, lean down so he can look in my eyes – 'the Mistress asked me specially to report your day's work to her. Seemed to think you'd be a quick learner. What's she going to say when she hears you're a lazy little bitch?'

His spit land on my face. His breath stink. His nose red like the Master nose but it bigger and ugly and got black hair that come out. I hate him. I hate him more than the Mistress. I think what it be like to spit in his face. But my foot burn – it feel like my whole body burn and shiver at the same time. Maybe it only 'cause it my firs' stripe. Maybe the other ones ain't gone hurt this bad.

His fingers grab my face on either side. They hurt my cheek.

'Ain't you got anything to say for yourself?'

'Sorry, Master Nagle.'

'What did you say? Speak up, girl, I can't hear you.'

His fingers squeeze so hard they 'gainst my bone.

Charity speak up then. 'It ain't her fault. It mine. I done spend too much time showin' her. We gone do better tomorrow.'

He smile wider. 'Yes, I believe you will.'

He let go of me, stand up straight. And I think it over then but it ain't never over. 'Walker, Sullivan, get her into the stocks.'

Maybe it 'cause I so tired that it take a second to hear him, to und'stand what he sayin'. Then they there – Walker on one side me, Sullivan on the other. Walker fingers soft on my arm, Sullivan harder, but I know neither of them ain't gone want to do this.

Nagle laugh, he shake his head. 'Not that one, you dumb fools! The other one – this one!'

He point the paddle at Charity and then he rub it down the side of her breast and her waist real slow. Walker and Sullivan let me go so fast I fall over on the barn floor. They walk over to Charity and they take her arms 'stead of mine. Her hands clench and I think she gone fight but she don't fight.

They pull her even though they don't need to 'cause her toes ain't grippin' the ground, her feet walkin', her shoulders straight and her head up like she could be walkin' anywhere. She don't shout, she don't scream. She don't look at Nagle and when she walk past me on the ground she don't look at me neither.

'Pete, go with them. And make sure they put her in neck first – not feet. She'll be out of there in five minutes with those skinny ankles.'

'Yessir,' Pete says. 'Got it. How long you want her out there for?'

Nagle tip his hat to the side.

'Till first light.'

Charity a'ready outside by then with Walker and Sullivan. Pete stop by the door.

'You want me to stay out there with her, make sure she don't try nothing?'

'You start and I'll come out later. I know it's a long night but I'm sure we'll think of something to keep us entertained.'

Pete look blank at firs' but then Nagle raise his eyebrows and he laugh and Pete start laughin' too. I look at Big Bill and his fists clench too like Charity fists. I think he gone do somethin' – to say somethin' – to run after them but he jus' stand there.

That why when Pete leave the barn I start to go after them but b'fore I get two steps Nagle stop me with the paddle.

'Where do you think you're going?' he say. 'We ain't done here.'

He weigh Nelly next and then Rose and after that Walker and Sullivan come back and he weigh them too. I look at Walker but he don't look at me. The whole time I ain't listenin' to who pick what, I 'maginin' Charity out there in the dark by herself with her head in the stocks. The stocks made for legs not necks and I scared she ain't breathin' right that she gone suffocate out there. There snakes down there by the swamp – Marjorie got bit when she out there and that only for an hour in the end. Charity gone be out there all night and it don't make it feel no better that Pete gone be with her. It only make it feel worse.

When the weighin' finish and we finish cleanin' the barn I want to go down to the stocks and it like Big Bill read my mind 'cause he put his hand on my shoulder and we walk back to the cabins t'gether with Walker and no one say nothin'.

Back in the cabin Rose and Nelly don't say nothin' neither, even when Linda and Marjorie ask where Charity at. And I thinkin' that maybe we ain't sayin' nothin' 'cause Big Bill got a plan and we ain't s'pposed to talk 'bout it. Only then it night-time and we all lyin' down sleepin' and I know in the next cabin Big Bill doin' the same and that there ain't no plan at all.

That night it ain't jus' the burn in my foot that stop sleep comin'. Or the pain in my hand. It 'cause ev'ry time my eyes close I see Charity with her neck in them stocks. And lyin' in the dark I make my breath deep as I can, deep breath down into my belly, my legs, my feets. Like the air in my lungs gone somehow go into her lungs. Like the air in me the same as the air in her.

And all night – that longest night – I pray. I pray that there no clouds out, that no matter what happen, no matter how many snakes Charity see, no matter what Nagle and Pete doin' to her, that she can still see the stars.

CASSIE

I figured out a million ways not to take the pills Alice gave me. It was easy. Angelina was supposed to make sure I took them every morning and evening but she was usually so busy doing laundry or cleaning, that once she'd seen me take them out of the bottle and put them in my hand she stopped paying attention. So the pills ended up wrapped in toilet paper being flushed away, or dropped down a drain on the way to school. Sometimes I put them down the garbage disposal. So apart from a couple of times at the beginning when I took them, the only other time I remember taking them was the night of Kristen Silverman's party.

I wasn't banking on Mom being home for dinner that night but she is and what's more she's cooking *and* we're having company. When I come in from school she has three books about macrobiotic cookery on the table and some giant new appliance on the counter she says is a steamer. The company is her 'friend' Jason from A.A. she says, and she can't wait for Ryan and me to meet him.

I'm on the phone to Gabi planning what to wear when I hear the bell but I don't go down to get it. Instead I wait until the last possible minute when Mom is yelling up the stairs that the food is going cold. Ryan is already at the table and next to him is some hipster guy who's way younger than Mom, even though his giant beard and thick glasses are supposed to make him look older. He stands up and holds out his hand which is sweaty when I shake it.

'Since I've met Ry already, you must be Cass,' he says in a voice too deep for his face, 'I'm Jason.'

I smile extra-wide so Mom can't say afterwards I didn't make an effort. 'Nice to meet you, Jace.'

Ryan and I catch eyes and he smirks and I pretend not to see the glare Mom gives me. Jason sits back down and continues talking about some book he's read which he promises to lend Mom. I don't tell him that she doesn't like reading books, unless they are ones she's written herself.

The dinner appears to be mostly raw vegetables and some weird soggy stuff that Mom says is fermented. Jason says it's delicious and talks about time spent on an organic farm upstate. Ryan is on his phone the whole way through dinner and barely eats anything. Every mouthful of food seems to expand in my mouth but I force it down anyway. I can't remember the last time Mom cooked and even though I hate it, some part of me is glad that she tried. When my plate is mostly clean, it's a relief.

'Well, what do you think guys? Did you like it?' Mom says in a weird, high voice.

'Really delicious,' Jason says. 'So flavourful.'

His plate is empty like hers. I've strategically placed my napkin over most of what's left so she won't see it but Ryan hasn't even bothered and his plate is full of green and brown debris. I pick up his plate, put mine on top of it, thinking maybe she hasn't noticed yet.

'It was good, Mom,' I say.

Ryan looks up from his phone. 'Is there any dessert?'

Jason rubs his hands together. 'Now you're talking, big guy! Yes, Lou, what's for dessert?'

Clearly, Jason has a thing for shortening names, but no one calls Mom *Lou* except Dad. When she stands up her cheeks are flushed and she fixes her hair behind both ears at the same time.

'Yes! There is dessert – I made some raw banana date nut pudding!'

Ryan makes a retching sound and I smack him on the arm.

'What?'

I thump his arm again, harder this time.

'Ow!' He snatches it back, rubs it. 'What's your problem?'

I don't know what my problem is except I know that if Dad was here – or Grandad – he wouldn't get away with acting like that, but they're not here. There's only me and Mom.

'Quit acting like such a brat – you've turned into such a selfish jerk lately.'

He laughs, raises his eyebrows. '*I'm* the selfish jerk in this family?'

Mom keeps smiling like she hasn't noticed the whole interaction. 'Try it, Ry, you might like it. You always have dessert.'

'That's right. Dessert – as in ice-cream or cake or cookies. I'll pass on the raw dates. Thanks.'

He gets up and heads for the door.

'Ryan, we don't leave the table until everyone's finished,' Mom says to his back. 'Or if we do, we ask to be excused.'

He's already in the hall and he doesn't come back. He says something I can't make out and I hear him take the stairs two at a time. Mom sits back down and looks like she might cry. Jason puts his arm around the back of her chair.

'Mom, I've got to go too – I've to meet Gabi soon. You remember I told you about Kristen Silverman's party tonight, right?'

Mom frowns. 'You did? I don't remember.'

'We talked about it last week. Her parents will be there. You said it was fine so long as I was home by midnight. Gabi's dad is going to bring us home.'

There are three lies in that sentence which makes it hard to look at her and I'm glad when Jason interjects.

'Hey, I remember what those high-school parties are like! Man, they were some fun nights.'

Mom is frowning more. 'There won't be alcohol there, will there, Cassie?'

Jason laughs. 'Of course there'll be alcohol – and pot! Come on, Lou, don't say you don't remember high school?'

I don't think I've ever hated someone more than at this moment. 'It was longer ago for her than it was for you!' I snap, standing to clear the plates from the table. 'Don't worry, Mom, there won't be alcohol or if there is, I won't drink it. You know I don't drink.'

Lie number four. I lean over to fill the dishwasher with my back to Mom so she won't be able to see it on my face.

Mom gets up from the table, walks around the kitchen island.

'Cassie, I hope you're telling me the truth. I hope you know better than to take a drink – I mean you know what alcohol has done to this family.'

My cheeks are burning. I can't believe she wants to have this conversation now, in front of this creepy guy.

'Yes, Mom, I know. I won't. Look, I have to go.'

I'm edging towards the door when she reaches up into the cupboard and takes out the pill bottle, shakes it.

'Aren't you forgetting something?' she says.

Looking back, I could have told her I'd already taken them when I came in from school. She's only doing it for show – to look like the diligent mother in front of Jason – and she'd been pouring over the steamer instructions earlier so it's not like she'd remember. But maybe that would have been one lie too many, or maybe it's seeing them like that in her hand reaching out to me. Whatever it is, I walk back, pour a glass of water and down the two pink pills, as if I do this every day.

Walking upstairs to my room, I imagine I can feel them taking effect already but that's got to be all in my head. I took them a couple of times in the beginning and I didn't feel all that much different and, anyway, whatever effect they're going to have it's not going to happen that quickly. I pull out my favourite Brooklyn Industry T-shirt, the jeans that I was wearing when Steve Sherman said I had a sexy ass and the belt that used to be Grandad's. I pick up my notebook from my desk drawer – it feels weird not to have a way to communicate with E.L., to leave her behind – but I'd need to take a pocketbook and I don't feel like it so I just scrawl *see you later* and hide it under the pile of books next to my bed. Even though Alice is fine with me writing to her, I know Mom hates it so it's easier to hide it and, besides, I don't want her to read what I write.

I want to tell you about the whole night but a lot of it is just like any other teenage party that ever happened so if you've ever been to one of your own you can probably picture it – bowls for chips and popcorn that after a bit people use as ashtrays, half full and empty cans of beer, the kids who are really drunk or really lame dancing in the living room, the cool kids having deep conversations in the kitchen or outside on a deck, the really cool ones getting it on upstairs in one of the bedrooms.

And me? I was kind of drifting. At first, I stick to the kitchen. I like the kitchen at parties because there are props – you can be getting something to eat or another drink and there's not enough room to dance even if you wanted to. Gabi likes the kitchen too and for ages we have the two counter stools beside the window and it's fun talking to her and I'm realising that because I've spent so much time in school writing to E.L. lately it's one of the first times we've talked properly in ages.

But then Scott Stroller arrives and even though he stands there pretending to talk to both of us we all know he's only really killing time to get Gabi on her own. She pulls at her hoop earring until her ear lobe goes stretchy and white and it's when I'm looking at her doing that I realise I'm starting to zone out. And I don't know if it's the pills or the second can of Coors Light or both but I definitely start to feel different.

Here's where the sequence gets a bit blurry. I remember dancing. And drinking something that wasn't beer, from a bottle. Then I am outside on the deck with Matt Stringer. I don't know Matt Stringer. I know that he's a senior and has jet black hair that is always perfectly gelled into a peak. I know he hangs out with David Price. He is talking about being on the swim team like I'm supposed to know that about him already and then he asks me what it's like to be the daughter of someone famous. I take the cigarette he offers me. I never smoke, but holding on to the railing next to Matt, pushing a line of smoke out of my mouth into the night air, it feels kind of right, kind of inevitable.

We started to make out somewhere around then. I don't remember how it starts only that I'd already flicked my cigarette away and next thing we're kissing, the railing digging into my back.

Afterwards Alice asked me if I liked it, liked him, and I said I didn't know. I didn't like it and I didn't not like it. It was just like the smoking – another thing I was supposed to do. And I told her how even as we are making out, even as his hand is trying to find its way under my shirt I still have that other feeling, like I am kind of separate, like part of me is watching me, floating above myself. Like part of me isn't even there.

I want to stop telling you the story right here – to have it fade to black – and it does in a way, but not like you expect. What happens next is a kind of suffocating feeling and I know that somewhere something bad is happening to E.L. – that she's in trouble.

I pull my head away from Matt's. I need space, air. I feel hands all over me, big hands, probing.

'What is it? What's the matter?'

Matt's voice is breathy and his gelled peak is tilting to one side.

'You good? This is good, right?'

His hand is inside my T-shirt now, on my skin, reaching around towards the back of my bra.

He doesn't wait for an answer but starts to kiss me again. Deftly he opens my bra. Our teeth bump. His kiss is wet, sloppy. I close my eyes and I try to get into it again but before I can the pain comes in my foot, sudden and fiery and fierce.

'Ow!' I yell, pull my face away.

'What? What is it?'

His arms have me tight, they won't let me go. I get my hands in between us, push on his chest.

'Stop!'

'Cassie, what's wrong?'

My foot is burning, on fire. I need to touch it. I push him hard, as hard as I can but he's too big, a big block of muscle.

'Get off me! Just get off me!'

'Geez! What the fuck? Calm down!' He's stepped back now, let go of me, his hands in the air as if I'm brandishing a gun.

There's a noise then and the door is sliding open and Kristen Silverman is there, Chrissy Peters is on the step behind her.

'What's going on?' Kristen asks.

She is asking me but she glares at Matt. He's shaking his head, still has his hands in the air. I get down on one knee, my hands on my foot, pushing into the pain.

'I was just – we were just making out. I swear, tell them, Cassie.'

The light from behind Kristen is too bright. I rip my Converse off, my sock, but there is no cut, no break, just white skin. But the pain is getting worse, blinding, searing, biting pain. I rub my foot, I close my eyes, open them again.

'Cassie? Cassie, are you okay?'

I don't know whose voice that is. I try to stand. It's too hot. I can't breathe. I'm on the ground even though I'm standing now. I can't be both at the same time and somehow I am. I hold on to the railing but it's like I can't feel it.

There's people all around me, a horse, rearing up. I open my eyes and there's snatches of Matt, of Kristen and Chrissy coming towards me, someone else now behind them. When I close them again I feel the man close on the horse, the pain seeping from my foot into my whole body.

'Get away from me!' I hear myself yelling out. I open my eyes, a crowd is forming, Kristen is coming towards me. 'E.L? Talk to me? What's happening? I'm right here – okay? I'm right here!'

Someone is saying something about a glass of water – other voices are there in the background too. There are hands on me, someone's hands and I am pushing them away – E.L. is pushing them away. There's yelling and another noise and when I look again Kristen is down on the deck, her hand behind her head.

'Ow!' she's yelling.

Chrissy is on her knees next to her. 'Are you okay? Don't move. You're bleeding!'

'Grab her!' someone else is shouting. 'She's going crazy!'

Someone comes at me. A guy, I don't know who. I remember kicking – I think I do – and afterwards Gabi tells me it was Danny McGonagle and that I kicked him in the balls but I didn't know that then. There's a girl too who I push out of the way so I can get down the steps and into the garden. I hop on my good foot – the one with the sneaker – but it slips on the grass.

I remember trying to run but the pain is too much. I remember falling and getting up, trying again. I am looking for trees with hanging moss and they are there and then they are gone and there is only creeper on a trellis on a red brick wall. I see cabins and I run towards them but they disappear so there is only a square of patchy grass, a barbecue with a cover for the winter.

I remember my hands scratching something – grabbing, pulling at something. I remember voices. I remember hands. And falling.

I remember falling.

CASSIE

It's Sunday afternoon and Gabi is sitting on my bed, going into great detail about Friday night, filling in the blanks I'd rather were left unfilled.

'When I came out the back – me and Scott – you were trying to climb the trellis,' she's saying, her eyes wide. 'There was this terrible sound – you know the kind of sound where you just knew it was about to come out of the wall. But you kept climbing up – it was like you were possessed, Cass. Don't you remember any of this?'

'No.'

She shakes her head. 'It was some crazy-ass shit, Cass-a-blanca. I mean, your fall was in slow motion. Like this.' She reaches out her hands and makes a free-falling motion. 'And I was calling out to you but I don't know if you even heard me. Did you hear me? You let your head just smack into the patio.'

My head is pounding. I can't believe I'm only allowed to have Tylenol because of my concussion. I shift in the bed but I can't get comfortable because of the ache in my ribs.

'You don't you remember anything?' Gabi says. 'None of it?'

'No, Gabs, I told you. Nothing.'

I've been over this with the E.R. doctors, with Mom and Dad. Saying I remember nothing is easier than trying to explain what the memories are really like – mine and E.L.'s all intertwined together. Even when Alice came over for the emergency session yesterday I didn't know how to tell her without her thinking I'm crazy, that had

I had some kind of breakdown, so I said the same thing: 'I started to kiss Matt and I remember nothing after that.'

Everyone agrees that I'm lucky to have gotten away with only a concussion and three cracked ribs but what still hurts the most is my foot. In the hospital they gave me an X-ray and then – when Dad insisted – an MRI but everything showed up clear. Apparently there's abosolutely nothing wrong with my foot.

'Did I tell you that Scott's brother knows Matt really well? They're on the swim team together. Do you want me to find out what he's saying about it?'

I shake my head. 'No! That's the last thing I want to know. Honestly, Gabs, I just want to forget the whole thing.'

'That's what Scott said – he said you probably wouldn't want to know – that most people wouldn't. He's smart, you know. Emotionally intelligent – not like most guys.'

Gabi's at that stage where she'll bring Scott into the conversation any way she can and if I have to hear one more thing about him – one more thing about that night – I think I might scream.

'Do me a favour, will you and see where my mom is? Dad said she was out at the store but she must be back by now.'

'Sure.'

'And can you ask her to bring one of those heating pad patches things? My back is killing me now too?'

'Coming right up!'

Gabi jumps off the bed and leaves the door onto the landing open. I hear her feet on the stairs, her voice calling out for Mom.

With the room empty there is oxygen, I can breathe. Since I got released from the hospital there's hardly been five minutes without someone else in the room and between the visitors and falling asleep all the time, I haven't been able to write to E.L., not even once.

Gabi's gone for ages and when she comes back she's not with Mom, she's with Dad.

'Where's Mom?'

'Your mom's gone out for a bit. She'll be back later.'

'Out where?'

He's over at the window, fiddling with the blinds.

'Just out with some friends.'

Out with some friends is code for being at an A.A. meeting and I think he's worried about Gabi knowing, even though she's texting again so it's not as if she's listening.

'So, you need something, Cass? Gabi was saying you wanted another heating pad?'

The good thing about being sick is that you can be honest with people, that you can pretty much tell them when to leave.

'Yeah, my back is killing me. If I could get that pain under control, I'd just love to sleep.'

Gabi looks up from her phone. 'I've tired you out,' she says. 'I'll let you get some rest,' and something about the way she says it and how quickly she grabs her bag makes me think she's been dying to go, that she's already made plans to meet Scott at Connecticut Muffin.

'I'll see you tomorrow?' She gives me a loose hug around my shoulders. 'I'll stop by after school. But call or text, you know – whatever you need, Cass-a-blanca, I'm here. Okay?'

'Okay.'

No one has said I'm not going to school tomorrow but I guess I'm not. And part of me is glad not to have to face them. I could do without ever having to face them again.

Dad sees Gabi out and I must've fallen straight asleep because when he comes back into the room, I jolt awake again.

'Cass, honey?'

'I was sleeping, Dad, I was about to sleep.'

'Okay, this will just take a minute. I just want to talk to you and your brother for a minute.'

It's only then I notice Ryan is behind him, leaning against the doorjamb. Dad comes in and gestures to Ryan to take the chair but he only comes in as far as the desk and leans against it, his arms folded, so Dad sits down instead. He takes off his glasses, rubs the top of his nose, which always means he's working up to say something. My heart must be going faster and every beat is a pulse of pain against my ribs.

'What's going on, Dad?'

'I told your brother this already but I wanted us all to talk about it together. We're going to make some changes around here. You guys are going to move in with me for a bit – when you feel well enough to travel.'

I'm not sure what I'm expecting him to say, but it's not this.

'Your place? But it's not big enough – you only have a one bedroom.'

'There's a two-bed coming available on the floor above next month, until then, we'll get by with the pull-out couch. Or I can get something else – another bed. A day bed.'

I look at Ryan but he's looking at the floor.

'But what about school?'

'You guys can get the subway. The R train goes right there.'

Again, I wait for Ryan to say something, to ask something. Maybe he feels my eyes on him because he looks up, but when he does he just blows his fringe from his eyes and looks away again.

'Why? I mean – why now? What about Mom? What does Mom say?' Under the covers my foot is on fire, the foot that showed up nothing despite all the tests. I reach down and knead it gently. 'Is this because of what happened at the party?'

Dad switches the cross of his legs, he shakes his head. 'It's not your fault, honey – none of this is your fault.'

'None of what? What's going on, Dad?'

'Mom's drinking again, that's what's going on.' Ryan says it in a deadpan way like it is something that was to be expected, something inevitable. Just another fact – and maybe it is.

Dad turns around to face him. 'Ry, we said—'

'What? You don't think Cassie deserves to know? You don't think she's going to notice Mom's not around?'

'When you said she was with friends I thought she was at A.A.! Where is she? What happened?'

Ryan pulls himself up onto my desk, swings his legs so his sneakers hit against the drawers in a way that I know will scuff the wood but I don't tell him to stop. 'Last night she said she was going to pop out to CVS. That was at nine thirty and she never came home. She's not answering her phone, responding to texts. I guess it must be a good bender if she's still going on a Sunday afternoon.'

'Ryan!' Dad stands up. 'Talking like that about your mother is not okay! Stop it right now.'

'Why not?' Ryan kicks the wood hard. 'I'm telling the truth and you know it. I heard you calling round the bars after you called the hospitals, the cops.'

Dad stands there with his hands on his hips. He looks from me to Ryan and back to me again. His mouth opens but no words come out and he closes it. Looking at them both I see suddenly how alike they look, the same dark hair, heavy eyebrows. I feel like what they're saying is floating above me, hovering around me – that I can't take it in.

'You mean it? That Mom's missing?' I say eventually. 'You don't know where she is?'

Dad wraps his arms across his chest like he's protecting himself from something. His eyes are rimmed with red and I don't know if it's from tiredness or crying or both.

'It's okay, Cass, she'll turn up eventually – you know your mother, you know she always does.'

I want to get out of bed, getting out of bed will help me think clearly – I can't think clearly in bed – but even if my ribs weren't throbbing the pain in my foot is too much and I don't think I could stand.

'Maybe she's at A.A.?' I suggest. 'Maybe you could call her A.A. friends? Jason? Or that other one – what's her name, Ryan? Margaret, is it Margaret?'

Ryan makes a snorting sound and Dad shoots him a look.

'We tried that, Cass. We called around. No one has seen her.'

'But maybe she went to other meetings. There's millions of meetings – she could be at one in Manhattan. Maybe her phone died. We don't know – you don't know for sure.'

Dad doesn't say anything and Ryan doesn't either, just kicks the desk, one two, one two. In their silence I hear the answer: if Mom was at a meeting, if her phone died, she could use someone else's phone. A pay phone. If Mom was at a meeting there's no way she wouldn't get in touch.

'Maybe she's hurt?' I say. 'Maybe she was mugged? Maybe she's at the hospital?'

Dad reaches across the bed and holds on to my hand. 'I checked all the hospitals, honey – no one has been admitted matching her description.' He smiles. 'That's good news.'

The bar must be pretty low for good news right now, is what I want to say, but the tiredness has come back, a sudden, heavy wave of it so I keep quiet instead. In my nightstand drawer there's a notepad and pen and as soon as they leave I want to write to E.L., to talk to her, to tell her what happened, to have her help me figure it out.

Dad is squeezing my hand and I open my eyes. 'It's going to be okay – all of this, you know. I don't know why this is happening but I do know it's going to be okay.'

I close my eyes again and he squeezes harder.

'We'll let you sleep now, but if you want anything – just call out, okay? I'll keep the door open.'

I nod and he lets go of my hand. I hear Ryan jump down from the desk and walk out onto the landing and when I snap my eyes open Dad's about to leave too.

'Dad?'

He turns back.

'We won't go anywhere before she's home, will we? I'd hate for her to come home and for us not to be here. I'd hate for her to come home to an empty house.'

He rubs his hand over the top of his head. His hair used to stick up all directions when he did that but now what's left is cut too short to move.

'Of course, sweetheart, we won't go anywhere until she gets back. Don't worry now, try and sleep. You need your rest, okay?'

'Okay.'

From the landing I hear Ryan's door close, the sound of his Xbox being powered up.

'He's mad at me, isn't he? He thinks it's my fault.'

Dad rubs his head again, shakes it. 'He's not mad at *you*, Cass, he's just mad – that's all. Like you probably are, like all of us. But I want you to know that whatever happens, it's not your fault.'

I nod.

'You know that, don't you?'

I nod again but something tells me he wants to hear me say it. 'I know. It's not my fault.'

He smiles a little smile and I do too. 'Get some sleep.'

Even though he said he'd leave the door open, he forgets and closes it anyway. I know it's only out of habit, I know he's not doing it to exclude me, to punish me, most of me knows that. But lying there with my foot throbbing and the ache in my head and my ribs, part of me doesn't know it. Part of me thinks he did it on purpose, because no matter what he says, he knows Ryan is right that Mom going missing is my fault. And that if anything bad happens to her – anything worse – that that will be my fault too.

E.L.

Benjamin foot get stuck in the spoke in the cartwheel. That what happen. We all in the field a'ready and then Benjamin lyin' on the ground and his eyes squeeze close and he moanin'. Benjamin brave. He never moan even when he gettin' lashed. When I look at his foot it bent funny and it swell big a'ready.

'Stupid boy!' Nagle shout. 'No, don't move the cart, that'll make it worse.'

Big Bill and Charity bend down to help Benjamin take his foot out but he moan more so they stop.

'We need a poultice,' Charity say, 'that take the swellin' down. Juba know how – she make the best poultice.'

Nagle look at Charity and then he look at Benjamin. Benjamin hold on to his leg and moan more.

'All right – you. Run to the big house and get Juba out here with a poultice.'

When I look up he pointin' at me.

'Come on – hurry up!' Nagle yell now. 'Run!'

He only care 'cause Benjamin pick real well and if he lose his foot he ain't gone be able to pick no more. The other night I hear Charity ask Big Bill what goin' on and that she hear the Master gone be sellin' slaves but Big Bill only say not to pay any mind to talkin' and what the Master doin' with his slaves no one else bus'ness 'cept his own.

I ain't been to the big house since the day with the piano and I ain't seen the Mistress since then neither. So when I come round the side and see her and the Master talkin' on the porch by the back steps I stop dead. I know I shoulda kept goin', that Benjamin in pain and he need me, but somethin' stop me. Somethin' make me freeze right there on the spot, crouch down on my hands and knees and crawl under the porch so they ain't gone see me.

'What about Benjamin? Or that other one – the really dark one. Sullivan? What about one of them?'

That the Mistress talkin'. Her voice sound mad but she a'ways sound mad.

'They're good pickers.' That the Master. 'We need them. Without them we won't be able to get a full harvest.'

'Well, if you're going to sell one who's useless in the field, you know who that should be – she's trained as a house slave. That raises her value.'

My heart stop. No breath come. They talkin' 'bout me.

The Master don't say nothin' so the Mistress keep goin'. 'It's the obvious thing to do, especially since Marjorie's doing so well in the house–'

'I told you before, we're not selling E.L.!'

The Master voice a shout and a bang come with it. After that there silence, no sound 'cept the cicadas and my heart beatin'. When the Mistress talk 'gain her voice sound madder than b'fore.

'Your sentimentality will destroy this place, if your drinking doesn't first. You won't even get rid of that old one – the blind one.'

She mean Elijah. Elijah use drive the carriage till he had an accident and now that Carlton job.

'You know I can't sell him. No one will buy him, not like this. At his age.'

'Give him his freedom then – isn't that what they all want? What these people in the north say they want?'

Under the porch I stuck. I want to stand up and run to Juba and tell her 'bout the poultice but if I run now they gone know I been listenin'. And anyway I ain't never heard no one talk 'bout slaves being free 'cept for Cassie.

The Master laugh. 'His freedom? He wouldn't know what to do with freedom. He's no family – he knows no free blacks, he's going blind. Freedom for him would be a death sentence.'

'So we just keep feeding him? Give him a roof over his head until he dies. You think we have the money for that?'

'What's the alternative, Joanne? He's been here for nearly forty years. More than either of our lifetimes! This is his home!'

Joanne. That mus' be the Mistress name. I ain't never heard it b'fore. Joanne. She don't look like no Joanne to me.

There sound of a chair bein' push back.

'His home? What about my home? This plantation has been in my family for decades. My father would turn in his grave if he saw how you're running it into the ground. He knew how to run a plantation.'

'I'm not having this argument again – I'm through arguing with some dead man.'

'If you don't have any respect for the dead maybe you'll give a thought to the living. What about your daughter? What kind of prospects will she have if you let this place go to rack and ruin? Or do you care more about these damn slaves than about her future?'

I wait for the Master to say somethin' back only he don't say nothin' and then there the sound of footsteps and I scrunch down even smaller when the Mistress walk right over my head.

The screen door squeak and I know she gone. There silence for a minute b'fore I hear the Master feets on the steps and I see him walkin' over t'wards the barn. He gone go out for a ride – maybe far as Charleston. Maybe he ain't gone come back for a while.

And then I r'member somethin' that musta happen so long ago I forget it till then. I r'member the Master takin' us to the barn – me and Miss Ellen – and I r'member him liftin' us up onto a horse, the two of us t'gether. And I r'member bein' so high up I 'fraid I gone fall and I hold on to Miss Ellen. And there someone else there on the other side me – a woman – and I holdin' on to her hand too. I try picture who there. At firs' I think maybe it Charity, only it don't feel like Charity hand, this hand feel diff'rent. And then, jus' like that, I know who in the barn that day: my mamma. I try picture her face and I can't but I can feel her hand and I know it her. It don't make no sense how I so sure 'cause I ain't got no other mem'ries of her but I sure. I sure as I sittin' there watchin' the Master walk 'way. I know she in the barn that day. I know I ain't 'maginin' it.

CASSIE

Mom shows up in a hospital on the Upper East Side of Manhattan late Sunday night. No one knows how she got there, only that she had a blood alcohol level of three point seven, which Google tells me is stronger than surgical anaesthesia. For the second time over the weekend Dad has to go to the Emergency Room and Ryan wants to go too but Dad won't let him and so he stays behind with me and Angelina, and we camp out in my room eating Chinese food and watching *Harry Potter and the Chamber of Secrets,* which we've all seen before.

It's almost midnight when Dad comes home and I must've been sleeping because I wake up when Ryan bounds out the door and down the stairs. When Dad comes in he tries to look cheerful as he tells us that Mom is doing okay, that she's in a detox and that tomorrow she's agreed to go to a rehab on Long Island for a month. And it's only when he asks Angelina to pack her a bag that I realise that we're not going to see her, that she's not coming home before she goes.

Dad stays over for the next two nights and Ryan begs him to just move in so that we won't have to move to his place in the city. I get why Ryan doesn't want to move – all his stuff is here, his friends – he wants to walk to school with them every morning and not have to get the R train, he wants to be able to hang out with them instead of coming straight home.

On Monday he comes into my room and asks how I'm doing and it's the first time he doesn't seem mad at me, but then he asks me to back him up, says Dad will listen to me and I know that's the only reason he's being nice. And he thinks I don't back him up to spite him, because I'm mad at him too but the real reason is that it's just too weird being in the house without Mom and anyway, some part of me thinks things might be better if we all start over somewhere else.

Dad's apartment is in a new building with a doorman and a huge elevator and a gym and pool. It has floor-to-ceiling windows with a view of the river and New Jersey beyond but only one bedroom, so until the two-bedroom upstairs is vacated, Ryan and Dad are sharing a bed and I'm on the pull-out couch.

'Are you sure you're comfortable enough? I can get another bed, a proper one – we'll fit it in somehow,' Dad says for the millionth time the first night. 'You're recovering and I don't want to make it any worse.'

'I'm fine, it's comfy. Nearly comfier than my bed at home.' I'm smiling because it's true. I like the pull-out bed, the way the arms and back of the couch make it feel enclosed, protected.

'Are you sure?' Dad says. 'Because the other option is you have the bedroom and Ryan takes that and I can just sleep on the floor. I don't mind.'

'Dad, how many different ways can she say it?' Ryan has his head in the fridge but I don't need to see his face to know he's rolling his eyes. 'She *said* it's fine.'

'Okay, relax over there, buddy,' Dad says, running his hand over his hair. 'I was just making sure.'

Ryan turns back towards us, holding the fridge door open so I can see the shelves, empty except for a few cans of soda and what looks like butter. 'When do you plan on going food shopping, Dad? There's nothing here.'

'What do you want? We can order in. Whatever you like.'

Ryan blows his fringe out of his eyes. 'I don't want to have to order in all the time, Dad. I want to be able to go to the fridge and make a snack. What if I'm hungry at three in the morning?'

'We're in the city now, Ry,' Dad laughs. 'The deli delivers at three in the morning.'

'That's the same deli who didn't have any avocado for a sandwich, right? Or even almond milk?'

Dad's about to lose it, I can tell by his face. I'm waiting for him to snap at Ryan and ask him since when have his late-night snacks included avocado and almond milk, but instead he just takes a deep breath, nods twice before he answers.

'Fine, buddy, I can do food shopping tomorrow after work. In fact why don't you come with me so you can make sure I get all the things you like? We'll do it together – what do you say?'

But Ryan doesn't say anything, just walks past him, and we both hear the bathroom door close, hard but not hard enough to be a slam.

For the next two days, Dad works from home to make sure I'm okay and I wish he wouldn't because the only thing I want to do – really the only thing – is to write to E.L. I've had two sessions with Alice since the party and she's told me she wants to take on a new approach where I've no more contact with E.L. – that I go cold turkey. When she says it, I nod, and agree, like it's no big deal and it is no big deal because I know there's no way she can hold me to it.

On Friday, Dad gets a call at 6.30a.m. and when he comes into the living room he's already in his suit and he says he has to go to the office, 'just for an hour', and I don't let him see how much I'm smiling because I know it's never just an hour.

It's great then, not only because my ribs are feeling better and I'm not as sleepy, but because I have a whole day to write back and forth to E.L.

At first I'm worried that she won't be there, but she is and I tell her all about the party and what happened with Mom and she tells me about the cotton fields and how she's picking as much as she can so Nagle the overseer won't beat Charity again and how she misses not seeing Miss Ellen every day, the way she used to.

And by the time it's four o'clock we've filled one whole marble journal and half of another one and I've forgotten to even eat anything and I know I have to get up and shower because Dad promised if I was well enough to go out, he'd take us to Serendipity for ice-cream.

Waiting in line for a table that night, I'm wishing that it was over and we were back home so I can write to E.L. and I wish there was more than one bathroom so I could spend longer in there and write to her on the small, flat notebook in my jeans pocket. By the time we get seated it's after nine and Ryan keeps making comments about it being a dumb kids' place to go so I have to pretend I'm excited so Dad doesn't feel bad. Over burgers and then ice-cream Ryan hardly speaks and Dad asks us questions about school and our friends like some weird distant uncle we hardly know and I think we're all really happy to get back to the apartment.

Dad helps me with the pull-out couch and I yawn really obviously so he'll get the hint to leave me alone but he doesn't seem to get it because he sits on the leather chair by the window, picks up the remote and starts turning it between his hands.

'So, Cass,' he says, 'how are you feeling now? Since Sunday, I mean?'

His voice is low and he glances towards the bathroom door – where Ryan is – and I know then that's what he's wanted to ask me all night.

I'm straightening the sheets properly around the corners.

'Fine – my ribs feel much better and my headache's gone.'

'Good. That's great.' He twists the remote control again, flipping it over and back. 'But I kind of meant ... you know ... emotionally, not physically. Alice said you're not going to be communicating – writing – to that, um, girl, anymore.'

'So much for client–patient privilege!' I fluff up my pillow but I laugh, to let him know it's a joke.

He laughs too, puts down the remote on the coffee table.

'So are you okay with that? Do you miss her – the girl, what's her name again?'

I pick up the blanket, fan it out in the air so for a second it obscures his face.

'E.L.'

'That's right. E.L. You know you can be honest with me, Cass. You know you can tell me the truth.'

He's stands up, folds his arms across his chest. He used to be so much taller than me, now, in his socks, we're at eye level. He thinks he wants the truth but really he doesn't, so I tell him what he wants to hear.

'You know it's funny, I thought I would, but I don't, Dad. It's been a whole week now almost and I feel better. I'm starting to feel much better than I did before.'

He smiles, the first proper smile I've seen all night.

'That's great. That's really great, Cass.'

'Thanks, Dad.'

We both hear the toilet flush and I have never been so glad for the sound. Dad reaches over, puts his hand on my shoulder.

'I'm here for you, you know.'

His face is flushed and mine probably is too. I hate this conversation. I nod a fraction of a nod. He leans forward and kisses my forehead and I think I'm going to implode with guilt but right then Ryan bursts out of the bathroom and Dad pulls away.

'Dad, can we watch a movie? *Lord of War* is on demand.'

Watching a movie will delay me writing to E.L. for at least two hours.

'Ry, I'm beat. I have to go to bed and I can't sleep with the T.V. on.'

'But it's not even eleven! And, it's a Friday night! Tell her, Dad!'

Ryan looks at Dad who shrugs. 'Sorry, buddy. Right now this is Cassie's bedroom so she calls the shots.'

'Why can't she sleep in the bed and we can sleep out here?'

'There's no room for us out here, you'd take up the whole couch bed to yourself.'

'I could give you the other cushions – you could sleep on the floor.'

'Ryan, come on. We can watch the movie tomorrow – I'm not sleeping on the floor.'

'But you said you would, the other night. Didn't he, Cass? You even suggested it.'

Ryan looks to me for support but I don't want to be in their fight so I look away. Dad laughs, like it's all a joke, but under the laughter his voice is hard.

'Come on, Ryan, be reasonable. That was different.'

Ryan stands with his hands on his hips, the same way I've seen Dad stand a million times.

'Why? What's different?'

Dad takes two steps towards Ryan, holds his arms out.

'I offered to sleep on the floor because Cassie has broken ribs and she might need the bed. That's what's different. I've had a long, hard week and you can't seriously expect me to sleep on the floor because you want to watch some dumb movie—'

'It's not a dumb movie!'

'I didn't mean that. I meant, expecting me to sleep on the floor so you can watch it – any movie – after the week I've had. It's just not fair!'

When I say things aren't fair Alice picks me up on it, says only children say that but I don't think it's a good time to point that out to Dad.

Ryan shakes his head. 'You know what's not fair? Her getting everything she wants and me getting nothing I want. Ever! That's what's not fucking fair around here.'

'Hey!' Dad calls after Ryan as he disappears down the hall. 'Watch your language! Don't walk away when I'm speaking to you! Get back here, now!'

But Ryan doesn't come back and this time it's the bedroom door we hear shut. And this time it is a slam.

'Sorry, Dad, I didn't mean to cause a fight. I just want to go asleep.'

'It's not your fault, honey – you get your rest. He's just mad at me that I've no T.V. in the bedroom. Maybe we'll pick one up tomorrow, we could use two T.V.s when we move to the apartment upstairs anyway.

There was a time when Ryan would've got in trouble for talking like that – acting like that – and not be rewarded with a T.V. but I don't say that. Instead I wait until Dad's done in the bathroom and I hear the creak of the bed before I take my notebook out.

I'm not tired – I could totally stay up to watch a movie – and I climb into the couch-bed, still dressed and pull the blanket up around me and I start to write to E.L.

***

I'm asleep and then I'm awake. I don't know where I am or what time it is. I don't know anything except that Dad is standing over me in a T-shirt and pyjama bottoms and he looks really mad.

'Dad?'

He has something in his hand, something he's waving at me.

'Not writing to her anymore? A whole week? Really?'

'Dad?'

He holds the notebook up, starts to read out loud putting on a strange voice that's nothing like his voice.

'"I couldn't wait to get home tonight and write to you. It's all so fake this family-time shit together, the only thing that's real is this – is you."'

I push myself up on the couch. 'Dad! Give me that! That's mine!'

He keeps reading.

'"It sound strange – stayin' at your daddy place. I can't 'magine what it like sleepin' som'place else without Charity lyin' next to me and Linda and Marjorie and Rose and Nelly up the other end. I don't think I be able to sleep none without Nelly snorin.'"'

E.L.'s voice doesn't sound like her voice in his mouth. It sounds wrong. I'm fully awake now, sitting up. I reach out for the book but he takes a step back, so I can't reach him.

'"I don't know how you sleep with all those people. Thank God I have my own room here. Ryan and Dad had a big fight tonight – I told Dad I wanted to go to sleep and he bought it. Just like when he bought it when I said I wasn't writing to you anymore!"'

'Give it to me! I can't believe you're going through my things! I thought I could trust you!'

He throws the notebook down on the carpet and I snatch it up and hold it to my chest. It's only then that I realise I'm still dressed, that I must have fallen asleep before I made it into my pyjamas.

'Trust me? You're one to talk about trust, Cassie, after what I just read out – you lied to me, you've been lying to me.'

'You read my private notebook! Trust goes both ways Dad. '

He sits down on the couch and I turn away from him, holding the notebook tight in case he tries to take it away again.

'Cassie, Cassie look at me!' His hand is on my shoulder but I pull away, burrow deeper under the sheets. 'Cassie – stop it! Calm down! I can't help you if you don't tell me the truth. That's all I want from you – don't you see that? The truth.'

'That's such bullshit, Dad.' I've never cursed at him before but it just comes out. 'You say you want the truth but then I tell you and no one wants to hear it. If I tell you the truth then I'm sick, I'm a crazy person – there's something wrong with me. Do you've any idea what that's like?'

He reaches closer, puts his arm around me.

'I tried telling you the truth, it's not like I didn't. If you'd believed me, trusted me, then I wouldn't have to lie. I don't want to keep lying.'

'Cass—'

I shake it off. 'All I want is for someone to believe me. Is that so hard to do?'

'Cass, it's okay, come here.'

He puts his arm back again, his voice is softer now. I let it stay this time.

'If Grandad was here, he'd believe me.'

And that's when the tears come.

***

I don't remember how long I cried on the couch only that afterwards we go to the kitchen and Dad puts the kettle on the stove and opens a packet of Pepperidge Farm cookies that he takes from behind the cooking oil on the top shelf of the cupboard.

'I was hiding them from your brother; he eats faster than I can shop.'

He laughs and I do too. After the tea is made we sit on high stools at his kitchen island watching the lights go on and off on the buildings across the river. Steam from the mug turns into water on the marble counter top and I make a pattern of it with my finger. He speaks first.

'Have you tried looking her up?'

I stop making the pattern, look at him. I think I know what he means, but I'm not sure.

'Looking who up?'

'E.L.' He says her name slowly. 'Have you tried to find out anything about her?'

I think of all my trips to the library, the hours of Googling. I want to tell him but it could be a trick – it could still be a trick.

'Yeah, a bit.'

'Slaves usually went by the last names of their owners. Do you know the last name of the owner of the plantation?'

His face looks serious, normal. Like it's not a trick. Even though behind him the microwave clock says it's 4.43a.m. he doesn't have that exhausted look he had earlier and I don't feel tired at all.

I scrunch my forehead, try to remember. 'No, I don't think so. But I could ask her.'

There's a flicker of something in his eyes and for a second my stomach drops because I think he's only humouring me, that he'll never believe me, but then it's gone and his eyes are his eyes again, focused on mine.

'So ask her. Find out as much information about her as you can. And if you want, we can try and look for her together.'

He says it real casual, like we're talking about looking for a flight or a hotel or a pair of sneakers. He's definitely humouring me, I know he is.

'I've already looked. It's impossible to find anything on the internet, believe me. I've tried.'

Dad nods, drinks some more tea. 'Have you tried Ancestry.com?'

I lick my finger, pick up the crumbs on the plate where the cookies were.

'It's expensive, you need a subscription. And a credit card. I don't have a credit card.'

Dad drains his mug of tea, puts it down on the counter. 'Well, even after that crazy over-priced ice-cream I think I still have some room left on mine. Want to give it a go?'

He stands up, nods towards the living room where his laptop is. I know he's humouring me; that he doesn't really believe in E.L. He's only doing this because I brought up Grandad, to show me that he can be like him. Or maybe he wants to score points against Mom, for him to be the one I open up to.

'What? Right now? In the middle of the night?'

He raises his eyebrows. 'Why not? I've no other plans – do you?'

I look at him and he looks at me. And that's when I decide. Even if he is humouring me, only pretending, if it helps me find out more about E.L., even help her, then who cares? Right then, at 4.49a.m., I can't see a downside, how it could be a bad thing.

'Okay.' I smile. 'Let's do it.'

And he smiles too. And I follow him into the living room and we sit side by side at the dining table while he powers up his laptop, and we start our search for E.L.

Together.

E.L.

She don't tell me what happen, Cassie don't, not then. But I know somethin' change, somethin' diff'rent. She askin' me all these questions all a sudden ...

What's your master's last name?

Is Riverside Hall the full name of the plantation?

How far are you from Charleston?

Do you grow anything other than cotton?

Are there any landmarks around? What can you see from outside the plantation?

She know what I can see, she see what I see, that the whole point. I tell her that and I tell her what I tell her b'fore that I ain't never been outside Riverside Hall, that there ain't no way I can leave. She get mad at me that I don't know the Master name and I stop talkin' to her till she say she sorry, that she jus' excited 'cause if she able to find out where I'm at then she gone be able to find out what happen, she gone be able to help me.

That when she tell me that her daddy helpin' her now, that they lookin' for me t'gether, but that make no sense. She from the future, som'place where slaves is able to write books and go to school, som'place where there ain't nobody sleepin' on planks of wood and workin' in the cotton fields all day.

One night after we come in from the field, I sittin' b'hind the cabin. It late and I should be in bed a'ready but Cassie so excited talkin' to me I stop there to be som'place by myself so I can hear her.

Slavery ends in less than ten years, E.L. There's this big war and eventually, when it ends, slavery is abolished. You'll only be in your twenties – you'll have your whole life ahead of you. So will Charity.

Ten years. I don't know nothin' 'bout no war or how to make sense of no ten years. All I know is that the wind blow the moss on the trees tonight and that in the mornin' the sun gone rise over those same trees and by the time it rise we gone be out in the field. I know it take a lot of suns risin' and suns settin' to make up ten years and that anythin' can happen b'tween now and then.

I look at the trees but I don't say nothin' to her and she keep talkin'.

So you see if I can find out where you are and your full name and everything then I can find out about what happens – how things turn out for you when slavery is over.

Things still turnin' out. I say that clear in my head so I know she hear me. Nothin' over. How it gone help me to know what happen?

I feel something, like she mad at me but she the one able to feel my feelings I ain't able to feel hers, at least I don't think I can.

It'll give you hope. When things are really bleak – really dark – you'll know that they'll get better. You'll have hope.

Hope. One time Big Bill and Charity have a big fight 'bout hope. Big Bill say there ain't nothin' good ever come of hope – that hope jus' 'nother word for pain. I ain't never seen Charity as angry as she get with him that night.

'Don't say that!' she say, her eyes all on fire. 'Don't even think it! No matter what happen, there a'ways hope.'

Thinkin' 'bout that it seem like a long time since I seen Charity look like that, talk like that. Ever since my firs' day pickin' in the field when Nagle send her to the stocks Charity ain't look like she got much hope left. She don't say much of nothin' to Big Bill these days or me either.

And that what get me thinkin' 'bout what Cassie sayin' that maybe even if I don't und'stand or b'lieve what she talkin' 'bout, that maybe it a good thing. That maybe Cassie gone somehow give me hope and maybe, somehow, I gone get 'nough hope not jus' for me but a little bit for Charity as well.

CASSIE

Getting E.L. to answer my questions is like pulling teeth. Anything I ask her, she says she doesn't know. And I know there is a lot she doesn't know but it seems like there is something else there too, that there are things she doesn't want to tell me or maybe even find out for herself. It's almost like she doesn't want me to find her, that she doesn't want us to help her.

Dad is almost as enthusiastic as I am – you couldn't fake that enthusiasm and I know he's not humouring me, that he believes me. Every evening as soon as he gets in from work he pulls up a chair and sits down next to me to see where we've got to on Ancenstry.com. One night he comes home with a cardboard tube and rolls out an old map of South Carolina. In the corner there's a date – 1842 – the year after E.L. was born. We haven't been able to find any trace of Riverside Hall but it might have had another name and that doesn't mean anything because lots of records were destroyed in the Civil War. But E.L. told us it's a whole day on horseback from Charleston, so Dad was really clever and figured out that it must be within a thirty- or forty-mile radius. That night with the map, he takes a compass and draws a circle with Charleston in the middle and the circumference forty miles away. It's amazing then, to look at that circle and know that somewhere in there is where E.L. is and that maybe someday she will see it too, that she will look at a map, exactly like this one.

Everything is better at Dad's, even going back to school isn't as bad as I think it's going to be and I just ignore the whispers of the other kids and think about the next part of the research that Dad and I need to do.

But things being better makes me worry more, not less. I worry that he's going to get bored of looking and that if E.L. doesn't give me more information to work with he'll lose interest completely – that's why I ask her any question I can think of. I worry that Ryan will figure out what it is we're doing and tell Mom on one of her weekly calls from the rehab, even though he doesn't seem to pay any attention to us since Dad got a T.V. for the bedroom where he can watch movies and play Xbox. And mostly I worry that when Mom comes home, we'll have to go and live with her and that will be the end of everything.

One night, sitting with Dad at our computers I work up the courage to ask him.

'You know how we have to go to the rehab for family time this weekend?'

'Uh huh.'

He's looking at a slave inventory on his screen and he zooms it in bigger.

'What if they say we should go back there – when she comes home? Back there to live I mean.'

He turns to look at me, takes his glasses off. The laptop screen lights up half his face.

'Is that what you want?'

'No!' I shake my head. 'I like staying here – it's awesome. I totally want to stay! Especially since the two bedroom is ready next week and I get my own room.'

'Good. So that's settled then.' He smiles. But it's not totally settled, not yet.

'But what if they make us? What if they say we have to live at home? That she'll drink if we don't come back?'

He closes his laptop and the room is nearly dark. I love it this way with only the lights from the riverboats and New Jersey across the water.

'When we go there this weekend, one of the things they're going to tell us is that we can't make Mom drink. Nothing we do can make her, just like nothing we do can stop her. So if you guys want to stay here, you stay here, that's it.'

He makes it sound so simple and maybe it is simple. Maybe it always was, maybe with Dad on my side, it can be.

'Sound good?' he says.

I smile. 'Sounds great.'

That night, lying in bed writing to E.L., I tell her all about the conversation with Dad and that there's no need to worry and that Dad and I have a really good chance of finding her, helping her. And it's only afterwards, when I've finished writing and I'm lying in the dark, that I think about Ryan and I wonder what he wants, if Dad has asked him. And I wish I hadn't thought about that because maybe he won't feel the way I do – and that means that maybe there is something else to worry about after all.

E.L.

Even though I tell Cassie I don't know the answer to her questions they make me get to wonderin' 'bout things. And when I get to wonderin', it like I can't stop. And I know I need to ask more 'bout my mamma and my daddy too. And there only one person I can ask 'bout things like that.

It night-time and we all in bed but I know by Charity breathin' that she ain't sleepin' yet. Maybe she stayin' 'wake for Big Bill to come in but maybe she ain't 'cause it seem like a long time since he come to see her in the night.

'Charity, you 'wake?'

She don't say nothin' but I know she hear me.

'Charity, there somethin' I want ask you.'

'Hush, child! There no need to wake the whole damn cabin!'

'Sorry, I jus' need ask you somethin'.'

'What?'

She turn over so she on her side, facin' me. I face her too. The white part of her eyes look big in the dark. We so close, it like her breath is in my mouth. Now I got her 'tension I scared 'cause maybe even if I get the courage to ask her, what if she ain't got no answers?

'What the Master name?'

'The Master?'

'The Master. What his name?'

'What you askin' 'bout the Master for?'

I tell a lie. In my head I ask God to forgive me.

'Miss Ellen told me that my last name the same as her name 'cause all the slaves have the Master name.'

Charity don't say nothin'. She jus' watch me and breathe in the dark.

'That true, Charity?'

She close her eyes, open them 'gain. 'It true and it ain't true. B'fore we came – b'fore we came here – we had our own daddy's names jus' like Miss Ellen has a name from her daddy.'

'So it ain't true then?'

Somewhere on the other side of the cabin someone moan. Maybe Rose or Linda. But it a sleepin' moan, no one wake up.

She shake her head. 'Sometimes the truth and the lie, they get mixed up.'

What Charity saying, it important, and I want to und'stand it, to make sure I get it right.

'So I have a name from my own daddy and that the truth and I got the Master name and that a lie?'

She look at me but she don't answer that question, she answer 'nother one instead. 'The Master name Carthy,' she say. 'That make your name E.L. Carthy. Your mamma, she Sophia Carthy. My name Charity Carthy. B'fore that your mamma and me we got the name Black.'

'So b'fore my mamma come here, her name Sophia Black?'

Charity nod. She smile.

'And what 'bout my daddy? His name Black too?'

She stop smilin'. 'I don't know much 'bout you daddy, E.L.'

'But if he on the same plantation as you and my mamma, then Black his name too? It have to be.'

She nod. 'I guess you right.'

'E.L. Black.' I whisper it but not too loud. It don't sound like my name. I try 'nother one. 'E.L. Carthy.' It sound better.

That when I think of 'nother question that Cassie ask me b'fore.

'Charity, what E.L. stand for?'

Charity face change, she look diff'rent – scared.

'Why you askin' all these questions all a sudden? E.L. stand for you. I a'ways done told you that.'

'I jus' wonderin' if it short for somethin' else, that all.'

Charity take a second to answer and when she do she whisper quieter than ever.

'Your mamma – she want to call you Ellen. And for a while she do but then Miss Ellen come 'long so she done had change it. So she name you E.L.'

It take a second for her whisper to get into my brain in a way that I can make it make sense.

'So my name use be Ellen Carthy but now it E.L. Carthy?'

Charity nod.

'And that my true name? Or my lie name?'

Charity reach out and she hold my hand tight, like what she gone say important.

'That your name, E.L,' she say. 'E.L. Carthy your name. Maybe it won't make no sense to you yet but sometimes, lies, they said so much that after a while it's like they true. That there so many lies that there ain't no way sometimes to tell the diff'rence b'tween lies and the truth. You und'stand?'

I ain't sure I do but I nod anyway 'cause it important to Charity and I want to und'stand. I think 'bout Cassie and I wonder if it lyin' to Charity, not tellin' her ev'rythin' that in my head.

Even as I lie there with Charity, holdin' her hand, I thinkin' 'bout what it gone be like to tell Cassie my whole name. Even though it a lie name, and it don't feel like my name, maybe she gone be please 'cause maybe it make it easier for her find my daddy, or for my daddy to find me after all.

CASSIE

I'm sitting at the kitchen island eating Honey Nut Cheerios and reading *The Great Gatsby* when Dad comes in. He's already in his suit for work even though I'm still in my pyjamas. Ryan is in the bathroom and even though he won't hear anything over the shower, Dad lowers his voice.

'I just got an email back from the Schomburg Center,' he says. 'They can see us this morning!'

'Wait. What?'

He's smiling; it must be good news. 'Remember, I told you? The library in Harlem that has a research centre. Where all the black history stuff is: books, photographs, even films.'

Now I remember. I've never even been to Harlem. 'You think they'll have stuff about slavery?'

'Absolutely. I asked the guy on the email. They have books and everything and a huge photographic collection.'

'You can see the photos?'

'Yes!' His smile gets wider. 'They have the originals – so many of them. We'll tell Ryan you're running a fever and we can get ready when he leaves for school.'

'What? We're going now? Today?'

'The appointment is for this morning! Ten thirty.'

'What about you? About work?'

'I just checked and there aren't any meetings that I can't cancel. I'll have Sylvia reschedule them. There's got to be some perks of being the boss.'

He winks at me and I can't quite believe I won't be going to school. Ditching school is the kind of thing Grandad would encourage but not Dad, never Dad, but then this version of him is new, different. Fun.

'Come on – hurry up. Get back in bed before Ryan is out of the bathroom.'

'He can't come?'

Dad raises his eyebrows. 'You're kidding, right? First of all he'd be bored out of his mind and, second, we can't risk him telling your mom. You know she'd flip out.'

I know Dad's right but it's funny how even after all the other lies I've told, lying to Ryan about this somehow feels worse. He knows I'm faking, of course he does. As my brother it's his job to know.

'I can't believe you're falling for it,' he says to Dad. 'She's *totally* not sick.'

'The thermometer says she is, buddy. She's running a fever of 101. You'll need to keep an eye on that, Cass, and if it gets higher call me.'

Dad's face is totally deadpan and he doesn't give anything away as he goes into the kitchen to rinse the thermometer under the water before Ryan can ask to see it. He looks at me and rolls his eyes. I pull the blanket up to my chin and try and look sick.

'Faker,' he says, but not loud enough that Dad can hear.

Dad leaves at the same time as Ryan and while they are both gone I get dressed. It's exciting not to be going to school, more exciting to be going somewhere to find out more about E.L. and I wish I had time to write to her about it but then Dad is back and we need to go.

We get the 1 train to the 2 and it gets up to Harlem really fast. Tonya from school is always going on about Harlem because her grandmother lives there. According to Tonya 125th Street has everything now – all the chain stores, Starbucks. According to Tonya everyone lives in Harlem these days.

The further uptown we get the more the train empties and by the time we get to 135th Street where the Schomburg Center is, Dad and I are the only white faces. Crossing the street to the library the wind is the coldest type of New York wind and Dad puts his arm around me a little bit. Inside it's like a furnace and the lady at the coat check waits patiently while we strip off all our layers. She's black, just like the lady at the security desk, and when we get to the third floor to the research centre the tall young guy with glasses who helps us is black too – in fact, so far we're the only white people I've seen in the whole building.

He hands us a tiny form to fill out where we get to choose which of the files from the slavery collection we want to see. They have names like *Runaway Slaves, Instruments of Torture, Plantation Life* and Dad is watching me, waiting for me to nod before he ticks each box.

'You think it's okay, us asking for all this stuff?' I whisper.

'Sure, why not? I don't think there's a limit.'

'No, not that.' I'm hoping Dad will get what I mean without me having to say it.

He frowns. 'What, Cass?'

'You know, they won't think it's weird or something…'

I trail off and his face clears.

'Oh, you mean because we're white?' He says it too loud, I wish he'd keep his voice lower. 'It's history, Cassie, it's part of all our history.'

Once we get the boxes, I am calmer. Everything is organised in folders and something about the order that makes me feel better. There are newspaper articles and drawings and photos all covered in clear plastic with a description on the back and a numbered sticker in the corner in case you want to make a photocopy.

Dad takes the box about slave auctions and sales and I take the one about plantation life.

'We can swap over at the end,' he says. 'Unless there's something in my box you want to see? As you go along show me anything you think is important, that might matter.'

I don't know what I want to see. What matters. Right now it feels like everything matters. I'm only hoping I might know it when I see it, that I might feel it.

'I don't think I'm going to need to see the auction one,' I say. 'E.L. was born on the plantation, so there won't be any record of her.'

'But it might help us find her mother. Didn't you tell me that her father was from the previous plantation she was on? That means she must have been pregnant when she was sold.'

Sold. The word catches me – the casual way he says it. I wait for it to catch him too, but he moves right past it like it is any word. He's still in his work clothes and he's put his glasses on now so the documents are reflected back in them. I imagine him suddenly at board meetings, business lunches, calm and in control. And that's when it hits me, that he's approaching this like any other work project, that our hunt for E.L. is just another job.

He pushes a page across the table to me. 'See here? It says when a woman was pregnant. Look.'

It's a copy of a newspaper clipping advertising a slave auction. He points to the line that says 'negress with child'.

Negress. I don't know if I'd heard that word before there, certainly never seen it written down. And the pages are full of words like that:

'mulatto', 'negro', 'overseer'. Words that are not part of my world, but were parts of E.L.'s.

I take a deep breath, try and focus on why we are here. 'You think we might be able to track her dad down? Like, if we found her mom, we might find a list of the men on the plantation and one of them would be E.L.'s dad.'

'I guess it's possible,' he says, 'I mean, you never know.'

The idea of that makes me excited. Imagining how I can ask E.L. to ask Charity for his first name. And if we find a matching name I'll have something to bring her – something concrete.

'That would be so cool – you know, if we found out who he is and we could help reunite them.'

Dad takes his glasses off. They've already made dents at the top of his nose and he rubs them with his fingers.

'What do you mean reunite them? Her father would be long dead, Cass.'

Immediately, I backtrack.

'I didn't mean reunite, I guess I just meant—'

Dad holds his glasses, looks at me. 'Every one of these people is dead, Cassie. No matter what we find here, whatever we uncover. We can't change anything that happened to E.L.'

I nod. 'I know that. Of course I know.'

A line comes in my head from *The Great Gatsby* that I'd read earlier, about not being able to change the past. It's Nick the narrator, he says it to Gatsby, who just laughs and says that of course you can. And I realise that Dad is still looking at me with a strange expression on his face so I start to take the folders from my box and put them in little piles along the table and eventually he goes back to his own.

The Great Gatsby is only a book, a novel – what Gatsby says about being able to change the past is something a writer made up. Just because it's printed in a book doesn't make it true.

But even as I'm opening the first folder I'm wondering what if it is? What if he's right? What if there's a way that you can?

***

The morning goes really fast and it's nice – that first part of the day – sitting next to Dad with the wind outside, doing something together and separately at the same time. As well as photos and newspaper clippings, my folder has funny line drawings with titles like *Negroes at Home* or *Negroes at Rest*. In the drawings the slaves are smiling, relaxing around a fire – in one, a man is playing a banjo and the other slaves are clapping their hands. In another, a woman is reading to a circle of children sitting around her and I think of Charity hiding in the barn and the Mistress tying E.L. to a chair when she finds out she can read. I don't know who drew them or who they were for, but from what E.L. has shown me they are nothing like real life.

By twelve thirty Dad has been through four folders but I'm still on my second. He's been making notes in his laptop as he goes along – dates, details, statistics, names. He works fast – nothing he looks at seems to slow him down. From time to time he's checked in with me to see if I recognise a name but I haven't recognised any names. I haven't recognised any faces either from the grainy photos I've been examining. I've seen cabins like E.L.'s and horses and carts like E.L.'s and children sitting in the dust, next to upturned wheelbarrows and men holding ladders and women with baskets and bundles on their heads coming in from the cotton fields. I scrutinise every one for something familiar, something I know and even though everything is familiar, nothing is Riverside Hall, only places that look like it. I stare at each one, into each slave's eyes but somehow the more I see, the less I seem to feel and by the end I hardly feel anything at all.

'I don't know about you but I'm starving,' Dad says, closing his last folder. 'Want to hunt down some lunch and then come back?'

I'm not hungry but I'm glad to be getting out for a while. 'Sure, that sounds great.'

Dad goes to make copies of the photos I've been looking at while I go to the bathroom. I don't need to go but I need to have the time away from him, away from that room. There is no one in the bathroom and I stare at myself in the mirror, like I've been staring at the faces in the photographs. I don't know if I want to come back after lunch – if I ever want to come back – but Dad has organised all this, has taken a day off for this, so I know I have to.

I pull my notebook out of my pocket, go to the page where I left off last night.

Do you want me to stay here and find out more?

I haven't explained what I am doing, I don't even know if she knows, but the answer comes back straightaway, without hesitation.

Yes.

Back outside, it's even colder than before so we go to the closest place for lunch – a self-service counter with more hot and cold options than I've ever seen. Dad takes one of the big containers and talks nonstop about the 1860 census from South Carolina as he fills it with some of everything. I look around to make sure no one is listening while I half fill my small one with Caesar salad and some pineapple.

'Is that all you're having?' Dad says, when we sit down, his mouth already full of fried chicken.

'I'm not that hungry.' I push the salad around and I try and figure out what I'm feeling by breathing into my stomach the way Alice always tells me to. Dad's support is exactly what I've wanted all along and he's excited now, motivated to research more. Plus E.L. told me she wants me to go back too so maybe that means we are getting close to finding something important. So it makes no sense that I don't want to go back there, it makes no sense that I have this feeling – this dread, this fear – as if something terrible is going to happen.

Across from me, Dad points at my container with his fork.

'Eat up,' he says, 'you don't have to keep up the pretence of being sick. I mean, I don't think we'll bump into anyone from your school around here!'

He laughs. There is chicken skin caught in his teeth but I don't tell him.

E.L.

It been comin' a long time. Somethin' bad been comin' – somethin' worse – ever since my firs' day in the cotton field, the day that Charity got put in the stocks. Maybe it been comin' since b'fore then.

Charity don't pick the way she use to no more. No matter how much Nagle beat her, cuss her out, lash her – it don't matter. Ev'ry night, when they put her basket on the scale, the number less than the number the day b'fore.

Ev'ry night she get beat. Ev'ry night Nagle tell her that she done better work harder tomorrow only when tomorrow come, Charity don't work no harder, no matter how hard they beat her. The more they lash, the less she cry. And ev'ry night after they done, we pick her up off the floor where she lie in her own blood and me and Big Bill help her to the cabin. Ev'ry night now, Rose ready with the brine and the washcloth and sometimes Charity beat so bad she don't even cry out no more, she jus' lie and while Rose try and clean her, me and Linda and Nelly and Marjorie sing to try and make her soul better even when her body broke.

The night Nagle bust into the cabin we singin' Swing Low Sweet Chariot. I r'member 'cause it one of my fav'rites and I close to Charity ear and I singin' all the words. Nelly see him firs' and she gasp and stop singin' and then we all look over. He look big in the cabin – tall. He got somethin' in his hand, somethin' I ain't never done seen b'fore. It a metal collar but not like the one the slave trader use. This collar thicker, heavier – it look like it go all the way from the bottom your neck to right under up your chin. And comin' out from the thick iron this collar got long spikes that stick out from e'vry angle all the way 'round, that make it look like some class of wheel.

Linda start cryin' out, 'no, no!', and she pull Marjorie b'hind her and go into the far corner but it ain't Marjorie he after or Linda neither. Nelly get up too and then even Rose get up and creep back to the others so I the only one left next to Charity. I gone stay with her no matter what they want do – that what I think – but then Nagle kick me outta the way and Pete push past me. Together Nagle and Pete sit Charity up, Nagle hold her neck while Pete fasten the collar 'round it. It so heavy when they let go her head fall down onto the ground and I scream out 'cause I think her neck gone snap like a tree twig.

Nagle turn 'round and crack me cross the face with his hand. 'Shut your mouth or you'll be next.'

The pain sudden and it shock. It been a while since I got beat, I been pickin' more, pickin' faster. The slower Charity pick the faster I pick like maybe it help her get fast too only it don't. One time Big Bill catch me emptyin' some my sack into hers and he make me put it back and tell me to never do that 'gain. But even though my face hurt bad, lookin' at Charity on the floor with her poor beaten back and the metal collar like a wheel that mean now she can't even lie down prop'ly I know I ain't got nothin' to be complainin' 'bout.

When Nagle and Pete there she don't make no sound but after they go she start makin' little cryin' noises. The noise she make r'mind me of the noise the cat made after they drown her babies in the river.

All night long Charity make those little cries. They ain't loud 'nough to keep you 'wake but that night no one get no sleep. The next mornin' I think Nagle gone take it off but he make her wear it into the field. It hot that day – the kinda heat make you itch inside your clothes when all you want do is sit with your legs in the river. I don't know how Charity walk with that collar – her body so thin it nothin' but bones and the collar so big and heavy she can't carry her head straight so her neck pull firs' to one side, then the other. She fall twice b'fore we even get to the field and the second time when Big Bill try and pick her up, Nagle give him five lashes right there even though he got a whole day's pickin' ahead of him.

She make it through the day. I don't know how she do but she do. She even get some cotton in her bag and not only what I put in there. She keep goin', keep pickin', even though by the time the day over there blood all down the front of her dress and even Nagle don't say nothin' when Big Bill lift her up and carry her in his arms to the barn for the weigh in.

They weigh her basket firs'. You can see it nearly empty, not even half full. She never got to teach me what the numbers mean but I know the size of the weights when it a good day and today it ain't a good day. I look at Charity but she ain't lookin' at the weighin' machine. She lyin' on the floor. Her eyes close.

It silent then in the barn. We all waitin' – for Nagle to roar, for somethin' bad to happen – but it seem like there nothin' bad that he can do that he ain't a'ready done. I sneak a look at his face and he mad, you can tell. But when he open his mouth to talk, he quiet.

'Take it off her,' he say to Pete.

'What? But she only picked–'

That when he get louder, start to yell. 'I said, take it off her!'

Pete move quick, he crouch down next to Charity and pull a key from his pocket. The collar make a creak b'fore it fall open and either side hit the ground hard so barn dust go up in the air. I think Charity gone sit up, roll 'way but she only lie there like it still on her neck or like her neck broke and I scared that maybe it is 'cause there lines of blood there where the collar been.

'Put it on that one.'

I lookin' at the blood on Charity neck, I ain't lookin' at Nagle so I don't see who he talkin' 'bout and it only when I hear Big Bill cryin' out that I turn 'round.

'No – you can't! Don't put that thing on her – I'll wear it, put it on me!'

Nagle lookin' at me. They all lookin' at me and Pete start walkin' over towards me and he got that heavy collar in his hand. Big Bill make a run at Pete and it take Walker and Sullivan both to hold him back. His face all dark and twisted up from the things he yellin' at Nagle but that only make Nagle laugh. And it like the whole world go quiet then 'cause I can't hear him laughin', I can only see his teeth, his mouth. And I don't hear Big Bill yellin' no more neither, even though I know he is. It like I can't see and hear at the same time and the only thing my mind see is Pete walkin' over to me holdin' that thing and it seem like he take a hundr'd years to get to me.

'No!' I scream and I go to run but it too late and Pete a'ready there, a'ready got hold my arm.

Big Bill still yellin', still pushin' 'gainst Walker and Sullivan. 'You ain't even weighed her yet! She did good today – look, you can see it!'

'I said, shut up!' Nagle lose his temper real bad then and he run over to Big Bill and beat him in the head twice, three times with the paddle. Big Bill try and make his hands go up to pr'tect himself but Walker and Sullivan still got them and blood start pourin' from his head.

I cryin' then, I ain't 'shamed to tell you. It too much, Big Bill bleedin' and Charity lyin' on the floor and the pain in my arm where Pete hold it too tight. Nagle wipin' the paddle on his pantaloons now to get rid of Big Bill blood and he smilin' but Pete ain't smilin' – he look scared like me.

'What are you waiting for?' Nagle say. 'Put it on.'

Pete open the collar wide like a mouth, put my neck inside. It heavy on my shoulders, even with his hands holdin' it. The metal cold. He hold it in place and reach for the key. He lock it but it big for my neck – too wide to touch the front and back at the same time.

'You idiot, not like that!' Nagle say. 'Any fool can see it's too loose for her. Make it tight – here, like this.'

Nagle throw his paddle down and push Pete 'way so he right close to me. The paddle nearly hit Charity and I see her eyes open, takin' in what happenin'. She try to speak but her voice nearly gone. 'No ... no, you can't,' she sayin', 'give it to me – give it back to me ...'

The louder Charity voice get the tighter Nagle make the collar. He twist somethin' so it touch my neck on the front and back and then the sides too. The metal hot now it so close to my skin. Jus' when it can't get no tighter, he make it tighter. I reach my hands up but there ain't no room for my fingers b'tween the metal and my skin.

'Please, Massa, stop!' It Rose yellin' that. 'She can't breathe – you're gone kill her.'

My chest move up and down too fast – like a fish gulpin' for air but there ain't no air. I open my mouth to scream but there ain't no sound.

Next to me Nagle smile. My neck gone be crushed. This collar gone break my neck it gone pull my head right off. On the floor Charity tryin' to stand up but she fall – she tryin' to say somethin' to me only I can't hear. I can't breathe. I can't do nothin'.

Right when I think I gone faint Nagle step 'way and Charity eyes lock on mine. And somethin' 'bout that – 'bout those two things – make jus' a tiny stream of breath come in.

Nagle fold his arms. Spit on the barn floor. He smile at Pete.

'Good job,' he say. 'That good enough for now. Right, who's next to be weighed?'

CASSIE

Looking back, the folder called 'Instruments of Torture' was always going to be tough going but I guess that's why they talk about hindsight being twenty-twenty.

At first, going through the drawings, the newspaper reports, the photographs, it's just like before and I don't feel much of anything. E.L. has told me about these things already or else she's shown me in dreams. I know about whipping posts and the Cat of Nine Tails and overseers on horseback and I leaf through the pages as if they are nothing, as if they have nothing to do with me.

One of the photos is face down and I flip it over. I know what it is before I check the description – I think I know – stocks with room for three sets of legs. I remember Charity, being stuck there all night, her neck skinny enough to fit inside the hole meant for a leg. I turn the photo face down again.

Dad looks up from the stack of photos he's going through. 'You okay, Cass?'

'I'm fine.' I smile, because even though my breath is a little shallow I am fine. I feel fine.

After the stocks there is a charcoal sketch of three young boys with ropes around their necks, strung up from the same tree branch. I turn it over quickly. The next is another sketch of a male slave, naked except for some underwear, lying face down on the ground. Three other slaves are holding him down and the overseer is standing next to them. I don't stop to see what it is the overseer is doing, I turn it face down along with the rest.

The next photograph is of something I've never seen before, something E.L. has never talked about. I pick it up and turn it to an angle trying to figure out what it is. It's some kind of iron collar with three crazy long prongs coming out at weird angles. Underneath is a description about how it was such an effective method of torture because when the slave was wearing it they couldn't lie down, couldn't sleep or even rest. And I can't tell you what more it said because it's right then I start to feel it – that choking feeling, like hands are closing around my neck, tight against my windpipe. The sudden panic of no breath.

'Dad!'

My voice isn't working but I must have made some kind of sound – let's say I did – because something makes him look over, push his chair back and jump into a stand all in one motion.

'Cassie! Jesus Christ! Cassie!'

I can hear him saying that, picture his face, but then the sound is going so I only see his mouth move. I can't hear him anymore and somehow my knees are on the floor and then my whole body and I don't know how I got there.

And Dad is leaning over me, his face close, his lips mouthing my name. And then he is yelling at someone else, someone I can't see. And that's the last thing I remember.

***

We are running through the field pushing back the long grass. It scratches our skin, our hands, our face. A long piece flicks back into my eye and makes it water.

Our breath is coming. Our feet hurt. Out in front our arms are black, thin. E.L.'s arms. I know what is coming next, I know where we are running, I know what is going to be hanging in the tree, but I don't look yet, I can't look until she looks. I know that now.

And right when I know she's going to look, she looks, both our eyes together, taking it in, the shape, slowly turning. And I know the shape is a body. I know that the shape is a woman.

The body slowly turns in the sunlight and I can hear my breath, the crunch of the corn under my feet. I can hear someone behind me, getting close, gaining on me. I can hear their feet, their breath, their voice – a woman's voice – calling out E.L.'s name.

But she doesn't turn around, we don't. We can't. And even though I want to turn away, to stop running, even though I want more than anything not to run towards this thing, more than anything not to see, I know that I have to. That I can't stop, that I have to see her.

And that's when I know. And when I do, I wonder how I could ever have not known.

Because it's clear to me then, as clear as the pain in the soles of my feet, as clear as the eye of the sun in the white hot sky.

The body in the tree, the woman turning slowly with her head on her shoulder. That woman is someone we know. Someone we have always known.

That woman is our mother.

***

I'm caught in no man's land between sleep and waking. Even when I open my eyes, I am still in the dream, some part of me is. My body is here, in this bed where it is freezing – so cold – and my eyes see someone at the end of the bed, in a chair, her head tilted back at an angle that looks like it hurts her neck.

Mom.

My mouth is dry, beyond dry. It feels like it is lined with cotton, cotton that's seeping every single drop of moisture from every cell in my throat.

There are noises – a machine beeping, the squeak of wheels on a tiled floor, voices. Mom stirs but her eyes are still closed. Behind her there's a big window with the blinds raised. The buildings outside are tall, not Brooklyn buildings, and behind them the sky is tinged with light. I don't know if it's morning or night, where I am, what part of the city. It's too much to try and work out and I close my eyes, start to fall into the dream again.

But something happens and my eyes spring open and all in one go I know what happened, I remember it all. And I know something terrible, something so horrific I can hardly even imagine it, has happened to E.L.

I push the blanket off me – it's thin, hardly more than a sheet – no wonder I'm so cold. As I swing my legs out I realise that I am attached to something – a machine, maybe more than one. Something is pulling from my arm, it hurts. Something is beeping.

Mom jerks awake.

'Cassie!'

There's a tube in my arm and if I'm going to move, to get out of here, I need to get it off and I'm pulling at the tape but it hurts. There are pads on my chest too – round ones with wires coming out and I pull at them instead and they come away, leaving long trails of glue.

'Cassie!' Mom's hands are on my arms, holding me down, pushing me. I push back; I'm stronger than she is. She turns her face away and yells louder. 'Nurse! Can someone help me? Nurse?'

Mom is stronger than I think she's going to be but I get some space between us, enough to take off more of the pads.

'Cassie, stop it! Stop! Nurse! I need a nurse!'

She's screaming now and the curtain pulls back like a magic trick and a black nurse in hot pink scrubs appears. Her whole face is a smile.

'Well, now,' she says. 'Look who's awake.'

I'm not sure how she does it but in seconds she gets Mom out of the way and me back down on the bed. With one hand she holds me down, while the other puts the sticky pads back on.

'Cassie, I'm Isabelle. You just woke up, you're in the hospital and it's understandable that you're feeling scared right now, but you just sit back there and relax and everything's going to be just fine.'

She moves slowly, deliberately. She has a softness about her that reminds me of how E.L. describes Charity and thinking about Charity makes me push against her again. The thing in the photo – the collar – has something to do with Charity. Is she dead? Is that what's happened? I grab for the tube in my arm again, but Isabelle's hand beats me to it and plucks mine away, holds it down on top of the blanket.

'There now – take a deep breath. That's right. And another. You're doing just fine. Your mamma's here. I'm here. Your daddy's been here and he's coming back soon. You're doing just fine.'

Mom is standing now at the end of the bed. One hand is rubbing her neck.

'I woke up and she was ripping all those things off herself – I didn't know what to do.'

Isabelle is plumping my pillows, slowly reattaching everything I pulled off. 'You did just fine. And she's going to be okay, she just got a little panicked – isn't that right, Cassie?'

'Shouldn't you call the doctor?' Mom says. 'She was having trouble breathing.'

'Dr. Mason's going to be doing her rounds very soon. Until then we might give her something to help her relax.'

'No – you can't! I don't want anything!'

They're the first words I've said and my voice comes out normal, not like the croak at the library. I try and sit up but Isabelle's hands are there again, soft and firm, pushing me back into the pillows.

'Okay then, if you don't want me to give you anything you got to show me that you don't need it – that you can relax on your own.'

Her hands fold my legs back into bed and tuck the blanket around them.

'You need another blanket? These ones are like Kleenex.'

I nod. 'Yes, please.'

When she goes to get it Mom is watching me, waiting for me to jump up again but I don't because I don't want a sedative – I know I need to keep my mind clear to get out of here, at least till Dad gets back, so we can help E.L.

'Here you go, honey.' Isabelle is back with two more blankets that she tucks over the first.

'I'm really thirsty. Can I get water? Or a soda?'

'Can she?' Mom says. 'Should we wait to see what the doctor says in case they need to do more bloodwork?'

'A little water should be fine – let me take her vitals and see what tests they want to do. Then we'll talk about a soda.'

I sit back, let her take my blood pressure, my temperature. I want to ask her what happened to me, how long I've been here, where Dad is and when he'll be back. Whatever happened must've been pretty bad for them to let Mom out of rehab. What if I've been in a coma for days? A week? What if E.L.'s been trying to get in touch with me – what if she needs me? My brain skips back to the research room, the pictures, the description and I feel my throat start to close like before but I take a deep breath.

Isabelle notices, pauses. 'Everything okay?'

'I'm fine. There's nothing wrong with me.'

She smiles that big smile again. 'That's right, baby doll – with that attitude you'll be back on your feet in no time.'

I smile back. She doesn't understand, none of them do. Just like before none of the tests they do are going to show up anything. I'm fine, there isn't anything wrong with me – I know that. But I know something terrible has happened. Something terrible has happened to E.L.

E.L.

That night the longest night. Big Bill carry me back to the cabin and lie me down on the floor. Rose and Nelly singin', the way we sing to Charity only I whisper for them to stop so they do. Charity lie down next to me on the floor and she put her hand on my chest real light.

'You gone be fine, E.L.' she say. 'You think you can't breathe only you can. You is. Don't panic – it only make it worse.'

I nod. I don't want to use no breath on talkin', even to Charity.

'Keep breathin', real slow. Like that. You and me – we breathe t'gether.'

So that what we do, all night, me and Charity, we breathe t'gether. Sometime even though my neck hurt like it gone break and my breath get panicky and fast, my eyes close, like my body want to sleep. And ev'ry time they jerk open 'gain, Charity still there and she still watchin'. She still breathin' with me. She don't leave me on my own.

Mornin' come and I think Nagle gone take the collar off, that it over now, only he don't take it off. He make me walk to the field the same way he make Charity walk. Even with Rose on one side and Charity on the other I only able to take two or three steps b'fore I need to stop and if it weren't for Charity and Rose I done fall on the ground. I hear Nagle close b'hind us on his horse and he laughin' and hittin' the ground near us with the whip. He laugh when we jump.

When we in the field Big Bill come over and try and talk to him. There bruises on his forehead and a gash on his cheek.

'Massa, please take it off the girl. She a good picker but she ain't gone be able to do nothin' with that 'round her neck.'

Nagle put his hand on Big Bill shoulder like they friends. 'She may be a good picker but she's not as good as this one.' He jerk his whip at Charity. 'If she picks more than two hundred and twenty pounds today, then the collar come off the girl.'

Big Bill look at Charity and she look at me. 'She still weak and beat,' Bill say. 'She ain't gone be able to pick two hun'red and twenty today.'

Nagle smile. 'Well she better pick it or die trying. 'Cause the girl ain't gone get out of that collar till she does.'

I can't tell you too much 'bout that day. Maybe I don't want to. Maybe that pain too much, the heat too much. I know I fell more than once. I know I black out and when I come to, the cotton tall all 'round me and the sun beatin' hard in my throat and my chest. I musta look bad 'cause Nagle 'llow Charity to give me water from the bucket but he don't let no one help me get up.

I know that sometime durin' the day I hear Big Bill and Charity talkin'. Arguin'.

'You gotta try, Charity.' That Big Bill's voice. 'You got to do your best by her.'

'You believe him? You a fool if you think he gone let her out – he ain't never gone let any of us out of nothin'.'

'You have to try! She only a child. Think 'bout Sophia.'

'I done nothin' but think 'bout Sophia ev'ry day my life!' Charity sound real angry now. 'You think I don't? You think I don't r'member what happen to her? I do this today and he ain't never gone stop usin' that girl to show his power over me. I do this today and Nagle gone do somethin' worse next time – he ain't never gone stop.'

After that I think Big Bill say that nothin' ain't gone change nothin' but I don't r'member real well 'cause maybe I black out 'gain.

Next thing I r'member after that is bein' in the barn and Nelly givin' me water that spill down my cheeks and onto my dress and she tellin' me they had to pull me outta the field on the cart 'cause I pass out and there ain't no way to wake me.

I lie on the barn floor and listen but I can't say nothin'. I don't know where my sack is, what happen to it or if I even picked any – I think I pick some. My head too heavy to pick up – it lie on one side like my neck broke and if I try to move it break a little more. Lyin' like this the door on a slant and I see ev'ryone else come in – Pete firs', then Sullivan and Walker then Big Bill and after him Jasper and Nelly and Benjamin. Charity last to come in and Nagle b'hind her. I can see a'ready from the way she carryin' her basket that it ain't as heavy as it been b'fore and I know she ain't picked anywhere near two hundred and twenty pounds. Her eyes lookin' all round the barn till she see me on the floor and then she look 'way. I close my eyes so I don't have to see if she look back 'gain.

What happen next, happen fast and slow – maybe I drift off for a second. Next thing I r'member Nagle shoutin' and Charity cryin' out and when I open my eyes Nagle there right above me and someone pullin' me cross the floor by my arm and I can't breathe and I know my neck gone break. I snap my eyes shut and pain 'splode then on my face – my chest – and when I open them I see the whip comin' down but closin' my eyes don't make it stop. People screamin' then and feets runnin' and pushin' and later Rose tell me I screamin' too only I don't know how 'cause I can't breathe. And with ev'rythin' happenin' I don't hear the horse outside or the sound of the barn door openin'. I only hear the silence that fall after that.

'What in God's name is going on here?'

That voice the Master. I want to see him but one eye is welded shut. I open the other one slow, jus' a slit but the floor the only thing I see.

'Nagle, I said what the hell is going on here? Answer me, goddamit!'

I never heard the Master shout like that b'fore. Nagle clear his throat.

'She's stopped picking, sir. Her weight – it's dropped up by half, more than half ...'

'The child?'

'No, sir. That one.'

'And beating a fourteen-year-old girl is your way to motivate her?'

The Master voice get closer and through my eye slit I see him crouch down next to me. His beard long today. He reach his hand out like he gone touch me but then he pull it 'way.

'Get this thing – this hideous contraption – off her! Get rid of it. Throw it in the bottom of the river! I will not condone this kind of thing – here – I will not ...'

The Master trail off and I mus' be dreamin' then 'cause for a minute I think he gone cry.

'But sir – the old master, he used to use it, he–'

'I am not the old Master! I don't care what he used or when he used it!' The Master stand up fast. 'This is my plantation now and if I ever see you using that ... that thing ... on anyone, for any reason, you're finished here.'

There silence in the barn – only the flies buzzing.

'Did you hear me, Nagle?'

'Yes, Master.' Nagle say.

I see the Master boots turn 'round on the floor. 'And get that girl cleaned up as soon as possible.' His voice gettin' further 'way now. I wish he stay – I want him to stay. 'I'm going to send some of the house slaves down to take care of her. And I don't want to see her back in the field tomorrow – or the other one either.'

It sound like Nagle gone argue but at the last minute he say somethin' else 'stead.

'Yes, Master.'

The barn door slam and outside I hear the horse whinny and then the sound of its hooves bein' turned 'round b'fore they gallop 'way. And then Pete there and he roll me over and do somethin' with his key and when the collar pop open it feel like the metal still there – that it still press 'gainst my throat.

'You and you – take her back to the cabins,' Nagle bark. 'Clean her up.'

Someone pickin' me up in strong arms – it Big Bill, I know his smell. There a hand on my forehead, it Charity hand.

'You a'right baby,' she say, 'we gone get you fixed up good as new. You gone be a'right.'

Her voice drift in and out like waves. I floatin' on the pain – on her voice – and I picture me and Charity in a boat, on the river, floatin' – up and down. Only then I r'member how her cotton sack a'most empty and how she look 'way from me in the barn and I change it so it me and Cassie in the boat, that we floatin' 'way t'gether to where she live 'stead. Far 'way from here.

'Cassie.'

I think I say it in my head only I musta said it out loud 'cause Big Bill slow down his walkin' to listen.

'What she say? You hear that?'

Charity stroke my forehead. 'She delirious. Poor baby. Let's jus' get her back to the cabin. She gettin' it even worse than her mamma use to.'

Big Bill start to walk 'gain.

'Well, let's hope she don't end up like her,' he say.

I hear him say that and I want ask what he mean. But b'fore I can, I fall 'sleep 'gain.

CASSIE

Dr. Mason is around Mom's age with a deep voice and permanent frown lines. When she comes to my bed she's surrounded by a semi-circle of medical students. She reads my chart and tells them that when I presented to the E.R., my heart wasn't beating.

'You're one lucky girl,' she says to me. 'Or a smart one, choosing to have this happen across the street from the hospital.'

A couple of the students laugh and she swivels around to look at them and they stop.

'I didn't mean that as a joke. If this girl had been a few blocks further away from a hospital, this story would have a whole different ending.'

Mom looks like she's about to ask a question but before she can Dr. Mason reels off a list of tests that they'll be running today. I know some of the names from *Grey's Anatomy*. I could tell her already that they're not going to find anything but I know that no one is going to listen to me.

'I was talking to the other doctor about the possibility of getting her transferred,' Mom interjects. 'Do you think that could happen before you run the tests?'

Dr. Mason's frown lines deepen. 'Transferred? Why?'

Mom fixes her hair behind her ears. Without any make-up she looks different, younger, and I wonder if any of them recognise her.

'We live in Brooklyn Heights, you see, and it would be ... easier, you know, to have somewhere closer. We have very good insurance,

I'm sure it would cover the ambulance ride, or we could pay for that out of pocket.'

Dr. Mason draws her clipboard up to her chest. 'It's nothing to do with insurance, ma'am. I'm sure it's very inconvenient having to come all the way to a hospital in East Harlem, but your daughter's health has got to be the priority here and she's not going anywhere until she has these tests.'

Mom's about to say something else but right then Dad appears around the curtain. I think he's going to be in his work clothes but under his jacket he has his old U Mass hoodie on, which I've only even him wear in the house.

'Dad!'

He nods at Dr. Mason and the students and comes right over to hug me around the wires and drips.

'How is she, doctor?' he asks.

'She's doing well – she's stabilised. We'll know more after today.' Even as Dr Mason answers, she's already moving away – they all are – to crowd around Mrs. Rodriguez in the next bed.

Dad pulls away, holds my shoulders. 'How are you? God, it's so good to see you.'

'I'm fine, Dad, I feel really good. I want to go home.'

He laughs. 'Did you hear that, Lou? She wants to go home! We'll get you home, Cass. We'll get you home as soon as we can.'

'Joe, can we have a word outside?' Mom says. 'I have to go to a meeting but I wanted to talk to you first.'

'Sure,' Dad says, 'I'll be right back, baby.'

Mom makes a big deal of kissing and hugging me goodbye, even though she says she'll be back after her meeting. I wish she would go home – at least for a while. I'm dying to get Dad alone, so we can talk properly about everything that happened. Dad knows what's going on, that E.L. is the one who's sick, not me. Dad will sort everything out, I know he will. But right when he comes back from talking to Mom outside in the corridor, the orderlies arrive with a trolley to take me for my first test – an angiogram.

'You'll be here when I get back, won't you? You'll wait, right?'

He smiles, squeezes my hand. 'Absolutely, honey. I'm not going anywhere, I'll be right here.'

And if he sees the tears that come into my eyes then he probably thinks it's because I'm scared about the angiogram but it's nothing to do with that. There's tears in my eyes because what he said is exactly what E.L. says – or what I hope she'll say, the next time I talk to her.

When they wheel me back to the room, Dad is in the chair by the window, looking at his phone. He stands up when he sees me.

'How did it go? Do you have any results yet?'

'It felt weird – but I'm fine,' I say, even though Dad is talking to the nurse and not me. It's another nurse – a Latina one whose name I forgot – and I wish it was Isabelle's shift instead.

'The doctor will come by later with the results,' she says. 'Depending on the results, they might order more tests.'

I try to catch Dad's eye and make a face but he's still looking at the nurse.

'But I thought they were doing a lot of other tests – my wife said they listed four or five.'

'It all depends,' the nurse says. 'The doctor will let you know.'

The nurse is clearly not going to give us any more information and I want her to go so we can talk on our own but she's much slower than Isabelle and it takes her forever to straighten up the bed and get all the machines back in place.

'You need anything?' she says. 'Water?'

'No, thanks. I'm fine.'

She checks her watch. 'You must be hungry. I'm going to check to see if you can eat yet – I'll be right back.'

I want to tell her I don't care about food but I know that'll just delay her so I only smile and say thanks. When she disappears, Dad sits down on the bed.

'How are you feeling, honey?'

'I'm fine, Dad, totally fine. Can you pull the curtain for a minute?'

'Sure.' He gets up and pulls it the full way around the bed. I know it doesn't give any privacy, not really, but it feels better somehow, being with just him.

He sits back down again, reaches for my hand, squeezes it. I squeeze him back.

'Dad, listen, how quickly can you get me out of here?'

'I know it's not the greatest hospital in the world, Cass, and we've been pushing to get a transfer but I don't think it's going to happen—'

I shake my head. 'Not a transfer, Dad. I mean *out of here*, out of here. We need to get back to work, we might not have much time.'

He frowns, looks confused. 'They're not going to release you until they know what happened with your heart. Didn't you hear what the doctor said earlier about the tests?'

I squeeze his hand tighter. 'Dad, come on – it's just me here. We both know what happened – that they're not going to find a thing wrong with my heart. Can't you sign a waiver for the tests or something?'

'Sign a waiver? Are you crazy? I'm going to make sure they keep you here until we know what the hell is going on.'

He's very convincing, I'll give him that. The sweatshirt, the blood shot eyes. I drop my voice to a whisper.

'Dad, come on. You know what happened – you saw it. It started when I was reading about the collar and I felt it, right then around my own throat—'

'Cassie—'

'It's just like the pain in my foot at the party was when E.L. got that lash in the cotton field. Or when the Mistress slammed the piano closed on her fingers. Don't you see? Something has happened to E.L. – something bad. I need to get in touch with her. I need to help her.'

He lets go of my hand, rubs his over his hair. He's got that look, the look he used to have when he didn't believe me – the one when he was scared of me – and I know that I should stop and let him speak, but somehow I can't.

'You saw it, right, Dad? You saw what happened? It was when I was reading about that collar – remember?'

'Cassie, listen, just slow down—'

'You saw me reading that part – I know you did – and you looked over to see if I was okay. And that's when I started to feel it; like hands, gripping my throat! I tried to pull them away – I remember that. You saw that.'

He's shaking his head. 'I saw you fall on the floor. I saw someone give you CPR … I saw things a father never wants to have to see.'

'Dad!' I reach for his other hand, the one still on the bed. 'Okay – I get that it freaked you out. Just bring the notebook in. I'll stay here for the tests if you can bring the notebook in – the one I had at the library. I can write to her, see what's going on—'

'Cassie.' Dad's voice is getting louder. Both his hands are on my hand now, squeezing it. 'Wait, take a breath, breathe with me.'

'—and once I know she's okay, then I can wait it out here. When we get home we can start to look for her again. Who knows, maybe this will help us find out more about her, maybe she's—'

'Enough, Cassie! Stop!'

He practically yells that part, holds his hands up. And I do stop. Swallow. My mouth is dry. My throat is sore. In the silence I can hear Mrs. Rodriguez's T.V. and I wonder how much she has overheard. When he speaks again, he's dropped his voice.

'Listen, we have to take this one step at a time, okay? There's a lot up in the air right now.'

'Like what? What's up in the air?'

'These tests – the results. We just need to take this one step at a time. We need to talk about where you'll be coming home *to* after you leave here.'

He says that last part in a rush, looks down at the blankets.

'What do you mean? You said ... you're the one who said I wouldn't have to go back to Mom's.'

He shifts on the bed. 'I know, I know what I said – but that was before. Before this.'

And then the penny drops; silently, slowly, I feel it drop.

'You don't believe me anymore, do you? You don't believe me about E.L., about what happened.'

'I didn't say that – I'm not saying that.'

'But you're not going to help me anymore.'

'Cassie, you're sick. You need help – a different kind of help than I can give.'

'I can't believe this. After all this, you're going to just abandon me? Abandon us?'

He's shaking his head. 'I'm here, Cassie, I'm not abandoning you. I'm right here!'

'Stop saying that!' I snatch my hand away and he tries to take it back but I won't let him.

He lifts up his glasses, wipes his eyes and I realise he might be close to crying. 'This isn't a game anymore, Cassie. Your heart stopped beating. Don't you get it? Your heart!' He's crying now, there are tears, right there on my dad's face.

I hit the bed, I can't help it. 'So that's what this was to you? A game? After all this time you don't even get it – it's not my heart that stopped, Dad, it's E.L.'s—'

'Fuck it!' He jumps up from the bed and for a second I think he's going to punch the wall but he hits his leg with his fist instead. I've never heard him say 'fuck' before. He takes a deep breath, unclenches his fingers one by one. 'Cassie please, just listen to yourself – just think about what you're saying.'

'You never believed me, did you? It was it all an act from the start, wasn't it?'

He looks out the window, at the rooftops, the buildings. He can't look at me. 'It wasn't like that, Cassie – I mean, I wanted to believe you. Fuck, I thought it might even help if you had an ally…'

I can't believe what he's saying. I don't want to hear it.

'… and I guess I thought – what if? You know. You hear of people having connections with spirits – dead people – all the time.' He looks up, behind his glasses his eyes are red.

'Like Grandad.'

'Sure – like your grandad.' He hangs his head. A tear drips off his face and onto the blanket. 'But it went too far – all this stuff about saving her, rescuing her. It went too far. If E.L. ever existed, she's long dead. I'm so sorry I encouraged you, that I took you to that stupid library. That was a ridiculous idea. I'm so sorry, baby.'

His shoulders are shaking as he cries. I want to hug him. I want to punch him. I want to run. I want to cry. He doesn't understand, he still doesn't get it and I'm about to tell him that but before I can the curtain is snatched back and Mom is standing there.

'Lou!' He stands up.

'Mom.'

She looks from me to him and back again. She doesn't say anything straight away and that's a bad sign. She has a packet of vanilla wafer cookies in her hand – the kind me and Grandad used to eat together – and she drops them on the bed.

Dad wipes his face with his hands. 'I don't know what you heard Lou, but—'

'Joe, can we talk outside?'

Dad looks at me. 'Cassie and I were talking, we haven't finished.'

'Now, Joe.'

'You can talk here,' I say. 'You can say whatever you have to say in front of me.'

But they both ignore me and he follows Mom out around the curtain.

As it turns out, I get to hear it all anyway – the whole floor can hear them, about how Dad has lost his mind too and that for once Mom thought they were in something together, and then Dad is yelling back, saying that they haven't been in anything together for a long time. And suddenly the fight is about her books and her book tour and Grandad is just coming into it when I hear another voice and then everything quietens down.

After that, I can't hear them but I don't want to anyway. Outside it is starting to snow, blowing in spirals up against the window. No one has thought to bring me in my music and if they had I'd put it on now, maybe I'd watch the flakes whirl and dance to Sigur Rós and pretend I'm in Iceland or the North Pole or anywhere except here. E.L. has probably never seen snow and she probably never will. The thought drifts in and right behind it is what Dad said, about her being long dead and that I can't do anything about it.

I pull the blanket up to my chin and the vanilla wafers Mom got me fall off the bed and onto the floor. Out of nowhere, I am suddenly starving and I want to reach over and pick them up – to eat the whole packet – and I would too, even though the stupid nurse never came back to say if I'm allowed. But somehow right then I can't muster the energy to lean down and get them, like it's all I can do to just sit there with the blanket bunched in my two fists under my chin.

It's all I can do to sit like that and not move and just to keep my eyes on the snow.

E.L.

The next mornin' I hear the bugle call but I can't hardly open my eyes. One eye stuck shut, the other open a slit. My whole body feel like it pounded into the floor. I r'member the collar and I take a panic breath, put my hand to my neck but it ain't there no more. It only feel like it still there.

'It a'right, E.L. You lie down, rest.'

That Charity voice and I see her outta my one eye – her hair fallin' down 'round her face. She smile but I don't smile back. I think of her empty bag of cotton and I close my eye.

'That's right, baby. You sleep more. We ain't goin' near no cotton field today.'

When I wake up 'gain, Linda there and she got some cornbread and a small pot of coffee. She grumble 'bout havin' to bring them down with so much else to do, why the Master say Charity ain't got to work today neither. Maybe I shoulda been wonderin' 'bout that too but I ain't wonderin' 'bout nothin'. When she leave, the cabin quiet and Charity sit b'hind me and prop me up 'nough so I can lean into her and eat some cornbread. We ain't never had the cabin jus' to ourselves b'fore and I wish yest'day never happen and I ain't never seen the way she look 'way from me 'cause if it ain't for yest'day this feel like the best day of my life.

'You still mad at me, E.L.,' she say when I'm done eatin'. 'Don't say you ain't.'

Even though it hurt, I push myself outta her arms, wiggle so I down on my plank 'gain.

'I don't blame you bein' mad. You should be mad. I mad too. It break my heart to see what he doin' to you.'

'Then why didn't you do somethin'?' The words come out b'fore I know they gone to, all raspy. My throat hurt. 'You coulda stopped him.'

She move 'round the front of me, down on the floor to where I can see her, her face close. She cryin'.

'E.L. I'm so sorry. I wanted to. You don't know how badly I wanted to. But I knew my pickin' ain't gone stop him. It only gone make it worse.'

I try turnin' my head but my neck hurt too much. Ev'rythin' hurt. I close my eye.

'If he knew that you bein' in that collar – that hurtin' you – would make me pick more or pick faster, that what he gone do ev'ry day. Don't you see? He use you to get to me 'cause he know how much I love you.'

She ain't never said that b'fore and even now it make some part of me feel better. Till I r'member it ain't true.

'Stop lyin'. You don't care 'bout me none.'

'E.L., open your eyes, look at me. I love you like you my own daughter – don't you und'stand that? Nagle do. He know ev'ry time he hurt you it hurt me twice as bad – you think he don't?'

'You ain't my mamma.'

I know sayin' that gone hurt her and I think maybe that gone make me feel better only seein' the hurt in her face, it only make me feel worse.

'Maybe I ain't, but I made your mamma a promise and I been doin' my best to keep it. And even if you don't und'stand now, you will when you older. Love a dang'rous thing E.L. If Nagle know for sure how much I love you then that the end, for both of us.'

She sound sure, but how can she be sure? It hurt to talk but I got to. I got to know.

'But he coulda killed me. Blinded me. You woulda let him.'

I cryin' now – tears comin' outta both eyes even the one sealed shut. She reach over, touch my neck. Her fingers gentle.

'I know the Master ain't gone let that happen. I know that he diff'rent than Nagle – diff'rent from the Mistress.'

Her fingers find the place in my neck that hurt real bad and they press so it feel better. I don't know how she a'ways know where the pain is and how to make it better, but she do.

'How you know he gone come?'

Her fingers press and let go, press and let go.

'I told Marjorie to tell Miss Ellen to tell him. But I ain't sure we can trust her so I tell Little Bill to tell him too. I pray that it gone be a day he ain't drinkin' too bad – that Little Bill see him in the stables.'

Her fingers like a rhythm, playin' me, and I don't know how the same fingers can be so gentle and so strong at the same time.

'But even if Little Bill tell him, how you know he gone come?'

'I jus' know, that's all.'

'But how? How you be so sure?'

What she say next come out all in a rush. 'I didn't plan on tellin' you like this – today ain't exactly the perfect day but maybe there ain't no perfect day.'

There silence while I waitin' for what she gone say next. And somehow I know what her words gone be even b'fore she say them.

'I knew he gone come 'cause he your daddy. The Master your daddy, E.L.'

Her fingers keep movin' on my skin, kneadin' like Juba knead the dough for bread. The rhythm the same like nothin' change, but right now ev'rything change.

'I don't know if you gone be more mad at me now, for not tellin' you b'fore. I was a'ways gone tell you. I was jus' waitin' till you older. But you plenty old 'nough. And in case anythin' happen to me – you need to know.'

'What 'bout my mamma ...?'

I don't know what I askin', I ain't sure, but Charity, she know.

'Your mamma love him. She thought he gone make her a free woman – he promise her that. And I think if he braver – if he ain't relyin' on the Mistress for money – maybe he woulda. Big Bill say that the Master love your mamma too and he known him his whole life.'

So Big Bill know too, course he do. I wonder who else know 'bout the Master bein' my daddy. Juba? Linda? The Mistress? Miss Ellen? Could Miss Ellen know?

'I think Master love you too – much as he can. He the one who insist your mamma call you Ellen, after his Mamma. You the firs' Ellen – till the Mistress had Miss Ellen and that made you E.L.'

Love a dang'rous thing. That what Charity say b'fore and her words come back now. It time to ask what I a'ways want to – what I think I know.

'What they do to her? My mamma?'

Charity fingers stop kneadin' and then they start 'gain. I close my eye and soon as I ask I think maybe I want close my ears too but no, I want to know. I have to.

'The Mistress knew – course she did. The woman a'ways know. She was so jealous of your mamma. She hated her. Your mamma – she was beautiful. Big eyes – jus' like yours. Light skin, like you too.'

I try and picture her face – I want to. I nearly can.

'I never trus' that woman. I r'member Sophia so please when she tell me she ain't gone be in the fields no more, that the Mistress ask for her 'specially to be her house slave. I knew somethin' up. The Mistress try so many times b'fore to punish her – make Nagle give her more lashes than anyone. Even set the dogs on her one time. Sophia, I say, you know you can't trust her. Sophia, I tell her, you watch your back.'

'What happen?' My voice a whisper.

Charity pull me closer into her. It hurt but it feel good too.

'She wait till the Master 'way – in Charleston. And then one day she say her ring stolen – it gold with a ruby.'

I picture the Mistress hand on the piano. I know the ring. Charity fingers still now 'gainst my skin.

'Nagle make us all line up in front of the house – field slaves and ev'ryone, even the chil'ren – you there too with Marjorie and Benjamin. And they make us empty our pockets and when we through with that they search the cabins. They found the ring in your mamma's blankets.'

'She took it?' I know the answer – I think I do – but I want to be sure.

'No!' Charity sound mad. 'Your mamma didn't take no ring. The Mistress – that bitch – she plant it there. She do it when we all line up, I bet that's when she do it. After they find it, Nagle and his mens string her up from one of the trees on the other side of the creek. Nobody 'llowed near her. When the Master come back – she a'ready dead.'

I close my eyes. I r'member the day Charity get mad when we washin' our dresses when I ask why we don't ever go to the other side. And I r'member somethin' else too – I think I do – runnin' through grass, my feet sore. Runnin' to get to her. My mamma.

'I'm sorry, E.L., I'm sorry that it happen. I'm sorry I the one who tellin' you all this but it seems to me you old 'nough now. It seems to me you got to know.'

I try and nod my head but it too sore to nod so I don't say nothin' else and Charity, she don't say nothin' else neither. I wait to feel somethin' – hate maybe – for the Mistress and Nagle or love for the Master – my daddy – but lyin' there so close to Charity in the quiet cabin, I don't feel nothin'.

'Cept for the pain it like I don't feel nothin' at all.

CASSIE

Have you ever felt so panicked about something, that it's all you can think about? That it changes everything, even the way you breathe? That night, in the hospital bed, is like that. If you saw me from the outside, I'd probably look okay, normal. And all the tests results are saying that too, but inside, things don't feel normal. Inside, I am panicking – I have convinced myself that E.L. is going to die. Or worse, that she's already dead.

On the other side of the curtain Mrs. Rodriguez's T.V. is blaring *Jeopardy!* and I know that I should turn my T.V. on too, that I should watch something – anything – but I don't. All day I had visitors and I wanted to be left alone and now they were gone I wished they were here.

Mom brought Ryan in after school and it was nice to see him but he hardly said a word the whole time. He perched on the window ledge instead of getting a chair and held his book bag on his lap. When Mom was in the bathroom I asked him if I could borrow a notebook and a pen and he looked out the window and acted like he hadn't heard but I know he did because he held the book bag tighter after that.

When they left Dad came in and he brought my laptop and the Harry Potter I'd been rereading but not the notebook from the library which was the only thing I'd asked for. I picked at my dinner and hardly said a word to him and he barely spoke to me either and after an hour was up he said he had to go to check in at the office and kissed me on the head and left.

The commercial break comes on Mrs. Rodriguez's T.V.. Only 7.10p.m. I can't just lie here for the next four hours thinking about E.L., panicking about E.L., and I think that's what makes me take the laptop from the nightstand. The stupid hospital is supposed to have Wi-Fi but like everything else it doesn't seem to be working and even if I could get online I know already that Dad will have cancelled our Ancestry.com account. But it's boredom that makes me open it – that and the hope that if I start writing something down it might make my panic stop.

There's a Word document already open – a half-finished geography assignment – and I close it down, open a new one. I type fast on the bright, white screen.

Where are you? I need you. Please. I need to know you're okay.

The cursor blinks. This is stupid. I know how stupid this is but I keep doing it anyway.

I'm in the hospital. That's why I haven't written. I can't leave the ward, no one will get me anything to write to you. They think I'm sick but I'm not sick. But I'm scared because I think you might be – I think I'm sick because something happened to you, because something is happening to you.

I take a breath. Writing it out makes me somehow feel better, like there is a little more space inside. I want to read back over what I wrote but it's hard to see with the shine from the neon strip light overhead so I tip the screen forward, closer to me, push it back again. And that's when I see it. See her.

It happens so fast – just a flicker on the screen – it might have been nothing, it might have only been my imagination. I pull the screen towards me, push it back again. Nothing. I do it again, slower this time. And she's there again.

You'll probably think I imagined it, when I tell you what I saw. You'll probably be like everyone else and think it was the drugs they had me on, or some weird reflection from the lighting. But I can't control what you think, I can only tell you what happened. I can only tell you what I saw.

Right there, in the screen where my face should be, is another face: a young black girl with wild hair and big eyes. Behind her I catch a glimpse of trees with moss hanging, smoke in the air from a fire. She is there and then she is gone. It's just me again.

I look around to see if anyone else saw but of course there is no one there, only Mrs. Rodriguez and *Jeopardy!* on the other side of the curtain and even if the curtain wasn't pulled closed she's probably asleep by now. My fingers fly over the keys – I am a musician, playing an instrument. I am triumphant. I am in control.

E.L.! I see you! I just saw you! Can you see me?

The cursor flashes. No words come. I push the screen back and forward again but this time it is only my face, my reflection. I try again.

E.L. I know you're there. What's going on? Talk to me! Answer me! I've been so worried.

There's a noise from the hallway – voices – and I am ready to slam the laptop closed but they pass by and no one comes in. I sit, my fingers poised over the keyboard. And when they finally move, it's as if they are being moved for me. They move slowly, letters coming up one by one, as if by magic.

I hear you, Cassie. I'm right here.

A whoop comes out of me – an actual whoop – I can't help it, and it's so loud one of the nurses could hear but right then I don't care.

Energy ripples through my body and I want to rip the blankets back, to jump out of bed, to dance, to punch the air, leap around the room, to grab Mrs. Rodriguez, shake her awake, tell her everything's going to be okay, that everything *is* okay.

But I am attached to two machines, so I can't do any of those things. Instead I take a breath and start to type. And when I start, I can't stop. I type and type and type and tell E.L. everything that's been happening – about the library and the hospital and the tests, all of it. The words keep flowing out of me and I tell her everything, every tiny detail I can think of except for what happened with Dad – I don't tell her about Dad. And when I'm done, I ask her questions too, about Charity and Miss Ellen and the Master and everything that's been happening but she doesn't answer. She doesn't write back.

Jeopardy! is long over by the time I've finished writing and *Wheel of Fortune* is over too and there's some reality show on Mrs. Rodriguez's T.V. And staring at the flashing cursor I feel lonelier than ever and more than anything I wish that E.L. would write and tell me everything too. And writing this now I see the irony, that how only a year ago this is what I wanted – this silence in my head – but now, when I have it, turns out it's not what I want after all.

A lot of time must pass because the nurse comes in and turns off Mrs. Rodriguez's T.V. and takes my vitals and the laptop turns itself off and E.L. never answers. I lie there a long time that night, before I fall asleep. I wish I had a pen and paper because I want to draw her face – the face in the screen – the shape of it, the wide set of her eyes, her wild hair. She looks different than how I'd pictured her in my head – I'd always imagined her as older, darker skinned, not as pretty. I've known her for what feels like a long, long time and now I get to see her too. And I guess that's the night the idea starts for real – the idea of getting back to her.

Even if Dad hadn't let me down I don't think I would have told him that. I knew it sounded crazy. But Grandad wouldn't have thought it was crazy. '*You'll see me again*' – that's what he'd said that day on Brighton Beach and for the millionth time I wished I'd asked him more about that, how it worked and what it would be like. Why wouldn't it happen like this? Why wouldn't it follow that if I could hear E.L. that I could see her too?

Books were full of ways you could enter different worlds, not just the Tír na nÓg books but the Narnia ones and even Harry Potter. If I could see her, I was getting closer – it meant the connection between us, between our worlds, was even stronger than I'd realised. If I could see her, I could get back to her. I didn't know yet, how I was going to make it happen, only that I had to.

No matter what Dad said – no matter what anyone said – I knew that if I could get back to her, then I could help her. And when I got back to her, I was going to set her free.

E.L.

I shoulda known. I shoulda known when Linda come back down 'gain, this time with some hot water and some soap and a rag. Charity think it for me – to clean me up – but Linda say that the Master say it for her to clean herself with and that she got a new dress for her too.

Even then, I don't get it, not right 'way. That night when I go over it in my head – when I tell Cassie – I know that Linda know. That Charity know. That ev'ryone know b'fore I do.

Charity clean me up firs' – even though the water and the rag for her not me – she take care 'round my shoulders and chest where the worst stripes are. She gentle. And then she open the cabin door and take me out onto the porch so I can have some air. I watch her wash like I seen her wash a thousand times 'cept this time it regular soap and not slave soap and there 'nough that she can soap her whole body and her hair as well.

She don't care that I lookin' that I can see the white bubbles the soap make, the knot of lines on her back. When she all soaped up – b'fore she wash it off, she put her hands on her hips and smile at me.

'Look, E.L., I like some white lady over here. I look like the Mistress I so clean.'

And she make a face and I laugh 'cause she want me to, even though we both know she don't look nothin' like the Mistress.

Jus' when she finish and she gettin' into the new dress, that when we both hear the noise of the mens comin' on they horses through the trees. One voice shout and it sound like Nagle, only Nagle ain't never here durin' the day, he a'ways out in the cotton field.

'Charity?' I say. 'That Nagle? What he doin' here?'

'It a'right, E.L.,' she say. 'Ev'rythin' gone be fine. Come on, quick, get back in the cabin. We don't want him sayin' you ain't really sick.'

She move fast, she half lift, half drag me into the cabin 'cause I ain't really able to walk and all the time she sayin' how things gone be fine, only she can't hide it from her voice – the fear – and I know whatever comin', it ain't gone be fine. Nothin' 'bout this feel fine.

She take me to the corner furthes' from the door where there the most shadow as if they ain't gone be able see us. I hear the other voices now – two diff'rent mens and Nagle too and I know they gettin' closer. I can picture them in the clearin' where a few minutes ago Charity been standin' pretendin' to be the Mistress.

'Charity, what happenin'?'

'I love you, E.L. R'member that. I love you and your mamma love you and somewhere in that white heart of his, I think the Master love you too.'

'Charity? You talk like you leavin' – you can't go.'

She grip me hard on the shoulders – she forget how bad I hurt but I don't want to tell her. Her eyes big and there tears in them.

'Don't be 'fraid, E.L. Say your prayers – trus' in God. He on your side – he on all our sides.'

The door bust open then and the cabin fill with light. I see Nagle shadow, some other man b'hind him.

'What are you doing over there, hiding in the corner. Get up on your feet!'

Nagle's voice light, like it a joke.

'Come on, get over here, girl. I have some friends I want you to meet.'

'Charity?' I don't know if she hear me. I barely hear myself.

She grip the tightest b'fore she let go.

'Trus' in God. R'member to pray, E.L., won't you?'

Nagle comin' up b'hind her and she hear him and stand up. Her eyes streamin' with tears. My eyes dry. I nod. I want to tell her I know, that I know 'bout trus' and God and that I love her too but love dang'rous, so I don't say nothin'.

Nagle grab her arm, spin her 'round. The back of her dress still wet from her hair. She ain't even put it up yet and her other hand reach to push it up only he drag her too fast to the door.

'Here she is, gentlemen,' he sayin'. 'The best cotton picker in all of South Carolina.'

'If she's such a fine cotton picker, then why do you want to sell her?'

Nagle close the door b'hind him so I can't see but I hear his voice.

'She has sass, I won't pretend she don't. She's a smart mouth and she can be stubborn as that mule out in the yard. But the right discipline – you'll have her picking faster than any man. Just between us, I think the Master here's a fool to be selling her and to passing traders too. He's a soft touch – doesn't know how to get the best out of his niggers.'

They footsteps goin' down the steps – they voices gettin' further 'way. I push myself up onto one knee, then the other and I crawl 'cross the cabin. My knees hurt on the floor, my neck and front hurt and there blood on my chest, comin' through my dress but none of that matter, not then. They slave traders and they come to take Charity 'way. That all that matter.

I make it to the door, crack it open and they standin' there on the other side of the fire pit, Charity and Nagle and the two mens. One tall and thin and he standin' with his arms fold 'cross his middle. The other one smaller and mean lookin' and he stand further back. Nagle say somethin' I can't hear and Charity pull her dress up over her head, take it off. The smaller one come in real close. He walk 'round her – slow. He feel her arms, the top her legs. He open her mouth and put his fingers inside.

I don't want look but I don't want look 'way neither. Charity open her mouth real wide and I wonder what she thinkin', why she don't bite his fingers off. I open the door the full way and when I lean on it I can pull myself up into standin'.

The short one take his fingers out her mouth and Nagle say somethin' that make the two mens laugh, the tall one firs', then the short mean one. Standin' there, Charity close to me and far 'way at the same time. I test my legs, my feets and I able to stand 'nough to take one step, two. I make it far as the porch rail. If Nagle look over and see me he gone say if I able to stand then I able to work, only that don't matter, not then. All I thinkin' 'bout is Charity and if my legs gone work well 'nough to get me to the other side of the fire pit and what I gone do when I get there.

My foot on the step of the porch when she see me. The look from her eyes stretch b'tween us. She move her head, a tiny move that she want only me to see and only I seen it. What she say this mornin' in my head, 'bout how if Nagle know she care – that she love me – he use that. He use that to make ev'rythin' worse.

She want me to go back in the cabin that what she tryin' to say. She don't want me to see her like this. She don't want me to r'member her like this. I don't know how I know exactly what she mean but I do. I know it more than I ever known anythin' b'fore.

I don't say nothin' – don't mouth no last message. I don't call out her name. I don't smile. 'Stead of all that I turn 'round and lean my weight on the porch rail so I can pull myself back up and inside the cabin.

And I get there slow and when I turn 'round, she still there with the two mens and Nagle talkin' next to her. And I look for a second more. I ain't cryin' then, jus' lookin'.

And then, I close the door.

Part Three

CASSIE

I'm in hospital for four nights and when I'm finally allowed to go home, it's to Mom's. All the tests were negative, just like I knew they would be. There's no medical explanation for what happened, no one can figure it out, and I wonder if there is any little part of Dad that thinks about what I said, that believes me despite himself. But we've hardly spoken since that awful day – the day I found out he was faking all along – and I'm nearly glad to be going back to Mom's after all.

Mom and Ryan are the ones who come to get me and she's organised a car service that takes a hundred years to get from Harlem to Brooklyn Heights. Ryan may as well not even be there, he has his headphones on until Mom makes him take them off and even then he's on his phone the whole time.

Pulling up outside the house is weird, like it's way longer than a month since I've been here. Mom is acting all fake and happy, like it's some special occasion and when she opens the door I see a banner that says *Welcome Home Cassie* in multicoloured letters strung across the hall.

'Taa-daa!' she says. 'What do you think?'

But I don't have to answer because at that moment Angelina comes out of the kitchen, wiping her hands in a towel.

'Welcome home, Cassie,' she says. 'You look good! Very good.'

She smiles and nods like that will make her words true but it won't. I look like shit – we can all see I look like shit. My hair is too long and no one brought me in the wax I use and the first thing I'm going to do is get a haircut. The hospital food sucked, I barely ate any of it, and when I finally got to change out of the stupid gown they made me wear and put my jeans on, my belt buckle ended up going to the next notch.

'What do you want to eat, Cass?' Mom says. 'Angelina can make you anything you want. You want a sandwich? A tuna melt?'

'How about tacos?' Angelina says. 'Ever since you a little girl, you love my tacos.'

Ryan pushes in behind me, dumps my bag on the floor and heads for the stairs.

'Ry, bring that upstairs for Cassie, will you, please? It's too heavy for her.'

Ryan doesn't roll his eyes but he may as well have. His irritation is written all over him, the way he jerks the bag over his shoulder, takes the stairs two at a time.

'Mom, I can carry it, I'm not an invalid.'

'How about pizza?' Mom says. 'We could order from Capizzi's?'

I start to take my jacket off. 'Thanks, but I'm not hungry, maybe later.'

'I could go for pizza,' Ryan calls from the top of the stairs.

Mom pulls my arm free of my jacket. Hangs it on the rack.

'Maybe just something light? A cup of tea? Milk and cookies? If you want pizza later, we can order in then.'

Upstairs, I hear Ryan saying something but I can't make out the words. There's the sound of something being dropped on the floor, a door slamming.

'I think I'll just lie down for a bit, Mom. I feel really tired.'

'Hospitals are like that, they make you feel tired – especially when you come home. Why don't you lie down on the couch, rest down here?'

That's when I start to get suspicious. Right then. She hates people lying around on the couch, she's always straightening cushions around them, making sure the throws are at the exact right angle they should be and not actually used for any kind of comfort.

'That's okay – I'll go lie down in my room.'

The truth is I want to write to E.L., to make sure that writing back and forth on my laptop works here just like it worked in the hospital. And all I want is for Mom to leave me alone but she follows me up the stairs, talking on and on about what it was like for her coming home from hospital when she had me, when she had Ryan. When her and Dad were first married and she had a burst appendix.

Ryan has left the door of my room open, my bag halfway across the threshold. I'm bending down to pick it up so I don't notice right away. Not until I stand up, not until I am fully inside and I look around.

My room is not my room anymore. The bookshelves are bare, empty. Every one of them. My books are gone. Every single book is gone.

I whirl around expecting to be face to face with Mom but she has hung back, is halfway down the landing.

'Mom? What the fuck? What's going on?'

It slips out – the 'fuck' – Mom hates me cursing but for once she doesn't say anything. I step into the room, around the bag. The shelves are cleaner than I ever remember them, not a speck of dust. Where the books should be there are DVDs, ornaments, framed photos: me and Mom on the beach in Montauk, the four of us in Disney World, Gabi's tenth birthday party, the one where we were all afraid of the clown. On the low shelves someone has laid out my art stuff, paints and brushes neatly stacked next to my oldest teddy bear, my favourite after Betty. On the shelf second from the top, there's a new lamp with the head rotated down so it will shine on my desk. There is all of that, but there are no books.

Mom has followed me into the room, her hand is on my shoulder. 'Sit down, Cass, take a breath, it's okay.'

'You think this is okay? Where are my books? Nothing about this is okay, Mom! You'd better not have done anything with my books!'

Across the hall, behind Ryan's door, the music gets louder. Mom glances at it, like she might be going to bang on it but thinks better of it. She takes my hand, sits down on the bed and tries to pull me down to sit next to her but I stay standing.

'They're not gone – just in storage. We thought it would be a good idea—'

She still has them; she hasn't given them away. Hearing that makes it easier to breathe, but still I snatch my hand back from her. 'Who? Who thought it would be a good idea?'

'Alice did. She talked to me and your dad.'

I walk over to the closest shelf. The one where the Tír na nÓg books should be.

'Alice? Alice wanted you to ambush me like this? Without telling me?'

Mom stands back up, folds her arms across her chest.

'Well, she wanted to talk to you first – for us to talk to you. But there wasn't ever time at the hospital and I didn't think it was the right setting for that conversation.'

I laugh, I make myself. 'Of course you didn't, because you knew if you told me I'd never have come home with you. You'd better bring them back. I'm not staying here – I'm not sleeping here – until you bring them back, not for one night.'

Mom takes a breath, looks out the window and back to me. For a second I feel bad for her, being alone breaking Alice's news.

'It's not forever, Cassie, just for a little while. Alice thinks it's important. She thinks they are some kind of coping mechanism for you, that they help you distort reality—'

My laugh is real this time. 'Mom, they're books! They're supposed to help you to escape reality. That's what they're *for*!'

She bites her lip, holds my gaze.

'I mean, seriously? Doesn't it seem a little extreme – taking away the one thing I have left that I love? Like I haven't been through enough? Like we haven't been through enough?'

As soon as I say it – *we* – I wish I could take it back but then I realise she thinks *we* is us – me and her, the family. She doesn't know I mean me and E.L.

She fixes her hair behind her ear. 'Honestly, honey, it seemed extreme to me too. But when Angelina and I were boxing them up we found so many of those ... letters ... the ones to that girl—'

'Jesus, Mom!' I kick my bag on the floor, I can't help it. 'That's why I don't want to live here – I've got no privacy, I can't trust you!'

Her face gets angry then, hard and angry. I knew this calm facade couldn't last. 'Trust is earned, Cassie, trust isn't something you're just entitled to. You told Alice – you told me – you weren't writing to that girl anymore, you promised!'

'Whatever, Mom. So I promised. What about *your* promises?'

I push past her, over to the window. I am trapped with her, trapped in this room. I need air.

'What are you talking about?'

'Oh you know – the promise you and Dad made to stay married. Your endless promises not to drink anymore right before you crack open another bottle of wine.'

She follows me around the bed, pulls me around to face her and for a second I think she's going to hit me again.

'Take that back! I'm your mother – you've no right to talk to me like that!'

'Or what? There's nothing left you can take away from me, Mom. I can't write to E.L., I can't read my books – there's not even any photos of Grandad in here. You've taken everything that makes me happy, Mom. What else is left?'

I yell that last part, right in her face. We are the same height now, almost the same. A bit of spit lands on her cheek and she wipes it away with her hand and I see that it's shaking. When she talks her voice is too.

'Your father, your brother. Me. We're what's left. But obviously we're not enough. I don't know why I'm surprised. You've never made it a secret that I haven't been enough for you.'

She starts to cry, puts her hands over her face. I think of Dad in the hospital, wiping his eyes under his glasses. What's wrong with them, both of them? I shouldn't have to see them like this. It's not right to see your parents cry all the time.

'I know you loved your grandfather, but please, please stop hating me, Cassie.'

And right then I don't hate her. I feel guilty because she's crying, I want her to stop. I feel sorry for her, but I don't know if that's the same thing as loving her.

'I don't hate you, Mom.'

Her shoulders shake and she sits down on the bed. 'Even the way you say that – like a robot. You can't even come here and comfort me. Your own mother, and you can't comfort me.'

I know what I'm supposed to do now, to sit next to her and put my arms around her and tell her it'll be okay. But I can't make my feet move, I can't make anything move.

'How about a couple of books, Mom? Just the Tír na nÓg ones. And the photo of Coney Island – the one with all of us. How about just that?'

She takes a Kleenex from her sleeve, dabs her eyes.

'The ones he gave you – of course you wouldn't ask for books me or Dad got you.'

'Mom?'

'Do you have any idea what it was like, seeing him doting over you, teaching you how to read all those books? When I was a kid, he didn't even know what grade I was in. He probably didn't even know if I *could* read.'

And that's when I hear it, something I hadn't heard before.

'You were jealous? You were jealous of *me*?'

She blows hard into the tissue, laughs. 'God, I'd forgotten how simplistic everything is when you're sixteen. Of course I wasn't jealous!'

I'm about to tell her that I'm not sixteen yet but she keeps on talking.

'I always encouraged your relationship with him, didn't I? I let him move in here, didn't I? Included him in meals and holidays – let him spend time with you and Ryan.'

'You *let* him?' I can't believe she's saying that, the way she's saying it. 'He was your father!'

'Yes, he was. He left us without enough money to eat sometimes, he hit me and my mother and my sister. He could've killed you and your brother that time he left you alone but you're right – he was still my father.'

Something told me she was going to bring that up about that night, I was waiting for it.

'Come on, Mom – that thing with me and Ryan, it was no big deal.'

She looks at me, her eyes hard. 'You were four years old, Cassie, your brother wasn't even a year, and my father left you alone in this house. At night. Don't tell me it wasn't a big deal.'

I turn away from her, I can't listen to this. I hadn't even remembered about that night until I'd sneaked a copy of her book, fresh and new from the stack in her office, scrunched down on the floor between the bed and the radiator to read it. Reading what she wrote, that scene where her and Dad come home and find me and Ryan locked in Grandad's room, distraught and crying, I could almost have believed it. But Mom was a fiction writer. And I was four when that happened. Old enough to read, to go to school almost. Old enough to remember if it was as bad as the way she described it.

'If that happened the way you wrote about it, how come you let him stay? How come you let him babysit all those Friday nights after that?'

She shrugs. 'He was so ashamed when he sobered up. Got right back into A.A. He said it would never happen again and it didn't. After a while, I guess I wanted to forgive him, to give him another chance.'

And all of a sudden, the anger inside is like a wave. Watching her sitting there on the bed with her lap full of shredded tissue, like she's the one everyone should feel sorry for, not Grandad who can never clear his name, not me, with everything I love gone.

'Just get out, Mom, and leave me alone!'

She looks up at me shocked. 'What?'

'Forgiveness? Another chance? This is such B.S. There's nothing about forgiveness in your book, only anger. Only hatred.'

'No? You don't think that taking care of him when he was sick – when he was dying – was forgiveness? I could've sent him to a nursing home, but I didn't! I nursed him myself, I took good care of him. You can't say I didn't. No one can say I didn't.'

Right then, she's not just sitting on my bed anymore, she's in Oprah's studio playing for the camera and there's something I read once about actions not meaning anything if there's no love in your heart but I can't remember where I read it, and anyway the energy of the anger has gone out of me now as quickly as it filled me up. I don't even feel like I have the energy to write to E.L. anymore, all I want to do is lie down on the bed, to close my eyes and block out this room that is nothing like my room.

'I'm sorry, Cassie,' she says. 'I know this is a hard time. A terrible time, for all of us. But this too shall pass, you know. Whether you believe it or not, it will.'

This too shall pass. That's got to be an A.A. slogan or something she heard in rehab. Grandad had a dishtowel with some of the A.A. slogans on it – *First things First* and *Live and Let Live* and I used to like our game together, picking one out for the day, but when Mom says them they sound stupid, fake. Like she's just repeating something she heard but she doesn't understand it, that she doesn't get it at all.

I don't say anything and she must take that to mean that the argument is over, because she comes over and kisses me on the cheek before she leaves the room. And lying there I wonder how what started with me being mad at her for taking my books away ended up being yet another conversation about how badly Grandad let her down, how she can justify blaming him for something else that's happened years after he died.

The anger starts to flare up again, and I think I'm never going to fall asleep, but it turns out I do, before I can even take my sneakers off. And the last thing I remember is hoping that I'll dream of E.L. and that if I don't dream of her that I'll dream of Grandad.

But I don't. I don't dream of either of them. I don't think I have any dreams that night at all.

E.L.

I stay there two days. In the cabin. Linda bring me food from the big house that she say the Master tell her to bring. Nagle stay 'way – it like he forgot I there. Rose and Nelly ask me all the time how I doin' and if the pain any better and I say it better even though it ain't. And now that Charity gone I don't think the pain ever gone go 'way 'gain.

On the third day Nagle grab Marjorie and tell her she gone be in the fields that day 'stead of the big house.

'But I gotta look after Miss Ellen,' she say. 'I'm a house slave now, I don't work in no fields.'

Nagle laugh. The way he hold her arm look like it hurt.

'Not anymore, you ain't. They want that other little bitch in there now. The Mistress asked for her 'specially. It's back to the fields for you.'

Marjorie look at me like she hate me more than she ever hate anyone and Linda look like she hate me too. I want to tell them it ain't my fault. That I don't want to be nowhere near the Mistress nor Miss Ellen neither. Even the Master. What Charity tell me that day 'bout my mamma and the Master gone from being a smoulder in my head to bein' a fire and I don't know how to put it out. I don't know how to look at them and not show them that I know.

It take me a long time to get to the big house that day. I still only see out one eye and my chest and neck hurt bad and I gotta stop twice to rest. Once I stop at the tree where Dolly live and when I take her out it good to see her white broken face. It good to know she still there, that some things stay the same. If I ain't pleased to see Miss Ellen she don't look too pleased to see me neither. When I come into her room she sittin' lookin' at herself in the mirror.

'My hair's all knotty today,' she say. 'I need you to work all the knots out. I need you to brush it until it shines.'

That what she say, not even no hello nor nothin'. She don't ask what happen to my face, why my eye swell close or 'bout the bruises 'round my neck. I don't know what she need such shiny hair for but I don't say nothin'. I pick up the brush, start to brush.

'Ow!' She jerk fo'ward, hold her head. 'Not like that! You have to be gentle, E.L.– patient. Marjorie was very gentle, she took all the knots out without me even feeling anything.'

'Sorry, Miss Ellen.'

I start 'gain, slower this time. She wish Marjorie was still here and I wish she was too. When I look up I see both our faces lookin' back at me from the mirror. We nothin' alike – she white as a ghost with her long yellow hair. She got her Daddy's eyes but her Mamma's mouth and this mornin' she got it more than ever, the way it all twisted up into a pout.

Lookin' at her I stop brushin' and she look like she gone say somethin' so I start 'gain b'fore she can. I keep brushin' slow, gentle and I look up 'gain at the two of us. My face a diff'rent colour, diff'rent shape, my mouth diff'rent, my chin. Maybe Charity lied. Maybe she wrong. There ain't no way we sisters, me and Miss Ellen.

My daddy on the old plantation. The Black plantation. He still there. There no way the Master my daddy. Charity wrong. She got to be wrong.

'What are you staring at, E.L.? What's got into you?'

She sound like her Mamma when she say that and I look down, back to her hair.

'Nothin', Miss Ellen. Sorry, Miss Ellen.'

And I keep brushin'. I don't look up no more. 'Cause I don't want her to see me lookin' and 'cause I don't want to look, to see. 'Cause b'fore I look down I see somethin' I ain't never seen b'fore. Somethin' I might even been 'maginin'.

I seen our eyes. They ain't the same colour – mine brown and her eyes green, like the Master. But there somethin' else 'bout them – the shape, the way they set in her face and my face. They set the way the Master eyes set in his.

I don't know how I ain't never seen it b'fore but I seen it that day. Me and Miss Ellen we do got somethin' the same, well as our name.

We got the same eyes.

CASSIE

Taking all the books from my room just showed what a dumbass Alice was, how after a year of talking to her twice a week, she still didn't really know me. That must have been my first birthday ever where no one gave me any books but it didn't matter, I didn't care. What Alice didn't get, what Mom and Dad didn't get, was that I'd read those books so many times I didn't need to see the words on the pages anymore – they were there, in my head and I could read them any time I wanted.

Dad got me a new MacBook for my birthday, like his, but I kept it in its box and kept using my old one because on that one I knew I could write to E.L. and that she would write back. I changed my password every day, just in case Mom was trying to snoop through my files the same way she'd snooped around my room. I used crazy combinations of obscure characters' names from my favourite books, throwing in random capital letters and numbers for good measure. I memorised them instead of writing them down – I wasn't taking any chances.

So things with me were mostly okay around then but they were worse with E.L. – things were pretty bad. It was getting harder to connect with her, she wasn't writing back as much, or as fast. Anytime I brought up Charity and asked how she was feeling about her being sold she'd say she was fine and change the subject, but she wasn't fine, I knew she wasn't fine. I tried to cheer her up by explaining about time travel and how I was going to be able to come back for her, change things for her, but she didn't follow what I was talking about. I wanted to see her again, so badly, like that night at the hospital. The lights were different at home and I was convinced that was the problem and I had Angelina buy hundred watt bulbs, then eighty then sixty. I even tried candles but no matter what the lighting, the time of day, no matter what angle I put the computer screen at, I never saw E.L. there again.

'I can't keep buying light bulb,' Angelina says. 'Every day, a different bulb. These are expensive, cost money. No more light bulb.'

'Okay. I get it, okay.'

I thought about going back to the hospital, to the room I was in, in case that had something to do with it, but although I wasn't officially grounded, it felt like Mom had me under surveillance and it would take forever to get up to Harlem. There were only two places I was able to be other than at home unless I was with her – school or therapy. Even Dad's apartment was off limits it seemed. If it wasn't for my laptop I would've gone crazy.

When I wasn't writing to E.L., I Googled time-travel books, movies and theories. I kept a file and wrote down everything I'd ever learned about magical worlds, anything that could be important. There was usually a device or a key or some point of connection. In the Tír na nÓg books, Oisin gets to Niamh on a magic horse that can go across the sea. In the Narnia books it's through the wardrobe. In *Back to the Future* it was Doc's DeLorean. I didn't know what it could be with E.L., there didn't seem to be anything to hold on to – anything consistent.

One day on the way home from school I stop at one of the African stores on DeKalb and I'm drawn to a percussion drum on a stick with yellow and pink tassels and I'm convinced that's it, the key to bringing me back to her. That night I rub the stick in my hands like

I'm trying to light a fire. It's fun watching the drum beat back and forth and I rub and rub until my hands are raw and Ryan barges in and tells me to keep it down because some people are trying to sleep. And I do it more quietly after that, but still nothing happens.

In the end, it turns out Alice and Mom did me a favour getting rid of my books. If it wasn't for them, I probably wouldn't have gone to the school library, might never have read *Slaughterhouse Five*. It wasn't even top of my list, if you want to know the truth. I wanted to read *A Wrinkle in Time* the most and then all the ones about mirrors giving access to another world. But they didn't have any of those, so I ended up with *Slaughterhouse Five*.

I'm reading it that day in the cafeteria when Gabi comes over. Or I should say re-reading it because it was very quick to read the first time and I felt like I'd missed a lot. They were clamping down on the rule about no computers being allowed in the cafeteria at lunch, so it was just me and the book.

'Hey, Cassie,' Gabi says, standing in front of me with her tray. 'How're you doing?'

We both hear it – Cassie. She never used to call me that, always Cass-a-blanca, or Cass-a-nova or some other messed up version of my name, but it doesn't matter because we're not friends anymore by then, not really. We didn't have a fight or anything, it just started after Kirsten Silverman's party when she was dating Scott Stroller and I moved into Dad's. We weren't walking to school together anymore and I usually went straight to the subway afterwards so I could get a head start on our research. She'd texted a few times and I guess I forgot to respond and when I moved back into Mom's she never said anything about walking to school together again and I didn't either. She probably walked with Scott these days and, anyway, I liked walking on my own because it gave me time to think about any dreams I'd had and how to save E.L. I didn't care that Gabi didn't want to walk together anymore, but still, it would've been nice to have been asked.

'Hi, Gabi. I'm fine. Really good, actually.'

I'm at the best part of the book, the part where the Tralfamadorians are explaining to Billy about the fourth dimension.

'What are you reading?'

I turn the book over so she can see the cover. She smiles. 'Oh, I've read that. It's kind of weird, don't you think?'

She laughs like she's just said something funny. She goes over and back on her ankle the way she does when she's nervous. I don't know why she's nervous.

'I like it. I like the whole fourth-dimension thing.'

She scrunches up her face, remembering. 'Oh right, I think I remember that. Is that about how all of time is real, the past and the future and everything?'

Despite myself, I smile. Gabi is one of the only people I know who reads as much as I do. Some of her books might even have been in the ones that Mom packed away. I'd forgotten how much I liked comparing notes on books with her. And now I remembered, I missed it.

'Yeah – they believe time is like this mountain range – the Rockies or something. So the past and the present and the future all exist at the same time and we get to choose which part we look at.'

'Right.' Gabi is nodding now. 'I remember thinking it would be kind of comforting if someone had died. You know, to think they still exist in the past somewhere.'

I put the book down, pick up a cookie from my tray and break it in half. 'Well, they do. I think they do.'

She thinks about that for a second. 'Well, I guess they do – in our memories.'

I take a bite of cookie. She glances over towards the window and I see Tammy Davis sitting at a table on her own, waiting for her. They're BFFs now, it seems. Tammy is dating Scott Stroller's best friend so I guess it worked out all round. I chew, swallow.

'No, not just in memories. I think the past exists just like that. Just like the book says. That we can see it if we want. If we know how to look.'

I don't fully know if that's what I believe yet, but I like saying it to her, seeing how it registers in her face. She says what I know she's going to say.

'It's a book. Fictional. It's made up.'

I shrug, take another bite of my cookie. 'Maybe.'

Gabi's twisting over on her ankle again. 'Listen, Tammy's waiting for me. You want to come over and eat lunch with us?'

Leo Schultz and Justin Caldwell walk past, behind her, and they're sniggering. They think I don't know they all call me Crazy Cass behind my back. They probably sent Gabi over here, to find out what is going on, to get the latest update. Well, now they have it.

'No, thanks.'

'You sure? It's been ages. I miss it, you know. Hanging out with you.'

She shrugs, glances over at Tammy again who is making eyes at her to hurry up.

'You'd better go. Tammy's waiting.'

I could've told her I missed her too and it would've been true, only I couldn't say it, not then. And for a second as she walks away I wish I had, I even think about taking my tray and following her over there, but the moment passes and when I start to read then the feeling goes away just like I know it will. And I get so into the book this time that I miss the bell and I'm late for biology and when I try and slip in the back Mr. Connors looks up and says, 'Nice of you to join us, Cassie.'

The whole class looks around there's an obligatory ripple of laughter and when I catch Gabi's eye she turns back to face the front. I look away too, super quick – I was going to anyway.

I just wish I'd been the one to look away first.

E.L.

Cassie changin'. Somethin' changin' and I don't like it. It scare me. She say she can see me through some screen – some window. I don't know what she talkin' 'bout – it don't make no sense. I think maybe she mean the screen door at the big house but when I tell her that she laugh and tell me it not that kind of screen, she talkin' 'bout somethin' called a computer screen.

Computers sound like demon boxes and the more she tell me 'bout them the less I hear. It get me to wonderin' if maybe she a demon after all – that maybe she a bad spirit who can come though the screen and get me. At night it hard to sleep 'cause I 'magine wakin' up and she there in the cabin with me. When I sleep I dream 'bout her and she look like Miss Ellen sometimes and then in 'nother dream she look like Charity only she mad and mean and she won't look at me. I wake up and my heart is racin' and I hope I ain't been screamin' out nothin' 'bout no demon. Marjorie a'ready hate me 'cause I took her job at the big house and that mean Linda hate me too. They don't need no other reason to tell Nagle so he drown me in the lake like the woman at the plantation five mile over.

B'fore, when I talk to Cassie we go back and forth. She ask me questions and she listen and then it my turn to listen when she tell me 'bout her Mamma and Daddy and school. But now she don't talk 'bout nothin' else no more 'cept for these screens and how she gone get back here. So I don't tell her 'bout Miss Ellen – 'bout our eyes bein' the same in the mirror and what Charity tell me b'fore she go. I don't tell her that ev'ry time I seen the Master I 'fraid to look at him now but that

I don't need to worry 'bout that no more 'cause he gone to Charleson for the whole winter and that he ain't never done that b'fore. I don't tell her that the Mistress bein' nice to me and smilin' and that one day she let me eat the burnt part of the peach cobbler in the kitchen even though Juba and Linda both want it too.

And I don't tell her 'bout what Miss Ellen say in her room that day. That thing that sound like a warnin'.

Ever since the Master been 'way, Miss Ellen been practisin' piano with the Mistress. Ev'ry day she in there playin' and playin' 'cept when she stop and they fight. It don't sound good – the music – it don't sound like it do when the Mistress play. But then I don't like hearin' the piano no more anyway ever since the day I touch the keys. Hearin' the music make the pain in my fingers worse and I don't ever think I gone be able to forget that day.

This day I up in Miss Ellen room layin' the fire when she come in like a hurricane and throw herself on the bed, She cryin' like a baby.

I jump up.

'Miss Ellen, what wrong? What happen?'

Her head in her arms and she don't look up. Don't stop to breathe.

'Miss Ellen? You sick?'

I reach out like I gone touch her the way Charity touch me when I cry, only I stop. This Miss Ellen – she ain't my friend anymore, not like when we was small. *She your sister*, a voice say. Maybe it my own voice, maybe it God, I don't know. I hear it plain as if the words said out loud. But I don't pay it no mind neither and I keep my hand back.

'She hates me!' Miss Ellen say. 'I'm never going to be able to play like her and she hates me for it! She's always hated me!'

Then she start cryin' 'gain, real loud.

'Who?' I ask. 'Who hate you?'

'Mamma!' she say. 'Who do you think? She hates me even more than she hates you!'

It hit me like a punch when she say that. Even though I a'ready know it, some part of me been tryin' to forget. When she nice to me and give me peach cobbler it easy to forget.

'She drives Daddy away. That's why he's hardly ever here anymore. Who could blame him? Who would want to be around her?'

She keep cryin' then – wailin' – so loud that maybe downstairs the Mistress hear. Maybe that the point. I stand by the bed and I don't know what to do so I finish makin' the fire and then I light it. Miss Ellen still on the bed and she sniffin' now.

'You want me fetch some coffee?'

'No!' She throw her arm down on the bed. 'I don't want any coffee!'

'You hungry – you want me ask Linda to make you a san'wich?'

She roll over on the bed, stare at the ceilin' fan. 'No. I don't want a sandwich, E.L. I don't want coffee. I don't want anything.'

I nod. I 'bout to leave the room when she call me back.

'E.L.?'

'Yes, Miss Ellen?'

She prop up on her hand then, lookin' at me from the bed.

'Don't you ever want more from life?'

Her face all messed up from her cryin' and fussin'. Her eyes red. Eyes like my eyes.

I look down. 'What you mean?'

'Something different – you know, something exciting?'

'I don't know, Miss Ellen, I ain't never thought 'bout it.'

It the truth I tellin' her but her face look sad.

'Do you ever think about what it would be like not to be a slave? To be free?'

She startin' to sound like Cassie now and that scare me – like she see inside my head or somethin'. It like she know I been thinkin' 'bout it lately. Like I been wonderin' what it be like to live somewhere else, with Charity, maybe with Big Bill and Nelly and Rose as well. Somewhere there ain't no bugle ev'ry mornin' where we gets to sleep in beds like Miss Ellen 'stead of on wood. Somewhere there ain't no lashin' post. But I can't tell her none of that.

I shake my head. 'I ain't never thought 'bout it, Miss Ellen.'

She sigh, roll over on her back 'gain like I dis'ppoint her.

I think she finish and I pick up the coal bucket to fill it up and she call me back 'gain.

'E.L.? Be careful – won't you. I wouldn't like ... anything to happen to you ...'

She ain't lookin' at me. My heart like a hammer. She talkin' 'bout Cassie. She mus' be. She know that they gone find out 'bout my demon and drown me in the lake. But how she know?

'Be careful around Mamma. Won't you?'

She turn her head so she look over at me 'gain. My fingers hurt even though the pain there older than the pain in my eye, my chest. I think 'bout what Charity say: love dang'rous but there ain't no one to love. Not no more.

I want ask her what she mean but askin' too many questions dang'rous too.

'Yes, Miss Ellen,' I say 'stead. 'I real careful.'

I wait for a second, in case she gone say more but she don't say no more. So I go then and fill the coal bucket and try to stop worryin' 'bout what she coulda meant.

CASSIE

The first thing I remember is the feeling of the grass, tickling my cheeks. I am face down in the grass – it is in even in my nostrils. I pull my head away. Sneeze. I know immediately where I am: I'm not confused, it doesn't take time to register, I can't explain it but I know when I look around I will see her. And there she is.

'E.L.?'

I've only ever seen her face in the computer screen, that one instant, but I know it's her – even with her eyes closed and her hands half-hiding her face.

'E.L.?'

She's mumbling a stream of words I can't hear. I look at her hands and realise she is praying.

'It's me! E.L., it's Cassie.'

I sit up all the way and bang my head off something hard.

'Ow!'

I rub where it hurts and look around. We are in a cramped hot space, outside but enclosed, and at first I'm not sure where we are until I see the light coming in from one side and the wooden pillars going into the ground and I know we are underneath the big house. I crawl on hands and knees towards her, careful not to hit my head again. As I get closer to her I can make out what she's saying.

'Lord, God, Jesus, help me. Lord, God, Jesus, take this demon away from me.'

It's her voice, definitely her voice, outside my head instead of in it. I'm so excited I want to shake her. I want her to see me too.

'E.L.?' I'm laughing now, giggling. 'E.L. it's me! Cassie! Look!'

She peeks at me with one eye, when she moves her hand I see the other one is swollen, bruised, but it opens slowly too. They take me in and I look down at myself to see what she sees: red and navy plaid pyjama bottoms, the red matching shirt. Already they have grass stains, dirt marks from where I landed and where I crawled and I wonder how I'll explain this to Angelina.

'It's okay, E.L. I'm not a demon. Don't be frightened.'

I don't know why I am not frightened, why I am the one reassuring her, only she looks way younger than me. Her grey-beige dress looks much too big for her and the sleeves hang from her skinny wrists. Her hand is on her mouth and she pulls it away slowly. I wait for her to speak. When she does, it's a whisper.

'Cassie? That really you?'

I smile. 'It's really me! It's really, really me!'

Her face is even lighter than I saw in the screen and that horrible word from the library comes into my mind, 'mulatto'. She's pretty. Even with the deep frown lines on her forehead right now, even with her eye partially swollen shut you can see how pretty she is.

'Why you come? Why you here?'

I laugh again, I can't help it. I'm here – I'm really here! I wish we weren't in this confined space. I want to dance, to swing her around.

'I don't know! I don't know what happened – I was just asleep and woke up here. I didn't do anything different. Did you? Did you do anything different?'

'Shh!' She puts her finger over her lips. 'They gone hear you. Please don't let them hear you.'

I don't know why it hasn't hit me before then that if we're here, under the house we must be hiding from someone. But it's not until I hear the terror in her voice right then that I get it – that there are people looking for us, that any moment they could find us and we could be beaten or whipped. Or something even worse.

I can't swallow. I hadn't been aware of the heat before but suddenly it is all around me. It is too thick – too hot – to breathe. The more I try the less air there is. I open my mouth all the way but there is no inhale, no breath.

'Cassie, what happen? You a'right?'

E.L. is watching me but it's like she's frozen, like we both are. There's no air. What if I can't breathe here, in this time? What if I die here?

I must have closed my eyes because I don't see her coming over to me but I feel her hand on my shoulder, on my back, making slow circles.

'Just breathe. You a'right. I'm right here.'

It's better, with just her voice, sounding the way I know it sounds – the way it's always sounded. I focus on the weight of her hand, the feel of my butt on the hot ground, my breath coming in and out, fast at first, then slow. When I open my eyes her face is inches from mine. She smiles. Her teeth are yellow. Some are missing. But it is still a beautiful smile.

Overhead a door slams. We both hear it and it feels like we move closer together. There are footsteps, one set, two. A voice calling.

'Ellen? Ellen? Where is that girl? Ellen, come down here at once!'

I've never heard the Mistress's voice in our dreams but I know it's her. And I'm about to say that to E.L. but she has her fingers to her lips again.

Somewhere a door opens. Floorboards creak.

'Ellen – there you are. Ellen, this is Mr. Barrett. He's come all the way over from Valley View to see E.L. and now it seems she's gone and disappeared. Have you seen her?'

'Charmed.' A man's voice says.

'E.L.'s not for sale.' Miss Ellen's voice is more Southern than her mother's: a slow Southern drawl. 'She's my slave and, besides, my daddy's the only one who can sell or buy slaves. And he's in Charleston.'

'Now, Ellen. You're only fifteen, too young to know anything about buying or selling anything.' The Mistress's laugh tinkles like a piano. 'I only asked you because I thought you might know her hiding places. Ain't that the trouble with negroes, Mr. Barrett – never around when you need them.'

E.L.'s eyes are shut tight again and I'm pretty sure she's praying in her head. I wish I knew the words to prayers too – wish I could remember the one Grandad always used to say – but right then none come, so I squeeze her hand instead. She squeezes back twice, three times. A signal. When I open my eyes she's gesturing to the other side of the house to where there is more shadow, hardly any light. Before I can acknowledge what she's trying to communicate, she lets go of my hand, lies flat on her stomach and half-slides, half-pushes herself towards where it is darkest.

In my chest, my heart stops, that's what it feels like, the fear like it has actually stopped my heart and the flow of blood and oxygen to all my organs. I can't follow her – there could be all sorts of bugs over there, spiders. There could be snakes over there.

Above us there's another creak and the voices get clearer, closer, and I figure out that they are on the porch now, outside. It sounds like they are right over our heads.

'Little Bill, come here. Run and find E.L. and make it quick. Mr. Barrett here doesn't have all day.'

'Yes, Ma'am.'

Little Bill's footsteps are fast and light on the porch steps. He must work in the house, that must be why I haven't seen him in the field. Where the light is, I catch a flash of his movement, streaking past.

I lie down on my stomach and follow E.L., try to copy her squirm, remember not to lift my head up. The ground changes, it is damper, less grass, more dirt. My pyjamas are filthy, I'll have to throw them away when I get home – *if* I ever get home.

Ahead of me, E.L. has stopped short, so her feet are nearly in my face. Her soles are thick, like they have a whole other layer of skin and there is a little stone embedded into her heel with a crusted outline of blood around it. I think of the dream, the pain in my feet after I wake up, and I wonder could that be what she feels all the time?

We are in the darkest part of the shadow of the house now, where the rows of hedges block the light coming in. E.L. stops and sits up so she is leaning against one of the pillars that hold up the house. She curls herself up into a ball – points to another pillar and mouths something. I lean against it, try and fold myself up as small as she has but I can't. My elbows, my knees, all seem to stick out. I pull everything in as much as I can.

Above us, a screen door opens and I hear the rattle of teacups on a tray. I can hear voices but not words so maybe they are inside again. There is no sign of Little Bill. Please let him be running to the cabins. Please let him be looking for us in the barn. The thoughts in my head are like prayers and I want to tell E.L. that I am praying, that she has taught me that too but even as I am thinking that another part is listening to a sound coming from the other side of the house.

Footsteps. I look over towards the brightness and Little Bill is there – his shape making a shadow through the sun filtering in. I snap my eyes closed.

'E.L.?' His call is soft. 'E.L., you in here ain't you? I know you in here.'

I squeeze my eyes tighter, like me not being able to see him will mean he can't see me, and a memory floats into my head – one of my own – of playing hide and seek with Grandad, hiding under the kitchen table, eyes tightly shut even though I knew he was down on his hunkers, right next to me. When I opened them, he had been smiling.

'E.L., come on out now. The Mistress looking for you. Some white man want meet you.'

I want to open my eyes, to peek at E.L. only I can't risk it. Any moment now Little Bill is going to see me – how has he not seen me already with my red pyjama top and my whiter than white skin? I am like a beacon in this darkness and he's going to see me and they'll find her and she'll be sold to this Mr. Barrett and it'll be all my fault.

'You know it gone be worse if you keep hidin'. You know she gone find you and then she beat you more. And me too.'

Without any sight I can hear everything. The sounds of Little Bill moving in, underneath the house. It feels like I can hear it all – the smash of every blade of grass, the dig of his fingers in the soil.

'Don't make me come all the way in here, E.L! Just come on out now.'

His voice is so close he's got to be able to hear my heart. I've stopped breathing, that's what it feels like. There is no breath in my body. I am dying to pee. I am going to pee right here on the grass. I am going to die right here on the grass.

'Oh, sweet Jesus! Oh, God!'

I almost think that is my voice crying out but it's not – it's his, Little Bill's. There's a bang, something hits wood. His head? My eyes bounce open just in time to see him turn around, crawling fast towards the light on the other side. I smile, look over at E.L. and her eyes are open too but she's not smiling. Her eyes are fixed to the ground to where there's a snake swiftly slicing its way across the top of the grass, barely bending the blades as it moves towards us.

Overhead I hear a man's laugh. Loud, deep. A woman's light tinkle. Down here, there is only the swish of the snake. No breath. No air. I scrunch my eyes tighter, tight, tight, tight until they can't close anymore.

And then, they are open, just like that, as if I have no control over them and maybe I don't. Above me the roof of the house is gone. It's been replaced by a ceiling, with a slow turning fan. My eyes follow the ceiling to the wall – bookshelves with no books, only picture frames, a teddy bear. On the other wall a T.V., switched off.

Somehow I am back. Somehow I am safe. Somehow I am home.

***

I wake up to Angelina pounding on the door. She is yelling.

'Get up, Cassie! You going to be so late! Get up!'

When I open my eyes she is in my room, pounding around the end of my bed to the window. She rips the curtains back. I hate being woken up like this. Grandad used to wake me up by rubbing on my back so the first thing I saw when I opened my eyes was his smile and a cup of tea he'd made for me.

'You awake now? You sure? You not going to sleep more?'

'I'm awake!' I'm yelling too. 'Yes, Angelina, I'm awake.'

Satisfied, she whirls out back onto the landing and I hear her across the hall, hammering on Ryan's door. And it's only when I look down at my pyjamas – my red top and my plaid pants – that everything comes back to me, that I remember.

I check the knees for grass stains, the front, but there are none and pulling back the covers there are no tell-tale signs on the bed either. In the bathroom I pull them off and check all over but the pyjamas are clean – rumpled but clean. It makes no sense, they were covered in dirt when I was there with E.L. and a small voice in my head says maybe it was only a dream, maybe I wasn't there at all. I push that voice away. I was there – I know I was – I've never known how this works and I probably never will. But I know I was definitely there.

There's no time to write to E.L. before school and first up that day is some big math test. I want to write to her so bad I would flunk it but we're not allowed to have our computers open and there's nowhere to write except on the single sheet of paper that I have to hand in to Mrs. Miller at the end.

At lunchtime I'm close to going home. If I fake that I'm sick I can get on the computer, lie in my room and write to E.L. as much as I want. But, then again Angelina might call Mom, and she might come home or send Alice over or take me to the doctor. And with all that attention I'll never be able to write to E.L.; they might even go through my computer, to look at the files there. I just need to hold on, to get through the afternoon. In the meantime I go over what happened last night in my head – every inch of it. I was there, I know I was – it wasn't like the other dreams. I saw her, I spoke to her. I know she saw me too, I know she'll remember and then I'll know for sure it was real.

It's Mrs. Palomino's class when I finally get a chance to write to her because she allows us to have our laptops open, so we can take notes. We've finally got on to *The Great Gatsby* and I'm wishing I hadn't read it so far ahead in the semester so that I'd remember it better. Mrs. Palomino is at the top of the classroom, talking about Nick, the narrator and I act like I'm noting down what she's saying, but really I'm writing to E.L.

E.L.? Are you there? I need to talk to you. It's really important.

The cursor flashes. Mrs. Palomino is walking around now and I wish I'd sat in the back row but I always sit here, by the window. Today, Faye Thompson is sitting in front and you can smell her B.O. but I don't care because maybe that'll keep Mrs. Palomino away too.

E.L. I'm at school, I don't have much time. I need to know if you saw me. Did you see me last night under the house?

Ms. Palomino has asked a question about Nick, and how his perspective changes the story. She's looking around, no hands are up. I scrunch down small behind Faye. When I look back down E.L. is there – has already written.

That really you? You really came?

My heart dips and swoops. She saw me. I knew she had! I was there! I made it back to her! I knew it wasn't a dream! I start to type and then I back up, delete. What if she's repeating what I'm telling her? I need to find out more details – I need to be sure.

What do you remember? Tell me anything you remember.

I glance up. Kristen Silverman is answering Mrs. Palomino's question, or trying to. I could answer it better. E.L. writes back quickly.

You don't r'member nothin'?

I do! Of course I do. I just want to know what it was like – what you saw.

Mrs. Palomino is on the move again. 'That's right, Kristen, Nick gives perspective to Gatsby – to all of them – in a way that would be different than if the story was told from, say, Gatsby's point of view?'

There's silence. I wish someone would answer – keep her busy. Someone on the other side, near the front. On my laptop E.L. is typing, very slowly. I'm afraid to look down and then I do.

You just come from nowhere. You scare me – I don't know it you. You look like some white boy!

I feel the back of my hair. I just got it cut, it's short – shorter than usual. She keeps writing.

And you sure done jump when you seen that snake.

I look up, breathe in deep. Faye smells really bad today and I pull my T-shirt up a bit around my neck, dip my head so I can breathe in my own heat, my own smell. My hair, the snake. She saw me. She knows what happened. She really saw me.

Mrs. Palomino is coming down this aisle again. Justin Caldwell is talking about Gatsby's car – of course he'd talk about the car. She must have picked on him, he'd never have jumped in to answer on his own. She's five desks away, four. I have time. I have to be sure.

What colour was my shirt, E.L.?

When I look up Mrs. Palomino is looking right at me.

'Well, Cassie,' she says. 'Can you think of any more?'

In front of me Faye shifts in her seat. I have no idea what Mrs. Palomino is talking about – any more of what. But Justin talked about the car, so it must be some kind of symbolism.

'The shirts,' I say. 'Gatsby's shirts.'

It's a horrible gamble and I can't read her face as she walks closer to me, right up to my desk.

'Go on.'

'That scene where he has his shirts in every colour and he throws them all around – it's heightened more because we see it through Nick's eyes.'

She walks behind my desk, leans on the window ledge. I flick to another open Word document. The one with *The Great Gatsby* in big letters at the top.

'What do you mean by it being heightened?'

She could be luring me further into a trap, I might not be answering the right question – she might have seen what was open on my screen before I could change it. I keep my voice calm, definite.

'It's heightened by the contrast between Nick's own frugality – his own appearance. The drab clothes he wears.'

There's silence for a minute and I hope I'm right. Not just about the question but about Nick's appearance. His clothes. Maybe I'm wrong, maybe there's no reference to how he looks, to his drab clothes, maybe I imagined that. My heart thunders in my chest.

'That's right, Cassie.' She sounds almost disappointed. 'The shirt scene is a very good example.'

She stays there for ages, leaning against the window ledge right behind me talking on and on about the stupid shirts and then she makes Faye read out from the beginning, about hearing the parties on the other side of the water. And Faye takes forever to read it, keeps stumbling over words and the whole time I'm dying to switch back to the other document, to let E.L. answer the question but I can't so instead I try and concentrate on remembering to breathe.

Two minutes from the end of class Mrs. Palomino walks to the front of the room to write our homework on the board. My fingers act like lightning, flick back to the screen where the question is still waiting to be answered.

And I'm worried that E.L. might have gone, that we might have lost the connection, that she won't remember the question. So I ask it again.

E.L. – do you remember the colour of my shirt?

I glance up at the board, memorise the homework assignment so I can write it down later. She wants us to rewrite a scene from Gatsby's point of view. One of the options is the shirts scene.

When I look down again, my fingers have just finished typing. E.L.'s answer is clear, the last word on the page. Three letters that make my heart leap.

Red.

I glance back at the board. Gabi has her hand in the air, asking a question about the homework and Mrs. Palomino is answering her; she's not looking at me, no one is looking at me. And when I look back at the screen, it's still there, the simple word that proves I was there. That she saw me. That together we can change her future – that together we can change her past.

E.L.

I a'ready scared that day she come. I been scared since what Miss Ellen done say 'bout bein' careful 'round her mamma and I know it ain't a good idea to be hidin' under the house and in my head Charity voice there tellin' me nothin' good never come from hidin'. But earlier when I seen the buggy with the white man in the back drivin' up the driveway it like I know inside somethin' bad gone happen. And it seem like all I know how to do is hide.

So one minute there I is hidin' and the next I look 'round and she there – only I don't know it her, I think it some white boy, scarin' me half to death. And if the Mistress ain't upstairs lookin' for me I woulda scream my head off only I know she lookin' so 'stead I close my eyes t'gether real tight, start prayin'. I pray God gone take him 'way – this demon – that he only my 'magination. But when I open my eyes the white boy still there and he smilin' like no white person ever smile at me 'cept maybe the Master.

'E.L.,' the boy sayin. 'It's me. It's Cassie.'

It Cassie's voice comin' outta his mouth and I think maybe her spirit done got inside somebody else only then I look 'gain and I ain't sure no more it a boy. He wearin' pantaloons like a boy with hair cut short like a boy but when I close my eyes it Cassie, it def'nitely Cassie. I open my eyes 'gain and I see it her – it ain't no boy after all.

A noise come from upstairs and b'fore I can say 'bout bein' quiet she look up and her face go whiter than b'fore. She look like she gone be sick.

'What's happening?' she say. 'What's going on?'

She talk too loud and I crawl 'cross grass to be next to her and when I put my hand on her she tremble like she freezin'.

We need to get to the dark part of the grass that hidden from the outside. I know the Mistress gone send Little Bill to find me and he ain't gone come all the way under 'cause he 'fraid of snakes ever since he been bit and he ain't gone risk seein' 'nother one.

'Come on,' I say, 'over here.'

I crawl – show her how. She follow me but she make too much noise and I want tell her stop makin' noise but Little Bill a'ready gone runnin' down the steps so there ain't no time to say nothin'. I get to the pillar and when I sit b'hind it she sit b'hind the other one. I look at her 'gain. She dirty from crawlin' her hands – her clothes. In the dark of the shadow she look whiter than b'fore. She whiter than Miss Ellen, whiter than the Master. She white like milk. She jus' 'bout the whitest thing I ever done seen.

We don't talk, jus' like she told you, we jus' sit there. I sneak looks at her. When she don't see me lookin' she look scared but when she see me, she smile. Her face shine with sweat that make a river on her neck. She got silver rings in her ears – three on one ear. She see me lookin' and she touch her ear. She smile. She pretty when she smile.

Little Bill at the other side now – he callin' out for me. He know I hidin' here. He nearly sure. I know he don't want to find me but he gotta look. On the porch the Mistress talk to the white man 'bout how it hard to get good negroes these days and that she don't know where I coulda done gone. And right when that all happenin', that when Little Bill and Cassie see the snake.

It ain't no rattler or nothin' – only a grass snake – but I guess Little Bill and Cassie don't know that. He turn 'round like the ground on fire und'neath him – crawl back out fast as he can. She done worse – she jump up and start to scream. If Little Bill ain't gone hear her scream he gone hear the bang her head make on the bottom of the house but he keep crawlin' 'way like he don't hear nothin'.

'Cassie!' I call out in a whisper. 'It a grass snake, it ain't gone hurt you!'

But she still wailin' and carryin' on and more than anythin' I want her to stop 'cause any minute the Mistress gone hear her and come down and find us but jus' as I reach out to grab her arm she gone. Jus' like that, she diss'pear – jus' as quick as she come in the firs' place.

Upstairs the Mistress and the white man talk on and on, back and forth, the way white folks talk, like they don't hear nothin'. And Little Bill he gone too so it only me and the grass snake and the sound my heart so loud I don't know how they don't hear that too.

I hear Little Bill call my name but his voice further 'way now and I know he gone run to the woods to look there and then the cabins and then maybe he look by the river.

I close my eyes. That ain't smart in case any rattler come but I keep 'em close an'way for a long time. I picture her – the white girl, Cassie – in my head. The girl that no one hear, maybe no one see 'cept me. And I get to thinkin' that maybe it only my 'magination. Maybe no one never been here at all.

But when I open my eyes and look over the grass all crumpled and broke where she sit and I know she ain't my 'magination. I know she real.

And I hope she gone come back.

CASSIE

It didn't escape me, the irony, that after all my searching for ways to get back to E.L. – light bulbs and mirrors and the little African drum – that the way back there was like the first way I'd ever seen her: through a dream. And just like from the start, I wasn't in control of when I'd see her again and what would happen next, but that didn't stop me trying to be.

The way I figured it, was that if sleeping was my way back to E.L.'s world, then the more I slept, the more chances I had of getting to see her. So I start to spend more time in bed, more time sleeping. As soon as I get home from school, instead of having a snack, or doing my homework, I go to bed for a nap. I get up for dinner and go right back to bed again. Half the time I can't sleep though – that's the problem – I lie under the comforter and the more I will myself to sleep the more awake I am. But even when it doesn't work, it feels good to be doing something. It feels good to be trying.

One afternoon I am lying awake in bed debating whether to get up and just write to her instead, when through my closed eyelids I see the light in the room change.

'Cassie?'

It's Angelina. I don't say anything, breathe like I am asleep.

'Cassie? You okay? You sick?'

I keep breathing, force myself to keep my eyes closed. I sense her coming closer to the bed.

I feel her fingers on my forehead. Cool. Gentle.

'You feel a little hot. Maybe you have fever?'

I open my eyes. 'I'm not sick, Angelina, I'm fine.'

'If you fine, then why you in bed at four-thirty in the afternoon? If you sick I need to call your mom.'

I push myself up. 'Angelina, I'm fine. I'm just tired. Can't someone just be tired?'

It's only when I see the reaction her face that I realise how that must have sounded.

'Sorry – I didn't mean to snap at you. I'm just having a hard time feeling like I'm under surveillance by Mom, that's all. I can't even take a nap in peace!'

She turns her head to the side and I think she's going to leave the room without saying anything but instead she turns back to me.

'Your Mom love you. She good woman. She worry.'

She nods along with every word, like it makes what she's saying more true.

'I know.' I hear myself say it and at that moment I do know. 'But she doesn't need to worry, I'm fine.'

After that, I'm more careful. I don't have a lock on my bedroom door anymore but I wait until Angelina's making dinner or doing the laundry. On Wednesdays she calls her sister in Mexico and that's the safest time. But she's not really the problem. The problem is that it's getting harder to sleep – not just in the afternoons but at night too – like the more I want it, the more elusive it becomes.

Alice is the one who brings up how exhausted I look in therapy that day and that's what gives me the idea.

'You look exhausted, Cassie. Have you still been having those dreams?'

She scoops her skirt up underneath her, shifts in her chair. For a horrible second I wonder if I told her about seeing E.L. under the house but then I know she means the regular ones, the ones where I am in E.L.'s body.

'No. I haven't had a dream for ages.'

She nods, waits for more.

'I'm not having dreams at the moment.'

That's not technically true. When I do finally fall asleep when it's closer to morning than night, I feel like I'm falling into the same dream. It's not expansive, like the E.L. dreams or a whole story like the Grandad one; it's a claustrophobic dream with only a few details that I can't seem to remember properly. There's a closed door – a locked door – with a high handle and a baby crying in the background. And the room is full of a smell that catches in my throat; the smell of dirty diapers.

'Where did you go right then?'

Alice is looking at me, her head tilted to the side.

'What do you mean? I'm right here.'

I smile. I like that I can use E.L.'s words like that and no one knows, like a joke only we will get.

'You know what I mean, Cassie – in your head, you went somewhere else.'

I look out the window. Today the tree branches have flecks of green, buds. Soon they will be blossoms in another spring. My whole life is passing me by while I'm looking out these windows. My life is passing me by – and E.L.'s is – and all I'm doing is skirting around the facts with people who don't want to know the truth. And that's when the idea comes.

'I was wondering if you can prescribe me some sleeping pills?'

Alice makes that face she makes when she hasn't quite got something.

'That seems a bit extreme for right now, don't you think? It would be good to talk about what might be causing this first. Do you have any thoughts on that?'

I push back in my chair. Could Angelina have told her about my naps? Trying to sleep in the afternoon? I didn't think so, but you never knew anymore.

'No. I don't think so.'

'What about your books? Could it have something to do with that?'

I shrug. 'I guess, I mean I always read to fall asleep.'

She's taken to jotting stuff down in a notepad – she never used to – and she writes something down then.

'You know how we talked about learning to do things without relying on your books so much? This might be one of those things – finding new ways to do the same thing.'

Every time she brings up the books I remember that I can't trust her. And that's what makes me start to lie. 'But I have been. I've tried having a hot bath, chamomile tea. Meditation and breathing exercises like you've been telling me to do.'

She shifts in her seat. 'Really? You never mentioned that before?'

I shrug. 'I guess it never came up. But this sleep thing is getting to me. The other day, two girls in my class asked me to hang out in Connecticut Muffin with them and I wanted to go but I was too tired, I just didn't have the energy.'

She keeps her face the same but I know she'll like that. She's always suggesting that I make some new friends. I take a breath, go in for the kill. 'And I fell asleep during math class. I'm worried about getting further behind, you know – especially with college applications next year.'

She's writing frantically in her notepad now. 'Integration' is her favourite buzzword at the moment – getting back into my life, school, friends – so I know I am hitting all the right buttons.

'Have you talked to your parents about this?' she asks.

I laugh a proper laugh. 'You're kidding, right? Between filming for *Oprah* and her new book and A.A., Mom is hardly there right now and since I ended up in hospital it's like Dad's scared to be on his own with me – he always finds an excuse to have Ryan or someone else around.'

I hadn't realised until I said it, that that's what Dad was doing, but it's true. I look out at the trees, the tiny buds. It's the truest thing I've said during this whole session.

'If I'm going to prescribe a light sleeping pill I'd have to talk to them,' she says. 'I'd have to clear it with them.'

'Okay, sure.' I keep my face blank. I need to make sure that I don't look like I care too much.

'Especially since we decided to go with a new strategy, rather than being on the meds like you were before.'

I cross my legs at the ankles, make sure not to fold my arms. 'Listen, if you think it's risky or something, forget it. I mean you're the one who knows what you're doing here.'

'No,' she says. 'I'm glad you brought it up. Let me talk to them. I'll let you know on Monday.'

My heart gives a little jolt of hope. Monday is only three days away – I'm seeing her twice a week by then. Mom will go for it, I know she'll go for any suggestion Alice makes. Dad is the wildcard – he's the one to watch – but since Schomburg he's been pretty much doing anything Mom wants.

She nods to the clock. 'We're out of time for today.'

And as I grab my bag and skip down her steps, I'm smiling, full of energy. Because it feels that when it comes to me helping E.L. that might just be the best session that we've ever had.

E.L.

Cassie changin' 'gain. There somethin' bad goin' on – I feel it. When I go in my head to talk to her it like she ain't there, I can't hear her mos' the time. And those times she there, she don't sound like her. She keep talkin' 'bout these magic pills that gone help her come back and make things better.

She been talkin' bout those magic pills for a while now – sometimes it feel like it all she talk 'bout. I ain't seen her since the day under the house with the snake – that firs' day Mr. Barrett come – the day they don't find me. And things changin' but they they ain't gettin' better. Things gettin' worse. Things happen and I want tell her, but even the times she there it like she don't know how to listen no more.

I miss her. Sometimes I think I miss her more than Charity. Charity gone – I know that and I don't 'spect nothin' diff'rent. But Cassie, she still there, sometimes she is. And it like, ev'ry time, I hopin' she gone be like she was b'fore but then she start talkin' 'bout these magic pills and she diss'pear 'gain. And sometimes I wish she really gone – like Charity gone, like Mamma gone. 'Cause if someone gone they jus' gone. And it hurt less than someone who keep comin' and goin' 'way 'gain. Someone who you think there but who ain't ever really there at all.

CASSIE

Alice prescribes Ambien and we have a whole session about how addictive they are and what I should and shouldn't do and what to watch out for. She gives them to Mom to monitor for me, and she gives them to Angelina. Angelina's only supposed to give them to me once at night – before bed – and at first I save the bedtime one for the next afternoon, so I can sleep after school, but then when I wake up for dinner I can't get back to sleep when it's really time for bed so that's why I need to get my hands on more.

Looking back, I can see that it was a bad idea to ask Isaac Morton to get some more for me; I can see how it looked bad. And taking whatever else he gave me when he didn't have Ambien was dumb, of course it was. But at the time I wasn't thinking straight – I was hardly thinking at all.

Have you ever taken sleeping pills? Well you know how have that feeling in the morning afterwards? That sluggish feeling where your body is on go-slow and your brain is being dragged behind like a dead weight. Well, I was like that all the time. And it was weird because even though I was never fully awake it felt like I never had a proper sleep either.

If you talk to Mom and Dad, they'll tell you I was addicted – even Ryan might tell you that – but it's not true, it's not what happened. I wasn't addicted to it, that feeling, the way your chest kind of feels warm and your breathing slows down and everything is a little further away, not too far – just far away not to hurt so much. Sure,

I liked it but that wasn't what made me ask Isaac for the pills, what made me give him money, what made me steal from Mom.

I did all that because of E.L. I hope you understand that. I wanted to get back to her again, more than anything. Things were getting worse for her, getting bad. I was the only hope she had – I knew that, even then.

It didn't make any sense to me – sometimes it still doesn't – but I knew that I was the only one. The only one who she could talk to. The only one who could change things.

The only one who could save her.

E.L.

It my fault. I shoulda listen to Miss Ellen. I shoulda gone with her. But I scared 'cause I don't want get in no trouble with the Mistress. The Master still in Charleston so there ain't no one to stop Nagle puttin' me in the collar and I scared that gone happen 'gain. I think the collar the worst thing that can happen then. I don't know there worse things than that.

They fightin' – Miss Ellen and her mamma – and I in the kitchen. Linda and me, we cleanin' out the pantry closet and Juba at the sink washin' ev'rythin. Upstairs we all hear them yellin' but we don't say nothin'.

'You've no right, you've no damn right!'

'Come back here! How dare you? I'm your mother. Your mother! Don't ever speak to me like that again.'

'You can't do this without Daddy and he won't let you do this. He'll never let you do this!'

Linda look at me and raise her eyebrows but still we don't say nothin'. The other night I hear Marjorie talkin' to her 'bout how Walker say he seen Miss Ellen out in the barn tryin' to talk to Benjamin and how Big Bill tell Benjamin to stay 'way from her 'cause she trouble and there ain't no quicker way to end up a swingin' nigger than bein' caught with the Master daughter.

'Well, your father's not here, is he? And we need some more money while he's away in Charleston, drinking all of ours.'

I never done hear the Mistress say that b'fore – anythin' like that. I stand closer to Linda. We on the jars of jellies and sauces now and I carry them to the counter where Juba wipe them down and empty out the ones nearly empty a'ready and Linda clean where they been with a wet cloth.

There noise of steps on stairs and then Miss Ellen bust in through the door. Her hair flyin' ev'ry which way and her face hot and red the way it a'ways get when she been cryin'.

'E.L., I want you to come with me. You can do that later.'

I put down the jars on the counter, wipe my hands on my dress.

'Where we going?'

'I want to show you how to ride.'

Juba shake her head jus' a little, not 'nough for Miss Ellen to see. None of the slaves ride, not even Big Bill. Nagle say it often 'nough how the only place the slave has is in front of a horse leadin' it or b'hind, shovellin' its dirt. Never on top. And maybe it 'cause of that or maybe it 'cause of the system we got goin' – me and Linda and Juba – that I don't want to go with her.

Miss Ellen at the back door now, holdin' it open. Her eyes flick over to the other door, the one into the hallway that lead upstairs to where her Mamma is.

'Come on now, E.L. – we don't have all day.'

That when I make the mistake. If I say yes, I'da been gone a'ready by the time the Mistress come in the door. But I don't say yes. I wait. And then the Mistress there and it too late.

'E.L. – don't you take one step! You stay right here. I have someone coming over to see you and I don't want him to have another wasted trip after that fiasco the last time.'

My back still hurt from where Nagle beat me with the paddle the day I hide – the day she can't find me.

'Yes, Ma'am,' I say to the Mistress. When I look at Miss Ellen the red from her cheeks spread down onto her neck. She gone cry now, I know she is.

'Fine,' she say. 'Stay, like the good little slave that you are, E.L. Clean the pantry! Every jar, every shelf. Clean them good, you hear? Clean them all real good.'

She slam the door then and the Mistress slam the other door into the hall. And me and Linda and Juba all look at each other and they start to talk 'bout how Miss Ellen Daddy spoil her so bad it no wonder she run wild. And I listenin' but I don't listen too. 'Cause I 'fraid of whoever she have comin' to see me and why. Miss Ellen done yell that the Mistress can't sell me without the Master but what if she wrong? What if she don't know?

It a while later when we hear the buggy pull up outside. We finish the big pantry closet and a'ready move onto the small one 'round the corner. In my head I pray. I pray to God and to my mamma and even to Charity that the noise from the buggy gone be the Master comin' home even though I know it ain't.

When the doorbell ring I know for sure it ain't the Master and my heart knock as fast as it knock the night Nagle come into the cabin and kick us 'wake and spill whisky from his bottle over us.

And b'fore the bell can ring 'gain I hear Elijah open it and there a man voice and then the Mistress voice – all sing-song like the piano, not like her screamin' voice from earlier. And both voices loud for a minute and then they soft 'cause they in the parlour and the door close.

Elijah stand at the top the kitchen steps – since he can't hardly see no more he a'ways 'fraid he gone fall.

'They ask for some ice tea and some peach cobbler in the parlour,' he say.

Linda wipe her hand on her apron. 'I fetch it for them right now.'

'Not you,' he say. 'She want E.L. fetch it.'

It feel like forever waitin' for Juba and Linda to make up the tray with the ice tea and the peach cobbler and san'wiches in case the white man hungry. And when it ready it feel real heavy. They watch me carry it up the steps and into the hall and I think the Mistress musta done hear the rattle of the glasses 'cause she open the parlour door b'fore I get to knock.

'Put that down there, E.L., that's right. Right there.'

I put the tray down on the table by the window next to where the white man sit. It mus' be nearly noon 'cause the sun comin' in full and warm and there a big square of light on the floor that almost cover the whole rug.

'E.L. don't just stand there. Say hello to Mr. Barrett.'

The Mistress got that voice on where I don't need look at her to know she smilin' and that make me more scared. I curtsey like I seen Linda do. I look down at the carpet.

'Well, well.'

The white man stand up. I don't know what to do next so I curtsey 'gain. He a big man, tall and wide, with a big belly. He older than the Master with white hair and white whiskers that he rub with his hand. He walk 'round me in a circle jus' like I seen the slave traders walk 'round Charity.

'You weren't exaggerating, Mrs. Carthy,' he say, 'She's quite the specimen. Very unusual in her appearance.'

'Yes, I thought you might appreciate her.'

They both stand b'hind me now and when I look up I see the big picture of the Master's mamma – Miss Ellen grandmamma look at me. Her name Ellen too and it only then I r'member that my name same as her name. That she my grandmamma too.

'I'm surprised your husband didn't bring her to Charleston with him. He could get a lot on the block for her, I should imagine.'

I know that why he come but it worse hearin' it out loud. My heart want to bang outta my chest. If I gone horse ridin' with Miss Ellen I be safe now. Maybe I get some lashes but that better than leavin' with this old white man. Than never seein' her or the Master or Linda or Juba or Big Bill or Benjamin ever 'gain.

The Mistress walk 'longside me. 'He had planned to and then he changed his mind. But I think he'd take a good offer, he said it himself right b'fore he left.'

Mr. Barrett walk beside her. Stop. 'You think, Mrs. Carthy? Forgive me, but you don't sound too certain? After your daughter's outburst the last time, you assured me you were acting on your husband's authority to sell this slave?'

The Mistress fix her hair straight. 'I am – I'm sorry if I suggested otherwise. He just – my husband – he changes his mind sometimes. You know how men can be!'

She laughs a high laugh but Mr. Barrett ain't laughin' none. He pick his hat up from the chair next to him. 'A man has a right to change his mind, ma'am, I'm sure you'll agree. This is a conversation I need to be having with your husband. It seems very clear that this has – once again – been a wasted journey.'

'Mr. Barrett, I'm so sorry.' The Mistress reach out to touch his arm.

He take her hand off his arm, fix his hat on his head.

'I apologise deeply for any misunderstanding,' she say. 'You're absolutely right, I can't give you a bill of sale for her today, only my husband can do that. But the trip doesn't have to be wasted ...'

He walkin' out the room. He a'ready walk past me.

'... I mean you could always ... see if she's to your liking or not. It's only fair to know what you're buying before you make an investment.'

He nearly at the door. When he there he gone call Elijah and ask him to bring 'round his boy with his horse and buggy and he gone ride out the gate and back to his own plantation. But then he stop. He turn 'round.

'I'm not quite sure I know what you mean, Mrs. Carthy.'

'Like I said, it's only right,' the Mistress say, 'for you to know something about an investment you're thinking of making. Take some time to find out if she ... meets your needs.'

He lookin' at the Mistress and then he look at me, standin' b'hind her. My cheeks burnin' and I don't know why.

'E.L., close the curtains.'

'Yes, Ma'am.'

I walk over to the window and close the curtains like she jus' askin' me to do any job. I don't know what he gone do but it like part of me do know, part of me a'ways been 'fraid of him doin' this. Of someone doin' this.

When I turn 'round the Mistress gone. The room feel diff'rent now, in the half dark without the sun. And Mr. Barrett take his hat off and he put it down on the couch 'gain. And then I know.

I don't fight him 'cause there ain't no point in fightin' him. Ev'rythin' hurt more when you fight back, ev'rythin' last longer when you fight back, ev'ryone know that. So when he tell me to take off my dress so he can see me, I open the buttons at the front and pull it up over my head the way I seen Charity do with the two white mens and Nagle out by the fire.

But when he come close and I can smell his smell, the sweetness of the ice tea and the smell of the t'bacco that make brown stains on his white whiskers, I take a step back, even though I know there ain't nowhere to go. And he take a step fo'ward and I take 'nother one back and we do that till my back 'gainst the piano and I ain't got nowhere else to step back to.

When he touch me I don't look, so I can pretend it my own hand on my skin or Charity hand only Charity never touch me the way he touch me, in the places he touch me. I squeeze my eyes close, real tight. His hands ev'rywhere, his fingers. They rough, they hurt. And then he stop and I think he finish – I think it done – but then I hear somethin' and I know he unbucklin' his pants. And when the bust of pain comes, hard and burnin', I cry out – I can't help it. That when he clamp his hand down over my mouth, hard. His face red and twisted and full of hate.

'Close your eyes, you stupid bitch,' he say.

I do what he want, I close my eyes, squeeze them, so tight, tight, tighter. And the more noise he make, the more he push and grunt, the more quiet I get, my breath barely makin' any noise, like I barely breathin'. And the pain burn so hard I think I gone split right up the middle, right in two. And he push so hard that my back gone break 'gainst the piano, gone snap like a twig branch. And the faster he go, the more it hurt, the tighter my eyes close.

And after forever it slow. After forever it stop. After forever he done.

When I open my eyes 'gain he wipin' hisself and fixin' his shirt inside his pants. His hair all mussed up, all long on one side now and he fix it so it cover his whole head. He look 'round for his hat and he find it on the couch by the back window and he fix it down hard on his head, jus' like b'fore.

I standin' there – I still bent back. I don't move, I don't know if I can move. My leg shakin' and wet and I look down and there blood on me and I lucky there ain't none on the rug. And he look at me, his eyes real slow over me and they diff'rent eyes than b'fore.

'Look at you. You're disgusting,' he say. 'Clean yourself up.'

And then he leave.

I don't know how long I stand there, it like I frozen or somethin' but then somethin' snap and I know I don't want the Mistress findin' me here, like this and I pick my dress up from where it lyin' on the floor and put it over my head. My fingers so shaky it take longer to fix the buttons but I fix the buttons and while I do I hear the noise of his buggy outside the window, of his horse and the whip 'gainst the horse back and the sound of the hooves 'gainst the ground as it pick up speed and drive 'way.

It hurt to walk – it hurt inside and outside and my leg hurt and the pain in my back real bad and it hard to stand straight. I practise not limpin', walk to one window and open the curtain and then the next to let the sun in 'gain. And I walk over to the tray and no one ate no cobbler or no san'wiches and the ice all melted in the tea now and I coulda done take some cobbler and hide it in my apron or eat it right then but I don't.

B'fore I leave I look 'round to make sure we ain't made no mess. But it a'right 'cause the room full of sunlight 'gain and the piano shine like it did b'fore and the square sunlight on the carpet move a bit but it look jus' like b'fore and it like nothin' bad done happen here.

When I go down the steps into the kitchen, Linda and Juba nearly finished the small pantry closet and they don't say nothin' when I put down the tray on the side and take my place in they line, takin' the plates Linda carryin' passin' them over to Juba so she can wash them, jus' like b'fore.

And walkin' back to Linda I see it – a drop of blood on the floor.

Jus' one drop – as bright red as the roses in the flower garden. Juba look down and she see it too.

'Clean that up,' she say. 'Don't go makin' a mess in my kitchen.'

She look 'way then, back to the sink and she keep washin'. She don't ask what happen to make the blood and Linda don't ask so I don't say nothin' neither. 'Cause even though it hurt down there where he been and even though my back feel like it gone break, maybe if I don't say nothin', maybe if I clean up the drop of red blood so no one see it, then maybe nothin' done happen? Maybe nothin' done happen at all.

CASSIE

There's a place I used to go with Grandad. At the end of Montague Street where everyone turns right on the promenade to walk towards the Brooklyn Bridge we would turn left. There's only a little bit of promenade left that way – 'a butt of promenade' he used to say – and nothing really to see from that direction, except the Brooklyn Queens Expressway underneath with the rush of cars and trucks and taxis and cars again. But Grandad always said views were overrated that sometimes not having a view to distract you made you see something else instead: that it made you see what was really important.

We would walk right to the end, where the railing curves around. If you stand there, with one foot on the side part of the curve and one on the front part, you feel like Kate Winslet in *Titanic* when she's at the front of the ship and Leonardo DiCaprio is holding her from behind. Except instead of Leonardo, I had Grandad.

That morning is the first time I go without him. It makes no sense that in over six years I've never been there, considering it was always one of my favourite places and only five minutes from our house, but it's like I forgot about it, like it doesn't exist without him. That morning feels different though. When I wake up with that pain in my back and the dream that's just out of my reach, my feet just take me there.

I know something terrible has happened to E.L., but I don't know what. These pills have made me sleep but they've killed our dreams – we've hardly even been writing lately and I hope it's not too late, that they haven't killed everything. My right foot goes on railing, my left further around the curve to the side. If I pushed myself a little higher, if I leaned a little further forward, I could fall. There is no Leonardo holding me today.

Most people hate that the BQE is there – the sound of it, the pollution – they say that it spoils the promenade. Most people say it was big mistake made by those planners all those years ago. But Grandad always said there was more than one way of looking at things. That you could choose to see the bad in something or the good. He looked at the BQE and he saw life, energy, the draw of the city. People making journeys, going to work, meeting friends, bringing things to sell or to build or eat or make. 'The roads of this city are like arteries – the blood flow,' he used to say, looking down. 'They keep it alive.'

It feels like a long time since I've let myself hear his voice in my head, let myself even really think about him, but this morning it feels good, hearing him. Standing there, above the traffic, I feel strong, powerful. Below me, the trucks and taxis and cars disappear underneath me, almost like they are becoming part of me, like I am taking in their energy. Standing there I can be anyone I want to be. I can be someone else; Kate Winslet in *Titanic* or a character in an action movie about to leap. I imagine myself jumping, landing on the roof of a truck, gripping the edges with my fingers as my body skitters with its movement as it flies into the city and beyond.

The pain in my back is just as intense as when I woke up, maybe even worse. It's her pain, not mine, just like the pain I felt in my fingers, my foot, my neck – my whole body is becoming her body it seems. I don't care though, the pain makes me feel close to her, connected. The pain is how I remember she is still there even when

I can't see her. I close my eyes and try to feel my way through the grey shape of the dream, to remember what she showed me, but the images are gone and I am only left with an empty place where the feeling should be.

It's getting windier now and I can feel my hair blowing forward, my T-shirt whipping up. The wind might make it easier to jump – to fall. The wind might carry me, might lift me across the traffic and gently place me by the water on the other side, or maybe it's so strong it might blow me right back up onto the promenade, it might even carry me home. But even as I let myself imagine that, I am stepping back down – one foot on the promenade first, then the other. E.L. needs me. I'm the one she needs – I've always been the one she needs. And right now she needs me more than ever.

I reach into my backpack, pull out the little bottle that Isaac Morton gave me. It bothered me at first that the pills were yellow – not white like the prescription ones from Alice, the ones that kept running out too quickly. But then that stopped bothering me and then nothing bothered me after a while. I unscrew the cap slowly but right when it is unlocked I screw it back on tight again like my body is fighting itself. It hasn't helped – these pills haven't helped – they've made everything worse and it seems like E.L. is the furthest away from me she's ever been now. I should've listened to her: she told me not to take the pills, to leave everything in God's hands, the way it had always worked out before. But I didn't listen. I had to think that I knew better – that I could help things along.

The traffic has slowed down. A blockage in the artery. I wish it was moving quicker, it would be easier to do this if it was moving quicker. I unscrew the cap all the way, tip it over so the pills are in my hand. I haven't taken one this morning and standing here with the wind off the water and the roar of the traffic my head feels clearer than it has in weeks. Fragments of E.L.'s voice, Grandad's voice, Alice's, Mom's, Dad's all swirl around me now in the wind. But there is no one there, only me. How do I know which voice is mine?

My fist clenches around the pills. There are fourteen of them. I don't have to count – I know already when I need to see Isaac again. I want to open my fist but I can't. It is glued together, stuck, the fingers welded tight, like I have no control, like the mechanical signal between my fingers and my head has broken down.

'Let go and let God.'

That voice is definitely Grandad's and that's the problem with memories – you let one in and next thing you know more have sneaked in behind it when the door was open. Next thing you know you can't keep them out at all.

I heard him say that a million times – it was one of the slogans on his dishcloth – but the first time I remember it was in Barnes & Noble when they didn't have the book we wanted. The book was called *The Boy Who Was Afraid* and it was Grandad's favourite book when he was a kid about a boy who built himself a boat on the river. He'd been telling me about it for days, and he'd promised to buy it for me, that we could read it together, but the woman behind the counter in Barnes & Noble was shaking her head and saying she had no record of it.

When we got outside I demanded that we go into the city to look for it in another Barnes & Noble and when he said there was no point, that she had checked all the stores, I had a meltdown.

'You don't know for sure! She mightn't know – she might have made a mistake.'

I yelled at him, like it was his fault, but he didn't get mad, he just got down on his hunkers and put his hand on my shoulder.

'I know you really want the book, so do I, and I bet one will show up sooner or later.'

'But where? What are we supposed to do?'

'We let go and let God.'

'That's stupid! That's not even a full sentence!' I kicked the kerb with my sneaker.

He smiled. 'I thought it was funny too, the first time I heard it but it just means we've done our bit, for today at least and now we hand it over to Him.'

It sounded stupid to me and I kicked the garbage can on the corner for good measure but if he noticed he didn't say anything, just took my hand to cross the road like nothing had happened and after a block or two I forgot to be mad. And the next Saturday, or the one after, we went to a yard sale on the corner of Pineapple and Hicks and in a stack of books Grandad finds one with a picture of a boy and a boat on the front with the title *Call It Courage*, and it turns out that's what the book's name was in America.

I wish I had the book with me now – that might make it easier, make the memory more real, but it had disappeared in Mom's clear out, along with all the others.

My hands are still tight around the pills, my fingernails dig into my palm. The wind makes my eyes water and I think maybe tears will come for Grandad but they don't, the water on my face is only water.

'Let go and let God,' I whisper. I take a breath, say it again. 'Let go and let God.'

It sounds silly. Ridiculous. I don't even think I believe in God, but as I say it my fingers open, slowly at first, then all at once.

And the pills start to fall, a line of them, carried on the wind away from me and down in a spiral, one by one, before they seem to catch up with each other and rain down hard all together. When my hand is empty I clutch the railing. They have gone too far down for me to see them but I imagine them bouncing off car roofs, windshields, flattened by tires. And now that I've let them go I want them again – to try and grab them back – but I know it's too late.

The traffic has picked up speed and I watch it long after the pills are gone. My mind is empty now – no Grandad, no E.L. – just me and the line of cars and trucks and taxis and cars. I don't check my watch, I already know I'm going to be late so it doesn't matter by how much. I just stand there holding on to the railing until the rain comes and starts to turn the promenade all around me from light grey to dark.

And when it gets too wet to stay there anymore, I pick up my backpack and swing it over my shoulder and head towards school.

CASSIE & E.L.

It rainin'. It don't hardly ever rain at night and this night I glad it rainin', this night I'm glad for the water on my skin.

It's dark. It's raining. I'm cold. Where am I? I don't know where I am.

I'm by the river and it swellin' with the rain, like it gone come over the bank. I here to wash, that what I tell myself but now I here I think maybe I here for some other reason. Bein' here make me think of Charity – the way we use to talk down here, the firs' time she show me how to wash out my dress. That when the pain come, diff'rent pain than b'fore. It too much, this pain. Too heavy. I can't carry it on top of ev'rythin' else as well. Not on my own.

It's impossible to see anything in this darkness, there's only black and shades of darker black that must be trees. Overhead there is no moon, only the night and the rain. Behind me I hear water, the river and I turn around, and that's when I see her about twenty feet away from me. I can only see her outline – the shape of a person – but I don't need to see her to know it's her. It can only be her.

I don't know how I hear her callin' me, over all that noise of the rain and the river but I mus' heard somethin' that make me turn 'round and look back. I think maybe it my mamma, callin' me from Heaven, maybe I can hear her 'cause maybe I dyin', maybe this pain inside what death feel like. But then I turn and see her. It ain't Mamma. It a skinny white girl who look like a boy, who look like a ghost and even though this time I know who she is, I don't know why she here.

'E.L!' I cup my hands around my mouth, shout against the wind. 'E.L.!'

She stands up, turns towards me and that's good because up until then I thought – I don't know what I thought – only I do know, I just don't want to say it. I start to run, my feet slipping in the mud and I look down to see they are bare, that in this downpour I am wearing my stripy Gap pyjama bottoms, that my white tank top is almost see through.

She runnin' toward me now and somethin' 'bout the way she nearly fall make me want start laughin' and want run to meet her too. But the pain win out over the laughin', over some white ghost demon girl from the future who here and not here. The river call me louder and I turn back to it. The water high, getting' higher. Charity a'ways say that one day she gone teach herself how to swim and then she gone teach me too. Tonight I glad she never did.

'E.L.!'

She turns away from me and I am screaming now. Over the wind I can't hear my own voice but I can feel the tear in my throat. She's disappearing. Where is she going? I put my hand over my eyes and I see her down on her hands and knees, right next to the water.

'E.L.!'

I make my legs go faster so I am running and sliding on the grass and the mud and one leg slides out of control and I am down on one knee, both hands. They sink into the mud as I push myself up, I have mud up to my elbows now but I don't care. I only care about getting to her.

But when I stand back up, she is gone.

Getting' into the water slow at firs', then fast. My foot in. The water cold. Strong. My other foot still on the bank – in control. My hands holdin' the grass still in control. But then the water swirl higher. It over my knees so my dress float on top. It up to my waist and make my dress sink. And then it grab me like a demon in the water. This water demon stronger than me. It pull me hard and pull me in. This demon in control now.

I must be ten feet from the edge when she goes in, slowly at first like she is easing herself into a pool but then a fast, sudden drop. Somehow she turns around to face me and I see her hands gripping at the grass and then the grass sliding away from her, the whites of her eyes bigger than ever, her mouth open, screaming something I can't hear.

'E.L.!'

Und'neath water it like nothin' I ever feel b'fore. Ev'rythin' slow down. My body light, not heavy and it like I turnin' and twistin' one way firs' then the next and nothin' hurt no more. My eyes close so I don't know which way up. Maybe I 'fraid only I don't r'member feelin' 'fraid. I don't r'member chokin' neither. I don't r'member feelin' nothin' 'cept for the slow water churn.

The edge of the bank is all mud now – no grass. It would be easy to slip in, to join her in the water. She's gone, no sign of her. How can there be no sign of her? But really there isn't – there's only the surface of the water, swirling brown with some bubbles, leaves, twigs. She's already gone. I'm too late. I've lost her.

The peace break. One minute there silence and the next – bang – it loud and I coughin' and there air now not jus' water and when my body know that air there, then air all it want. My arms hit the water in front and it splash up in my face. I can't get no air. I can't breathe. The rain, the water make ev'rythin' loud. I want breath. I want breath more than anythin'.

When she breaks the surface she is close to me, two feet away at the most.

'E.L., over here!'

Scrambling down the bank I don't think about what I am doing, what I plan to do. My feet sink into the mud, water swirls around my ankles, my shins. This isn't the pool at the Y. If I go in after her I am not coming out – neither of us will be coming out.

'E.L!' I lean as far as I can towards her. 'Grab my hand!'

Cassie right there. I see her face. I hear her callin'. It her – it really her. All a sudden she real close to me but then she gone and the water pourin' over my face 'gain. This time there ain't no peace – it too fast, pourin' in ev'rywhere, fillin' me up and then somethin' change and I back in the air 'gain, coughin' and chokin' and feelin' like I gone be sick.

When she goes under, she goes under deeper, and I know if I don't get her out, this will be the last time. My right hand searches the bank for something to hold on to – a tree root, a rock, anything – but there are only reeds. I grab a handful and stretch my left out as far as I can towards her. She is splashing, flailing. Her head is tipped back and her mouth is wide open, her eyes wide too, the white parts so white in the dark. Her panic becomes mine. I'm too far away. I lean out more – my bones are stretching, my tendons are. My fingers on the reeds are slipping but my other fingers graze her, almost connect with hers before her hand disappears under the water. I think I've messed it up, missed our only chance and then the water pushes her closer to me somehow. All around her, the rain is making pock marks on the water and I can barely see through it but I reach out a little more. I am sinking into the mud – the mud is holding me – I let go of the reeds and then I grab her with both hands.

Lookin' back I think maybe that the firs' time a white woman touch me – touch me without hurtin' me – only I ain't thinkin' that then. I ain't got no time for thinkin', I only coughin' and splashin' and tryin' to get breath into my heart pumpin' so full of fear. Her hands, they hold my wrist tight, they pull me up only I don't want go up. Goin' down easier, the last time weren't so bad, the peace start to come 'gain. I think the next time I go down it gone be peace all the time. I think it gone be peace forever.

She's going under, she's pulling me with her, and I'm screaming her name over and over, even though her head is disappearing under the water and she can't hear me. Is this how it ends? Do we drown here together? I remember thinking that – a fleeting thought – wondering if I die here am I dead back in Brooklyn too? And maybe it's thinking that that makes me lean closer still, pull her towards me, one hand over the other hand, so I am holding her elbow, her upper arm. The water is up to my chest but I have her this time. I really have her.

Cassie stronger than she look. Her grip on me hard, like Nagle grip. It hurt. My arm, my shoulders, my head out in the air now, back in the rain and the noise. There no peace here. When I try and talk a cough come out at the same time.

'Let me go, Cassie.' Her grip tight. Her face don't change. I don't know if she hear me so I say it 'gain. 'This ain't got nothin' to do with you. Let me go.'

Her face is out of the water her mouth gasping for breath. I don't let go, I still have her. She is saying something that I don't hear at first. And then I do.

'Let me go.'

Maybe reading this, you know what you'd do then, or maybe you think you do. I might have thought so too but that night, in that rain, up to my chest in that river, afraid for my own life as well as hers, there wasn't much time for thinking. There were maybe three seconds, or even less, when I looked at her, the two of us locked together like that, the rain pounding all around us, that's maybe how long I paused. And maybe during those three seconds, maybe I heard Grandad saying 'let go and let God' but if I did hear him, I didn't listen. I didn't let go. I couldn't. I wasn't ready. And so I pulled harder.

I ain't got no strength lef' to fight her. I ain't got no strength to do nothin'. She pull me and the water demon pull me. Whoever gone win this fight it ain't gone be me. Her hands on my arms, under them, on my shoulder. She pullin' and she pushin' and she grabbin' all at the same time. Somehow I outta the water and she got me on the bank. Her hands on my back and she push me. Roll me. I open my eyes and I on the grass now. My breath full of water, I coughin' water, bein' sick water.

I don't know how I got her out. I doubt I could do it again but I did, somehow, and right after she is on the bank I realise I am the one in trouble now, with my right leg stuck knee-deep in mud and the water rising. The water swirls around my chest, higher then, as far as my neck. I wish there was the moon overhead, stars, but there are only clouds. I jiggle my leg and feel the mud suction around it more. My body is aching, exhausted, ready to give in. From nowhere I remember something I saw on T.V. or on YouTube, something I am desperate enough to try.

I take a breath, duck my head under and pull with both hands, making space down each side of my shin. Something loosens and I feel my leg slide. I'm almost out of breath and I burst back to the top, use the momentum to hit the air and let it carry me forward so I can throw my arms over the bank.

I hope E.L. will grab my hands, that she'll pull me out like I did for her, but she is lying the other way, her back to me and I hear her throwing up. I grab on to the reeds, take a breath, throw myself forward, bicycle my feet. I push forward on my stomach, flopping forward an inch, two. I am not graceful, this is not pretty. I am out of the water now, on the bank. I am covered in mud. My heart is pounding. I've done something to my foot and I don't know what yet. Next to me E.L. is still coughing, spewing water. Rain pounds the ground around us.

No one is there to see our struggle. No one will wrap us up in warm blankets or thank me for saving her, or talk about courage, bravery. No one will call me a hero but that doesn't matter, none of it matters; all that matters is that she is safe.

Lying on the bank, gulping in the hot warm air, I don't think I'm a hero. In a way that I can't explain I feel like I never had any choice, but to save her. That saving her was somehow linked to saving myself.

***

The day after the river dream is a Thursday. At first I don't remember that I even had a dream but walking to school I feel my ankle is sore – like it's sprained – and I know that something must have happened, even if I don't know what.

English, geography and math all crawl by and then it's finally lunchtime. I smuggle my laptop into the cafeteria, sit in the corner with my back to the room so no one will see it. When I start to write the dream comes back in images and feelings: I see her head disappearing under the water, feel the stretch of every sinew in my body as I try and reach her, the suction of mud on my leg.

What did you think you were doing last night? You could have died – you know that? You could have drowned.

The screen is a patch of quiet in the chaos of the cafeteria. All around me there is laughing, voices shouting, calling, talking, but E.L. remains silent.

You really would have done that? You really would have just left me?

I realise then that I am holding my breath and I know I must be mad at her because I only do that when I'm really mad. But she's mad at me too – I can feel it. She wishes I'd let her drown. If I hadn't come, she'd be dead and that's how she wanted it. And somehow it's only then that it sinks in, what happened; I saved her. I take a deep breath and the knowledge sinks in deeper. I did it. I changed things, I really changed things.

Art class that afternoon is perfect and I sit in the far corner so as not to have to speak to anyone, to think. I'd saved E.L. and that meant if I changed things for her once I could change them again. If she's fifteen right now, that means the start of the Civil War is five years away, it's nine years till it ends. She won't last that long – I know she won't. I have to get her out.

'That's very atmospheric, Cassie.'

Miss Roberts' voice comes from right behind my shoulder, so close my hand jerks a stripe of paint across the page and almost spills the water.

'Sorry, I didn't mean to startle you.'

'You didn't.'

'I like your use of the dark blues and blacks – I can almost feel the river churning, the rain falling.'

'Thanks.' I want to put my arm across the painting but I can't because she's looking really closely and besides the paint is still wet.

'Is that a hand?' she asks, her fingernail light above the paper. 'Is that someone's hand right there, coming out of the water?'

'Yes.'

'So, someone is drowning in this churning river?'

I shift in my chair. 'Yes.'

She waits for me to say something else but I don't. One thing I've learned from all these shrinks is how to ride out questions and only answer the parts you really have to. Miss Roberts doesn't have a chance.

'Powerful,' she says.

'Thanks.'

I sit back from the table, make it clear that I won't paint any more until she moves away and on to someone else and eventually she does. And it's only then I look at the painting properly myself, really see it, and that's when I notice that I'm not in it – there's only E.L., only her hand coming out of the water. I'm not there to pull her out, to save her. No one is.

There's something else too that I only see then; the hand stretching out of the water for help, it's white. It's not a black hand. I keep looking at it – the hand – as if it's going to change colour. It seems weird the way I got it confused like that, but I wasn't really paying attention, wasn't really thinking about it.

Still, it gives me the creeps, that hand, and I decide to make it dark brown even though it messes the whole picture up because the paint isn't dry and the colours all start to run into each other. I know it's stupid to get the creeps from a picture, from something I painted, but I do. Because looking at that picture, the way I painted it, you wouldn't be sure what was happening.

Looking at the painting, you wouldn't know which one of us is drowning.

E.L.

Cassie keep on askin' questions. She don't never stop. Askin' if I a'right. Askin' where I at. Askin' why I gone and jump in the river.

I don't say nothin'. I don't answer. It ain't none of her bus'ness. I never ask her to pull me from no river. I never ask her to save me. I never done ask her for nothin'.

All this talkin' to her – it a waste of time. She don't know nothin' 'bout what it like here with Charity gone and the Master gone and Miss Ellen who may as well be gone too for all I see of her. Cassie don't know what it like ev'ry day when ev'ry sound ou'side make me jump case it Barrett back in his buggy. Jus' 'cause I ain't seen the Mistress since, jus' 'cause she been in the parlour playin' piano all the time, don't mean it over. That don't mean he ain't gone come back 'gain.

Truth is, I wish she never done pull me from that river. I wish I drown that night. 'Cause drownin' better than this – anythin' got be better than this.

But there no sense tellin' Cassie all that. She think she done a good thing. She don't get it. She jus' don't get it at all.

CASSIE

Ever since I pulled E.L. from the river, she has stopped talking to me. She doesn't answer me when I write to her on the laptop. I've even risked writing to her in my notebook but she doesn't answer that either. Every night I go to bed hoping to see her, hoping that I might get back there. Ever since the river night I am prepared – I sleep in my clothes, sometimes even my sneakers – but every morning when I wake up I know I've just been here, nowhere else. That my dreams have been only mine.

Despite her silence, I know somehow that our connection isn't permanently broken. Even though she doesn't answer, I can still feel her there, listening. I know she's still mad, but I know that I must have saved her for a reason. That I didn't just save her to leave her there. And I know that if I can save her once, I can save her again.

I start to go to Barnes & Noble every day after school the way I used to when I was hiding Mom's memoir in different sections of the store. If Angelina notices she doesn't say anything so I don't either. Every day I go to the history section where they have a million books on slavery, on the Civil War – way more than the library – and I sit between the shelves and start to read.

That's where I read about Henry Ward Beecher and Plymouth Church and I want to hit myself in the head that day, for being such a dumbass, for not having remembered before. Plymouth Church is on the corner of Orange and Hicks, three blocks from our house. We took a school trip there in sixth grade; an old lady gave us a tour. I remembered a lot about the day – how hot it was in there, how me and Gabi couldn't stop giggling and Mrs. Jonas gave us the evil eye from the other side of the group which made us laugh even more. There was a pew where Abraham Lincoln had sat, I remembered that, how we all took turns sliding in to sit down for a few seconds and getting up again. But apart from some kind of auction about buying the freedom for some slave girl, I didn't remember anything the old lady said. I wished I'd listened more, that I could go back in time and do it all over again, write down every word she said. I wished I could call her up and ask her for a tour with just me.

After Barnes & Noble, I start to take a detour by that church and if the garden is open and there's no one around I go in and sit on one of the benches. Sitting on that bench thinking about what I've been reading about the Underground Railroad, things seem to come together, to fit. Maybe they've always fitted and I'm only starting to see the full picture now. This church was a major stop on the Underground Railroad, the place where so many slaves were freed and I'd walked past it for years. Every day, every step I took on these sidewalks, probably had me walking above some secret tunnel, some hiding place, a basement where a slave or even a family of slaves had been waiting for their freedom. No wonder this had seeped up from the sidewalks into the soles of my sneakers, up through my legs and into my body, my head, my heart. No wonder E.L. had come to me.

Since E.L.'s silence there haven't been any dreams either and I never feel like going to bed so I stay up late reading more about the Underground Railroad on the internet, about the conductors who helped the slaves escape. *Slaughterhouse Five* is two months overdue from the school library but I don't bring it back. When I finally get in bed, I take it out and turn to page sixty-two, my favourite passage, where Billy describes how the Tralfamadorians see time. It makes so much sense, that everything that happens is permanent somewhere, that the past exists, just as real as the present exists and the future too. I love the part about how when they look at a dead body they don't feel bad because they know that in plenty of other moments that person is still alive – still living. That there's no need to mourn, because no one ever really dies.

I love that part because it totally ties into Grandad's gift and I wonder over and over if he'd read it, what he'd have thought of it. I think of what Gabi said about it that day at school: 'It's a book. Fictional. It's made up.' Grandad's gift wasn't made up – I'd seen enough people leave his room smiling, thanking him, shaking his hand, to know that. And reading that part of the book again and again, something about it finally helps it sink in: that Grandad's gift wasn't just his, that now it is my gift too.

After I've read all the books on slavery and the Civil War at Barnes and Noble I move onto the section where there are books about mediums and the afterlife and getting in touch with dead people. That's the section I'm sitting in the day I see Ryan and his friend Jack.

They are at end of the aisle and Jack has a book in his hand but I can't see what it is. It's open and he's showing something to Ryan. Ryan is talking, in an animated way that I haven't seen in what feels like a really long time. Jack points at something else and Ryan laughs a laugh that lights up his whole face.

They turn to come into my aisle, closer to me and I'm enjoying just watching them, my brother and his friend, laughing together when over Jack's shoulder Ryan sees me. His eyes land on mine. I smile, lift my hand, wave.

Something in his face changes and Jack sees it, turns around, sees me too. Ryan takes the book from Jack's hand, puts it on a cart, on top of a pile of other books.

'Come on,' he says, 'let's get out of here.'

Jack hesitates, picks up the book from the cart again. But Ryan has already walked away around the corner, and he takes another glance at me, puts the book back.

'Hey man, wasn't that your sister?' I hear him say as he follows him out of sight.

I don't know if Ryan answers him but whatever he says or doesn't say I don't hear it.

That night over dinner I think about bringing it up but he won't catch my eye and anyway that would mean saying I was in Barnes & Noble, which would lead into a whole thing with Mom asking me what I was doing there, so I don't say anything. And later, I pause outside his room and my hand nearly knocks on his door, but inside I can hear him playing Xbox, so I don't.

I'll say it to him the next time it happens, that's what I tell myself. Or better still, when I see him, I'll go over to him, talk to him, say hi. Be normal. But I don't know if it's normal for your brother to ignore you in public, to be ashamed of you. And there's no one I can ask about it. And it turns out there is no next time. Because for all the hours and hours I spent in Barnes & Noble, after that day I never see Ryan there again.

***

By then Mom and Dad are having an ongoing argument about Alice. Mom says that she's making no progress and that after eighteen months we should be seeing some improvement. Dad says these things take time – 'especially in cases like Cassie's'. He says that last part in a low voice, because he's in the kitchen, but I overhear it anyway because I'm on the stairs. And it seems like he wins this round because no one says anything about seeing anyone new, so I still go twice a week and every other week I end up seeing her three times because that's when we have our family sessions.

Ever since that first session we all sit in the same seats and, on the day I want to tell you about, Dad is in the room first, even before Alice. He looks tired. His stubble has grown and he needs a haircut too. He looks younger when he gets his hair cut.

'Hey, Cass.' He stands up and gives me a hug, holding on too long so it gets awkward. I pull back first, then he does. 'Where's your brother?'

I shrug. 'On his way, I guess.'

I hope Dad won't ask why we never come together and he doesn't. He sits back down and I sit in the chair I always sit in. Dad crosses his foot over his knee, picks at his laces.

'How are things? How are you feeling?'

'Fine.'

Without Alice, there is no one to tell me that 'fine' is not a feeling. Dad nods. Smiles.

'Good. That's good. Seems like this is the only place we ever see each other these days. Want to go see a movie this weekend? Maybe Saturday?'

There are footsteps on the stairs then and Alice comes in, Ryan behind her. Dad gets up to hug Ryan and he pulls away even quicker than I did. He takes his usual seat, throws his backpack on the floor.

'Me and Cassie were just saying we might see a movie this weekend,' Dad says. 'What do you think, buddy? That new Bourne one is out.'

I wish he wouldn't say this stuff in front of Alice. Just because she's by the window fiddling with the air conditioning doesn't mean she's not listening. Only on Tuesday she was asking me about Dad, if I felt 'betrayed' by him. At first I thought she was going to ask if I felt betrayed because of what happened after the Schomburg incident and for once I thought she might really have been on to something. But she was talking about him leaving Mom and as usual she was 400 million miles off the mark.

'I didn't say I'd definitely go, Dad. I don't know yet what I'm even doing this weekend.'

'Ah, but you will though, won't you? We could go for pizza after. John's?'

It's sad how pathetic he looks with his hands clasped between his knees like he's begging us.

'I don't know. Maybe.'

He smiles. 'Great! How about you Ryan?'

'I don't know. I said I'd see Jack.'

'I'm sure you won't be with Jack all weekend? We can go when you're not with Jack.'

Ryan looks at his sneakers and makes a non-committal noise. Alice scoops her skirt under her knees and sits down.

'Or Jack can come. I don't mind if he comes. I'm sure Cassie won't either.'

I see an out and I grab it. 'Actually, I do mind. I have no desire to spend my weekend with Ryan's lame little friends.'

Ryan jerks his head up to look at me. 'At least I *have* friends.'

I wait for Dad to tell him to take that back but he doesn't. We sit in silence then, the four of us, waiting for Mom to arrive. After what seems like an eternity, we hear her on the stairs – fast footsteps. When she comes in she is out of breath.

'I'm sorry. Sorry I'm late. The traffic on the BQE was appalling.'

There's a silence and I'm waiting for Dad to say something but it's Ryan who speaks next in a bored voice.

'You say that same shit every single time, Mom. The BQE is a highway. Highways have traffic – yet it always seems to come as a surprise to you.'

'Ryan – watch your language!'

'It's therapy. I'm allowed.'

He leans back in his chair so the front legs are off the ground. The tips of his sneakers are on the floor, balancing him and I think Mom is going to tell him to sit on his chair properly but she just sits down on her own, puts her bag on the ground. Now there is only one empty chair – E.L.'s.

Alice has been looking at Mom and then she turns to Ryan. 'You sound mad at your mom, Ryan?'

Mom rolls her eyes. 'He's thirteen – he's always mad at me.'

'Does it bother you that she's late?'

'Why wouldn't it bother him?' Dad jumps in. 'She's late for every session. Doesn't it bother you?'

Alice ignores him, keeps her eyes on Ryan.

'Ryan, are you angry with your mom?'

His arms are folded and he's looking into the corner. Usually, he doesn't say much of anything in these sessions and I know he wants Alice to leave him alone, is trying to figure out the quickest way to do that.

'Sure,' he says. 'We're here on time. It's bullshit that she's always late.'

'Why don't you tell her how you feel?' Alice says.

'I just did.'

'No.' Alice shakes her head. 'You didn't. Why don't you tell her in the way we are learning to talk to each other?'

Mom fixes her hair behind her ears, makes a kind of tutting noise. Ryan's eyes flick to her and back to the floor. When he speaks it's in a robot voice, mimicking the way Alice has modelled for us to talk.

'Mom ... when you are late ... I feel mad.'

I can't help but smile and I want him to look over, to smile at me too, so both of us can be on the same side like we used to be. Only he doesn't look over, and it suddenly seems like a really long time since we've been on the same side.

'Well, I'm glad someone's smiling.'

That's Mom's voice and it takes a second to realise she is talking to me. 'What?'

'I just mean it's ironic that we come here and you're smiling. I can't remember the last time I saw you smile at home.'

Alice sees that I'm about to respond, but she beats me to it.

'You're saying that your experience of Cassie in the sessions is different than at home, Louise?'

Mom makes a face. 'I'm saying that she doesn't smile at home. I can't remember the last time I saw her smile.'

'That sounds hard. Can you tell us a little about what your experience of Cassie *is* like at home?'

Alice uses words like that a lot – 'your experience'. It's her way of pretending there's no wrong and no right, just people's experiences.

According to Alice, we can all live through the same event but have totally different experiences of it.

Mom folds her arms. 'I don't know where to start. There was all the stuff with the lightbulbs and the candles – and then that African drumming all night. I'm constantly getting calls from the school that she's late, once that she didn't show up.'

I turn around to face her. 'Come on, Mom – you told us all about the lightbulbs and the drum weeks and weeks ago. If you're going to pick on me to divert attention from the obvious question as to why you're late every time, you need to come up with some new material.'

I laugh and glance over at Ryan. I should get a smile for that last remark at least, but he's still not looking at me.

'Oh there's plenty of new material – don't get me started on new material. The school calling up every other day about you being late, not showing up—'

'Louise,' Dad says, 'go easy.'

'Go easy? Try fielding all the calls from the school, Joe. Then tell me to go easy.'

'I just don't think it's helpful, starting the session with such a critical tone, that's all. And I think Cassie has a point about diverting attention from you. We *were* talking about you – why it is you're always late.'

'Jesus Christ, Joe!' Mom's voice spirals higher. 'I'm sorry, okay? I'm sorry for being *five minutes* late. What do you want me to do? Flagellate myself? Throw myself out the window? The parking is horrible around here. None of the rest of you have to park.'

Dad makes a snorting sound.

'What?' Mom demands.

'That's so typical you. Throw an apology out and take it back immediately. Don't they tell you in A.A. that doesn't count?'

I try to catch Alice's eye. I told her in our one-to-one session about Mom missing meetings. In the beginning she went to seven a week, then five and last week she only went to two. I asked Alice to bring that up today, and if she's going to, now would be a really good time.

'You know what's typical of you?' Mom is leaning on the back of her chair, one finger pointing at Dad.

'Tell me!'

'Fixating on the small things, rather than the real issues—'

Dad sits back in his chair, folds his arms. 'Is that so? And you have your finger on the pulse of the real issues?'

He raises his eyebrows, sort of smirks. That face drives her crazy; he knows it does. It's a dance and they both know every move. I'm staring at Alice now but she looks unfazed. Maybe Mom is right, maybe she is a shitty therapist.

'Call me crazy if I think the real issue is that our daughter is sitting here, emaciated, dressed head to toe in black. That between sleeping and being on that damn computer she hardly leaves her room – let alone the house. That her art teacher said her paintings are showing signs of suicidal ideation.'

The silence after she said that is louder than anything anyone has said so far. I didn't know that – that thing about the suicidal ideation – and I want to laugh at how wrong Mrs. Roberts got it but I know laughing will make it worse.

'But you're right, Joe, it's much better to focus on me being five minutes late.'

After rehab Mom got her hair cut short but she still goes to fix it behind her ears, even though she doesn't need to anymore. Alice watches and then turns to me.

'How does it feel to hear your mother say that about you, Cassie?'

It's the seriousness of her voice that makes the laughter bubble up – giggles at first, then a snort, then full-blown laughing.

'You think this is funny?' Dad says, but Alice shoots him a look and he stops.

I clamp my lips together, shake my head, but the laugh fizzes out.

'I'm sorry,' I manage.

'What are you sorry for?' Alice asks.

I start to speak but when I try, laughs come out instead. Knowing they are all looking at me, being centre of their gaze, makes it worse, feeds the laughter and keeps it coming. This is so ludicrous, all of it. If only I could tell them the truth – if they'd believe me – it would be so much simpler. But they don't want the truth – anytime I bring up E.L., no one wants to hear it.

No one says anything while I am laughing and eventually I stop. There is silence.

'What are you feeling now?' Alice says.

'I don't know.'

'Guess, if you had to guess.'

Mad, glad, sad, lonely and scared. They are the five feelings that Alice talks about, week in, week out. I am laughing, so it must be glad.

'Glad,' I say. 'Happy.'

Alice nods slowly. 'What's making you feel happy right now?'

I shrug. It's okay to have the feeling and not be able to explain it. 'I don't know.'

There's a crash and we all look around. It's Ryan's chair legs, banging hard on the floor.

'This is bullshit!' He jumps out of his chair, walks into the middle of the circle. Alice is startled out of her therapy face and for a second I see a real emotion: fear. She's never said we have to stay in our chairs but no one's ever got up in the middle of a session before. He looks so tall. I didn't notice he'd got so tall.

Dad is first to react. 'Ryan, sit down.'

'No.' Alice is composed again, waves a hand at Dad. 'It's okay. What's bullshit, Ryan?'

'I want to go ... Can I just get out of here?'

The colour is high in his cheeks and he's rubbing his forehead with the heel of his hand the way he always does when he's upset. My mind brings up other times I've seen him rub his head like that – in front of the T.V. the day the towers fell, the Christmas Dad left, at school when Justin Caldwell kicked his backpack across the hall and called him a faggot. And now he's doing it because of me.

Alice doesn't tell him he can leave or that he should stay. Instead she asks him a question.

'Ryan, what's bullshit?'

He's pacing, circles, figure eights. He walks over to the window, back, behind his chair. When he gets like this, his words get jammed up inside. He's never had to tell me that, but I know, he's my kid brother and I know.

'All of it. You!' He points at Alice. 'You're supposed to be making her ... better.'

'Ryan, calm down, honey,' Mom says.

'Calm down?' He leans on the back of his chair, grips it. 'You talked about her wearing that black shit all the time. Did you know she wears it all to bed, Mom? Even her fucking sneakers! Did you know that?'

I don't know how he knows that but judging from Mom's face she didn't. I don't need to look at Dad to know he is sitting with his arms folded, his head bowed.

'We come here week after week and you guys fight and we all talk about this bullshit but no one talks about what really matters, what's really going on. She's getting worse. Don't you all see she's getting worse?'

'She's not taking those sleeping pills anymore, Ry,' Dad says. 'That was a big thing, that she stopped abusing the pills.'

Ryan lifts the chair in his gripped hands, slams it down on the floor. Hard.

'It was never about the fucking pills, Dad. Don't you see? There's something wrong with her – I saw her talking to herself in Barnes & Noble the other day – there's something majorly fucking wrong with her and none of you are doing a fucking thing about it.'

His cheeks are a flame of colour that's spreading out towards his ears. Any minute now, he's going to cry. He turns in a circle, like there is nowhere to go, and maybe there is nowhere to go. He sits back on the chair, hides his face in the crook of his arm. What he says next is barely audible.

'Someone needs to do something … to stop this.' He gulps in a breath. 'My sister is fucking dying or something and none of you are doing a fucking thing to stop it.'

And just like I knew they would, that's when his tears come. Despite myself, despite everything he's been saying, part of me wants to get up, to walk over and put my arms around him. To comfort him like I always used to when he was a little kid.

But he's not a little kid and it's a long time since I've comforted him and I'm not sure he'd want me to now. And even if he did, I don't think I can. I don't think I remember how to do that anymore.

CASSIE

I found out by accident that I could take things back to her but, once I knew, I couldn't believe I hadn't thought to check before. That night I'd been listening to *Astral Weeks,* over and over, trying to fall asleep and when I wake up 'Beside You' is playing, but I'm not in bed – I'm somewhere else.

It's daytime and I'm in the forest, all around me there's those trees with the moss hanging making strips of shade in the sunlight. I whip my head around but I can't see her and suddenly I am terrified that someone else will find me first. I yank the headphones out of my ears and my breathing comes a little easier without the music. My sneakers are on my feet. It feels better to be dressed. I turn off the music, put it in my pocket. Around me there are forest noises, birds, cracking of twigs, the sway of the moss. And in the middle of those noises I hear another sound – the rhythm of footsteps. For a second I freeze, as if standing statue still will mean I can't be seen. Then I think about climbing the tree, am trying to find a handhold on the smooth bark when the footsteps get closer. They are behind me now, whoever is there must see me. I grab on to a low branch but it's too far and my fingers slip off – grazed by the bark – and my sneaker slides against the trunk.

'Cassie?' There's a voice behind me. 'Cassie, that you?'

I turn around and it's her – thank God it's her. It's the first time I've seen her since the night at the riverbank, the first time we've had any contact since then. And I'm so relieved to see that she's smiling because that might mean she's not mad at me anymore.

'Thank God it's you! I was terrified it might be Nagle or someone.'

She laughs. I don't remember seeing her laugh before and it's quiet, like breath.

'What's so funny?'

'You ain't figured it out yet?'

'Figured what out?'

'They can't see you – I the only one who see you. So it don't matter who come along so long as I ain't talkin' to you. Then I gone end up in the lake like that house slave from the Morristown plantation.'

She laughs that soft laugh again.

'How do you know? I mean, are you sure?'

'That day under the house. You don't see 'cause you had you eyes close but Little Bill – he look righ' at you and he don't see you, even though you whiter than white in the dark. If he don't see you I figure no one can.'

She's still smiling – she looks so different when she smiles, with the sun lighting up her eyes, her skin, nothing like the girl I pulled out of the river. She hitches up her skirt, crosses her legs and sits right down in one motion, right where she's standing. There could be snakes around here – how does she know there aren't? But I take a chance, lower myself down too.

'So how are you doing? I've missed you. You haven't answered me for weeks.' I pull at the grass between us instead of looking at her. When I glance up she has stopped smiling and she's looking at the space between us too. 'I thought something might have happened to you.'

We both know what 'something' means – another episode by the river that I'm not there to stop. But then again, with Nagle and the Mistress around, it could mean anything else too.

'I was worried about you, E.L.'

I look over at her and her fingers are skimming the top of the blades of grass in front of her but she still doesn't say anything so I try again.

'Every time you cut me out like this, it hurts – I thought we were in this together.'

That's supposed to make her feel bad – guilty – about not getting back to me but when her head jerks up to look at me her chin juts out and there is the flare of anger in her eyes.

'We ain't in nothin' together – you make no mistake 'bout that.'

Her right hand grips at the grass and pulls it from the ground. Her last three fingers are at a funny angle from the knuckle part, like the bones are growing in a weird way. I didn't notice that before. Looking at her fingers makes me remember the pain in my own when I woke up after that day at the piano. My pain lasted a few days, but it went away – it's not something I live with every day.

'Listen, I know it might not feel that way all the time – I get it. You're stuck here, I get to come and go. But every spare minute I'm not with you, not talking to you, I'm doing research, I'm making plans to get you out of here.'

She's looking down at the grass again, her right hand systematically pulling chunks out and laying them to one side, her left balanced on her knee.

'I've been reading all about the Underground Railroad and how many slaves they helped to get up north. It's amazing, E.L. – you wouldn't believe the number of people who risked their lives to free slaves like you.'

'I don't know nothing 'bout no railroad.'

'I know. It's a secret. It's not a real railroad – more like a collection of people with access to boats and trains and things. But I bet someone here knows!' Despite myself I am getting excited. 'I bet if you asked Big Bill—'

'Don't you know nothin'? Don't you never listen to nothin' I tell you?' She spits the words out. 'Big Bill do his job best he can. He ain't got no time for folks talkin' 'bout 'scapin'. 'Specially 'bout some make-believe railroad.'

Her face looks hard – so different from how she looked just a few minutes ago. Above her dress her collar bones stick out. She is so thin. I think of our full fridge, wish I'd brought back food for her. And then I remember the iPod. I take it out of my pocket, unwrap the headphones from around my neck and put it in the grass between us.

She's frowning. 'What that?'

'It's called an iPod. It plays music.'

'How you play it?'

She picks it up and makes to strum the wire connecting the headphones and I'm about to ask what she's doing and then I realise she thinks it's an instrument, that she can play music on it. I want to laugh, but I hold it back.

'No, it's not an instrument. I mean it *plays* music. You know, like, like ... a radio.'

Her frown deepens and I realise I'm probably about half a century too early for that reference to work.

'This little box – it holds the music inside. Hundreds of songs. You choose which one you want.'

That's when she throws it at me, like it burns her to touch it. She slides away from me, back across the grass. 'That one of your demon boxes? You bring one of your demon boxes back here?'

She looks like she's going to get up and run. 'No, E.L. – wait, it's not a demon box. It's okay – wait.' I open my mouth to explain, to say something that will make her feel better and not for the first time it hits me how much further away she feels when we are right next to each other. Writing back and forth, all I ever feel are the ways we are the same, but, face to face, looking at each other, it's like we only see our differences.

I reach out, pick up the iPod and take a breath. I make an effort to talk really slowly. 'I understand how crazy it must seem to you, E.L., and I'm not even going to try to explain how it works. But this is called an iPod and it has music on it and where I'm from it's really normal and everyone has them – the same way everyone here has ... a bucket or clothes.'

She still looks suspicious, but she hasn't gotten up to run. 'Not ev'ryone has a bucket. I use share Charity's – now I got my own.'

'All right – okay. And yeah – it's like that with this. My brother used to share mine. And then he got his own. My point is it's just music, E.L. – nothing bad. No demons. Please, just listen. Just trust me.'

I pick up the headphones, put one in my ear and hold the other one out to her.

'Why I gone trust you? Some white girl from the future. How I know you ain't tryin' trick me?'

Part of me wants to shake her then, for saying that, after everything I've done for her, but another part of me thinks about Mr. Barrett in the parlour, about Charity standing in the circle of white men.

'I guess you won't know for sure until you try. But if I don't care about you – if I wanted to hurt you – why wouldn't I have let you drown that night? Why would I have risked my life trying to save you?'

He eyes are on me now, listening. What I say next is important.

'I'm doing everything I can to get you free, E.L., and you should believe that because that's the truth. But until I do, music is the best thing I can give you. Like Charity used to say about reading – music can set your soul free, your mind, no matter what they do with your body.'

I take the earphone from my ear and hit play so we can both the tinny sound of 'Beside You'. I place the iPod gently on the grass between us and something tells me to swivel around so my back is to her. Facing the trees, I think I hear something behind me, I think I hear her move. I don't know how much time I have, if the iPod will come back with me or stay here with her when I do, or if it will vanish entirely into some middle place. The sun has moved and it's beating down on us now and I can feel sweat make a line down my back under my T-shirt, feel it pool inside my sneakers. More than anything I want a drink of water – the one I know is next to my bed. I'm wasting my time here. I'm wasting my time on her. I want to go home.

And then I feel something touch my shoulder, her hand. I turn around.

She is sitting right behind me, the iPod in the lap of her dress. One of the earbuds is in her ear and she holds the other one out to me with the good fingers of her right hand. She is smiling.

'You want listen too?' she says.

I smile. And I take it from her. And I do.

E.L.

The music change. It keep changin'. One minute it slow magic music like what we listen to t'gether and then it somethin' diff'rent. This music ain't like nothin' I ever heard b'fore. This man shoutin' – he angry. Cassie show me how to push the button so the machine know to move the music on to the next one but I don't. Somethin' make me want to keep listenin' to this one.

I'm in the forest next to where I seen Cassie that day. I'm glad she come back. I'm glad we talkin' 'gain. Not jus' 'cause of the music but it good not to miss her no more. There 'nough people to miss without missin' her too.

It quiet – that happen b'tween each music. Firs' I think the machine broke but Cassie say when it stop workin' it ain't gone mean I done broke it. She say the box gone empty all the music out and when she come back she take it home and fill it 'gain. It don't make no sense to me but I try and r'member to trus' her.

Music on 'gain, slow this time. A woman. I like the man and his shoutin' better and I push the button and then he start all over 'gain. I wish I knew what he shoutin' 'bout, I wish I catch all the words. Cassie say there a lot cuss words in his music but I don't know what kind music got cuss words in it. I like the part where he shout 'bout losin' hisself and havin' one shot, not missin' it. That my fav'rite part.

I'm standin' now by the tree, I can't sit down and listen to him – it ain't like listenin' in Church. And my body want to move – my hands do, my feets. And I look 'round and there ain't nobody there, only me, so I let them.

It hard to tell you how it feel – that feeling. It fill me up – that the best I can tell you. Dancin' like that to this music it like I ain't tired. I ain't hungry. I don't feel the pain I a'ways feel in my back or my fingers. And I wish I know all the words 'cause I want to sing it. I want to shout. I want to scream.

Sometimes it leave me tired after I listen but not tonight. The sun like a fire b'hind the trees and then it get dark and it time for me to go to the cabins. I wrap the wire round the machine like Cassie show me and I put it in the tree trunk, next to Dolly. The music still in my body and my head and I wonder if that what it like for the Mistress, if that why she spend all her time playin' piano. Juba say she even play at night now when she s'pposed be sleepin'. But I don't want waste time thinkin' 'bout the Mistress so 'stead I take Dolly outta her tree and I swing her 'round by her little hand. I throw her in the air and catch her.

'Listen to it, Dolly.' I say. 'You ain't done never heard nothin' like it b'fore!'

I crazy. I know I crazy and knowin' that make me laugh so loud. I don't care. It feel good to feel crazy. It feel diff'rent. Actin' crazy, I don't feel so scared.

I kiss Dolly where her face all broke and fix her yellow hair. I put her next to the machine. It real dark now but I ain't scared. I ain't scared of steppin' on no snake. I ain't scared Nagle gone find me. I ain't scared of no one.

Cassie talkin' more 'bout this secret railroad that help people 'scape. Ev'ry time now she tellin' me a diff'rent story. A slave who covered hisself with onions so the dogs don't smell him. A slave who hid in a crate and they all think he cargo. Two slave that dress up like they white ladies goin' to a funeral and no one 'spect a thing.

I don't know who they is – all these slaves who 'scape. I ain't never heard of no one doin' that. Even Charity never say nothin' 'bout that. More than anythin' I wish she here and thinkin' 'bout her make the music feelin' empty out a bit. I wish I told her 'bout Cassie when I had the chance. I wish I knew what she think I should do.

Through the trees I see them all in the barn. It time for the cotton weighin'. From here I hear Nagle laugh then the sound of a lash. Someone cry out – a woman – and it sound like Nelly but maybe it Marjorie. Marjorie hate me now 'cause she back in the fields and if she gettin' lashed then it my fault. For a second I think 'bout sayin' sorry to her later but then I r'member what Charity say down by the river, the day she grab my face and my promise to her never to say sorry for somethin' that ain't my fault.

And all a sudden what she want me to do clear as the moon hangin' there in the sky. Charity want me to leave. She tell me to take a chance. To run 'way. To try. It like the man say in the music – he only got one shot. We all only got one shot. Maybe Cassie the one who help give it to me, but it my shot. And I the one who gone take it.

CASSIE

She's sitting in the living room watching *Grey's Anatomy*. No one watches *Grey's Anatomy* anymore. She looks up when I walk in, makes room on the couch next to her, but I walk past her over to Grandad's chair by the fireplace. I curl my legs up under me. She's wearing sweatpants – she never wears sweatpants.

'This guy and his wife are both in comas,' she says. 'I'll fill you in at the break.'

'Okay.'

I'm not here to watch the show with her but I watch it anyway. Or I pretend to be watching it. Really, I am watching her. The way she holds her glass, cupping it, draining it. The way she leans over to refill it before it's fully empty. The bottle is more than half gone now, three quarters gone. That's how I found out what was going on, when I walked into the kitchen yesterday and saw Ryan emptying wine down the sink.

'What are you doing?' I asked, even though it was pretty obvious what he was doing.

'She's drinking again.' He said it like an accusation, as if I was the one who had done something wrong.

The smell of wine filled the kitchen as he rinsed the bottle inside and out.

'Well? Aren't you going to say something? Did you know?'

As he turned to put the bottle in the recycling bin I wasn't surprised to see the flush in his cheeks and I know whatever I say is going to be the wrong answer.

'No. I didn't know.'

He made a fake laugh. 'Sure. Why would you? You've got too much going on in all your parallel universes to keep track of. Who cares about what's happening in your own actual home?'

He'd walked out of the kitchen then so even if I had wanted to answer him I didn't have a chance. Watching the *Grey's Anatomy* characters on screen in their shiny world with their shiny problems that will be resolved by the end of the episode, I replay his words in my head. On the couch, Mom laughs at something, drinks another sip of wine like what is happening is nothing. Maybe it is nothing.

At the commercial break she mutes the sound.

'Remember when this first came on we used to always watch it together?' She's smiling, her eyes are soft.

It seems like a hundred years ago but I do remember, the two of us sitting close munching on Kettle Corn, Dad coming in every now and then to roll his eyes or make a sarcastic remark about the plot.

'Yeah.'

'That was when it was really good – this show. Those were fun times.' She's smiling as if in her memory, things were perfect, as if there was never anything wrong. But even then the bottle was out – not on the coffee table, but on the kitchen counter – and I remember waiting to see which commercial break she'd offer to refill the popcorn bowl and come back with a refilled glass as well.

'Honestly, I never really liked this show. It was always lame.'

It's not true – that comment – it's supposed to hurt her and it does. She holds my gaze for a second before she sighs, takes another drink of wine. On T.V., two girls are laughing in a changing room. It's a dumb commercial for tampons. If I'm going to say something I have to say it now, before the break is over.

'I can't believe you're drinking again!'

She puts the glass down on the table. 'Ah, so that's what this is about.'

'What did you expect, Mom? That after rehab, months in A.A., that we're not going to say anything? To notice? You're not even going to talk about it?'

She runs her hand through her hair. 'Look, I tried A.A. and I discovered I'm not an alcoholic. It's good news, Cass. But you're right, I should have talked to you about it.'

The show is back on and her fingers move towards the remote. If she even touches the volume button I'm going to pick it up and throw it through the T.V. screen.

'Oh, so that's how it works? You say you're not an alcoholic, that you don't have a problem and that's that? What about the time you ended up in hospital?'

She holds up her glass. 'I'm having a glass of wine to unwind watching T.V. after a hard day's work like plenty of people do. No one's ending up in hospital. Does that look like a problem?'

I don't say anything.

'Look, you're right in a way. I was having a hard time going out. All those media events where they keep refilling your glass and I couldn't keep track. I couldn't control that but I'm not going to drink when I'm out anymore. Just the odd glass of wine at home. That's it.'

'Does Dad know?'

She picks up the cork, motions towards the bottle.

'If you want me to, I'll put it away right now. Cork the bottle. I'll even throw it down the sink if you want, if it upsets you that much.'

'Actually, it doesn't upset me. It upsets Ryan.'

She raises her eyebrows. 'It upsets Ryan?'

'Yes.'

'And since when are you so concerned with what upsets your brother? As I recall from one of our last family therapy sessions, *you* were the one who was upsetting him.'

I hate this part of her, the way she can take a conversation that's about one thing and twist it so then it's about something else. I stand up.

'Forget it, I don't care what you do. Go back to your wine and your dumb show.'

I almost make it out of the room. I walk around her, behind the couch, am at the door when she says what she knows will reel me back in.

'Funny how you forgave your grandfather so quickly, when he picked up again – but with me, of course, it's a different story.'

I am right there, at the door. It would be so easy to walk out, into the hall and up the stairs. E.L. is waiting for me, we are back talking to each other every night again since I brought her the iPod. We are planning, finally planning, her escape.

'I'm not having this conversation, Mom.'

One foot is in the hall, I am almost out. I can't see her face, only the top of her head over the back of the couch.

'You know what I learned when I was in A.A., Cassie? That's what's called denial – never wanting to talk about things, walking away from conversations you can't handle.'

That's what does it, grabs me back in like a fish hook that's hooked deep into my heart, and it's easier to be right there, back in the fight with her, as if somehow it will be more pain to set myself free.

'Give me a break – I can handle any conversation you want to have. I'm not the one who can't handle conversations! *I'm* not the one in denial!'

The words are spilling out now and somehow I am back at the end of the couch. She is smiling.

'Oh really – so you're finally ready to admit that what I wrote about in my memoir was the truth? That your grandfather left you and Ryan alone, locked in his bedroom, so he could go out drinking.'

I want to pick up her stupid bottle and hit her over the head with it.

'Are you for real, Mom? What's wrong with you? I never denied that happened. It just wasn't a big deal – I barely even remember it. And you even say in the memoir that he was back in A.A. the next day.'

'No big deal? Really?' She refills her glass. 'You wet the bed for months after that, do you remember that?'

A smell memory hits me: a thick rubber bedsheet, the tang of pee.

'I was four, Mom. Kids wet the bed.'

'Not you.' She shakes her head. 'You never had before. You changed after that. Do you remember that vacation house we rented in Maine? The time Ryan was playing around and he locked you in the bedroom and then the key broke? You screamed your head off. Dad had to break the door down. I remember wondering afterwards, if that was connected to it as well.'

'Whatever, Mom. I'd leave the psychobabble to Alice, if I was you.'

The words come out fast but not fast enough so I don't register that my heart has kicked up a notch, two notches. I remember the house in Maine, my hand on the doorknob, twisting, pushing, pulling. Like the bathroom doorknob in Gabi's house that came off in my hand the time I got stuck in there, the only time her mom had ever yelled at me – to stop being hysterical, that she was going to get me out. Of course she did get me out and I was embarrassed afterwards but I hadn't locked it since, always kept it a bit ajar even when her brothers and Dad were home. Not that it meant anything.

'Did it ever come up with Alice? Did you ever tell her about it?'

She puts her glass down on the table again. It's empty now, the bottle too, no need to pour it anywhere. I almost told Alice about the dream last week – reaching for the handle, the baby crying in the background, the smell of his pee. I'd almost told her but something stopped me and I'm glad now, that I hadn't.

'What we discuss is private, Mom. I thought you knew that.'

Grey's Anatomy is on the final break and I wish I'd never said I didn't like it, wished I'd sat down next to her on the couch and just watched it like she wanted me to and we could have avoided this conversation entirely.

'I can imagine it though – you telling her how wonderful your grandfather was, what a terrible mother I am.'

I feel a twist of guilt as her words graze the truth.

'She probably sees me on *Oprah* and thinks, what has she got to share with the world? She can't even look after her own daughter.'

She's started crying, doesn't bother to hide it. Her make-up will be a mess. I saw Angelina the other day using Oxyclean on a pillowcase, trying to get out the mascara marks.

'Mom, she doesn't think that.'

'All I'm asking for is a level playing field. That's all, Cass. He was a human being – just like the rest of us. I can't compete with some idealised ghost. None of us can.' She glances up at me; she's reading my reaction. 'It's not my fault you lost him, Cassie.'

On T.V. the credits are rolling and already the next show is coming on – the screen split in two like it's too much to feel the end of something without something new to fill the space. This is the room we sat in that morning, me and Ryan together on the couch and Dad got down on his hunkers and told us that Grandad had gone to Heaven while Mom was standing by the window with Auntie Cathy, the two of them holding hands.

That was the day, the day I'd always been dreading but I never blamed her that he died, that she hadn't done enough. Not once. But there was another day – the day I sneaked the memoir from the pile, the day I read what she wrote, the day I couldn't stop turning those pages no matter how much I wanted to. That was the day – the worst day. That was the day I really lost him.

I don't say anything. I don't try and explain something she'll never understand but I don't comfort her either. I don't take the empty bottle of wine to the kitchen to rinse it out and recycle and when I walk out into the hall I don't run. I take the stairs slowly, not two at a time.

And I don't slam the door of my room. I don't throw myself on the bed. I don't wail. I don't cry. I don't scream. I don't even sniff.

I take my laptop out of my backpack and I power it on. I open a new document. And I start to write to E.L.

E.L.

Mornin' time the best time to find Big Bill on his own. He a'ways up b'fore the bugle no matter how late he work the night b'fore. Charity say his mornin' time like his little bit freedom. That bein' up b'fore the bugle make him feel like he got choices.

He washin' by the fire pit wearin' only pantaloons, no shirt. I fill my bucket from the barrel by the cabin door and bring it over. I leave it on the floor by where he standin' and he look 'round, surprise.

'Thank you,' he say.

I smile but I don't say nothin'. I ain't never spoke to him like this b'fore, not jus' him and me. He pick up the bucket, throw it over his back. Some water splash my foot.

'That feel good,' he say. 'It gone be sticky today.'

I nod.

'You mus' be glad you back in the big house – 'specially on days like this.'

It a question but I don't know how to answer so I don't say nothin'. 'Stead I look down at my feets.

'Is there somethin' you want tell me, E.L.? Somethin' on your mind?'

He standin' right in front of me now. He so tall. He strong, the strongest slave at Riverside Hall. If he ain't done 'scaped then no one gone 'scape.

'You know anythin' 'bout up north?' The words come out real fast. 'They say there a railroad that go there. That slaves free there.'

He look 'round but there ain't no one near us. At firs' I think he mad but then he bend down so his big face close to mine.

'Who been fillin' your head with all this? Charity? She told you 'bout this b'fore she leave?'

My heart make a jump like it 'live 'gain. Charity know 'bout the trains. That mean it true. Cassie ain't lyin'.

I shake my head.

'Then who told you?'

Now he sound like he gone get mad like the time in the barn when he catch Charity teachin' us 'bout readin' but I don't care how mad he get I ain't gone tell him 'bout Cassie.

He look 'round 'gain, keep his voice real low.

'Don't let no one hear you talkin' 'bout no railroad, 'bout goin' up north. You don't know what they do to slaves they hear talkin' 'bout things like that.'

'So it real then? It true that slaves 'scape?'

He stand up real tall. He take a rag from the fence and wipe his face and neck.

'Some do. Them who got a lot of help and a lot of money. Even then, mos' end up dead. Anyone hear you even talk like this the Master gone sell you som'place you don't want be. R'member what happen with Charity?'

It make me mad then, the way he say that. Like I ever gone forget what happen with Charity.

'The Master ain't never gone sell me.'

I ain't plannin' on sayin' that. He dryin' himself on the front and then he stop.

'Why you so sure that?'

My heart goin' real fast. I think 'bout sayin' somethin' else but the way he look at me all I can think of is the truth.

'Charity. She told me–'

'What she done told you?'

'She told me that he my daddy! That Miss Ellen my sister and we got the same name!'

He throw the rag down on the floor. It land near my foot but I don't pick it up. He shake his head.

'She done told you all that, did she? She tell you how many masters father children on they plantations? That some plantations got six or eight half-white babies like they master? Maybe he your father but that ain't the same thing as being your daddy.'

'But Charity – she say you tell her he love my mamma. She think maybe he love me too–'

Big Bill laugh. He pick up the rag 'gain, shake it out. I feel more mad than b'fore and that make me brave, brave 'nough to say more.

'What you laughin' at? You sayin' that ain't true?'

He smile but it ain't a real smile. 'Love? There ain't no such thing as love here, child, maybe som'place else but not here.' He rub the part of his chest where hair grow. 'He don't love none of us and 'sides, he broke – there ain't no money to buy no one no freedom. Any day he gone start sellin' us. He have to. Why you think the Mistress so mad? Why you think she hide 'way playin' that piano all damn day long?'

I don't know the Mistress play the piano more when she mad. And if she mad I think it 'cause Miss Ellen never 'round the house no more. Or maybe 'cause Mr. Barrett don't like me none and that why he ain't come back.

Big Bill lookin' at me like he waitin' for me to argue with him or say somethin' else but I think I done said 'nough.

'You don't know nothing, E.L. You only a child. I sorry you lost your mamma. Lost Charity. But don't make this harder on yourself. Don't make this no harder than it a'ready is.'

He done dried his whole body 'cept his back. And when he turn 'round to go to the cabin I see there more lines on it and they fresh, more red than the others. Watchin' him walk 'way I wonder what he do to get the new stripes. I wonder what they do to slaves they hear talkin' 'bout the railroad and goin' up north. And how it gone be any worse than that.

CASSIE

She's in my mind all the time now. Not in a bad way – not like before when I was trying to make her quiet. She's there in a way I can talk to her – we talk back and forth – without paper, without notes, without the laptop. Which is just as well, since I had to sell it.

I say 'had to' sell it but I know that really, it was a choice. After she talked to Big Bill, E.L. finally believed for sure about the railroad but she was even more scared than before and she kept asking me where she was going to get the money from. The first thing I thought was about bringing her back cash, but it looks too different and that's when I had a better idea: to bring back gold. The first laptop I pawned was the one that Dad gave me for my birthday – it was still in the box – and I got two bracelets, a necklace and another necklace with a locket in exchange. It seemed a lot in the store, but not when I got home, and that's when I decided to pawn the other laptop too – the one I wrote to E.L on. I got a cool gold watch for that one – an old one on a chain – so now at night I've started to sleep with that in my pockets, along with the other jewellery and the packets of almonds and string cheese and Ryan's iPod because I know the battery in my one must be long dead by now.

The gold you have? It gone be 'nough?

That's E.L.'s voice. She must ask me that fifty times a day and the truth is I don't know. I know the conductors on the railroad are good people, that they don't take any money. But I also know most of the slaves ran into people they had to bribe, with money and with other things too. I don't want to scare her more, but I want to tell her the truth.

I don't know yet if it's going to be enough but I'm going to get more. I'll make sure you have enough.

I have no idea how I can get more money. Mom is mad as hell with me for getting my laptop stolen – that's what I told her – and she refuses to buy me another one. I counted on the fact that she'd forgotten about the one Dad got me for my birthday and she had but I was surprised that Ryan didn't remember.

I know I need more gold and every day I have this terrible image of E.L. running out of money, getting caught, punished, worse. She's the one taking the big risks, not me. She's the one putting her life on the line and I need to support her any way I can.

How I gone find folks to help me? This is another thing she asks all the time. Big Bill say you need help.

We're not going to take any risks until we have someone – a name at least. I've been scouring books and the internet. There's got to be someone and I'll find him. Don't worry. You're not going anywhere till we have a name.

What if I get lost? What if I can't find the person who gone help? What if Nagle catch me?

As soon as I answer one of her fears another one jumps in, that's what it feels like, and sometimes – like today – it's exhausting. I say what I always say, what calms her down.

It's going to be okay, E.L. God wants you to be free. He has a plan and he's going to give us all the help you need. He hasn't brought us this far to let us down now.

I've started to say that to her twice, three times a day. I don't know if I even believe in God, but she does, and hearing it makes her feel better for a while, which means I feel better. And the more I say it, the more I start to believe it too.

There's no turning around now, no way back. Only forward and the only way we're going to get there is together. I have to believe that. I want to believe that. I do believe that.

Even on the days I don't.

E.L.

When I tell Cassie no slave ain't never done 'scaped I ain't lyin'. I forget 'bout Jasper 'cause he ain't never done 'scape from Riverside Hall. And anyway, I don't know if it count that he 'scape from his old plantation 'cause they catch him and bring him back. So I don't never even think of askin' him. And if it ain't for that day in the barn I prob'bly ain't never think of askin' him at all.

I hear the noise b'fore I seen them. I supp'sed to be gettin' peaches for Juba to make cobbler.

'Be quick,' she say, 'don't waste no time now', and I been runnin' from the big house. I ain't stopped to listen to the music 'cause the machine die and that mean no more music till Cassie come back. And it mus' be 'round noon 'cause after the bright outside I don't see nothin' in the barn 'cept blackness at firs'. And that when I hear them.

The noise like breathin' – fast breathin' – but there another noise too. Someone cry out like they bein' hurt. At firs' I think it one of the animals, I think it the horse but he in the field pullin' the cart. And then it ain't so black no more and my eyes see what make the noise right there in fron' of me. And it ain't no horse.

It happen real fast. Tellin' you here, it like it slow, but it ain't slow. If it slow like this I woulda close the door and I woulda told Juba there weren't no more peaches left and I wouldn't care how mad she done get with me later when she find out I lyin'. But 'cause it happen fast by the time I seen them I a'ready in the barn and it too late to leave. His back to me and I know it Jasper straight 'way from his skinny dark back shiny with stripes – he got more stripes than anyone. His pantaloons down 'round his knees and there other knees hooked round his waist. White knees.

I know them knees. I know them legs and the blue skirt pushed up and the arms 'round his neck and the mouth open showin' pink inside makin' them sounds. I done heard many sounds outta that mouth but I ain't never heard noises like this.

B'fore I know I goin' to, I runnin' 'cross the barn.

'You stop it! You let her go!'

I reach up my arm to hit him and I ain't thinkin' 'cause even though he skinny he strong, he a'most as strong as Big Bill.

'You leave Miss Ellen alone!'

He turn 'round – grab my wrist real hard. And he musta let her go 'cause she yell out and fall back 'gainst the wall and down onto the dust.

His grip on my wrist hard like metal. I squirm to get 'way, but he too strong.

'Let me go! I gone tell the Master! I gone tell the Master what you doin' to her!'

That prob'ly not too clever to say that 'cause when I do he drag me closer and clamp his other hand on my mouth. It cover part of my nose too so I can't breathe.

'E.L!' Miss Ellen gettin' up off the floor. 'Jasper – let her go!'

I try to catch the skin of his hand with my teeth but he hold me too tight to open my mouth – he hold the bone of my jaw tight, like he hold my arm. His face close and it cover in sweat. His scar shinier than rest of him. When he speak it move.

'Little bitch tryin' to bite me!'

There no air. It like bein' in the collar. I can't get no breath. When I think that, that when Charity voice come in my head clear as anythin': 'You can breathe, E.L., breathe slow, breathe with me.' I pull my head back so there a tiny space b'tween my nostril and his hand. I breathe slow. I breathe with Charity.

'Let her go, Jasper! You're hurting her!'

Miss Ellen hair a mess and her face red. She closin' up the buttons at the front of her dress but she don't look hurt. His grip on my wrist loosen but his hand on my mouth stay the same.

'Little bitch gone tell your pa,' he say. 'She gone tell ev'ryone.'

'Let her go. Let me explain it to her. We can trust her.'

They talkin' like they forget I here, even though they talkin' 'bout me. Real slow, he take his hand 'way from my mouth. He ready to clamp back soon as I do any little thing only I ain't doin' nothin' 'cept takin' big gulps air. Then he let go my wrist and I hold it with my other hand. I don't want see his face so I look at Miss Ellen.

'E.L., you can't tell anyone – this has to be our secret.'

Jasper righ' b'hind me. I feel his breath. I wish he go so I can say what I have to say but he still there and I got to say it anyway.

'He hurt you, Miss Ellen – we got to tell you daddy. You don't need let him hurt you.'

'See? I told you!' Jasper grab my arm tight 'gain.

'Wait!' Miss Ellen hold her hand up. 'He wasn't hurting me, E.L. I wanted him to do this.'

That don't make no sense, why she wan' do that, but I don't get to say nothin' 'cause she keep talkin'.

'Me and Jasper – we love each other! But you can't tell anyone. Anyone, E.L. – especially Daddy. He'd send Jasper away and I couldn't bear it.'

That when I know Miss Ellen musta gone crazy 'cause if her daddy find out he gone do a lot worse than send Jasper 'way. And I want say that but b'fore I can somethin' happen inside and I know I gone be sick. I pull 'way from Jasper and when I cough, vomit come out. The coughin' take me down to my knees and more vomit come. It spray on the floor and back up onto my face.

I feel somethin' on my back, somethin' push me.

'Filthy nigger bitch!'

'Stop it, Jasper! Don't do that!'

'She a'most get me – she doin' that on purpose!'

Miss Ellen down on the floor now, next to me. 'E.L., are you all right? Breathe. Jasper – get her some water. Run, will you? Hurry!'

More coughin' come and more vomit come and I see Jasper pull his pantaloons back up and run out the door. Miss Ellen hand on my back. Soft. Slow, like Charity hands. The cough come 'gain but there less vomit and then only coughin' and no more vomit. That when I feel that I shakin'.

'Sorry, Miss Ellen,' I say, 'I ain't been sick on purpose–'

'I know. It's all right.'

'It a mess. I gone go clean it.'

I try stand up but her hand push me back down.

'It's all right, E.L. Jasper can clean it up. You had a shock. You can stay here and rest.'

'But Juba – she send me for peaches.'

She still rubbin' my back. 'I'll bring her the peaches. I'll tell her you're running an errand for me.'

She smilin' like it all so easy. She ain't never done my work for me b'fore. Her hand make circles on my back. She ain't never touched me like this b'fore neither.

'You just need to promise me you won't tell anyone, E.L. No one. Not Daddy or Mamma. Not even Marjorie.'

I don't know why she say that. Marjorie the last person I gone tell somethin' like this. There ain't no one I tell somethin' like this to 'cept Cassie, and she don't count.

'I promise.' I say. I look at her, I want say more. I want to ask her how she can do that with him, why it don't hurt her. She look at me and it like she see the question even though I can't find no words to ask it.

'When two people love each other it makes it different. It's not the same thing as ... as ...' She stop, look at the floor. 'When you find someone you love – you'll see. It won't feel like the same thing. Do you understand, E.L.?'

She smilin' like she want me to und'stand and I nod like I do, but I don't. And I don't ask what she mean when she say it not the same thing, 'cause I think I know. I think she talkin' bout what happen in the parlour with Mr. Barrett and I don't know how she know what he do when he come over but I think she do. And it don't make no sense to me what she sayin' 'cause there ain't no love in what he do to me. There ain't nothin' but hate and pain, mine and his all mussed up t'gether.

'You won't say anything to anyone, E.L., will you?'

Her hand on my back stop. The heat come through my dress. There a noise at the barn door and we both jump but it only Jasper with a pail. The water slop over the side and onto the floor.

'No, Miss Ellen, I won't say nothin'. I promise'

'Thank you, E.L. It'll be our secret. Just between the three of us.' She smile and then she take her hand 'way. 'See, Jasper, I told you we could trust E.L.'

Jasper look at me with that scar that look like he smilin' only he ain't smilin'. He dump the water on the floor.

'That for you to clean up this mess,' he say.

'Jasper, you do it, will you? E.L. isn't well. She's going to rest.'

For a second Miss Ellen sound like her mamma and I don't know if she see the flash of anger in Jasper eyes b'fore he look 'way but I do. He pour water on the vomit and kick at the dust with his foot.

'Nagle gone be lookin' for me. He gone beat me,' he say.

Miss Ellen stand up, put her hand on his neck, real gentle jus' like she had it on me.

'Let me look after Nagle,' she say.

She kiss him on the side of his mouth – right on his scar – and when the kiss finish she fix her dress b'fore she put her shoes on and she walk out of the barn leavin' me there with Jasper. I think he gone say somethin' to me but he don't say nothin', he keep cleanin' and I sit and watch him. And it only when he done and gone too that I r'member Juba and her peaches. Miss Ellen done forgot to take them and by the time I bring them to Juba she so mad she don't stop huffin' and puffin' till the Mistress come in and ask what the matter and Juba straighten her dress and say she jus' upset 'cause the cobbler takin' longer to make than regular and she look at me but I lucky 'cause she don't say nothin' else.

Later, when I see Jasper he got a fresh stripe 'cross his shoulders and he ain't been so lucky 'cause I hear Nelly talkin' to Linda 'bout him disappearin' from the field and gettin' a beatin' from Nagle when he come back. And I think Miss Ellen done forget to talk to Nagle too, jus' like she forget the peaches and I wonder what she doin' that she forget ev'rythin' so quick 'specially for someone she s'pposed to love. And I wonder if he mad with her or if the stripe worth it for what he get to do with her in the barn? If he got so many stripes that it don't matter to get one more?

Lookin' at his face I try to figure it out but there ain't no tellin' 'cause lookin' at his face it impossible to know what he feelin' or if he feelin' anythin' at all.

CASSIE

Dad finally gets me and Ryan to go to the movies with him. It's over a month since he suggested it in the therapy session and to see how excited he is about it makes me feel guilty and irritated all at the same time.

On screen there's a trailer for the new Harry Potter movie: *The Order of the Phoenix.*

'We can go see that when it comes out,' Dad says in what's supposed to be a whisper.

'Dad, shh, everyone can hear you.'

'It's the trailers! We're allowed to talk.'

He looks at me waiting for an answer but I stare at the screen. On his other side Ryan is shovelling popcorn into his mouth, ignoring us.

'Is this going to be the fourth Harry Potter movie?'

He says it in a real whisper this time and the flick of guilt is there again.

'The fifth.'

'We've seen them all together so far, haven't we? We should go see this one together too – we should make a pact that we see them all together, the whole series.'

I want him to shut up. He sounds desperate and there's no way the group of kids behind us didn't hear. I slump lower in my seat.

'Can we just watch this, Dad? I'm trying to watch this.'

I hate the way he looks so wounded, like my response has physically hurt him. I nearly say something when he turns back to face the screen but I don't. Ryan has a fist of popcorn that he lets fall into his mouth a piece at a time. Some of it falls down his shirt but he doesn't seem to notice. I hate the way he eats lately – like an animal. I hate that he just seems to opt out of talking when we're with Dad and leaves the whole conversation to me.

The one good thing about being at the movies is that I get to talk to E.L. without anyone bothering me. Over dinner it was tricky – I kept finding myself beginning conversations with her, trying to listen or talk, and then I'd realise Dad was saying something, waiting for an answer. It happened twice, three times, and the look on his face was worse than the wounded look earlier: it reminded me of the way he looked at the hospital that day, and that was the worst look of all.

On screen the movie has burst to life with a car chase that is now turning into a chase on foot down narrow alleys and up flights of stairs. I glance at Dad and he's enthralled. I close my eyes. It's easier to pick up the conversation if I close my eyes.

I think you can leverage that – what you know about Miss Ellen and Jasper.

E.L. has been telling me about it – finding them in the barn. It's what we were talking about during dinner. I think it might take a minute for her to come back, but she's there straightaway.

What that mean – leverage?

Use it. You know – you have something over them. A secret. You can use it to get stuff you want. Maybe he can tell you something about the Underground Railroad?

I flutter my eyes open and the scene has changed. The hero is with a woman now, in an elevator. I close them again.

I don't know, Cassie. I promise Miss Ellen I ain't gone say nothin'. And I scared of him.

I know, E.L. But he's probably scared of you too. You're the one who has power over him. You're the one who could get him sold.

Or killed. The Master find out – he gone kill him.

Sure, he might – if he ever actually gets back from Charleston!

There's silence then and I know I messed up, saying that thing about the Master. Despite what Big Bill said I think she still has ideas of some kind of reunion with him, maybe even that he'll set her free. She's never said that, but somehow I know.

I open my eyes to check the movie. They are in another country now – Germany maybe or Holland. In the light from the screen Dad and Ryan look like older and younger versions of each other, eating popcorn with the same rhythm. I go back to E.L.

You told me that Jasper had tried to escape before from his old plantation. I know he got caught but he was going somewhere – he might have had some information. Even if he has a name, I can look it up and find out if there's any record of this person helping other slaves.

I don't know. Maybe.

When she gets like this it's better to leave her alone and come back to it later. She's scared of Jasper; I know that's what's going on, but I don't push it. We're so close now, that's one of the only pieces of the puzzle left. The other day I found a copy of a slave pass online and I doctored it to include E.L.'s name and printed it out on yellowed paper that looked like parchment. Every night, the slave pass and a map go in my pockets now, along with the gold and the food. I've had to start wearing my black hoody to bed as well, so there's space to put it all. When I have everything on, the last thing I do is spray myself all over with perfume so that when I trade clothes with E.L. that will put the dogs off the scent.

Getting ready for bed is way more work now than getting up in the morning, and that's why I'd refused to stay in Dad's new place tonight. It came up again, over dinner and he was obviously pretty hurt about it, not that he said that directly. Instead, he just made these little half-remarks and sighs about how he'd been excited for us to see it, and how he did up the second bedroom in my favourite colours. When he went to pay the bill, Ryan started on me too, saying that it was only one night and could I not do something for someone else for once? He didn't get it. It was only one night but what if that was the night I went back to her? I wanted to tell him that. I wanted to tell him that I'd like it too – spending a night in a new room, wearing pyjamas in a new bed, without stuff digging into me, without the smell of perfume keeping me awake. I wanted to tell him that sometimes it felt like my whole life was spent doing things for someone else. But I knew he wouldn't get any of that, so I didn't answer him and he walked away, mad as usual.

Dad's elbow bumps mine by mistake and I jerk open my eyes. He is looking at me.

'You okay?' he asks in his non-whisper.

'I'm fine.'

I smile. I look like I'm okay. And I am okay. Me and E.L. both are. Our plan is nearly complete, we're nearly there. We don't need him, his help. It turns out we never did.

'I thought I heard you say something? Were you saying something?'

'No.' I shake my head, stare at the screen. 'I didn't say anything.'

Ryan is staring straight ahead, pretending not to notice. Behind us I hear someone say, 'Shh.'

Dad stares at me and I stare at the screen. Every now and then he glances back over and I know it's too risky to do anything else other than watch the movie, that he'll probably quiz me about it later. So I keep my eyes open and every time I hear E.L.'s voice I tell her I'll talk to her later and when she won't quiet down I take a mouthful of popcorn that I crunch down on extra hard to try and drown her out.

E.L.

He down by the river. I don't 'spect to see him down here. He s'pose to be comin' in from the field or weighin' cotton in the barn but he there standin' with his back to me. When I get closer I see he got a fishin' pole in his hand.

It three, four weeks since I seen him in the barn with Miss Ellen. I think after what I know he gone be diff'rent 'round the fire in the mornin' or at night but he the same as he ever was. Mos' the time he don't even pay me no mind.

He ain't seen me yet. Mos' the time when I collectin' branches for the fire I stay in the middle of the forest – I don't hardly ever come over here, to the edge. Bein' down by the river r'mind me of the day Charity hit me and what she say 'bout Mamma. And it r'mind me of the night Cassie come and pull me outta the river. No, there ain't no good mem'ries down here.

It ain't too late to turn 'round, go back b'fore he see me. But somethin' make me stay, somethin' make me walk over to him.

He got his shirt on so I can't see his stripes but I know they there und'neath. I try to 'magine Miss Ellen hand on his stripes, touchin' them. Maybe she even kiss them the way I seen Charity kiss Big Bill stripes one night when she think we all 'sleep. Miss Ellen ain't said nothin' 'bout what I seen in the barn since it happen neither. She ask me to make up her fire and empty her bath like she a'ways do. Like nothin' any diff'rent.

The branches light in my arms. I need to go get more but I keep walkin' over to where he standin'. I think 'bout when I tell Cassie the secret – 'bout findin' them in the barn – she say that secret give me power. She say he mus' know somethin' 'bout gettin' free, even if he done been caught.

I righ' b'hind him now. Real close.

'Jasper.'

My voice so low I barely hear it and I think he ain't never gone hear me over the sound of the river. I 'bout to say his name 'gain, but he turn 'round, real slow.

He look at me like he ain't surprise to see me. He don't say nothin'. I keep walkin' then stop. I closer than I ever been to him 'cept that day in the barn. I take a deep breath and make my voice louder this time.

'What you doin'?'

'What it look like?'

'You snuck 'way from the field?'

He shake his head and look back at the river. The rod twitch in his hands and he steady it.

'Yup.'

'You ain't worried 'bout what Nagle gone do he find you ain't workin'?'

He don't look at me. He keep his head turn so it face the river. The ear near to me got a piece missin' from the top like a triangle and I r'member hearin' Linda tellin' Rose and Nelly that he got tore apart by dogs b'fore he came to Riverside Hall. I 'bout to ask him 'gain when he turn his head 'round and laugh. He nods at the branches in my arms.

'That what you call this? Work? You think you workin'?'

Collectin' branches part of my work and he know that too but there somethin' 'bout the way he ask that make me think that sayin' yes the wrong answer. That I don't even und'stand the question.

'A workin' man – he get paid the end of the day,' he say. 'He sow his seeds, tend to his crops, harvest them, sell them – he get paid. His labourers – they get paid. They buy food. Clothes for they family. Tobacco. They rest and then they work some more.'

His rod jump and twitch and he grip it and step back.

'Workin' and slavin' – there a diff'rence. Dumb girl like you don't know that, but there is.'

'I ain't dumb! I know there a diff'rence!'

He laugh. 'You ain't never even set foot outside these walls. You don't know nothin'!'

It make me real mad when he say that.

'Jus' 'cause I grown up here don't mean I some dumb girl. I know things!'

'Oh yeah? What you know?'

'I know all 'bout the Und'ground Railroad!'

I ain't planned to say that but the words – they jus' jump on out and then they there on the grass b'tween us like fish floppin'. I know this ain't the way to do this. I know I gotta be careful 'bout how to trade his secret for mine.

His small eyes look smaller. 'What you know 'bout the Und'ground Railroad?'

I in too far now, I got to keep going.

'I know there people who help slaves 'scape up north or to Canada.'

Somethin' change in his eyes and I know he 'mpress I know 'bout Canada.

'What people? White folks? You mus' be dumber than I thought if you think white folks helpin' us.'

He laugh 'gain. It do sound dumb. Maybe Cassie wrong. But then I think of all them things she been tellin' me. All them stories. And I think that maybe he testin' me. I hold the branches closer, stand tall.

'Some white folks and some free slaves–'

'There ain't no such thing as a free slave!'

He right, they ain't slaves no more. I think of the word Cassie use.

'You right. They ain't slaves. They African-Americans. Them and the white folks help slaves get on boats and hide them in their barns and churches. Sometimes in tunnels under the ground.'

He frown like he confuse' but he listenin' now.

'Who told you 'bout all this?' he say.

Now it my turn to stay silent.

'I said, who told you all this stuff 'bout the railroad?'

He start to look real mad. It gettin' dark and if I ain't back with the branches I gone be in trouble. I think 'bout runnin' back to the forest without sayin' any more but then I think of Cassie and all she doin' to get me free and I know it time to be brave.

'None your bus'ness. Why don't you tell me ev'rythin' you done know 'bout it? Who in Charleston to talk to 'bout it.'

'I don't know no folks in Charleston to talk to.'

'I know you do – I know you try 'scape b'fore. And you gotta tell me. You gotta give me a name to help.'

He sneer. 'Why I got tell you?'

''Cause if you don't I gone tell the Master 'bout you and Miss Ellen.'

I say that part real fast. My heart beatin' faster than the words. It seem like his face get darker. All 'round us it dark now too, a'most night. His face so black it like it part of the dark so alls I can see is the white part his eyes and the shine on his scar.

'You think you can blackmail me?' he say. 'You think the Master gone b'lieve you?'

Inside I feel cold. Scared. Small. But he don't know that 'less I let him see. I stand tall, hold the branches tight. I make myself smile.

'The Master like me. He listen to me. He trus' me.'

He laugh. His laugh last a long time. The rod jerk and he hold it only in one hand now like he forgot he s'ppose be fishin'.

'He trus' you? The Master trus' you?' His teeth white in the dark when he smile. 'What 'bout Miss Ellen? What you think she gone do? She gone deny it and you think her pa gone take the word some slave over the word his own daughter?'

I could tell him the Master my daddy too but if I tell him my secret I ain't got no power no more.

''Sides,' he say. 'You promise her you never gone say nothin' and you ain't never gone go 'gainst that. She ain't never gone forgive you if you do that.'

I hold the branches tight 'gainst my chest. 'I think you wrong 'bout that – her forgivin' me. You righ' 'bout the promise, she make me promise three times not to tell him. But you ever hear 'bout denyin' somethin' so much, sayin' you don't want somethin' happen – that sometime that exactly what you do want?'

'You crazy!' He shake his head. 'You jus' plain crazy if you think she want her pa to know she whorin' 'round with the blackest slave here.'

'Maybe,' I say. 'But I known her a long time and I think more than anythin' she want him to pay her some mind. I think she darn near do anythin' for him to be here 'stead of 'way in Charleston all the time.'

My heart beat fast sayin' all that but I know I gotta say it. I don't know if it true, not for sure, but I been thinkin' a lot 'bout the Master and somethin' Miss Ellen say to me one time 'bout her being invisible. And even if I ain't right, maybe I right 'nough so that Jasper think I is.

His laughin' stop. 'You talkin' crazy talk. She love me. She told you.'

'Maybe I wrong, but you sure I ain't? She love you so much why she let you get stripes from Nagle that day? She love you so much she gone be able stop them hangin' you from a tree?'

Jasper throw down his rod on the grass. My heart beatin' so loud he mus' hear it. What I thinkin' sayin' all this? What I thinkin' sayin' all this here where he can kill me and throw me in the river and no one ever find me? But then I hear Cassie voice – 'you doin' great E.L.', she say. And I keep goin'.

'You give me a name – someone in Charleston gone help me – I won't say nothin'. Then when I gone you ain't gotta worry no more.'

Jasper shake his head.

'What make you think I ain't gone tell them 'bout you plannin' on runnin' 'way?' he say, 'I can tell the Master 'bout that – tell Nagle.'

He right, he could, but I shake my head like he shakin' his. 'Who you think they gone b'lieve? A run'way slave who ev'ryone know no good? Or a house slave who ain't never got in no trouble? You tell an'body 'bout me leavin' and I say you lyin' and that you tryin' to get rid of me 'cause I seen you and Miss Ellen in the shed.'

His face twist and he kick his fishin' rod and I think he gone grab me or hit me or somethin' and I jump back but I don't need to 'cause he don't do nothin'. 'Stead he bend down like he gone pick up his fishin' pole but the river done pull it 'way into the water. That when he walk real close to me so his skinny face a'most touch mine.

'I wrong 'bout you. You ain't such a dumb slave after all. You cunnin'. You sly.'

I want step back but I don't want him knowin' I 'fraid. His mouth too close. I don't know how Miss Ellen kiss that mouth.

'But that don't mean I gone help you. Tell the Master. Tell him an'thin' you want. Hangin' from a tree ain't the wors' thing to happen to a nigger som'place like this.'

He turn 'way, spit on the grass.

'I jus' need a name,' I say. 'Please, Jasper – jus' give me a name.'

Soon as I say it, I know it wrong. He hear it in my voice – that I 'fraid now, that he got the power back.

'I ain't givin' you nothin'. If you gone try 'scape, you on you own. You ain't gettin' no help from me.'

There ain't nothin' more to say then so I jus' turn 'round and start walkin' toward the forest where it dark and there gone be snakes out by now. There tears in my eyes but I ain't gone let him see. The tears ain't 'cause of bein' sad, they there 'cause I mad – mad 'cause I let Cassie down, mad 'cause I let me down.

Halfway to the forest he call out my name and my heart jump 'cause for a second I think he done change his mind. I turn 'round too quick and he standin' there in the same spot watchin' me, jus' a dark shape 'gainst the dark b'hind him.

'You know I doin' you a favour!' he shout. 'Even if I give you some name it ain't 'nough. You need money – gold. A lot. You ain't never gone be able get your hands on money like that.'

The money Cassie's part. My part the name. I wonder what he say if

I tell him that – 'bout some white girl from the future who gone bring me gold in the night? He done gone think I really crazy if I tell him that.

I turn 'round, keep walkin' to the forest. I don't need look back to know he still watchin', can feel his eyes on me the whole time. And when I safe in the shadow of the trees I look 'gain and even though it too dark to see him I know he ain't moved, that he watchin' me still. I know he gone keep his eyes on the place I been for a long time.

CASSIE

I don't know which one of us is more disappointed about Jasper – me or E.L. She's on the verge of giving up – I know she is – and I feel like that too, even though I don't tell her. Without a name, a contact, she can't go, it's too risky. But then I think of what happened in the parlour and Charity leaving and her mother hanging from the tree, and I know we have to find a way.

The other obstacle, of course, is gold – I still don't think we have enough and it keeps me awake at night thinking endlessly about it; how I can get more. But it's in math class that the idea comes to me and immediately I know it's what I have to do: I have to stage a break in.

As I copy down equations from the board, I work out the details in my head. The plan is so easy, I don't know how I didn't think of it before. The only complicated part is making sure that everyone is out at the same time. Along with mine, Ryan's schedule is the most predictable: school and then chess club until five thirty on Tuesdays and Thursdays. Mom's schedule seems to change week to week, but between travelling and meetings and whatever else she does these days she's rarely been home for dinner lately, sometimes she's not home by the time I'm going to bed. Which leaves Angelina, who is nearly always there – finding a time when she's not there is going to be the hardest part.

It becomes an obsession, all through lunch and in geography and history and even in Phys Ed, I'm trying to figure out some way to get her out of the house. I go over and over plans – I could ask her to go to the grocery store or the pharmacy or the dry cleaners but she always does those things in the morning, when we are at school and, anyway, it mightn't give me enough time. I skip Barnes & Noble so I can focus on it at home, try and figure it out. There has to be a way to get her out of the house, I just need to think more. I'm thinking about it so hard when I open the front door, I don't realise at first that the alarm is beeping to be turned off. And it's only turning it off that it hits me, what it means.

'Hello?' I call out, walking through the hall. 'Angelina, are you here?'

I already know she's not here; the alarm wouldn't be on if she was here and the house has that empty sound, just me and air. No radio, no T.V., no bumping dryer, no sound of her voice on the phone. The kitchen is empty like I know it will be. Sometimes she sits in the garden on the phone but it's the fall, too cold to sit outside and I can see through the patio door that the garden is empty too.

I'm about to go down into the basement, just to make sure she's not sorting laundry down there, when I see the note on the kitchen island.

Rosa sick. Gone to emergency room. Sorry. Call later. A.

Rosa is Angelina's granddaughter who is three, or maybe four, by now. I like Rosa – the way she is so curious and not shy and how she squeezes her eyes tightly closed when she laughs. But that day – and I'm not proud of this – I don't give her a second thought. I don't wonder why she's in the emergency room or if she'll be okay. I don't think about calling Angelina to find out how she is. Instead, all I can think about is that God has answered our prayers – mine and E.L.'s. It's Thursday: Ryan is at chess club, Mom is out. I check the calendar on the wall and it says she has a meeting at 2p.m. with

Mia, her publicist, which means she won't be back till dinner at the latest.

All of which means today is the day I need to do it. Today might be the only day I get.

I take the stairs two at a time, go straight to my room. I need something to put everything in and I grab a bag from the back of the closet door. It's the navy and red US Open one that Ryan and I both got when Dad took us there two or three years ago. It was a fun day and I like the bag because it reminds me of it, and I hesitate until I remember I don't have time for hesitation, so I take it and run to Mom's room.

The curtains are still closed and it smells of her perfume but too strongly, like the perfume's covering up some other smell. The bed's not made and when I turn on the light I see the dirty clothes everywhere – by the side of the bed and overflowing out of the hamper. Angelina must not have cleaned in here – must never clean in here – because there's an empty wine glass on the bedside table, a candy bar wrapper on the floor. It's disgusting and I want to shut the door and pretend I'd never seen inside but E.L. is counting on me and I know what I have to do.

There's a layer of dust on her vanity table and on the jewellery boxes piled on top of each other. I start to open them – the ones with the store names on them and the big wooden one that Dad brought back from his work trip to India. And at first I'm careful, sifting through the earrings, the rings, necklaces, bangles, trying to discern what looks old enough, valuable enough but then I remember that a thief isn't going to take his time to do this, so I dump them all into the US Open bag. That's the scariest moment right then, because after that there's no going back and I freeze for a second. Part of me wants to take everything out, to try and sort it all back to where it belongs, but then I think of E.L., and everything she'll have to go through, and I know I have the easy part, compared to her.

I take it all: diamond earrings. Her sapphire pendant. A bracelet with sparkly blue stones. This is where the money is, I can pawn these, get a lot of gold for stuff like this. I'll probably have too much to fit in my pockets, but maybe I can find some kind of bag that I can strap securely around me so I can make sure I can bring it back to her. As my hands are opening boxes, throwing jewellery on top of jewellery my brain is already whirring through the possibilities. Maybe I can put some pieces in my socks.

The bag is heavy now, I have enough, more than enough, but I need to make it look like a proper break in. I open Ryan's door. As usual his sneakers are lined up by colour, his books, his Xbox games are all sorted alphabetically. His Xbox, would a thief take his Xbox? For a second I think about it but it's too heavy and besides there's nowhere I can hide it. Some thieves are on foot – this thief is on foot.

I'm about to close the door when something makes me turn back, grab his bookshelf from behind and push it over onto the floor. He doesn't have nearly as many books as I did but still, in the silence of the house the crash feels like an earthquake. I'm not scared anymore, I'm exhilarated now, more full of energy than I can remember being in a really long time. I grab the other bookshelf and do the same thing. I leave the door open. He hates when his door is left open.

My room is next – I can't ignore my room. My shelves are attached to the wall but I swipe my hand along them sending the photograph frames and candles flying. I yank open the drawers of my desk. With my laptop gone there's nothing of value. I don't really wear jewellery anymore and I cleared out most of my old stuff last summer. The only thing left is Grandad's signet ring and the silver necklace I got for my confirmation. I throw the confirmation necklace in on top of the others, leave the box. I hesitate with the ring. But the ring is gold. It's something E.L. could use. And even if I don't give it to her I need to make it go missing just like everything else, I throw it in the bag.

My heart is pounding, I'm going through the other rooms in my head: the silver cutlery service in the dining room, Mom's office. But no, I have enough. My alarm clock says it's 4.53p.m. – Ryan will be home soon and there's no telling when to expect Mom. Back downstairs, I am about to pick up the phone in the hall when it starts to ring. My heart stops – I think it actually stops. My first thought is that it's probably Angelina, that she's on her way home, that the thing with Rosa was a false alarm. I stand frozen in the hall until the answering machine clicks on. Silence. Whoever it was hung up. A telemarketer. It has to be. It's okay. Everything is okay.

Maybe I don't have to call 911, maybe I can just leave and let Ryan find everything – but no, he'd be scared and, anyway, I'm always home by now. I reach for the phone and take a deep breath. And that's when I realise that the US Open bag is still in my hand.

'Fucking idiot!'

I say that out loud, slam the phone down and run back upstairs and into my room past the open drawers and the mess on the floor. I stand on my stepstool so I can reach the very back part of the closet, push it in there as far as it'll go, down behind a storage box of summer clothes I never even took out last summer. The police won't look there, will they? What if they have a search warrant? But I'm being stupid, search warrants are for the criminals. We're not the criminals, we're the victims. But I get back on the stool and push the bag back further and pile my winter sweaters over it, just in case.

Back downstairs again. Five o'clock by the clock in the hall, one minute past. My breath is shallow, fast and I try and breathe deep – the way Alice is always reminding me to, into my stomach. I run my hands through my hair, look around.

'What have I missed? Is there anything I've missed?'

I don't know if I'm talking to myself or to E.L. but that's when I remember I've forgotten the most important thing of all, the thing that they always look for in that first part of *Law & Order* – how the criminals got in in the first place. I can't believe I didn't think of it until now.

The door could've been open when I got home but no, that would mean someone who had a key, someone we knew and that's not the kind of burglary I want this to look like. As the thought forms in my head so does a memory of an argument Mom and Dad used to have about the glass panels in the front door – the ones he said needed to be replaced by something stronger, the ones she said we needed to keep because they were an original feature. It seems like forever ago since that argument, since I'd actually even noticed the door. As I turn to look at it, I'm so happy to see that she won this argument, that the reds and greens and clear glass are still there.

I've never broken glass before. It seems like the kind of things you should have done by the time you're coming up to seventeen, but I haven't. I wish I had something – a hammer, some kind of instrument – and I look around the hall for something but there's nothing. And then I remember whatever I use to break the glass needs to be found outside, the glass needs to be in the hall, inside. I'm glad it's dark, that it's November, can't imagine doing this in broad daylight. The first rock I pick up is too small, the next one is heavy, it feels right. At the top of the steps I glance around but there's no one to see me. I close the door but I don't lock it, just in case. I pull my sleeve down so it covers my hand, swing it back, close my eyes.

The first time I miss, I hit the wood. The next time my eyes are open but I hit it too lightly, I tap the glass so it makes a scraping sound. Who knew breaking glass would be so hard? E.L. comes into my mind, how scared she was approaching Jasper but that she did it anyway and I take a deep breath, swing my hand back, close my eyes again.

The glass smashing is only a tinkle but it's the loudest sound I've ever heard. I wait for someone to yell out, to come running, for police sirens, but nothing happens. I throw the rock back into the garden, reach inside gently through the broken glass and reach around to where the handle is, covering my fingers with my sleeve. It's awkward but I can do it. My heart is about to explode and I realise I've stopped breathing again. Dad was right all along, anyone could have done this. I shuffle in with the door as it pushes the glass on the floor. I take my hand back, real slow. Shake the shards of glass from my sweatshirt cuff onto the carpet. I've done it, I've really done it.

The clock says ten past five and for some reason that time seems absolutely perfect. I pick up the phone and dial 911.

E.L.

I on my way back from the big house when I stop in and check on Dolly and the music machine like I a'ways do. Even though I know the music machine ain't gone work till Cassie come back I try it anyway but it still sleepin'. I thinkin' 'bout Cassie and how maybe she gone come back soon, maybe even tonight, when I hear the noise – a branch crackin' like someone step on it.

'Who there?' I call out.

There silence then but I feel someone eyes watchin' me. I know someone there.

'Cassie? That you? Come out! Don't play 'round.'

I don't know what make me say that 'cause Cassie ain't never played 'round b'fore, she ain't there and then sudd'nly she there, that how it work. So I shoulda known it someone else, even b'fore I hear the voice that come outta the trees.

'Who you talkin' to? Who Cassie?'

It Marjorie. I know b'fore she step out from b'hind the tree.

'What you doin' watchin' me? Hidin' in the trees?'

My heart race like she catch me doin' somethin' wrong.

'I ain't hidin'.'

'Standin' b'hind that tree sure look like hidin' to me.'

She walkin' over to me now right up to where I standin' in the clearin'.

'You the one hidin'. A'ways sneakin' 'round, a'ways late back with the firewood. Who you talkin' to? Who this Cassie?'

'What you talkin' 'bout? You don't know what you talkin' bout.'

'Don't I? What you got there?' She point to where I hold Dolly b'hind my back. 'What in your hand?'

I glad the music machine sleepin' in the tree. I glad it ain't workin' 'cause if it been workin' then she woulda seen me dancin' and I don't know how I ever woulda 'splained that.

'I ask you a question, E.L. Jus' 'cause you a house slave 'gain and I workin' in the fields don't mean you ain't gotta answer. Don't mean you can pret'nd I ain't here.'

She mad at me. She sound mad. She walkin' closer to me now. She only a year older but she taller, bigger – she a'ways been bigger than me.

'It jus' somethin' Miss Ellen give me,' I say.

'She give you somethin'? Or you stole it, like your thievin' mamma?'

She reach b'hind and try get Dolly but I snatch her 'way in my other hand. I ain't fast 'nough though, 'cause quick as a flash her hand switch and she got my hand with Dolly in it.

'My mamma ain't no thief! Let go!'

Her fingers work down over my hand and onto Dolly. She grip tight and I grip tight. We both pull.

'Let go! Leave her 'lone – let go!'

That me, that my voice and maybe I shoulda been the one to do the lettin' go but I don't and next thing there a horrible noise and we pull apart. In my hand I got Dolly body – her little legs, her dress, her arms. Marjorie look down and she look surprise – she got Dolly head.

'Look at that – she look like Miss Ellen with her blonde curls. But her face done be all broke.' She poke her finger in the hole in Dolly face and I try snatch her back but Marjorie hold Dolly high over her head where I can't reach her.

'Give her back – give her back to me! She mine!'

Marjorie put her finger in the broke part Dolly cheek.

'You broke her. Look at that. You done broke her cheek.'

Her face change and she look at me. She don't look mad no more, she look scared, and she throw Dolly head down on the grass like she on fire.

'Oh, my God!' she say. 'Oh, Lord in Heaven!'

I down on my knees then, pick up Dolly head, line it up to hold it 'gainst her body.

'Oh, Lord in Heaven,' she say 'gain. 'I heard 'bout this but I ain't never done seen it with my own eyes. I can't b'lieve what I seein' – she a demon doll!'

I look up and Marjorie standin' there with her hands over her mouth like she seen some ghost.

'What you talkin' 'bout?' I say. 'She ain't no demon – she jus' an old doll b'long to Miss Ellen. She give her to me back when we only chil'ren after the Master broke her face.'

But Marjorie shakin' her head. Her fingers rub her own cheek.

'That place – that place where she broke. That the same place where Miss Ellen get struck by branches when she out ridin' that time a few months back. The time she came back all bloody and Juba had put a poultice on her face and it took a long time healin'.'

I r'member seein' Miss Ellen with a bandage and hearin' that she done have an accident on her horse but that when I in the fields pickin' so I don't r'member real good.

I confuse. I scared. I don't know what Marjorie sayin' yet – not e'verythin' – but I can tell it gone be real bad.

'You put a cuss on her? Didn't you? You stole her doll and put a cuss on her face 'cause she put you out into the fields.'

'No!' I shout that, real loud. 'No, you crazy! There ain't no demon doll. I ain't never do nothin' like that on Miss Ellen.'

But Marjorie backin' 'way, real slow and she talkin' real quiet.

'Cassie the name of the demon, ain't it? I been watchin' you, E.L. – I seen you talkin' to yoursel' when no one here. I seen you dancin' out here like you poss'ssed. I know you had a demon in you – I jus' know it! My mamma say not to say nothin' till we can prove it. And now we can.'

That when she run at me real fast and I know she want get Dolly. Firs' I turn 'round, start to run but then somethin' in me change and in the hand not holdin' Dolly I swing at Marjorie head, hard as I can. My knuckles sore when they hit some bone in her face and she musta trip on some tree root at the same time 'cause she fall to the side and yell out like she hurt bad. As she fallin' she grab my other hand and Dolly go flyin' – rollin' 'cross the grass.

'I told you Miss Ellen give her to me. Her face broke. Ask her yourself! Jus' ask her!'

Somehow I on top of Marjorie then and I yellin' at her and slappin' her and she squirmin' to get 'way and scratchin' my skin on my arms and face but I got hold on her too strong. And I ain't proud to say this but I want tell the truth, what really happen, and the truth is that I keep on hittin' and slappin' her long after she stop scratchin' and tryin' get 'way. And all the while I screamin' like I never done scream b'fore – 'bout Dolly and Miss Ellen and even my mamma – and the way I screamin' then it like Marjorie right, it like I do have some demon inside me.

I don't know how long I scream but after while the demon go quick as he come and I roll off her and onto the grass. My breath come fast and hard. She cryin' and she breathin' fast too so I know she ain't dead or nothin', that I ain't killed her even though the demon part of me seem to want to.

I get up and go find Dolly head and her body. There ain't no way to put 'em back t'gether and I think 'bout buryin' her but I don't want Marjorie to have any way to find her so I sit there 'gainst the tree and hold both parts in my hand.

And after a bit Marjorie get up. She limpin' and she got to hold on to the trees so she walk prop'ly. There blood on her face and on her dress. Maybe there blood in her hair. She don't say nothin' to me and I don't say nothin' to her neither, jus' watch her limp 'way through the trees.

I wait till after she gone to take the music machine from the moss bed in the tree and then I walk down to the river even though it dark and I still ain't brought back no firewood. And I hope Cassie ain't gone be mad 'bout what I gone do and I wish she there to talk to but it like when I talk to her she ain't answerin' so I need to do this on my own.

I throw Dolly into the water firs' – her head and body t'gether – but they come 'part straight 'way. Her body sink firs', a'most 'mmediately but her head float along for a bit till the water fill in under her cheek and it turn face over then down and the river suck her under. After watchin' that, I think the music machine gone be easier that it gone sink like a stone but it float too on the surface of the water and it still floatin' till the river carry it 'way 'round the bend.

And I don't know what I feelin' then, by myself in the dark. Maybe I feel sad 'cause Dolly gone, but that don't make no sense after losin' all the people I a'ready lost to care 'bout some broken doll. I know I wishin' I could go back in time – back to b'fore when I in the clearin' and if I know Marjorie there I ain't never taken Dolly outta the tree, I woulda gone straight back to the cabin and none this done ever happen.

I wonder what goin' on back in the cabin – what Marjorie tellin' Linda and if Rose and Nelly fixin' up her bruises and what they gone think. And I scared. I scared 'bout what gone happen next.

I scared that lettin' the demon take over when I hittin' Marjorie gone change e'verythin'. I scared that I done somethin' that I ain't never gone be able to undo.

CASSIE

My butt is numb from sitting on the cold step for so long and then everything happens at the same time. Just as I hear the sirens the phone rings and it's Mom calling me back. And as I'm trying to explain to her what's going on, the cop car pulls up and two cops jump out, almost knocking over Ryan who has just appeared on the sidewalk.

There is a black cop and a white cop, both with guns drawn. The white cop – the older one – calls out to me.

'Miss, did you call 911?'

I don't remember getting up but I'm standing then and somehow my hands are in the air. Ryan drops his backpack at the gate and runs past the cops, towards me. The black one, turns around and points his gun at him.

'Don't! He's my brother! Yes – yes, I called 911!'

Ryan is saying something and the white cop is saying something and at the end of the line Mom sounds hysterical and I hang up on her. Both cops lower their guns and the white one talks again. He's almost fully bald with a thick brown moustache and a belly that hangs low over the top of his pants.

'Miss, I'm Officer Doyle and this is Officer Clinton. Can you confirm your name and why you called us?'

'I'm Cassie Lazzaro and this is my brother, Ryan. There's been a break in – I found a break in.'

I'd rehearsed that line and it sounded better before, in my head. Officer Clinton is putting his gun away. He smiles, he has a nice smile

– he must be the good cop. 'You can put your hands down, now. We need to secure the scene so you guys are going to have to wait over here, on the sidewalk.'

My hand is on Ryan's shoulder, gripping him tightly, and even though he's on the step below me, we move together like one person. Officer Clinton's arm is outstretched, between us and the house as if that will protect us from whoever might be inside.

'Can you tell us what happened?' Officer Doyle is asking. 'Take us through exactly what happened.'

'I got home and I saw there'd been a break in. There was broken glass and the door was open.'

'When? What time?' Officer Doyle asks.

'Five ten.'

'You remember that exactly?'

'Yes – I saw the time when I made the call.'

'Did you go inside?' That's Officer Clinton. 'Did you see nyone?'

'No, I saw the broken glass and I got scared.' I sound convincing, I think I do. 'I've always been told to call 911 if anything happens, anything like this…'

'You called from your cell phone?' Officer Doyle nods towards the phone in my hand that's lighting up again with Mom's number. For a second I think about lying but I know enough to know they will know. That the call has been traced.

'No. The house phone – in the hall.'

'I thought you didn't go inside?' Officer Clinton says. He's frowning. He doesn't seem nice anymore. He knows I'm lying.

'Just for a second, just to use the phone. I was only in the hall.'

'So you did go inside?' That's Officer Doyle, and the questions are coming too fast now. I feel my face go red but before I can answer him, Ryan has another question instead.

'What about Angelina? Where's Angelina?'

'Angelina?' Officer Clinton picks up the questioning again as Officer Doyle steps away to say something into his radio.

'Our housekeeper,' I say.

Ryan interrupts, starts to push back past me up the steps. 'She's inside, she's got to be!'

Before he can get any closer, Officer Clinton has manoeuvred him down the steps.

'Let go of me – she could be in trouble, she could be hurt!'

Officer Clinton is saying something to calm Ryan down and on the radio I hear Officer Doyle calling for back up. I think of all the real crimes happening now, right at this very moment, all over the city and for a second I close my eyes. When I open them, Officer Doyle is standing next to me and he leads me down the path to where Ryan and Officer Clinton are at the gate. I don't like him with his belly and his moustache; he reminds me of someone, someone else I don't like and I can't think who.

'Did you hear what I said?' he says.

It's only then I realise that he's asked me a question, is waiting for an answer.

'I'm sorry, what did you ask me?'

'I asked if you have a home security system. An alarm, motion detectors, cameras – anything like that?'

He smooths his moustache down at both edges as he speaks and suddenly it hits me who he reminds me of: Nagle, E.L.'s overseer. This cop is just like Nagle.

Beside me, Ryan is on the phone, then he hangs up. 'She's not answering, Angelina's not answering! She always answers!'

Clinton and Doyle are both looking at me now, waiting for an answer. Officer Doyle's radio crackles.

'A home security system?' I repeat.

'The alarm, Cass!' Ryan practically yells at me. 'They want to know was the alarm on?'

On the sidewalk, people have started to gather, the Lugos from two doors down, Mrs. Campanaro from across the road, some kids I don't recognise on bikes. Seeing all their faces reflected in the flashing lights I can't think, I can't think of the right answer.

'Yes. I mean … no! No, it wasn't on.'

'You're sure?' Officer Clinton says. 'You're absolutely sure?'

'Yes, I'm sure. Positive.'

Officer Doyle has stepped away, is on his radio again. When he steps back, he moves his head closer to Officer Clinton's. 'ETA five minutes,' he says.

I think there's going to be more conversation but there isn't. They turn away from us, draw their guns again and start up the path, their steps in rhythm with each other.

'She's got to be in there! If the alarm wasn't on that means she's in there!' Ryan's shouting now and he goes to run after the cops but they are already at the top step now, in the door and someone – maybe Mr. Lugo – pulls him back. I start to shake – or maybe I'm shaking already – and it must be the cold, because I know there's no one in there, no real danger, I'm the only one who knows none of this is real.

A woman I recognise from down the road puts her arm around me and Ryan is on my other side. He's nearly as tall as me now –

we're almost the same height – I hadn't noticed it on the steps. I put my arm around him and he lets me pull him in close to me so I can feel him shaking too. We watch as lights go on in the living room, the dining room. Soon they will find the note in the kitchen. They'll find it and they'll know where Angelina's gone, that she's safe and this part of the nightmare will be over.

'Angelina's okay,' I say to him. 'I know it.'

He's looking down at his phone, hits redial on her number. 'How do you know?'

'I just know – I feel it. I know she's okay.'

He glances across at me and back to his phone. 'If she's okay why wouldn't she have called the cops? Why won't she pick up?'

I can't think of an answer to that that wouldn't give away what I already know so I just squeeze him tighter. The cops will find the note, they have to find the note. Any second now, they're going to come out here holding it and run down the steps and show it to us and Ryan will whoop with relief and I will too. That's what's going to happen. That's what's going to happen next.

But that's not what happens next, in fact what happens next is a bit of a blur. As a light goes on upstairs there's more sirens and another squad car arrives, followed by a third one. I don't know how many cops there are any more, how many are in uniform. They all run up the steps and through the open door. Then my phone's ringing again and this time it's Dad asking the same questions that Mom asked even though he's already spoken to her and knows the answers.

'Tell him about Angelina,' Ryan is saying in the background. 'Ask him if he's been in touch with Angelina.'

Dad's still talking, saying he'll be there soon and I'm waiting for a gap in the conversation when Ryan grabs the phone from me.

'Dad? Have you heard from Angelina? She's missing. She won't pick up her phone.'

He pulls away from me, one finger in his ear so he can hear Dad. The woman on my other side has been replaced by a woman cop with curly hair. Another cop in a windbreaker with CSU written on it is pushing us all back further onto the sidewalk, so he can unroll yellow tape across the gate.

'I'm Officer Hernandez,' the curly haired cop is saying, 'let's get you into this car over here, sit you down.'

But I don't want to sit down, I want to stay with Ryan, and that's what I'm trying to tell her when Officer Clinton appears in the lit hallway. Behind him I see a cop in a suit on the phone. The CSU cop is walking up the front steps.

Ryan hangs up on Dad. I pull away from the female cop. Officer Clinton jumps down the steps and heads in our direction, lifting the yellow tape so he can join us on the sidewalk.

'Is she there? Did you find her?' Ryan says.

Officer Clinton nods at Officer Hernandez, like he is giving some secret message to her even though he is talking to us. 'The house is empty, there's no one there.'

He's going to tell us now about the note. All those cops in the house, they have to have found the note.

'Angelina's not there? Are you sure? Can I look?'

Officer Clinton puts his hand on Ryan's shoulder. 'I'm afraid not, right now it's a crime scene. No one allowed in here except for us cops.'

'What did you find inside?' I hear myself asking. 'Is much missing?'

'Some jewellery was taken it looks like – not much else. Looks like the work of amateurs. Don't worry, we'll get these guys.'

'But what about Angelina?' Ryan is close to tears.

'Maybe she's at the store?' I say, 'She could be anywhere, maybe she had to leave suddenly for some reason?'

I'm trying to find a way to suggest they look again for a note, without actually saying it, to make Officer Clinton think it's his idea. But before I can figure out how to do that, Officer Doyle is back with another cop in a suit, the one I saw talking on the phone.

'Detective Franklin, this is Cassie and Ryan Lazzaro. Cassie reported the break in.'

Detective Franklin has gelled hair and soft hands. 'Call me, John. Cassie, you said the alarm wasn't on, you're sure about that?'

I nod. 'Yes, I'm sure.'

'One hundred per cent sure? You couldn't have made a mistake?'

He raises his eyebrows, half smiles, like it's the easiest thing in the world to have made a mistake. This is my chance, my last chance to tell the truth, but it will look too suspicious if I change my story now.

'No. I'm sure. One hundred per cent.'

'And she's usually home? At this time she'd be home?'

'She's *always* home when I get in!' Ryan says. 'She'd be making dinner right now. And if she ever goes out, she *always* puts the alarm on and she *always* answers her phone.'

Detective Franklin writes something in his notebook.

'Sometimes she leaves a note,' I say. 'You know, if she has to go out.'

'There was no note,' Officer Doyle butts in. 'We would have found a note.'

For a horrible second I wonder if I could have put it in my pocket but, no, I didn't touch it. It was right there, right on the counter. She'd left it secured under the fruit bowl but when I picked it up, I put it back down again. Maybe it blew off when I shut the door. Maybe it floated onto the ground, is hidden under the fridge.

'You're sure? It's not worth looking again?'

Detective Franklin pauses from whatever he is writing down. He is looking at me. I have to keep my mouth shut; I can't say anything more about the note.

'There were signs of a struggle upstairs,' Officer Doyle says. He looks more like Nagle than ever, his tiny eyes, his doughy face. 'The most likely possibility is that she may have interrupted them.'

The bookshelves. The stupid bookshelves in Ryan's room. I could kick myself. I look at Ryan, wait for him to say something, to ask something, but the colour has drained out of his face.

'But there was no sign of blood.' Detective Franklin smiles. 'That's a good sign, that so far there is no trace of blood.'

We all hear it – the *so far*. Every crime drama I've ever seen blends into one in my head and I imagine them right now with some weird machine that can show up blood that has been cleaned away. This isn't my life, our lives, our house. This is someone else's. This is something from T.V.. I wish it *was* T.V., that I could hit the pause button, that I could talk to E.L., tell her what's happening, ask her what I should do. But there's no time, there's no time for anything and the only thing to do is keep going.

'So what happens next?' I hear myself ask.

'We're dusting for prints right now. We're going to need a full description of your housekeeper to get out on the wires straight away, oh and a recent photo.'

'A photo?' I repeat. 'I don't think we have a photo. Ryan, do you a photo?'

He shrugs. Shakes his head.

'Okay then, what was she wearing when you last saw her?' Detective Franklin says. 'Do you remember?'

I try and think if I even saw Angelina that morning. She was there, she was always there. She must have made my breakfast, but I didn't remember seeing her.

'Something white?' I say. 'A white shirt?'

'Jeans.' Ryan nods twice. 'She always wears jeans with these little zips at the bottom and white sneakers. I don't think they have a brand.'

Detective Franklin writes that down.

'What about next of kin information, family, friends. Anywhere she could have gone.'

'Her daughter!' Ryan says. 'Maria! Maybe she's with her? Do you have her number, Cassie?'

'No. I wish I did.' That's the truth, the first true thing I've said. If I had her number, we could straighten this out. More than anything I wish I had Maria's number.

'Mom would have it – I'm going to call Mom.'

Ryan starts to dial. Officer Doyle is on the radio again and Officer Clinton is on the street behind us, trying to disperse the crowd so the traffic can get past. Officer Hernandez is over by a squad car, talking to another female cop. I lower my voice, turn to Detective Franklin.

'All this – you really think it's necessary? Officer Clinton said it looked like amateurs, just a regular break in. I know my brother's upset but Angelina often steps out for things. She could be anywhere – she could just be at the grocery store.'

He closes his book, looks at me in a way that I don't like.

'Do you know something, Cassie? Is there more that you're not telling me?'

I swallow. 'No. I've told you everything. Just my brother can get a bit hysterical, I don't want all you all wasting your time and it turns out she was in Duane Reade the whole time.'

His eyes are glued on mine; he won't look away. 'If that happens, that will be the best outcome to this. And clearly, we all hope it does. But we can't ignore the fact that she's missing, the signs of a struggle, that you can't contact her. Any one of those things is concerning, but the fact that you're so sure the alarm was off, indicates she was home when this happened. Which turns this from a burglary into a kidnapping investigation.'

It's a joke. He's got to be joking. Only he's not.

And right then, right at that moment when it seems things can't get any worse, right then, Mom and Dad both arrive at the exact same time.

E.L.

When I get back to the cabin that night Marjorie 'sleep. Linda look at me funny but she don't say nothin' and Nelly and Rose don't say nothin' neither. I got some scratches and cuts from where Marjorie cut me but no one offer to help me clean them up and no one ask how I got them.

The next mornin' I up b'fore the bugle and when I get to the big house Juba shuckin' corn in the sink. She look surprise to see me.

'What you doin' here?' she say.

'I don't sleep too good last night,' I say. 'Reckon I get here early.'

Her hand pause on the corn. 'I don't mean 'cause you early. Marjorie done got here half hour ago. I think that mean you back in the fields.'

My heart race but I don't say nothin'. Charity a'ways say Juba got the biggest darn mouth of anyone for miles 'round.

'No one say nothin' to me – not Miss Ellen and not Nagle so I here to do my work.'

Juba shrug. Go back to cleanin' corn. 'I darned if I know what Marjorie doin' here then. Maybe you want ask Linda but she with the Mistress right now – tryin' to get her take a break from that piano and eat some breakfast.'

It only then I register the piano music playin' in the back'round.

'She playin' early this mornin'.'

'She done been playin' all night too.' Juba pick up a new piece corn. 'She ain't played this crazy since the time right after her mamma die and her daddy want her to marry Mr. Cleve at Morristown plantation.'

Juba say that like she want me to ask more 'bout what happen and 'nother time maybe I would have but today I itchin' to get upstairs to where Marjorie at with Miss Ellen so I take a clean apron and hat and head on up. At each step I get more scared and I wonder if I shoulda jus' run now, outta the house and outta the gate and take my chances. At the top I see Miss Ellen door close but I hear her voice even though I don't hear what she sayin'. Someone else say somethin' too. It mus' be Marjorie. My hand go to knock and then it stop midair. It shakin'. I make a fist, say a prayer, knock.

'Come in!' That Miss Ellen and when I open the door I see she sittin' by the window and Marjorie there standin' in front of her. The bed ain't made and the fire ain't set.

'Good mornin', Miss Ellen.'

'Good morning, E.L.'

She smile like ev'rythin' normal, her voice sound normal, but the air b'tween us don't feel normal. It don't feel nowhere near normal. Marjorie turn to look at me and I see her face all cut up down one side and there a yellow and purple bruise round her eye. I don't say nothin' and Marjorie don't say nothin' neither. It Miss Ellen who break the silence.

'You can set the fire, please, E.L. Then fetch me some tea.'

Happiness run like a thaw in my body when she say that 'cause if I here settin' the fire and makin' tea it mean she don't think I poss'ssed by no demon and it mean I ain't gone go back to no field.

'Yes, Miss Ellen.'

But then somethin' make me hes'tate. Today Thursday, and that the day Miss Ellen a'ways want me draw her a bath firs' – b'fore the fire or makin' any tea. Drawin' a bath mean I gotta stay here though and maybe she want me to leave so she can talk more to Marjorie.

Miss Ellen sense somethin'. 'What is it, E.L.?'

'I jus' wonderin' ...' I stop. 'Is there somethin' Marjorie helpin' with that I can do for you, Miss Ellen?'

Miss Ellen stroke her hair down over her shoulder. It gone real long. It look more knotty than usual too and I wonder if that 'cause of what she were doin' in the barn with Jasper. It gone take a long time brush all of that out later.

'Marjorie and I were jus' having a talk. Your duties are as usual.'

Miss Ellen smile and Marjorie turn look at me. She smilin' too. I don't like it none when she smile.

'Yes, Miss Ellen.'

I go downstairs and outside to get the wood for the fire. Linda in the kitchen now with Juba and she watch me when I walk past but Juba tellin' some story 'bout the Mistress in the old days so neither one say nothin' to me.

And when I get back upstairs Marjorie gone and Miss Ellen still sittin' by the window where she sittin' b'fore, lookin' at the cotton field and I think maybe she lookin' for Jasper. After I set the fire I make the bed and then I brush her hair and it take a real long time with all those knots. She mus' be tired 'cause she close her eyes and keep 'em close and in the mirror she look diff'rent without her eyes like my eyes. She look jus' like her mamma.

And lookin' at her refl'ction I see the scar on her cheek where she musta been hit by those branches and I don't know how I never thought to ask 'bout it b'fore. I think 'bout talkin' to her 'bout what happen with Marjorie and r'mindin' her 'bout how she gave me Dolly and how 'bout her daddy break her little china face that time he mad but I know she mus' r'member that. Whatever Marjorie done tell her Miss Ellen gone know what really happen. She gone know I ain't no demon. She gone have set Marjorie straight 'bout ev'rythin' and that why she mus' be back workin' in the fields where she b'long.

And thinkin' all that I feel better, like ev'rythin' forgotten and ev'rythin' gone be a'right 'gain, I even feel safe for a while. But later when Marjorie come in from the fields she keep lookin' over at me, ev'ry time I turn to look at her she a'ready lookin' and she got this smile on her face jus' like the one in Miss Ellen room. And she don't never usually smile at me. And somethin' 'bout that don't feel no good. Somethin' 'bout that make me scared and I want ask Cassie what to do, but jus' like what happen b'fore, Cassie ain't there, so I all by myself 'gain.

CASSIE

Everyone is talking at once – Mom, Dad, Detective Franklin, Officer Doyle.

Mom is drunk, she takes my hand and holds it too tightly, brings it to her mouth and kisses it.

'Who's missing?' she says. 'Who's missing? Everyone is here.'

'Your housekeeper, ma'am, Angelina ... Sanchez.' Detective Franklin consults his notebook even though he has said her name fifteen hundred times already. 'When your daughter came home and discovered the crime scene, she wasn't home. We think she's missing but maybe she told you of some plans for today? Maybe this morning she told you she had somewhere to go?'

Mom kisses my hand again, starts to cry. 'My baby walked in on a crime scene. A crime scene! She might have been killed!'

'Lou, come on, calm down. Cassie's okay,' Dad says. 'Just answer the detective's question – did Angelina say anything this morning? Anywhere she might have been going?'

'I can't believe how callous you are, how casual!' Mom says it to Dad, but turns around to the other cops as well. 'Our daughter was in danger—'

'Mom, I was fine, I was always fine.'

'Maybe you can be calm about that, maybe you can be cold, but not me. I'm just not like that!'

Detective Franklin is nodding at Officer Hernandez who is slightly outside the circle but who makes her way over to Mom. 'Mrs. Lazzaro, it's natural to be upset, everyone's upset. But your daughter is fine. We're worried about your housekeeper though – anything you can remember about her whereabouts today, her movements would be helpful.'

'Do you have Maria's number?' Ryan says. 'You must have it!'

'Maria?' Mom shakes her head. 'I don't know what you're talking about, I don't know any Maria?'

'Angelina's daughter!' Dad's voice is practically a snarl and he steps away, takes a breath. 'Do you have Angelina's daughter's number?'

By then Officer Hernandez has managed to stand between me and Mom but Mom still won't let go of my hand. 'If you let me have your phone I can check?' she says. 'I can search.'

Mom fumbles in her bag and hands over her phone. Officer Hernandez starts to search through the contacts.

'You don't have too many numbers in here,' she says. 'Do you have another phone?'

Mom shakes her head, looks up at the house and back at Officer Hernandez. 'I lost my phone last week. In a cab. I haven't had a chance to update the contacts yet.'

'What? Again?' Dad rolls his eyes.

'That means you won't have her number,' Ryan says. 'Dad, do you have it?'

Everyone looks at Dad, I never even thought of asking Dad.

'No, I don't think so. I don't think I've ever had it.'

He starts to go through his phone anyway and we all watch him.

'You should have it,' Mom says. 'You should have her number.'

'Why?' Dad says. 'Why would I have *your* housekeeper's daughter's phone number?'

'Oh, now she's *my* housekeeper now, is she?'

'Yes, she is. Since I don't live here anymore!'

Mom turns to Officer Hernandez and drops her voice to talk in a confidential tone that we all can hear. 'She's been our housekeeper for eight years – it's not even two years since he moved out. But he was at work so much, he was hardly ever here even when he lived here.'

'Lou, please,' Dad says. 'Not now, not here.'

'Ten years,' Ryan is saying. 'Angelina came when I was four, that's nearly ten years!'

Mom's finally dropped my hand and moved hers onto Officer Hernandez's arm. 'He hardly ever sees the kids now – you saw how he wasn't even worried about what nearly happened to our daughter tonight ...'

Dad turns to walk away but he can't get far because of the yellow tape. His hands are clenching and unclenching and I know that he's trying not to lose it in front of the cops.

'... sometimes I wonder does he even care about the kids anymore ...'

That's what does it and he swings around so fast for a second I think he's going to hit her.

'Of course I fucking care!' His voice is shaking. 'How could you say I don't care?'

That's when Detective Franklin steps in between them, puts his hand lightly on Dad's chest. 'Okay, just settle down. Everyone's upset, let's take a minute. Take a time out. Officer Hernandez, can you get Mrs. Lazzaro some coffee?'

She starts to lead Mom away and that's when my brainwave comes. I need to get inside the house. I need to find the note myself. Detective Franklin has turned to talk to Officer Doyle who I can't look at now without thinking of Nagle. Officer Clinton is standing off to the side, alone and I walk over to him.

'I need to go inside,' I say. 'I really need to pee.'

'I'm sorry, sweetheart, but they're not finished yet. It shouldn't take too much longer.'

'But I really need to go. I mean *really*. You know, girl's stuff.'

I make a face to indicate the severity of the situation and he looks around, helpless, but there is no one to come to his rescue. And he might have let me if that busybody Mrs. Lugo hadn't popped up behind me.

'You can use ours,' she says. 'Come across and use ours. We can make you some hot tea as well, if you like.'

Mom is by the squad car drinking coffee from a polystyrene cup and Dad is talking to Detective Franklin. Ryan comes with me to the Lugos' house. I've never been inside before – never said anything more than hello to them before – and it's weird being there because the layout makes it feel like being in our house but the antiques and old paintings make it feel like being in a museum. The bathroom has an old-fashioned, wooden, toilet-roll dispenser and a wooden seat. As soon as I sit down, I exhale, try and talk to E.L.

Oh my God. Can you see this? You see what's happening? Tell me what to do – I don't know what to do!

I wait but she doesn't answer me, I can't hear her at all.

Please, E.L., please. I need your help – I'm scared. I'm really scared.

There's a knock on the door. Ryan. 'Hurry up! You're taking forever.'

'Okay, hold on. I'm coming.'

When I come out, Mrs. Lugo is waiting at the end of the hall, offering to make tea, sandwiches, to give us cookies. And part of me wants to say yes to all of it, to stay in her kitchen that looks so cosy and old-fashioned, but through the front door I hear the noise of raised voices and there is some kind of commotion outside. From the bathroom, Ryan has heard it too and he rushes down the hall, his belt still unbuckled. I follow him out onto the sidewalk and Mrs. Lugo follows me. He sees her before I do.

'Angelina!'

He runs across the street and elbows his way through the crowd on the other side. When he gets to her, he throws himself at her and she catches him, like he's a little kid, puts her hand on the back of his head that he buries in her shoulder. She's saying something that I can't hear as she rubs his hair and from the shake of his shoulders I can tell he's crying.

I've stopped at the edge of the crowd and Angelina sees me, hanging back. She smiles and it's crazy but even though I knew she was fine all along, I find myself crying too. I run over, join their hug on the outside. She's talking fast in a mixture of Spanish and English, the way she always does when she's upset, and I don't know what she's saying but it doesn't matter.

'Thank God you're okay, Angelina. Thank God you're okay.'

I want to ask her about Rosa – how she is – but of course I can't and, anyway, Detective Franklin is next to us, trying to get her attention too.

'Miss Sanchez, I just need to go over some details, for you to answer some questions.'

Angelina disentangles herself from me and Ryan, though he stands close to her. She blows her nose. Her eyes are big, scared looking. She hates cops, I'd forgotten that. She looks around for Dad in the crowd.

'What happen?' she say. 'Why all the police?'

'There was a break-in. A burglary.' Detective Franklin makes his voice slow and loud. 'Were you home?'

'Home?' She looks around at the crowd. I catch her eye, smile. 'No. I go to hospital. Rosa fall at school. She have accident. They call me. I leave note.'

At the word 'note' Detective Franklin looks at me but I pretend not to see. Instead I ask what I've been dying to know all day. 'Is Rosa okay? Is she going to be okay?'

'Who's Rosa?' he asks, but no one answers.

Angelina starts to cry. 'I don't know. She still there. She hit her head – here.' She gestures to her forehead. 'She ... how you say ... unconscious. Asleep. She need more tests, but they won't give because she no insurance.'

Dad makes his way over to her, holds out his big hankie.

'Come on, we'll get down to the hospital. We'll get this sorted out.'

'You can't be serious,' Mom says from behind me. I turn around and she has a red blanket around her shoulder, the cup in her hand.

'What?' Dad says.

'You're needed here, Joe. With your family.'

'There's nothing I can do here – look at all the cops, they have this under control.' Dad gestures around. 'Rosa could be critical, she needs help.'

'You heard her, Joe – they don't have any insurance. What are you going to do? Pay for it all out of pocket?'

Angelina is looking at Mom now and there's fear in her face but something else too.

'I don't know – we can't just do nothing, Louise,' Dad says.

Mom walks up so she's standing next to me, closing the circle tighter. She sways a little.

'What I want to know before anyone goes anywhere is why the alarm wasn't on? You didn't put the alarm on when you left the house, Angelina. That's how this happened!'

My heart drops then, into my stomach, down further than that. Angelina rubs her eye with her hand.

'I put alarm on. I always put on.'

'Not this time. There was no alarm and that's how these, these ... cocksuckers ... broke in. Looted our home. Cassie interrupted them, she could've been attacked. Killed.'

'We don't actually know that she interrupted them,' Detective Franklin says.

'I think I put on. I always put on. I'm sorry Mrs. Lazzaro.'

Dad pats Angelina on the arm. 'We know, it's okay. It could happen to anyone, running out to the hospital like that. No harm was done.'

As soon as he says that, I know Mom is going to react badly, and she does.

'No harm was done? No harm?' Her voice is rising to a hysterical pitch now. Behind me I can feel all the eyes watching, all the neighbours. I wish they would open the house, let us have this argument in peace. 'I hate to disagree with my husband – soon to be *ex*-husband – but I think a lot of harm was done.'

Angelina puts her hand through her hair. She is doubting herself, I know she is, and I want to shake her, to tell her not to, to tell her the alarm was on. 'I'm sorry, it won't happen again.'

Mom waves a hand in the air. 'You're right, it won't. Because you're fired.'

For what seems like the first time in the longest time there's a second of silence before everyone starts yelling at once.

'Come on, Lou, you're not thinking clearly—'

'Please, please, Mrs. Lazzaro—'

'You can't fire Angelina!'

'—sleep it off, you'll feel differently tomorrow.'

'—please, it not easy get another job. I won't make mistake again.'

'You can't do this, Mom!'

Ryan lunges at Mom and Officer Clinton has to drag him back. Angelina is crying and shouting in Spanish now and Mom is at the centre of it all, turning circles to get away from Dad, from Ryan, from Officer Hernandez, talking about how the safety of her children has to come first and it's not her problem if Angelina gets deported to Mexico.

And in the midst of the craziest part of this crazy night, I know there is only one thing left to do, to tell the truth. It takes a split second to decide and when I do I shout it; I shout it from the top of my lungs.

'Angelina, didn't do anything wrong, Mom. You can't fire her. The alarm wasn't off – it was on. The alarm was on when I got home.'

I have their attention now, Detective Franklin's, Dad's, Angelina's, Ryan's, all the cops, all the people behind me I can't see. I am the centre of their silence and I even have Mom's attention too. They are all waiting and with them all looking at me I think I can't go through with it, but I take a deep breath because I know I have to.

'I was the one who turned the alarm off. There was no break in. I did it – I needed the money for E.L., to help her escape. I staged the whole thing.'

And before I know I'm going to, I close my eyes and start to cry. And once I start, I can't stop. I don't think I'm ever going to stop.

E.L.

I emptyin' out Miss Ellen bath water down the drain by the back steps when I see him. He crouch under the house and in the shadow the white parts his eyes look whiter than ever in his face.

'E.L.!'

He whisper my name but it still sound loud out here where he ain't s'ppose to be.

'E.L., I need talk to you.'

He ain't never use my name b'fore and by the look on his face it somethin' important. Prob'ly he want see Miss Ellen. Prob'ly she decide she don't want see him in the barn no more. I throw the water down too fast and it bubble up over top of the drain makin' a garglin' noise.

'What you doin' hidin' here? Nagle find you ain't in the fields you gone get more stripes.'

'I don't care none 'bout no stripes. I need talk to you.'

He gesture for me to come under the house too and move back so he make room. I look 'round over my shoulder to see if Benjamin out by the barn but there no one there.

'Miss Ellen upstairs – she a'ways done sleep after her bath.'

'I ain't here talk to her, E.L. – I here talk to you.'

It don't make no sense that Jasper gone risk gettin' stripes to talk to me but the longer we stay here arguin' the more chance someone gone see us so I put down the bath and get down on my knees to shuffle in b'side him. He move back so there room. It nice under here

– cool and shade – and I r'member the last time I hide out under here and I wonder what happen if Cassie d'cide to come 'gain.

'What you want?' I say. 'They got us cleanin' down all the curtains and beddin' today and if I don't get back they gone be givin' me stripes.'

'Stripes the least your problems,' he say. 'You got more be worryin' 'bout than that.'

He look at me then look 'way. He look scared even with his scar smile. I ain't never seen him look scared b'fore.

'What you talkin' 'bout? What I got to be worryin' 'bout?'

I know b'fore he say it what he gone say but I need to hear it. Need to be sure.

'I know what done happen with you and Marjorie. Miss Ellen done told me. Marjorie done told her 'bout the doll and how you usin' it to put cusses on Miss Ellen. They think you got some spirit inside you, E.L., that you workin' some black-magic voodoo or somethin'.'

Tears in my eyes, jus' like that.

'They want do that test in the lake – like what happen with that slave on Morristown plantation.'

'But Miss Ellen ...' I start talk, then the tears come. 'She know! She know what happen with the doll – it *her* doll. The Master done broke her. Why don't she say nothin'?'

Jasper look down at his feet where they crossed in the grass.

'She know I ain't doin' no voodoo! Why don't she tell Marjorie then ev'rythin' gone be a'right?'

Jasper shrug. 'I don't know. 'Less it maybe 'cause I tell her 'bout you threatenin' to tell her daddy. Maybe it suit her better if you ain't here no more.'

Upstairs we both hear somethin' on the back porch, the sound of feets. They slow and heavy and I know it Juba and that she lookin' for me. The bath sit there where I left it, real bright reflectin' the sunshine and I wish I done pulled it in with me but it too late now. I wait for her to say somethin', to call my name, but the feets go the other way 'gain and back into the house.

'I gotta go,' I say, soon as she gone. 'I gotta get back to work.'

'Wait,' Jasper say and he grab my arm. 'What you gone do?'

'I gone do like I told you. Get back to work and make a start on the curtains and–'

'E.L. – you ain't listenin' to me! You ain't heard a damn word I done say. The only reason you ain't out in that lake now 'cause they need some special demon catcher that Morristown use and he ain't able get here till tomorrow. You want live, you gotta leave tonight.'

Demon catcher. Hearin' that make the tears start fresh. I wish Charity here – that I able to run tell her what goin' on. Charity know what to do next.

'How I know I able trus' you?' I say. 'You tell Miss Ellen that I gone run 'way!'

'You tell me you gone see me hang!' he say. 'That why I tell her.'

'So why you gone help me now? Why you want me 'scapin'?'

He shake his head. 'I don't know for sure. 'Cept that when Miss Ellen tell me 'bout it I feel real sick in my stomach. 'Cause I know she know you ain't got no demon inside you. And I know she do the same to me jus' as quick.'

From somewhere upstairs piano music start up – slow and haltin' not like the flow of the Mistress music. Miss Ellen been done practisin' – she ain't sleepin' and she gone be wonderin' where I hidin'.

'I gotta go now,' I say. 'She gone know somethin' up otherwise.'

He nod. Let go my arm. 'You ask b'fore 'bout someone in Charleston who can help. There a white man called Cunningham – work on the dock. Black hair and whiskers – you find him.'

'Cunningham?' I say his name slow. 'He part of the Und'ground Railroad?'

I can't b'lieve what he sayin'. Even after ev'rythin' Cassie tell me up till now, even after what Big Bill say, some part me can't believe it actually true.

'Tell him Jim send you.'

'Jim? Who Jim?'

'You r'member a few months back some white man come here – he fix pots at the big house? He sharpen knives. Then he ask if can fix anythin' round the slave cabins?'

When he say it I r'member. A white man in a blue pantaloons and a blue shirt.

'That Jim. When he fix a hole in my pail and he tell me 'bout Cunningham. He say to say Jim sent me.'

Upstairs we both hear the feets 'gain. This time there a voice too, Linda voice and she hollerin' my name.

'E.L.? E.L.? Where you at? You better come quick girl or you gone be on the wrong side Juba. She gone tell the Mistress if you ain't back inside here in two minutes flat!'

Her feets walk fast over to the other side of the porch where she prob'ly gone yell out the same thing. She know too. She mus' know 'bout the demon catcher from Morristown who gone come tomorrow night.

'I gotta go,' I say 'gain. 'Thank you. Thank you for tellin' me.'

He nod. He reach out 'gain, squeeze my arm.

'You go tonight. Promise me you go tonight.'

I nod. I trus' him. I ain't sure why I do, but I do. And I don't know how I gone leave tonight or how I gone find Cunningham in Charleston but I know I gotta try. With or without Cassie, I gotta try.

CASSIE

Officer Doyle wanted to put me under arrest and Detective Franklin probably would have gone along with it if Dad's hotshot lawyer friend hadn't shown up just when she did. The initial charge was wasting police time, but they became pretty convinced that there were drugs involved – that that must be why I'd done it. It didn't help that every time I tried to explain about E.L. Mom got hysterical and kept talking over me, as if she'd prefer them to think I was an addict than to think I was crazy.

Dad was the one who brought up Redfern, who seemed to know all about it, almost as if he'd been planning for something like this. He has their number in his phone and while he's talking to someone in admissions to make sure they can take me in the morning, his lawyer – my lawyer – has Detective Franklin off to the side, saying how I'll be better off somewhere like that, not going into the system where I would only get worse.

It's almost eleven o'clock by the time we're able to get back into the house, past midnight when I am getting to bed, on the night that would turn out to be my last in Brooklyn for a long, long time. And I almost just get into my pyjamas, I almost don't bother with the cheese strings and the almonds and the map and the slave pass and the gold. It goes without saying that I had to hand over the US Open bag, to give everything back, and shoving the bracelets and the necklaces that are all I have left into my jeans feels like a waste of time, but somewhere there's a nagging thought to do it anyway, so I do.

Dad must have stayed over because he's the one who comes in to wake me up. And for a second I've forgotten everything that happened the night before, I've even forgotten that he doesn't live with us anymore, but then as he cracks the blinds open and light filters in I see it in his face – the creases of sadness and guilt and blame – and everything comes rushing back.

'It's time to get up, Cassie. I don't want any messing around. They're expecting us at eleven, which means we need to be on the road by eight.'

He's expecting me to fight him, to argue, I can tell by his tone, and I might have if I hadn't felt my feet right then, realised that my toes were free to wiggle under the comforter. And I don't need to look down to know that I'm not wearing my jeans, my top, my hoody, that under the covers I am naked except for my bra and panties even though I went to bed fully dressed.

I can barely wait till he leaves to rip the blankets back, just to be sure and then I am sure, I see it as well as feel it: my clothes, my shoes, the gold, the food, everything – everything is gone! I jump up on the bed, bounce, once, twice. Three times. I want to do a backflip but I don't know how. I want to whoop but I keep it in. As I bounce, flashes of the night before flicker back – E.L.'s face in the moonlight, the forest around us. And after all this time I can't believe it worked – I can't believe it really worked!

I don't have much time, Dad will be back any minute. I lie back down, pull the comforter over me, close my eyes.

E.L., where are you now?

I wait for an answer, but there is nothing.

E.L., talk to me. Is everything okay?

I lie there but there is only silence and I grab my emergency notebook from under the mattress, scribble out the words.

E.L.? I don't have much time. Please just let me know if you're safe, if everything's okay?

The pen in my left hand is stubborn, silent, and Dad is knocking on the door. 'Cassie, come on – I don't hear the shower! We'll be leaving in twenty minutes, whether you're ready or not.'

'Okay, Dad, I'm coming. I'm up, I swear!'

I throw the covers back again, take the notebook over to my suitcase with clothes spilling out on the floor. It was late when I packed last night and I couldn't even remember what I'd put in there – just clothes really, and sneakers and the photo of the four of us at Magic Kingdom. And I smile as I think about how much harder packing would have been if I still had all my books, trying to decide which ones to take. But without them, without my laptop – even my music – packing was a synch, it was probably the easiest case I'd ever packed in my life.

I shove the notebook deep inside, under some sweatshirts and it's good to know it's there, that we can talk later. But then it hits me: later I don't know where I'll be. Sure, I know it's an institution upstate, some private place that Dad said will be really nice and Mom said they can't afford, but all I really know for sure is that everyone there will be sick, crazy. That I'll be all alone. The fear then, is like a wave, it almost takes my legs from under me. I hold on to to the edge of the bookshelf and take a deep breath. *This too shall pass* was one of the slogans on Grandad's dishtowel and I can almost hear him saying it, I think I can. And with another breath the wave is less, like it has broken over me and I am steady enough to bend and zip up my case.

Maybe, after all this time, I'm ready now. That's the thought that's there in my head. Even though I don't know where we're going, what it'll be like, maybe I'll find something else there. Something different. Maybe, like E.L., I'm finally ready to go.

E.L.

In my dream that night I see Mamma. I don't think I know what her face look like no more but in the dream I know it her straigh' 'way. She smilin'. Charity a'ways say that Mamma got a smile that light up a whole room – a whole day – and she right 'bout that. And Charity in the dream with Mamma. And she smilin' too.

When I wake up Cassie there and this time it like I know she gone be there – I ain't surprise. In the dark cabin she like a ghost. Marjorie roll over, open her eyes but it a'right 'cause she don't see Cassie jus' like I know she won't and she close them 'gain.

We don't say nothin', there no need. I shuffle off my board, get up slow. The door creak like it a'ways creak when it open but no one wake up, no one move. I go out firs', Cassie next. My heart beat fast. Walkin' down the cabin steps I r'member one night wakin' up and Big Bill and Sullivan there doin' somethin' by the fire – pullin' the skin off some animal and the blood on the ground, black as oil. I scared that night and Big Bill tell me to go back to sleep that ev'rythin' a'right. I stop outside the mens cabin. Inside Big Bill prob'ly sleepin' and I know I prob'ly ain't never gone see him 'gain and part me want say goodbye even though I can't. Somethin' tell me that inside Jasper 'wake, that he hear me. But we done said goodbye a'ready,

I walk past the fire all set for tomorrow – that my job now Charity gone and I wonder who gone do that when I gone too. Cassie b'hind me and we walk the trail as if we goin' to the cotton field and in front of me I can a'most see Charity – the shape her shoulder make 'gainst her dress, how she able to carry the basket on her head and never once done drop it. Halfway down I turn off into the trees and walk some more till we reach the clearin'.

I turn 'round, smile at Cassie. She smile too.

'I didn't realise how big this place is,' she say. 'I thought we were going to be walking forever.'

'This place far from the cabins and the big house too. Nagle gone be blowin' the bugle real soon – I don't want them to see or hear us.'

'How do you know?'

'You see the light in the sky over there? Dawn two hours away, maybe less.'

'Come on then, we don't have much time.'

As she say that she start takin' her clothes off. Her shirt firs' that she throw on the grass and then some other shirt under that shirt.

'Don't just stand there, E.L., come on. Get undressed.'

By the time she sayin' that she startin' to undo her pantaloons. In the moonlight her body look like white silk. She wearin' somethin' 'round her breasts like Miss Ellen's corsets only smaller. She skinnier than Miss Ellen, so skinny you can see her ribs. She a'most skinny as me. I don't never r'member her bein' this skinny be'fore.

She talkin' fast and loud and she pull her clothes off real quick. 'I got everything! I checked my pockets, I can't believe it worked! I have the map, the gold – your pass, I'm so happy I remembered your pass! Here, put this on!'

She throw her shirt at me and I reach out to catch it and my dress fall down to my waist and I pull it back up straight 'way. After ev'rythin' we been through it funny but I shy now. I seen Miss Ellen without clothes plenty times but I ain't never taken my dress off in front no white girl b'fore. Cassie ain't shy. She push her shoe off with her other foot kick it off. She pull her pantaloons all the way down – hop on one leg to pull them off.

'E.L. what's the matter with you? You just told me it's not long until dawn. Come on – hurry up! After everything we've been through to set this up, don't tell me you're having second thoughts?'

She smilin' a big smile but she look diff'rent than when I seen her b'fore. Her face skinnier too – not jus' her body. And maybe it jus' the shadow of the trees but even her eyes look diff'rent, like they sinkin' into her face.

'You a'right, Cassie? You look real tired.'

'I've never felt better, E.L. – I'm so excited. I know it's scary but this is it! This is huge! We're going to set you free! We're going to save you!'

All 'long we been talkin' 'bout savin' me and sudd'nly I thinkin' 'bout Cassie and who gone save her, what she need be free from? But I don't know how to say anythin' 'bout that so I don't say nothin'.

Cassie walk real close to me – reach for my hand.

'I know what happened here with Marjorie, E.L. – I saw it. And what Jasper told you too. I know you're scared and I get it, but you have to go tonight.'

I look down at our hands holdin' each other, hers and mine, diff'rent colours but the same size. Same shape. She reach under my chin, make me look at her.

'We're not going to get another chance.'

For the second time the tears there 'gain, like when they start I don't know nothin' 'bout stoppin' them.

'Come on, don't be sad. Look at me here – I look ridiculous. You can't look at me and not laugh!'

And all a sudden I laughin' 'cause she do look funny, half in and half out her pantaloons with only that little corset on.

'Okay,' I say, like she a'ways say. I like how it sound. 'Okay.'

I let go of her hand and the dress. It fall down 'round my feets. I ain't wearin' nothin' else but I don't stop to think of her lookin' 'cause I tryin' to put her shirt on. It like nothin' I ever wear b'fore – it not even like the shirts the mens wear and my arms get stuck in it. It smell nice – like flowers – but the smell too strong and I start to cough.

Cassie laughin' 'gain. 'Sorry there's so much perfume on it. I wanted to be sure to throw the dogs off. Here – put your head through here.'

She hold the hole open and my head go through. It smaller than my dress, it fit good. The material soft.

'Here,' she say, handin' me the pantaloons, 'now these.'

I ain't never worn pantaloons b'fore and I ain't never seen pantaloons this narrow, ain't never seen no woman wearin' them. I hold them out and put one foot in the leg the way I seen the mens do. It hard to stand and I nearly fall 'cept Cassie there to hold me. I try the other leg but Cassie say I pull it up too far so I pull a bit down 'gain and put the other leg in. When they on, Cassie close metal part at the front and a button.

'They're a little big on you,' she say.

I pull at the waist like she do. 'You ain't got no suspenders?'

'Suspenders?' She laugh. 'No. They're big on me now too. Don't worry, they won't fall down.'

I put my hands in the pockets at the side. They move down a bit but she right, they don't fall. I feel diff'rent. Strange. I don't feel like me.

'Here,' Cassie down on the ground now. 'Put these on.'

'No,' I pull my feets 'way. 'I ain't wearin' no shoes, I wear Miss Ellen shoe one time and I don't like it.'

But Cassie keep pushin' the shoe on. 'These are different – Nike Frees. Like you're hardly wearing shoes at all. You'll like them, trust me.'

The shoe feel nothin' like Miss Ellen shoe – it soft, light, like feathers. I 'llow her put the other one on too.

'There,' she go. 'How's that?'

I take a step and then 'nother one. It feel like walkin' with someone else feets. I step on the root of the tree and I feel and don't feel the shape under my sole. I take another step onto the leaves, where they crackly and I hear the crackle noise but I don't feel it and it feel like somethin' wrong.

'I don't like it. I wanna take them off.' My voice sound like maybe I gone cry 'gain.

'It's okay. They just feel different, that's all. Walk around a bit, let your feet get used to them. It's important so the dogs won't smell your scent.'

I walk to the next tree and then the one after that. I think I gone fall over and I want take them off. Wearin' them like my feets forget ever'thin' they know – ev'ry root, ev'ry piece of earth. My feets know where the ground soft and where it hard. They know the quickest way to the big house and the slow way home. How they gone know in these shoes?

'Well,' she say, 'any better?'

She walkin' over to me and she havin' trouble with her steps too and she goin' real slow. She make a face and I know she done step on somethin' hard. She got my dress on and she look funny in it. If she can do it then I can too.

'It gone be a'right.'

We by the tree now that a'ways Dolly tree and it make me sad that she ain't there. And I think Cassie gone ask 'bout the music machine but then I r'member she saw what happen last night so she a'ready know.

'Sorry I had throw 'way your music machine.'

Now it her turn shrug. 'Don't worry, it's fine. It was an old one anyway. I'm sorry I forgot to bring back Ryan's.'

'And I done want give you Dolly so you got somethin' to r'member me by. You know – jus' in case. But now she gone too.'

I don't say jus' in case what but she nod, like she und'stand. Like she been worryin' too 'bout whether we gone be able to talk to each other when I gone.

'That's okay. When I was a kid my favourite teddy bear was called Betty,' she say. 'When I said bye to my grandad I gave her to him so he wouldn't be on his own. But I don't need anything to remember you by E.L. No matter what happens I'll always remember you.'

She reach out then and she put her arms round me, she hug me. It the firs' time we done that and it seem strange that we part of each other but we ain't never hug b'fore. She the one pull 'way firs' and talk fast, all bus'ness 'gain.

'The map is in your front right pocket, but you know the start, right? You remember?'

'Out the back gate, follow the river till I get to the road.'

'Which way?'

I pause, she done taught me this so many times but I get my right and left mixed up ev'ry time. I lift one hand. 'This way – the way the river flow.'

'Yep, that's right. And at first sign of daylight what are you going to do?'

I smile. I know this. We been over this a hundred times.

'I climb a tree. I climb a tree up real high to where the leaves thick and I stay there till it dark.'

'Good.' She smile too. 'That's good. I don't think there's any way the dogs will follow your scent over all that perfume so even if they send them out, even if they're at the bottom of the tree, don't be scared, wait it out, okay?'

'Okay.'

'Your slave pass is in the left pocket. If anyone sees you just show them the pass and say your Master sent you on an errand to Charleston. The food is in the back – the cheese and the nuts and the gold is in the other back pocket and the sweatshirt pocket there at the front, that's why it's heavy.'

There too much to r'member. The longer we talk the more the light start to seep into the sky. And then I know it ain't the time for no more talkin'.

'I gone go, Cassie,' I say. 'It time.'

She nod. 'Yes. It's time.'

'Maybe you come walk the firs' part with me? Jus' till you got go home?'

She shake her head. We a'ready talk through this. I a'ready know the answer but she tell me 'gain.

'I'm in your dress – remember? What's the point in going to all this trouble to dowse you with perfume so the dogs pick up the scent from me?'

She shake her head like she mad that I don't r'member but I know she ain't mad.

'I'm gone miss you,' I say.

Her eyes shine and it look like she the one gone cry now. 'I'm gone miss you too.'

That the last thing she say and I don't say nothin' back. She nod. She don't let no more tears come and I don't neither. I wave at her and turn 'round like I walkin' to the big house but then I dip 'round the side past the stables where Benjamin keep the horses and it so quiet I swear I can hear 'em breathin'. Ev'rythin' quiet – my feets on the ground quiet, my heart, it quiet now too. I gettin' use to the shoes now jus' like Cassie say. They still don't feel like my feets but I can walk. And even though I ain't got no music machine I can hear Cassie music in my head. And it like the shoes walkin' to that music. And that they takin' me somewhere.

At the edge of the trees it the scariest part. The back gate lock like it a'ways lock but it ain't that high and I know I can climb over. Lookin' at it I don't know why I ain't never even thought 'bout climbin' over b'fore. I look b'hind but there ain't nobody there. There ain't nobody there and there ev'rybody there. Cassie, Charity, Big Bill, Miss Ellen, Jasper, the Master, Nagle, the Mistress, even my mamma. They all there, on this side the gate. I don't know what on the other side; but I know it got be better than this.

I reach up high with one hand, grab the bars with the other. My foot find 'nother bar. I pull myself up. And I start to climb.

CASSIE

We are standing under a tree. It is raining. The rain is getting harder, so heavy it is bouncing up from the ground, making mud out of the dirt road. Afterwards there will be that smell, the smell after the rain, but not yet, now it is still raining.

We are looking up – E.L. is looking up – at the branches that reach wide, at the rain falling through, bouncing off the leaves. I've never been as conscious of the rain as I am at this moment that isn't even my moment. I've never listened to rain quite the way I am listening now, with her ears. I've never heard each individual drop fall, all the drops that fall together – on us, on the road, on the plantations, on all of everything. On all of time.

We tip our head back, something is digging into our neck and I realise it's the laces of my sneakers tied together, that she has them hanging there instead of wearing them. Overhead her arms reach up, as if to catch the rain, skinny wrists out of my hoody top. The rain is slick on our face. She closes her eyes, we open our mouth. I smile. We laugh. We taste the rain.

***

That's the dream I have the first night at Redfern and every night after that – for months I have that dream. It always ends right there, right when I'm wondering why you're not wearing my sneakers, why we are outside in the daylight, why we're not hiding. I will myself back to sleep, to go on to the next part and find out what happens, but I never can.

They took the notebook away that first morning when Dad and I got there. We're not allowed to have anything like that, no pens or pencils – at least not unsupervised – nothing we can hurt ourselves with. That's how I know, all those months later when I find your letter, that it's really you, that no matter what the shrinks say, you really existed, because I couldn't have written that letter. Even if I wanted to, I couldn't have written it.

As soon as I put my hand in my dressing gown pocket that morning and feel the paper there, folded up tight, some part of me knows it's from you. The bathroom door has no lock so I lean up against it, and open up the paper slowly and when I see your writing my heart does a jolt and it's hard to breathe. It's been so long since I've seen it, so long since I've heard your voice and the craving I thought had dulled – that my shrinks were working so hard to dull – is there immediately, like it was waiting all along under the surface and had never gone away.

If my room-mate Isabella hadn't started knocking on the door, I might have read it there and then but I don't want to rush it, to skim. Even though more than anything I want to know what happened, I don't just want to *know*. I want to *feel* it, like before. I want to feel it all.

All day long your letter burns through the pocket of my jeans. Through one-to-one and through group, through lunch and study period, through Dad and Ryan's visit, I can feel it, waiting there, waiting for me. Knowing that you are still with me, that in my pocket is everything I've been longing for, is like mixing hope and fear all together. It's not going to be good news, I know it's not, even as I hope it will be. But whatever it says has to be better than your silence. And in that place where we have no privacy, where everything is watched, recorded, analysed and nothing can be just mine, this letter from you is just mine.

And so I wait. I wait until we are all in bed. Until lights out. Until Isabella's snoring is steady. Until the footsteps in the hallway have silenced. And then I take it out from under my pillow, real slow. And I hardly breathe as I unfold the paper. And I take out the tiny pink reading light that Mom smuggled in for me and I click it on.

And I begin to read.

E.L.

Cassie, you there? You hearin' me? I hope you is. It feel like somethin' diff'rent. It feel like somethin' change since I left Riverside Hall, like I can't hear you no more and I thinkin' that maybe you can't hear me neither. I don't know if there any point in tellin' you what I want tell you but I gone try.

There so much I want tell you – it only two days and one night since you come but those two days feel like nothin' I ain't never known. You think I gone be fright'ned, don't you? I think that too and in the beginnin' I am, in the beginnin' ev'ry little sound make me scared. I hear a dog or a horse and I think it Nagle – I know it him. I think they able to smell me, even with your clothes, your perfume, that they comin' after me but they ain't comin'. Nobody comin'. Nobody come so far.

Wearin' your pantaloons, eatin' the food you bring me, wearin' them bracelets and necklaces, I feel like I somebody else, not plain old E.L. I know the gold is to sell, I know it ain't for wearin', but I wear it anyway 'cause it don't make no diff'rence and I ain't never worn no jewel'ry b'fore.

I follow the river like you say. That firs' mornin' when I see the sun I climb a tree like you say. I keep wearin' your crazy shoes even though my feets want be free. And even though I tired I can't sleep – I can't stop watchin' the river and the birds, I even watch the flies. I don't never r'member Riverside Hall havin' so many birds as they do here. Here they small birds on they own and birds in twos that go jumpin' from branch to branch and then they these big groups of birds that all fly t'gether and I don't know how they all know to fly the same d'rection but they do.

And when it get dark and the stars come out, at firs' I sad 'cause the birds all sleepin' and they ain't gone come with me when I walk by the river. But then I get to lookin' at the stars over my head and listenin' to the water next to me and, even though it the same river as Riverside Hall, this river sound like it singin', it don't sound the same at all. And even without your voice in my head, even with no one else 'round for miles, on that walk I don't never feel 'lone.

I know I shoulda keep walkin' – that you say to walk at night – but I tired 'cause I ain't slept all day and it so peaceful there. I lie down in the grass jus' for a few minutes – jus' to listen to the river and watch the stars. And when the birds done wake me up with they singin' and I feel the sun on my face I know I shoulda find a tree to hide out in 'cause it dang'rous but I don't want do that. I can't really 'splain it but I don't want hide no more.

Don't be mad, Cassie. I don't want you to be mad. I know it stupid takin' your shoes off – tyin' them 'round my neck – but I want know what the earth feel like under my feets. This earth. Free earth. 'Cause I think it gone feel diff'rent jus' like the river sound diff'rent and the sky and the birds all diff'rent. And you know what? It do.

I think 'bout you a lot, walkin' 'long in the sun. And I think 'bout my mamma and 'bout Charity and 'bout what we learn at Church. And with the birds and the grass and the river and the sky it seem like I might see my mamma walkin' 'long the opp'site direction. That maybe we gone meet somewhere 'long this riverbank. That maybe right here, right now, maybe this what Heaven feel like.

Don't be mad, Cassie. You done so much. You done help me so much you don't even know. But lookin' at the water and the reeds ripple in the wind it got me thinkin' 'bout the night you save me and what coulda happen to you. And all you done for me and what it doin' to you.

And that this your time now – it ain't mine. It never was.

Earlier it rain. It rain so hard that by time I find a tree for shelter my skin wet under your clothes but I stand under the tree anyway. And standin' there it like the firs' time I ever hearin' rain, like the rain makin' music on the leaves jus' for us. I 'magine you bein' there with me and I see you put your head back, I see the rain roll down your face, I see you laughin' and I do the same. If you done seen me you prb'ly think I crazy then, laughin' at the rain, lettin' it land in my open mouth, lettin' it land in my eye.

I think I hear you laughin' with me – like your voice mixed up in the rain and Charity voice and even Mamma, even Mamma there, and she laughin' too.

I want tell you that, so you know. So you know you all there with me. So you know it all been worth it. So you know that standin' there under that tree, laughin' at the rain, I know what it feel like – what you been talkin' 'bout all 'long.

'Cause right then, under that tree, I finally know what it mean to be free.

Epilogue

CASSIE

I've read this letter, the only one I have left from you, over and over. I've folded it and unfolded it so many times there are tears where the folds are, so it's almost like four pieces of paper, instead of just one.

Here, on Trá Mór, I need to hold on to it tight so it doesn't blow away. It snaps in the wind and I wonder what Mom would do if she found it, if she'd be mad at Redfern for overlooking it, at me for deceiving her, for deceiving them all, all over again.

The tide is so far out today, I don't think I've ever seen it out so far. With the wind in my ears I even can't hear it but there's barely any navy blue between the white lines of foam and I know that means it'll be crashing hard against the rocks, along the sand.

The wind blows harder and I am glad I stole Ryan's Kangol hat from where he'd left it on the chair in the kitchen. In my hand, your letter flaps like crazy. Overhead the sky is almost totally white – just a tinge of blue – and even though the sun is caught behind a cloud, it feels like the most glaring sun I've ever seen.

Don't look directly into the sun. Grandad would always say that. I can hear his voice in my head, saying it now. Is it my imagination? My memory of one time or a hundred times that he said that? Does it really matter if it's his voice or some version of mine?

What should I do with E.L.'s letter? I ask him in my head, not out loud. *Help me. Show me what to do.*

I've hardly finished the question when I hear my name being called. A voice carrying it away on the wind.

'Cassie!'

I turn around. It's Ryan, shading his eyes with his hand.

'Cass!'

He's in shorts, despite the cold, and he starts to run towards me. Even from this distance I can see the flush in his cheeks and I stand up fast, taking care to hold on to your letter.

'Ry? What's wrong? Is everything okay?'

He smiles and in that smile I feel my heart release again, breath come in again, and I see now that he is holding something in his hand, over his head – a rugby ball. He's wearing his rugby shirt too – the one he bought at the airport – and it is tight across his shoulders, his arms. Running towards me on the beach, my little brother is still my little brother, but he's becoming someone else too – he's becoming a man.

'Here!' he calls out. 'Catch!'

All at once a memory comes – one of mine, not yours – me and Ryan scrunched together on the floor, too close to the T.V., leaning against Grandad's legs behind us. On the screen the players in green are pushing and sliding in the mud, pumping their way forward towards the white line.

'These are the hard yards,' Grandad says.

Ryan pulls his arm behind his head and throws the rugby ball at me like it's a football. I want to yell at him that you're supposed to pass backwards in rugby, not throw it like that but the ball is high in the air now, and I want to catch it more than I want to tell him he's wrong.

His throw is way off, I'm sure it is, much too far to the left but then the wind catches the ball and pulls it back on course, towards me and I wonder if that was luck or if he planned it.

The arc the ball makes is slow and fast at the same time but when it starts to drop it picks up speed, hurtling out of the air. I'm watching it, I'm standing under it. I want to catch it, I know I can catch it. I remember how to catch it – the way Grandad showed us in Prospect Park.

I open my hands and I don't know if I knew as I was doing it, that opening them to catch the ball would mean letting your letter go. There's a second – no, a millisecond – where the paper is in the air, an inch, two inches above my hand and I probably could have snatched it back again if I'd acted quick enough. I probably could have grabbed it in between my fingers. I probably could have saved it. But I didn't. I don't.

The wind has it now – your letter – and it flutters by my feet for a fleeting second before it disappears around me, behind me, back down the beach. I picture it dancing over the damp sand but I don't look around because looking around will mean taking my eye off the ball. So I keep my hands open the way Grandad showed us all those years ago and I keep my eye on the rugby ball – closer, closer, so close now. And when I catch it, my fingertips burn a bit from the rubber but I don't drop it, I pull it into me, the way Grandad showed us and I still don't look back.

When it is secure, I hold the ball in two hands over my head, victorious. Ryan's close to me by then, slowing down, smiling, squinting into the sun.

'Nice hat,' he says. 'I was looking for that.'

I touch my head. Smile. 'It suits me better. You know you threw that ball all wrong? It's rugby – you're supposed to pass it backwards, remember?'

'I knew that,' he says. 'I know. I remember.'

And without saying we're going to, we both start to run down the beach, towards the far out waves, falling into pace with each other. He hangs behind me and I pass the ball back to him and he catches it easily. I fall back then and I catch it too. And we run like that, one forward, one behind, passing back and forth like Grandad showed us until our feet are sloshing in pools of water, the remains of waves caught between the hard ridges of sand. Together, we turn around and start to run the other direction, away from the glare, away from the waves, away from where your letter might be caught on a rock, or soaking in a pool, or in four pieces now, instead of one. We run, my brother and me, passing the ball back and forth, we run towards the dunes, towards the village, towards the cottage where Mom is probably home from her A.A. meeting by now waiting for us, where she might already be making lunch.

Together we run, back towards family, back towards home. Back, towards life.

Acknowledgements

I would like to thank the following people for their help with this book:

Susanne White for being the first to let me know about the Brooklyn Heights' history and for steering me towards Plymouth Church to find out more.

Lois Rosebrooks, former historian at Brooklyn Heights' Plymouth Church, who was so informative and generous with her time.

All the staff at The Schomburg Center for Research in Black Culture.

Jim Urbom for insight, encouragement and being my writing buddy at Schomburg.

Ciara Geraghty for our writing retreat in Donegal and being a wonderful sounding board as always.

Ita Hughes for giving me a writing haven to work on this book over Christmas 2015.

Bernie Furlong, Eileen Kavanagh and Emma McEvoy for being my shout-line sounding board.

Patrick Phillips for allowing me to use his beautiful poem, 'Heaven'.

Donna Condon, my copy-editor, and Claire Rourke, my proofreader.

Joy Tutela at the David Black Agency, whose thoughtful and insightful feedback helped to make this a better book.

My editor, Ciara Doorley, whose steadfast belief in me has been so important for my development as a writer, and all at Hachette for their professionalism, loyalty and hard work in promoting this novel.

My students at the Irish Arts Center who were the first public audience for this book, and all my students who inspire me every day with their dedication, curiosity and willingness to take risks in their own writing.

For much of the writing of this book, I was recovering from an injury and surgery that followed. Thanks to all of you who kept my spirits up through this difficult time, and especially to my physio, Katherine Albright, and my surgeon, John G. Kennedy, who both got me through the 'hard yards'.

Finally, thank you to all my friends and extended family on both sides of the Atlantic – you make this all worthwhile. Special thanks to my wonderful mum and dad who continue to support me in so many ways, especially over the past twelve months, to Aisling O'Sullivan, who cheers me on daily from afar and Denise Pauling, who cheers me on daily from a few blocks away.

And of course, to my wife, Danielle – for watching endless movies with me about the American South, for working our holidays around visits to plantations, for your lovely homemade meals especially around deadline time and, most importantly, for loving me through it all.

Note to Reader

New York,

October 2016

Dear Reader,

Let's get back to the start, to where the idea for the book came from. Just like my other novels, the premise didn't come fully formed. It came in fragments, almost like the narrative itself. The first germ was when I was in Charleston, South Carolina, on holiday a couple of years back. My wife had food poisoning – actually it turned out to be stomach flu, which I would contract a few days later – and I found myself with some unstructured 'wandering time'. 'Wandering time' is always a good source of ideas for me, particularly in a new city. I found myself wandering into squares, old churches, onto open porches where I could rest from the heat in a rocking chair and sip some sweet iced tea. And I found myself wandering into the Old Slave Mart Museum.

Probably much like you, I have seen films and television programmes about slavery. I have read books. I felt reasonably well informed about the events in the South that led to the Civil War. Living in New York and working in a soup kitchen where about 80 per cent of the 1,000 people served every day were African-American, I wondered sometimes about the legacy of slavery and its ripple effect through the generations. But I had never been in a place like this – a place where the horror of human beings being bought and sold seemed sealed into the cold stone walls – and it was here that the knowledge, become more than knowledge. It became something I knew I wanted to write.

Soon after, a character started to form. A young girl – a slave girl on a cotton plantation. I tried to push her away, this character. I couldn't write this story – it just wasn't my story to write. If I wanted to write a narrative of a child's experience of a traumatic historical event, I had plenty of options to choose from much closer to home. I had no business writing about slavery. I would be setting myself up for failure to even try.

As any writer knows, the more you try and quieten a character, the stronger their voice gets. So while I was searching for a new idea – a real idea that I could start to work on for my next novel – I wrote about this character on the side, you know, just to get her out of my system. As I wrote, her story unfolded: her name was E.L., she was an orphan, born into slavery. Something terrible had happened to her mother.

While E.L.'s story poured onto the page, the idea for my 'real book' was coming much more slowly than I wanted. I found myself drawn to a shabby café in Brooklyn Heights to work on it. The fact that it was a forty-five minute subway ride from my apartment made it inconvenient, to say the least, but when I'm drawn to a place to write, I've learned not to question it. And it was in that shabby café that another character started to emerge; an Irish-American teenager named Cassie, a loner and a book lover who was growing up not far from where I was writing. In a way that I didn't yet understand, I knew almost instantly Cassie's story was somehow connected to E.L.'s.

When I wasn't writing, I spent time worrying about what shape the narrative was going to take with these two intersecting lives. I worried that I wouldn't get E.L.'s voice right, that the girls' lives were too different to be in the same book which would lead me back to my original worry that I shouldn't be writing this book at all. But when, one day, a friend I met for lunch told me how Brooklyn Heights had been the heart of the anti-slavery movement in New York and my shabby writing café was mere blocks from a famous church where abolitionists gathered and a young slave girl had been granted her freedom in a public 'auction', I began to worry less. After that, as I headed to the café to begin my day's work, I thought about how under the very paths I walked, there were old tunnels and cellars that had housed escaped slaves on the run and it felt like a sign, a vote of confidence. And the momentum of the story came faster than ever.

As you've now realised, the central question of the book is whether or not E.L. is a real person and, ultimately, whether you believe she exists purely inside Cassie's mind or outside of it as well, doesn't really matter. At least not to me. If, having read this book, you learned a little more about slavery or you changed your perspective on mental illness or you found yourself thinking more about what freedom means to you in your own life, then that would make me happy. That would mean I've done my job!

Yvonne Cassidy

What if uncovering the past led to a future you never imagined?

How Many Letters Are in Goodbye?

'A compelling story of tragic loss, self-discovery and love'
Sunday Independent

YVONNE CASSIDY

It's been almost eleven years since Rhea Farrell last wrote to her mother.

It was a Friday night ritual – until Rhea's father decided it was stupid to write letters to a dead person. That was the summer before the accident. The summer before Rhea began to keep her first secret.

Now about to turn eighteen, far from home and alone on the streets of New York, Rhea finds herself the holder of many more secrets. So, just like she used to do as a little girl, she begins a letter with the words 'Dear Mum' and tells her mother the things she can't tell anyone else. But is it enough, to confide in someone who can never answer? Or is it the only way she knows how to say goodbye?

Also available as an ebook

Carla Matthews travelled to New York as a student for the summer but when the time came to head home to Ireland, she decided to stay. She had fallen in love with musician boyfriend Eddie, with the city itself, with the idea that here she could become someone new, someone she couldn't be in Dublin anymore.

Eleven years later, Carla feels stuck. She never did return to university and has almost forgotten her dream of being a writer. As she begins to wonder if this is how it will always be, she receives a phone call from home that changes everything.

Now Carla must return to Dublin, to her mother and sister, to a city and a life she hardly recognises anymore. Faced with some difficult choices, Carla begins to discover what it truly means to come home to herself.

What Might Have Been Me is a compelling story of love and belonging, and of how, in the midst of devastating loss, a family finds a way to piece itself back together.

Also available as an ebook

'You know that moment between sleep and waking? I read somewhere that the first thing that comes into your head is what you desire or fear the most. I don't know if that's fully right though because for years when I opened my eyes I used to think of Mark.'

I'm JP Whelan and I said that my shrink. He's always trying to get me to talk about what happened all those years ago, when we were just kids.

Here's where I'm supposed to tell you about all that, about my life with Katie and Abbey in London or before then, back in Dublin, with Dad, listening to the Beatles and how those were the only times I really felt safe.

But then I'd have to tell you about Dessie and what happened with Mark.

But, it doesn't all fit into some neat little box, my story. I wish it did. So if you really want to know the truth, you're going to have to find out for yourself, because even now I'm not sure what the truth is.

Also available as an ebook